THE DEVIL'S
WORKSHOP

THE DEVIL'S WORKSHOP

Donnally Miller

Dreamy Moon Press

THE DEVIL'S WORKSHOP

copyright © 2018 by Donnally Miller.

Cover art, layout, and map by Candace April Lee

Published by Dreamy Moon Press

21616 Winter Park Court

Venice, FL 34293

ISBN 978-1-7321030-0-9

Library of Congress Control Number: 2018902981

For Bernice

"Life is short, but the days are long."

—Colophus of Demarest

CONTENTS

PART ONE
OPENING

A Grave at Midnight 1

New Acquaintances 13

A Fresh Pair of Boots 24

The Toss of a Coin 32

Witchcraft in the Woods 38

Something Saved and Something Lost 47

A Dance by Moonlight 67

In the Belly of the Beast 87

Piracy and Pillage 108

Two Vagabonds 118

PART TWO
MIDDLE GAME

The Eye of Maddibimbo 128

Once More under the Sun 143

Freedom and Its Discontents 152

The Full of the Moon 161

A Man Must Have a Purpose 176

Counsels of War 188

Coldblood Farm 198

The Devil's Kiss 221

CONTENTS

PART TWO
continued

Lost Bastard Island	229
The Fight in the Forest	244

PART THREE
ENDGAME

Dodgy Eyeballs	272
The Specter of the Wolfman	298
Heartbreak Hill	313
Sorrow and the True Nature of God	323
In the Devil's Workshop	351
Love Conquers All	366
Buttockracy	374
Obsession	380
Story's End	394
A Meditation on Ladybirds	402
Acknowledgments	414
Author's Note	414

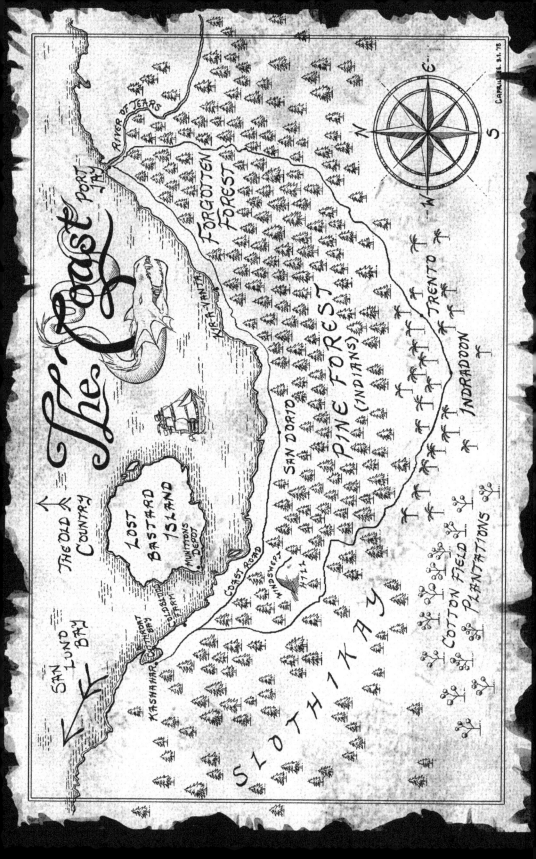

PART ONE

OPENING

The First Chapter
A Grave at Midnight

THE MAN STANDING at the top of the hole was little more than a darker shadow etched against the gloomful, dreary night. A sullen wind lashed the branches of the trees behind him as he rubbed his hands together, trying to work a little warmth into the ends of his fingers. "Can you not dig any faster?"

Tom leaned on his shovel and stretched his tired shoulders, sending aching pains through every weary scrap of muscle. "True it is I cannot."

The rain was in Tom's eyes and down the back of his neck. It pooled in the dirt at his feet making a mucky muddy mess of his shoes, and making each shovelful of soggy dirt heavier than the last. It dripped from the branches above and ran in little waterfalls down the sides of the hole he was digging. Standing as he was at the bottom, looking up against the dark background, the face of the man above was cast in shadow by the broad brim of his hat. Taking the haft of the shovel in his calloused hands, he tossed another spadeful of mud onto the mound he'd been erecting at the hole's side.

"Time's a-wastin'," the man said. "You've dug enough. Deep enough on a night like this. Desist."

"That's a welcome word. Welcome and long looked for it is."

"Now clamber up here and give us a hand lowering this item into the ground." The man was walking towards the horse and cart as Tom heaved his body out of the muddy hole and got himself to his feet. He walked over, still stretching his shoulders and his elbows, and looked at the long wooden box in the back of the cart they'd come in. It had a grim air about it, that box, and Tom thought once or twice he'd heard something inside it moving around, but he'd known better than to ask what it held. The man hopped in the back of the cart and made some furtive movements with his hands, twisting them now this way and then another. "Here, I'm at the front," he said. He gave a shove and the long casket slid out the back. "Can you grab ahold of that?" Tom grabbed it but he wasn't prepared for how cold it felt, bone chilling cold, more frigid than a block of ice. It sent shivers from his fingers all up his arms. "Good. Get that, and I've got this end," the man said as he hopped off onto the ground, still holding the box. He was a short man, and the end he held was lower than Tom's. At one point he asked to stop so he could adjust a certain object in his pocket, and then they went on. When they came to the hole, Tom lowered himself in holding the casket, but the top wasn't nailed shut, and it opened a little, almost as if something inside was trying to get out. In the ghostly moonlight he saw a man's face. It was a hard, chiseled face, and then the short man clapped the lid shut and the sight was gone. All the same, it was a face he thought he knew, but the back of his mind was empty as to where or how.

The man jumped into the hole still holding his end, making a muddy splash. As the box hit the bottom, with a vigorous leap and a scramble Tom was back standing on the edge of the hole, and he was aiming a pistol at the man now standing below him.

"Now I think we'll have it out and be done. I'll have that fifteen dollars of which we spoke."

"I am right disgusted with you. You never thought I'd pay?"

"A hole dug to hold one man can just as well hold two. And a sly man likes of you might bury something and want no one else the wiser. Maybe a sly man thought that way would see to it any who helped wouldn't be able to speak of what was buried. So a man must take a care, and I'm taking a care now. We'll have just what we agreed on."

"Here's your fifteen dollars." He held out a bag. "I said I'd pay, and I keep my word. Take it from my hand if you dare come that close."

"Throw it here."

He threw it with a snort that wrinkled his lips.

Tom carefully picked up the bag and opened it, making sure he kept the man well under observation. Once satisfied as to its contents, he hung the bag on his belt and said, "Take off your clothes."

2

"True it is I will not be doing that. A night like this in the dismal stinking woods, I'd die two times of the rheumatism. I will not be taking off my clothes."

"They've got to come off."

"You've got the cart, take it and take yourself away. I'll follow on foot. A sad night it'll be for me, I can tell you. Walking all the way, and I've the corns like you wouldn't believe. But I'm not taking off my clothes. You can shoot me dead. I'm not taking them off."

"We're at an impasse."

"What I'll do, I'll take off my shoes. An impasse, he calls it. I'll take off my shoes, will that satisfy you? You big bad man holding me up like you are?"

Tom stood silent, and his silence held a note of perplexity. "Go on," he said at last. "Take off your shoes. And your pants. That'll take us to the fair."

"Bad enough it is I take off my shoes in the thistles as you wouldn't believe. Thorns that've been waiting since the start of time just to stick into the nice toes of a man like me. Well, Lord knows, this is the night they've waited for. I'll take off my shoes." He said this undoing his laces, "but I won't be taking off my pants." He threw his two shoes onto the pile of mud Tom was standing beside. "Go ahead, take the cart, take my shoes, I'll fill in the hole and come to town with my two feet torn to tatters and the blood running down my stumps that'll be all that's left. But I'm not taking off my pants."

"Take off your pants."

"I'll not be forgetting this. You'll have to watch your backside from this day till you die, you will. There'll be one not going to rest till you're regretting this night's doings as much as he. I've shown I'm a man who keeps his word. There was no need for any of this. I'd have given you the second fifteen and driven you back to town like I said."

Just then it looked as though the box tried to open again, and the man hit something inside it with his shovel. Tom decided it was time to go. He said, "You stay in that hole, mister, you stay till I'm gone. I'll be keeping an eye on you, so just sit there and don't think about following where I go. I'd say this is a good night's business. And it's hard on me but I'll let you keep your pants."

Tom walked back to the cart and unhoppled the horse. He threw the pair of shoes in the back of the cart and then took the reins and put the horse in the way of an amble back to town. As he rode away he heard the crack of a shot, and a bullet whizzed past his right ear. He put his head down and whipped the horse to a gallop. *Damn*, he said to himself, *I should've taken his pants.*

He thundered past the rood at the crossroads, and as he made the last turn approaching the town the rain had let up and there were first signs of light slipping craftily into the sky towards the east. He saw ahead of him Katie Jean waiting under the dripping arms of a sheltering beech. He brought the cart to a standstill and got out to sit beside her.

"Where you coming from, on such a dull and unentertaining night as this?" she asked.

"I had a bit of a queer business I signed up for. Put some money in my pocket this night before I'm shipping out."

"And that was a better use of the night than to spend it in the arms of one who won't be holding you for two years now. I see your point."

"Lord knows I'll be missing you. Thought I might want to get some practice at it. Get that running start I've heard about. Kiss me, Katie."

"The whys of a woman with a sailor man are soon answered."

"That was a kiss?"

"Reckon it was."

"I couldn't know if I felt it, or if it was one of those gnats I see maybe it landed on my cheek, celebrating the dizzy wonder of being a gnat."

"I was crying in my bedroom. And you was in the pub making an address to your two best friends, whiskey and stout, and I fear they've settled their disagreeableness and have decided you're the lad."

"That they have. Those friends of mine were having their tricks. I was in a sure shmother and I didn't know if I'd be able to get out of it. But there was this character, a Mr. X he called himself, wouldn't go by his full name, he had me by the ear now, and he was promising he'd give me thirty silver dollars just for a little night's work. He'd

4

give me fifteen up front, and the other fifteen when the job was done. Well before you'd know, I was on the cart with him and driving the horse out of town to a little place in the back of beyond where he told me to dig him a hole."

"And what was in the hole?"

"That I'd rather not be saying."

"Mr. X, and a hole you dug, and you'd not say what's in it. You have a way of telling a story with the story left out."

"I'll tell you I dug the hole and I collected my thirty dollars."

"And where's this leave Mr. X?"

"The last I seen he was in the way of filling the hole, but those are his shoes in the cart."

"Funny man, Mr. X. He gives you thirty dollars and a pair of shoes to dig him a hole just so he can fill it up again. I've got a powerful feeling something's been left out of this tale, and I've a sneaking suspicion it might be a Mrs. X what I'm not hearing of."

"There's no Mrs. X at all. Or if there is I saw neither hide nor whisker of her this night."

"It'll be an easy thing to learn who you were with. I'll keep a look out for someone with no shoes, and when I find her I'll be asking if her foot fits into one of those. Kind of like an old girl I heard tell of named Cinderella."

"It'd be Cinderella on an awfully bad night. Those are a man's shoes."

"Never knew you to be too particular once you'd had a few."

"I'm glad it was you said that not me; it makes a poor reflection on yourself."

"O damn you!" Katie Jean hit him on the cheek.

"Whoa, whoa, let's not part like this. You know I have to be going. I've signed on the Queen of Bel Harbor and she's bound away on the morning tide." He put his arms around her. "Two long years till I'll be back, and every empty night of those long years will be filled with the thought of you."

"Thoughts of me and whoever's handy in those ports you'll be landing in. I know who you are, Tom. I know you better than you know yourself. But I'm grateful I found you this morning because

I'd not have you going without me having a last look at you, and I'd got ready a gift, a little token you might call it, to carry with you, to remind you who's waiting for you here on the shore." And with that she gave him a little box.

"Oh, Katie, you shouldn't have."

"Yes, I know I shouldn't have, and now I've done it I'm half sorry about it, but here, take it and be gone."

He opened the box and inside was a watch for his fob pocket. The outside bore a design of knots and tangles, and when he opened it the little second hand was ticking round, and on the inside of the lid was engraved "From your own darling Katie." He was struck speechless.

Katie went on, "Because you're always missing your appointments and complaining you don't know the time, well now you've no excuse. I saved up for it and I –" here she broke down for a moment. Then she continued, "And I'm a silly girl for thinking of you at all. But I was waiting to give it to you last night and you were never there and I can tell you because I checked and the watch is a good one, there was not ten minutes that passed I didn't cry a tear for you."

"Katie, Katie, oh girl. You've struck me sore. I wish you hadn't done this. Why is it a woman's kindness hurts so much, and what a selfish idiot I am, that you've got this for me and I'm standing here and my hands are empty and I've nothing for you. And you got it engraved. I'm feeling as worthless as a man can feel. I know you've no pity for me and I've none for my own self, but you've struck me sore you have. Why did you have to do it?"

"Because of the love I have for you, Tom." She kissed him.

"I'll cherish this, I will. You shouldn't have done this, but I'm glad you did. I will keep this and hold it dear all my days." He looked at the watch. "And if the time it tells is true, I've no time to be spending with you. I'm afraid I'll be missed on the docks."

"Of course the time it tells is true. You think I'd give you a gift of a watch and it not tell the right time?"

He got up, putting his hat back on his head. "This is the last one. No more voyages after this. I promise you that." She looked at him, and tried to save it in her mind just how he was. The cut of his hair, and the little smile that tried to say more than he'd allow, and all the way he stood there in the morning sun, wincing from the water still dropping off the leaves. "This is the one that'll make my fortune and no mistake. There's no mistaking at all. Oh, Katie, it seems the only time I love you is when I leave you. I haven't the words to say what's in my heart. It'll be just a shell of me on the ship because the best part of me will be here still with you. And if I could have your face in front of me like this all the days of my life I'd be a very blessed man."

They kissed, and held each other for a lengthy moment, and then he got back in the cart and drove off; but before turning the next bend he looked back, and Katie Jean was still there, still looking, following with her lonely eyes, till he turned the corner and was gone.

He left the horse and cart tied in front of the saloon, figuring Mr. X would be sure to find them there. It crossed his mind to sell them – the cart wasn't worth much but the horse might be – to get his own back for that bullet Mr. X had sent in his direction. But he was tired, and there wasn't much time. He'd gotten what he'd bargained for and didn't see any point in angering Mr. X more than he had already. He was chewing these thoughts over as he neared the quays, where he found there was a scene of great busyness. People were scurrying back and forth, carrying packets and parcels and bales and not noticing who they were stampeding next to in their desperate bustle to see that everything was taken care of and stored right and proper. The smell of the tar and the salt was overwhelming, and there was a multitude of ships of all sizes and rigs. Sailors were singing and going aloft, hanging to threads far over Tom's head, and there was wonderful figureheads, some that had been all over the ocean and back, and many old sailors with whiskers and rings in their ears. Mariners from up and down the Coast and beyond could be seen. There were gnarly, hirsute natives of the Gongorran Plateau, and tall green-eyed Jacquanauts from Terra Berra. Tom found his ship, the Queen of Bel Harbor. She was a mighty and a splendid galleon, almost a floating castle, and she loomed over the vessels docked next to her. It was plentiful goods she'd carry, and it would be a profitable voyage for certain. The boatswain was a man named Ramsey, dressed in stout blue cloth, who piped him aboard but hadn't much patience for a seaman on tired legs who had to be told twice which way his cabin was. Tom did his best to stay out of his way, and neither of his cabin mates being present, he unpacked his kit, chose a lower bunk for himself, and stretched out to get some sleep before he'd be wanted on deck.

Sometime later a weary, disgruntled, and very footsore traveler came limping into town. Muttering an incessant string of curses under his breath, he found his way to the saloon, where he was relieved to see his horse waiting patiently, with his cart, tied to the hitching post. Seating himself on the edge of the horse trough, he put his feet in the water and massaged his toes and his instep. As he did so his eye was caught by a young man with red hair seated in a splint-bottomed chair leaned precariously against the wall behind him. His hat was slouched forward, covering the top of his face, and he was idly blowing on a harmonica, exploring a few sounds, but nothing quite approaching a melody.

"Hey, Stranger, Miss Deirdre's wondering where you been," the young man said, putting the harmonica to one side.

"Let her wonder."

"She saw your cart, couldn't understand if you was back, why you hadn't paid her a call."

"I wasn't back is why."

The only answer was a few tuneless notes from the harmonica. The traveler stood and retrieved his shoes from the cart. He rubbed off the mud and slid his feet into them. He was in no mood to bandy words. As he strode past the young man he gave a kick to his chair leg that sent him sprawling, and then throwing the saloon doors open he walked decisively to the back, where he mounted a stair and rapped on the door of Miss Deirdre's office.

"Enter."

He opened the door. Miss Deirdre was floating two feet from the ceiling. She wore a long gown that trailed between her legs, and a silver belt around her waist, and on it thirteen bells. She held her arms extended over her head as she moved gently across the room, her long raven locks hardly moving in the almost undetectable breeze. Barely turning in the direction of her visitor, she said, "A mighty burden was

8

in your hands under cover of night. The veil of darkness is now long withdrawn, and what have you to say of it?"

"There's many a corse I've put to bed, but never before was there one that so kept wanting to sit up. It was a good piece of work getting that one underground, I'll have you know that." A devil with the head of an ostrich and the legs of a toad sat up in the corner and gave him a wicked grin.

"The Son of Light is in the grave?" Her outstretched fingertips just touched the wall, and she pushed off and started gently gliding towards the other side of the room.

"He's in the grave sure enough, and can't you come down where a man can look you in the eye? A man'd get a woeful crick in the neck talking to a body slithering about up there." For just a moment he saw the water she floated on, a sunny river filled with weeds and shimmering fish. She seemed to turn and swim down towards the level where he stood at the river's bottom and then the vision was gone and she was seated in an armchair that had appeared near to hand. She inserted a cigarette into a cigarette holder that must have been eight inches long. Then, lighting the cigarette, she inserted the other end of the cigarette holder in her mouth, and as she inhaled a grateful puff of smoke, she gestured him to sit in a caquetoire that had shown up just behind him.

"He blocked me at every turn," she said. "I can hardly believe he's dead. The time has come to spread my wings . . ." She took another puff, and expelled the smoke from her mouth with evident satisfaction. "Now, for reasons that are quite compelling, but which I haven't time to go into, Hell will be coming to the Coast. Are you ready?"

"Aren't I just?" He sat back and produced a snuff box from his waistcoat pocket. Proceeding to take a good snort in each nostril, he continued, "The pirates of San Luno Bay are starving for a fight. And I've the bait for them. The emerald eye of Maddibimbo has been purloined. The ones who did it knifed the thing out of the idol's face. They've left a trail for the angry priests to follow, but they have a date set to sell it in the back streets of Kashahar."

"Whom would they be selling it to?"

"That would be a shady gentleman wouldn't want his name recorded in this here transaction. But the point of the matter is I'll be letting Crazy Dog and his buccaneers know where the exchange is to take place, so when the thieves arrive, they'll find the pirates waiting on them."

"I take it these are the same pirates that were raked by the guns of Lost Bastard Island only a fortnight ago, smuggling their rum into Cutthroat Bay."

"They would be the ones. And I'm thinking the munitions depot on that island has been recently enlarged. Is that the case?"

"It has." She leaned forward and made a point of capturing his eye. "General Hobsbawm has been recruiting in the Panhandle and all round the Forgotten Forest. The force he's raised is substantial, though ill-trained and young , liable to run at the first chance. This time they're minded to put the blasted Indians down for good. I also know that Half Moon and his braves have been smoking the holy mushroom, and while dancing round the totem of war and death they've called on their bitter ancestors for help, and aren't they just that thirsty for a chance to drink some soldiers' blood. But to get the army marching into the Forest, maybe a fire at their back will do the trick."

This is how it always starts, he was thinking, and a satisfied glint came to his eye. *Mankind is that blood-thirsty an animal. His instinct is always to make sure there are no survivors.* The devil in the corner had produced a tarnished trumpet and was tooting away. "So I'll be off to Kashahar," he said. "But on my way, there's a new lot of slaves coming to the markets of Indradoon, and there's rumors of rebellion I'll be whispering into some willing ears. I suspect there's many won't go docile into that sweating hellhole of misery and subjugation."

Little whirlpools appeared where the top of the water would have been and started dancing round the room, casting ripples from the light that came through the windows. Miss Deirdre stood, and spreading her arms invoked the obscene deity she worshipped and cast her wicked spell. "A new age is come. We're in the Devil's workshop now. Send me demons, send me the dangerous, the resolute, those fierce to upset the continuity of earth. Send me gremlins to undermine and rabid beasts to overwhelm the great convexity of this globe! Send me those who would destroy, dismantle, and demolish!" Tiny horned demons appeared in little explosions of light throughout the room, some floating in the air, others perched on the furniture. They howled icy shrieks of glee, turning somersaults in the air.

A sound as of wings muted by great distance seemed to happen just at the top of the traveler's skull. He could hear it there, like a monstrous bird flapping incredibly high in the sky but somehow still inside his head. The flapping horror hovered lower, seeming to settle now somewhere behind and just above his right shoulder. He looked behind, jumped up and started to run. He was running through the whirlpools of light and in between the demons dancing round his head, and when he looked behind he saw ferocious talons taking shape in the gloom above him. Just at that moment with one impassioned scream Miss Deirdre vanished in a startling fizzing burst of crimson motes that scattered through the air and disappeared before they'd hit the floor, leaving only her cigarette holder hovering tentatively in mid-air with the cigarette still lit. The whirlpools and the demons that had been tripping round the room were gone like smoke. The devil in the corner hid his trumpet somewhere in his posterior and went out with a pop. Suddenly the room was empty save for himself. Where there had been chairs there were now piles of rotten sticks. Miss Deirdre reappeared for just a moment to catch her cigarette before it hit the floor, and then was gone again. He looked about himself, muttered something under his breath, and strode out the door. He descended the stair and cast his eyes round the unfriendly saloon. A few of the faces at the bar went so far as to look up from the bottles they held before them.

"I need a man who'll ride with me to that fly-infested blister on the land they call Indradoon. I have business in the slave markets there. Fifteen silver dollars in your pocket now and another fifteen when the job is done. A man can't be fairer than that. Who'll ride with me?"

There was a general resurgence of interest in the contents of the drinks. The traveling man cursed and walked out onto the boardwalk outside. The young man with the harmonica was still there. In fact he'd acquired a banjo as well, and was picking at it in a desultory fashion, as much as to say I know I can't play this very well but neither can you.

"Fergus," said the traveling man. "You're mine."

"Not me. Nossir."

"Come off that nonsense. Have you fed my horse?"

"No."

"Why not? What have you been doing all the time I've been dallying with Miss Deirdre?"

"Haven't been doin' nothin'."

"No, I see. Well look sharp. Get Dobbin a good feed of oats, and unhitch him from this cart. We won't be needing that. Have you a horse of your own?"

"No."

"Of course you do."

"Said I don't."

"What did you do with your horse?"

"I never –"

"Did you sell him for that banjo?"

"A horse'd be worth a lot more than a banjo."

"I've seen them that weren't. So what you're telling me is, I've got to get you a horse, is that the long and the short of it?"

"No, don't get no horse. I'm not goin' nowheres."

At just that moment, a black stallion no one could recall having seen before ambled up and whinnied in a companionable manner. Fergus kicked the side of the building and said, "Gol darn it, Miss Deirdre, I hears you."

The traveling man added, "Now all you need's a saddle."

Fergus went off mumbling, "That Miss Deirdre's in my head and all, it's like she's squeezed my thoughts down till they're not much more than a little oil that spills out my ears. And she's taken up the rest of my head for herself."

"I wouldn't fret. It's not as if you're losing much. That banjo's got more brains than you do. Now come on." He unhitched the horse.

That afternoon the two of them were out of town, on the road to Indradoon.

Chapter Two
New Acquaintances

Katie Jean slept alone, with only her thoughts for company, and some of the thoughts that kept her company these nights were making her very sad. Unlike the other lasses, she'd not chased after boys from the farms that sat along the river, no, a life of churning butter and keeping the cows contented was not for her. She'd given her heart to a sea-faring lad who bore a fever and a magic she'd thought took on the right and unmistakable shape of her desire. And now when the man was gone to sea, she had these thoughts that came to her at night to chase the sleep away. Some were thoughts of poor lonely Tom, out on the windy sea, and the ravages of the work he'd be enduring. And then there were thoughts of herself and the work she had to be doing. And the sum and the lot of all these thoughts was a great sadness with no way of ending for two long, empty years.

So after a night of tossing and turning in the sheets, punctuated by moments of staring at the ceiling, it was her custom in the morning to walk to the roof of the mansion where she worked, where there was a veranda enclosed by a wooden railing. From there she could see far off the constant turning and pounding of the waves, and she could hear the snarling they made as they tried to snaffle up the shore. Sometimes a little sob would rise in her throat, and sometimes she'd let it come out, as a tear or two drifted down her cheek. It was the tribute she paid to the persistence and steadfastness of her loving heart. And much as she wished that she could have done different, she believed the tribulations suffered by a loving heart were the reward of living life with a passionate intensity, and that her struggles were a blessing. At least it's what she told herself.

Tavish, the boot black, butler and general factotum, watched her cry. He was a tall man of dark aspect, several years her elder. He'd been in service to the Lanchesters all his life and was the owner of an unfortunate face, one eye being larger than the other giving it a queer, misshapen look. Also his nose had broken and not healed well. His voice was harsh, and he had thick lips. He wished he could touch her, but he was certain that was not his place. Instead he scanned the town below. There was a noise being made by a batch of boys who were taking delight in torturing a dog, and it gave him a sick feeling all the way through the middle of his stomach. What was it about people that made them think they weren't doing anything unless they were doing something cruel? It was a sore distress to him. He pointed the disturbance out to Katie, and the mood she was in gave fuel to her natural womanly anger at the pointlessness and brutality of men.

When Katie left the roof, she descended the stairs to speak to her employer and her mistress Madam Arabella Lanchester. She spoke of the boys taking their heartless pleasures by distressing a poor animal, and asked if there wasn't something that could be done.

Madam Lanchester took a distant view of the actions of those she considered lesser than herself. In fact, nothing they could do would surprise her, and she took a grim satisfaction in the confirmation of her low esteem for the human rabble. "You can hardly expect them to display the least sensitivity to the feelings of other species. Be thankful they don't see fit to indulge their malicious inclinations by tormenting a small child."

Katie said, "I'm in the way of thinking we should put a stop to their fun before it reaches that point. It seems there's a wildness and a fury that's come over people in the night and I don't know what to make of it at all."

"I'm of a like mind. Tavish."

"Yes 'm," said Tavish.

"You're the man of the house. Can you see what can be done for the rescuing of this poor animal. We'd be beholden if you'd take this matter in hand."

"And I'll go with," added Katie Jean.

So that's how Katie came to be holding a good thick stick as she followed Tavish down the hill towards the boys whom she'd made the true objects of her festering anger. The dog had been a poor one, even before being singled out for abuse, just a poor starved mutt really, little more than a friendly rat that had been promoted. He was probably some little one's pet, with a name like Bowser or Winky, who'd wandered from his proper friends and now found himself in the clutches of a gleeful gang of bored brutes. He'd tried to ingratiate himself, giving them his fawning gaze, and wagging his bit of a tail, but now his forepaws were tied to a wire, and his body was dangling down, his poor hind feet unable to find purchase on the ground below. His front legs were likely broken by the weight of his body, and he was whinging in a desperate fashion, still hoping to appease the excited rabble who were set on his execution. The ringleader was a lout with an unruly mop of black hair, and he wore a vest and had buckles on his shoes, as if he worked in a clerk's office. He was poking the little animal in the stomach with a stick, eliciting excited shouts from his audience every time the dog howled and flinched.

"Now that's enough of that," Tavish strode into the midst of the crowd. "Put that stick down," he told the boy, using his most commanding tone of voice.

"And who are you?" said the boy. He was backed up and reinforced by a resounding chorus of jeers from the younger ones who didn't want their fun taken away just as it was getting to the delicious point of it all.

"This is my dog," said Tavish, "and I'll not put up with anyone treating him poorly."

"You're a liar!" The boy was now threatening to poke Tavish with his stick. "I've seen you round the town. You've got no dog." One of the urchins threw a stone in Tavish's direction.

Katie saw fit to wave her own stick, which was a good bit thicker than the one the boy held. While the boy was distracted, Tavish untied the dog's legs. The rabble, seeing their prize on the point of being carried away, put up a vociferous clamor. The leader jabbed Tavish with his stick. One or two boys tried to grab the dog by the tail and pull it back. Katie was infuriated. She waded in and the next thing she knew she was wielding her stick like a truncheon round the skulls of the offending mob. She'd knocked one or two of them back off their heels, but she had the feeling more were coming up behind her. She whirled to take account of them, and knocked a couple of sconces into the gutter. Then she turned back to give a really good bash and at that moment felt a restraining hand on her shoulder.

"Easy, girl, easy," said Tavish. "I think you've driven them off."

She looked around. Nothing was moving, except the poor dog, who was trying to lick his damaged paws. The boys were huddled together and giving her a gaze of earnest apprehension, as if to ask what was she so worked up about? She stared them down.

"What's got into the lot of you?" she asked, waving her stick. And they kept their eyes on the stick. "You're horrible," she shouted, "torturing a poor dog that's done nothing to you. All you're doing is showing how mean and ugly you are. Haven't you got the sense to see that? No. Of course you don't because you're stupid too!"

At this, one of them threw a small rock.

"Who threw that rock?" she said. Her spirit was up now. She marched towards them, waving her stick. "You're mean and ugly and stupid! And what's worse, you smell bad!"

Tavish pulled her back. "Let's not get into a contest of who's got the best insults. We'd not win." He lifted the damaged puppy and held Katie's hand as the two of them backed slowly away. Once they were certain of their escape they dashed back to Lanchester Mansion, where they laid the pup down and tried to minister to it.

"You're a right terror when your back's up, ain't you?" said Tavish, as he tied a splint to the poor beast's paw.

"I don't know what you're talking about," she answered.

"They'll remember who cracked their skulls, and I'm thinking maybe they'll be hurrying the other way next time they see you with a stout staff in your hands."

"I don't see that I did anything so extraordinary." The dog gave a little whimper. "Oh, this poor one," she said, turning her attention to the animal, "I'm afraid he'll never walk really sound again."

"I feel a mood's come over this place," said Tavish. "Like on a sunny day when a cloud comes to cover the sun and there's a shiver and a little breeze. Do you know what I'm feeling?"

"No I don't. I think you're a silly man with your feelings and your shivers. All I did was knock a few heads, and they were heads that needed knocking. We'll have to be giving this poor boy a name since he's ours now. Think I'll call him Tommy, in honor of my own Tom who's out on the wild waters."

So they named the poor mutt Tommy Dog and they kept him with them in the house. That spring Tommy Dog came back to life. Katie's daily routine now had to include taking the time to be certain he was walked and fed. She made him a bed at the foot of hers where he curled up in the night, and in return he gave her what companionship he could.

That was the outward event that made a change in Katie Jean's life at that time. But there was also another more interior change that came to pass. Katie was dismayed to find that her customary monthly blood did not come flowing from her the way it always had. She waited to see if perhaps it was taking somewhat longer, as on occasion it had done before. But truly there was no sign of it. She thought of the casual indiscretions she'd committed with Tom, and started to tremble a little with thoughts of what she'd done. She was altogether feeling more tired in the nights, and then one morning when she woke coughing up her last night's meal she roused herself to a good bout of bashing her stupid self for ever getting mixed up with a man who'd run away as soon as he'd kissed her, and then another good bout of wondering whatever she could do about the trouble she'd inflicted on herself now. She didn't feel this problem was in the nature of one she could discuss with Tavish, and much less with Madam Lanchester, because she'd have her out of the house if she ever found out, so her only confidant was Tommy Dog, but his begging eyes and twisted paws gave no indication of the right route to follow. She found herself walking through her chores, looking sideways at her days with the hopeful thought that at some point in the future she'd be able to look back with the grandest sort of satisfaction on how she'd sorted this problem, but with the most desperate kind of worry in the present as to what she was going to do.

In her walks through the town she started having a feeling that the people were no longer quite the people she had known. At first she was liable to put this down to her own moods, which had become a little bit flitty, fleet and darting and at times seemed a bit wounding even to her. But she couldn't dissolve away the sounds of broken crockery, and the harsh edge to the words she heard spoken, and the way sometimes the housewives looked at the blades of their knives and contemplated their husbands' throats. So she found herself taking her stick along for even the shortest walk through the town. And once Tommy Dog was up to it, she'd take him along as well, though what protection he could offer was a question she hoped not to have answered. One time she had to drag him snarling from a mop of black hair and a vindictive pair of eyes she remembered well. *Let that clod follow me*, she thought. *I beat him once, I'll beat him again if it's what he's a mind to.* But there was no mistaking the feeling that something was coming. It was in the air. Like the rumble of distant thunder that startles the stillness of a quiet afternoon.

While Katie was taking pains to settle her troubled heart, Tom, adrift on the ocean's tumbling currents, was coming to terms with his cabin mates. Where work was to be done on deck Vincenzo, who had the other lower bunk, was the best and most to be relied on seaman any could hope for. His agility at mounting the mast to reach the rigging was unequaled, and the speed and dexterity with which he would tie and untie the sheets had impressed all the crew most favorably. There was, however, about him a darkness and a willingness to hurt that made him one to be approached gingerly. The incautious were likely to find themselves on the pointed barb of a sarcasm, or apprehensive of some elusive yet undefined threat that had come tantalizingly close to actual expression. He was mostly to be found in the company of two others of similar makeup, one Diego, the surgeon, and the carpenter, who went only by the name of Mr. Chips. The first evening out from port there was a brawl on deck and a seaman was stabbed in the forearm. Diego had ministered to his patient as best he could, cleaning the wound and applying several stitches, but the Master had berated him for the unsteadiness of his hands, and this put him in a foul humor. He was recounting the events to his two mates, and Tom happening to pass at that moment, he thought he might take the opportunity to start a fight, so he asked

Tom why he'd jostled his elbow, and when Tom answered there'd been no jostling, Mr. Chips inquired if Tom was calling his friend a liar.

Tom said, "There's been enough nonsense for one night. I don't see the need to be manufacturing more."

At this Vincenzo took on himself the role of peace keeper. "Now, friends, Tom's my cabin mate. Like he says, there'll be no nonsense." He gave a sly smile. "There's no need for us to be doing harm to one another. The wind and the weather are up for that, surely. A wet spot on the deck at night, and a man could slip and be overboard before he'd ever have the chance to holler 'chuck.' Or a sheet that's a little frayed up top, where no notice is given, suddenly a man's falling twenty feet head first and breaking his neck. Why should we be fighting one another when there's already distress and destruction waiting at our heels?"

"Thanks, friend Vincenzo, your reassurances leave me feeling a good deal more fearful than I was before."

"Hah," and he gave Tom a poke in the ribs and not a gentle one, "you've no need to worry. I can assure you if ever it should happen that I'd want to do a man in, he'd have no warning of it beforehand." He winked and passed on.

Tom's other cabin mate was a native of Slothikay who'd taken the name of Brutus. His face, like that of many from that region, was disfigured by a multitude of tattoos, in particular an open staring eye in the middle of his forehead, a decorative motif favored by many from that district. This, as well as what was perceived as a casual regard for discipline, had put him under a bit of a cloud with the Master. However, he was by nature gentle as a lamb, and Tom had found him knowledgeable in his discourse, with a surprising sagacity and a scientific understanding not to be expected in one of such meager learning as his appearance connoted. He also bore with him always a small idol of Maddibimbo the one-eyed monkey god he reverenced, and in the evenings would frequently bow down before it and offer up prayer in a pagan tongue Tom could not comprehend. The idol was a hideous figure of a hairy monkey with a long tail and one lonely eye set in the center of its head. The hole representing the eye had in the past been filled with a chip of green glass, but this had fallen out and gotten lost shortly before shipping out on the current voyage, an event which Brutus apprehended was a portent of some calamitous consequence. He had been many years on the sea and had acquired a thorough knowledge of boats and tackle and rigging and all things maritime, but more than that he claimed acquaintance with certain mysteries of the pelagic depths, and asserted that he was on a familiar footing with nautical powers that some seamen regarded as illusory.

Tom and Brutus would sometimes discourse on the roundness of the world and the stupidity of men, in the mornings when the sun was shining brightly and the ship was turned into the wind so the salt surf sprayed into their faces and the chop dumped them first up and then down. One such morning they were washing down the deck when Tom, tearing himself from his inner visions of Katie, inquired of Brutus why it was that a man with such a surprising depth of knowledge as himself had labored so many years and yet had not risen above the level of a common seaman. Tom was certain that Brutus's accomplishments merited a greater distinction than that which he possessed.

"The answer is a simple one, and can be given in one word," was Brutus's reply.

"And what word would that be?"

"Rum."

"And a fine word too. A word fit to be held between the teeth and to sit on a man's tongue."

"To some it is."

"In your case, Brutus, I've not observed you to be a drinking man. Or perhaps you're one of those so accomplished in the art of imbibing that the effects are not evident, and you're walking about all the day with a skinfull of comfort and no one the wiser."

"That would not be me. I'm a brawling and a battling drunk. I'm a bitter and a bashing drunk. I'm truly better sober, but always I have the thirst. I'm a man of many faults, though I strive to amend them." And then he sat for a moment, looking at the bucket of soapy water before him. The only sounds were the calls of the seabirds, and the creaking of the rigging, and the slop of the waves against the hull. Ramsey strolled by, casting an eye in their direction. Ramsey,

Tom had concluded, was a man consumed by some inner struggle or antagonism, one he never spoke of, but which gave evidence of itself in facial twitches and fidgets of his fingers. This morning he seemed lost in an internal soliloquy and it's questionable whether the presence of Tom and Brutus registered on his conscious mind as he made his rounds of the ship. After he had passed aft, Tom took one of his silver dollars from his pocket and tossed it in the air. It was ever his idle habit to intervene in the tussle of the heads and the tails. He made note of the fact that this morning tails were in the ascendant, and replaced the coin in his pocket.

Then, seeing Brutus had paused to watch what he was doing, he explained, "Just a thing my hands like to do. My fingers want some occupation other than growing the fingernails."

"Growing the fingernails . . ." He chuckled and resumed his work. "There are many things like fingernails, things that grow, and would not stop . . . There are things that would cover the entire world if they could."

"Yes . . . And I think I know what you're speaking of. They're called ideas."

"Actually I was thinking more of a sponge, like this one." Tom looked blank. Brutus went on, "Your sponge lives forever by making more of itself. "In that way it's like your fingernail."

"I see."

"It's the first trick life ever taught herself. Divide and conquer."

"Now that I don't see. What's your meaning of divide and conquer? I've washed with many a sponge, but how does it divide, and whom will it conquer?"

"These sponges were torn from an animal – I'll reconsider – not an animal – from a sea-fungus that was born and still lives and goes on living," said Brutus. "The first living thing, so the wise tell us, was a single cell. That cell divided, and there were two cells identical to the first. So like they were, they were the one thing."

"Right. I'm with you."

"And those cells divided again, and so on. What I mean when I say divide and conquer. So the first cell is still living, and all the other cells are the first cell as well."

"Very good. So that's the divide, but where's the conquer?"

"Your sponge continues to live until it is destroyed, but never will it die. The cells of the sponge divide, the sponge grows larger and still larger. If there was nothing to stop it, the whole world would be one sponge."

"Brutus, it's a pleasure to converse with a philosopher such as yourself who's inspired by a sponge and a bucket of soapy water."

"There are lessons in everything, if only you look."

"Never was spoken a truer word."

There was a pause as they moved to another portion of the deck, wringing suds from their sponges and stretching their backs.

"Life's second trick was a bit more perplexing. To this day we've never yet seen to the bottom of it. Life's second trick was to die."

"And a foul trick that was, I'm thinking," said Tom.

"And certain it was not."

". . . I should have known there was a paradox lurking. So make your meaning known."

"Without death there would be no reproduction by means of sex," said Brutus.

Tom could not fathom this. "I'm not quite following you. I've had sex, but I'm still alive. Not to dispute a philosopher so lofty as yourself, but you might want your philosophy to correspond in some degree with the actual facts and daily events of existence. Not that sex has been a daily event of late."

"Tom, at some point, so the wise tell us, a living being, instead of reproducing itself by dividing, united first with another being. The active blood of the male united with the passive blood of the female to form a third being. The third being was a reproduction of neither the first two; it was an individual unto itself. And the two parents still lived, until they died, and they passed altogether out of existence. Unlike the sponge, who is always with us. So in this manner love and death were brought together into the world at one and the same moment, and since that time there's no having one without the other."

"Your explanation is clear, and I'll confess it's a wonder I never thought to see it that way myself."

"Truly they are the two sides of the coin that fate and chance are always tossing."

"So they are . . . "

And with confabulations such as this and others, Tom found a place among his mates. The days were bright and clear, and the work was tiring but bracing as the Queen of Bel Harbor sped on her way towards the port of Kashahar.

CHAPTER THREE
A FRESH PAIR OF BOOTS

THE TRAVELING MAN sat in the loggia of the Trento Hotel and looked with great sorrow on the ruin of his shoes. Since the night he'd let Tom get the better of him and haul his shoes away on the cart, they'd undergone a transformation for the worse. They'd spent the night out in the rain and been covered with mud, and that hadn't done them as much good as you might imagine. After he'd recovered them and worn them a bit they'd repaid him by giving him blisters, and rubbing the skin raw on several of his toes. He was altogether dissatisfied with his footwear, so when they'd reached Trento, still a day and a half from Indradoon, he'd sent Fergus in search of the best boot maker the town could offer.

It hadn't taken him long. He'd returned with a cordwainer named Smith who had measured his feet and had also proven to be a fount of information. Smith informed him that a gang of slaves had escaped and set up a camp in the vicinity of a vast and gloomy swamp not far to the southeast, judging that the difficulty of the terrain would deter most pursuit.

"Are they likely to be finding more recruits?"

"See that one?" Smith pointed out a gentleman who was accompanied by a slave bearing a lamp. "See how close he's keeping his slave? I don't actually see the chain, but I feel as if it's there, and he might almost seem to be making haste to reach his destination. Never before have I seen the masters in a hurry. The Marshal's the one supposed to round up any who get away. Our Marshal – " here he spat, "he's put his strategy in place. He's got hisself so drunk he's locked in his own jail. Seems he plans to observe these heinous reprobates from that post, and he's well prepared to capture any that should stumble into a cell."

24

"I know the plantation owners have their own teams of men."

"Don't they. And they would like to replace those with slaves also. Have the slaves keep the slaves in line, but they haven't figured out yet how to make that work. So there's still some employment for free men, mostly bravos from the coast or the odd castoff from the army."

The traveler contemplated the town square with its venerable palms and colonnades. "How would I find my way to the encampment of these freed slaves?"

"They are not freed. They are escaped."

"Sorry. Where is the encampment of these escaped slaves?"

"Why would you go there? I wouldn't if I was you. They'd slit your throat as soon as look at you."

"Why would they try that? I've little they could steal."

"I only know they have much to fear, and when men are afraid they look for someone they can hurt."

"You've learned that lesson wrong way front. We look for those that are afraid so we can hurt them, like wolves to a deer. Do we not?"

"But why would you want to go among them?"

"I have a great work to do and they are a weapon ready to my hand. Mankind has a passion for destruction, but from time to time needs to be pointed in the proper direction."

"No, creation, not destruction. Of all living creatures, man is the one that makes."

"And what he makes is destruction. The boots you're making for me, are they made to last?"

"Of course they will last. The boots I make are of the very finest quality."

"But they will wear out in time."

"They will last you the rest of your life."

"And after my life, what then?"

"After your life, why do you care?"

"So what man makes, he makes for just a little time, because he knows he will die. He knows all he creates will perish. Every brick he places on top of another, another will come and knock down. Nothing will last. The children demolish what their parents put up,

25

and they call this progress because every step forward is a means to destroy more and yet more. He says I'm making the greatest civilization the world will know, and he looks about and sees only the things he's wasted and used up. If God is the creator, man is the destroyer. And I'm just here to help him along. So can you show me the way to these escaped slaves?"

"If you'd like, I'll show you tomorrow when I return with your boots."

So now he sat, awaiting Smith's reappearance and enduring Fergus's rendition of a popular ballad, accompanying himself on the banjo. He sang,

> My mother was a Western woman
> > Skilled in grammary,
> She taught me young to pluck the harp
> > The sword was not for me.
> The words she sang still haunt my mind
> > Her antique voice still charms,
> As I wander the world in search of a love
> > And a woman to hold in my arms.

Trento was a small town set amidst miles of cotton fields. At its center sat a paved piazza lined by rows of palms. There was a fair amount of money and commerce in Trento, though not immediately apparent, being wealth of a lazier, less bustling variety than that found in Port Jay, which he'd just left, the sort of wealth that could sit down and appraise itself in the mirror and think *Damn, I'm good looking. Think I'll just set here awhile and take in the view.*

When Smith arrived, the new boots of cordovan leather were found to be quite acceptable. The traveler walked them up and down the piazza, gave Fergus his obligatory kick, and then pronounced them decent. Setting off with Smith his boots were christened in the swampy waters of a grove of mangroves, this being the difficult terrain Smith had spoken of.

The leader of the escaped slaves was a heavily muscled black named Famularis. His right cheek was marred by a cross that had been deeply burned into it, and there was a good deal of puffiness about his left eye. It was an altogether motley group he led, mostly women and youngsters. They'd erected a few tents and looked to be feeding themselves by foraging for fruits and berries and bringing down the occasional turkey vulture or white-tailed deer. It must have been scant fare they were surviving on, and the water here looked stale and foul. The traveler had had to assure Famularis of his good intentions and had submitted to the surrender of his pistol and his two sharp knives, and they were now huddled round a guttering fire, roasting a haunch of venison, with a few rays of glimmering twilight still slanting through the ancient cypresses. The sounds of the forest were hushed, just a few birds still calling. Bats flittered in the gloaming. Famularis shoved another log onto the dying fire, and turning to his visitors asked them why the smartest thing he could do wouldn't be just to kill them and take their possessions. He especially made note of the jaunty pair of boots sported by one of his guests.

"That wouldn't take you very far, would it?" asked the traveler. "You've a problem, seems to me, that'll not be sorted by a pair of boots. You're cut off from your family, and any friends you had were probably killed or most certainly disciplined. How was it that you came to break out?"

"I was to be whipped for killing a man, Massah. But I seized the whip from the yobbo's hand and beat him with it."

"Don't call me master. Who was the man you killed?"

"Yes, Massah. Another slave. That's why I was only to be whipped. He thought he could take my things and lord it over me. He was the white man's tool. The Master put the knife into me but it was he who turned the knife. It was he who put me out to work each morning and then took my woman behind my back. He thought he could build his little empire in the white man's dust but he was wrong and I killed him."

"Who was your master?"

"Lord Merriwether."

"An upstanding and a God fearing man," said Smith.

"Yes, Massah. And a whoremonger, and a rum runner, and a slave dealer," added Famularis.

"I see he has reason to fear God," said the traveler with a wicked grin. "So now you've broken out, and you've taken some with you. But you can't move from here without falling into the arms of those who are hunting for you, and you can't stay here. Either you'll starve or they'll come for you and burn you out. You can't stand still. For you to stand still is to die. You have to make a move now, here on the last day of April. All you've got are girls and boys."

"They was the house slaves convenient to be led out. The field hands was under the gun and could not get away."

"Maybe I'm thinking the girls and boys you've led here will start seeing the truth of the matter, that they'd be better off where someone will take care of them, even if it comes at the price of a good whipping."

"The truth of the matter? I freed them. They is loyal, to me."

"Right now one of those young ones is thinking what can he get for the price of your head. You sit still you die."

"Has you been hungry? Has you been whipped? Has you seen your brothers and your sisters – allathem — dead before they's twenty years old? No. I don't think you has, and a little bit I hate you for that. Has you been sold away from your mama and your papa? Don' tell me the truth of the matter."

"Truly do you think you're better off here where you're scrounging for the crust of existence? Or wouldn't you like a good master who'd take care of you and see your needs are met?"

"Here we is free."

"No, you're slaves still. What a man wants is not to be free. A man wants food in his stomach and a house to live in, good clothes to put on his back and a woman to take them off for. Very little of that have you got. There's no man on God's earth wouldn't give up that empty word free in return for that, and isn't that the bargain we're all of us making every day, to sell our freedom for the best price we can get? There's no way to live but to live in chains."

"The greatest good a man can claim is his freedom. I is free to make myself; I is not made by my masters. The only one who can enslave my soul is me. And what is your name anyway?"

"Leave my name out of it. I do not want my name invoked. You can call me Mister X."

"I don't want to sit here all night and listen to the gibes of a nameless one. If you can talk to me you can tell me who you are. I tell you I am free now. True, all the day I scrounge to meet my needs, but they is my needs, not those of my master."

Smith saw fit to interject that if he wanted to remain free, Famularis would have to leave this spot, since Merriwether and the other owners were sure to be coming.

The traveler brushed this aside. "What brought you here, and what keeps you here, is your hate: hatred, nothing else. If you were smart you'd be a good slave, but you hate your master and you hate his whip, and you hate them both so much you'd wipe out their whole stinking race before you'd go back to being a slave. Everything inside you says it's right to hate him, so hate him you must. This is your strength. This is your army."

"If I was smart I'd be a good slave? Really do you say this? Then I'm glad I am not smart. But also I am not stupid. I know what your friend says is true. I cannot long survive here. I must move, and all these I must take with me. It is not an easy thing. I need more like me. There is others, I know, who would join if they thought they had a chance of something better."

"There are others. For many years, for decades, the masters have brought you and those like you across the ocean to pick their cotton and grow their food. But the crop they've been planting is you, and now it's time to reap the harvest. There are others being brought this very moment to Indradoon to be sold in the markets there. I will lead you to them. They haven't been broken. They'll be hard, and yearning, like you, to be free. Your hatred is the spark to ignite them."

Famularis took this in and pondered it for some time in silence. Lifting the roasting haunch of venison from the fire he offered it to his guest.

"Save it for yourself," he answered.

"You will not share my food? I's not worthy?" He glanced at the traveling man, then stared at the grass around his feet. It was difficult for him to look white men in the eye.

"You need it more than I."

"Massah Smith?"

Smith silently declined. The last glimmers of sunlight were gone. Their faces were lit solely by the flickering flames licking at the meat.

"Where are these others?" asked Famularis.

"Close at hand."

Famularis thought awhile, as though musing over a difficult puzzle, while he chewed slowly. "Very good. I would still much like to kill you and take your boots, but you can keep them for now . . . And I think it will all be simple. Once there is enough of us we can live our own way. This forest has many riches; she can provide. We will live together and all be friends. There is no need always to grow this cotton. We will grow the fruits that spring from the earth."

"The fruit of revenge is death. There is no other fruit that grows more fertile from this soil. Return to me my pistol and my knives. We're friends now."

At a signal from Famularis his weapons were handed back to him. With his artillery on him he felt more like his true self. "I will lead you to the others, and they will be a knife in your hand, a knife to put to your master's throat, and isn't that a throat worthy to be slit?"

"You will lead me to them?"

"Certain it is that I will."

"Swear to me."

"I swear."

"Not that. Tha's just words." Famularis took a dagger from his belt. "We will swear with the oath of blood. We will be close as brothers." He slashed the dagger across the palm of his hand, raising a riband of blood. He held his palm out to the traveler, who drank from it, tasting the salty iron tang that filled the man's veins. Then eagerly, as though gleaning a reward unlooked for, the traveler slashed his own palm and held it out to Famularis. When they were done, they sealed the wounds with ashes from the fire.

Famularis said, "Now we is bound by blood. You will lead me to these slaves who is to be sold."

"Certain it is that I will."

"Lead me tonight. I's ready."

"You're not ready. Tonight is too soon. Tonight I will return to town. I will be back with the morning's first light. Prepare your campground to move."

"What is there to prepare? All we have we carry on our backs. We will be ready."

As Smith was steering the traveler back towards town, they came to a large clearing. The traveler gazed at the immensity of the stars above. Like a shiver down the back of his spine he sensed before he saw them the witches, cavorting in their gaudy evil, dancing before the stars, making them go dark and then light again, as they passed in front. In that clammy silence he could almost hear their dismal cries, and almost fathom their worthless, empty hearts.

CHAPTER FOUR
THE TOSS OF A COIN

ON THE SAME EVENING the traveler spoke with Famularis, the Master
of the Queen of Bel Harbor was dining with Ramsey and his First
Mate in his cabin at the stern of the ship. These were men of commerce, their ears never weary of the prattle of chaffer, so conversation
turned on matters of merchandising, as to what profit would be reaped
from the wines and silks and the richly-tinted featherwork, a specialty
of Port Jay, the ship carried in her hold. Also there was discussion concerning a certain laxness of discipline that had been observed amongst
the seamen. The First Mate put it down to simple rudeness, but the
Master felt there was more to it than that. He felt that the brawl on
deck the first night out, when one man had been stabbed in the arm,
the drunkenness he'd observed on occasion, even in the case of the surgeon, and other such manifestations of an impulsive character should
be brought to a halt by the arrest and punishment of a prominent individual who could be made an admonitory spectacle to the rest of the
crew. He'd observed this to work wonders on other occasions where it
was the character of the men that was at issue.

At the same time, the gimbaled oil light in Tom's cabin before the
mast illuminated an altogether different scene: three berths and the
floor, albeit the illumination afforded the upper berth, where Brutus
slept, was little and dark. The cabin was not spacious, there was just
about room for one chair, and then the floor for those that chose to
squat.

Tom, Brutus and Vincenzo were perched on their berths conversing of the day's events. None of them being needed up above, the
moment gave a wanted chance of communal contentment. Vincenzo lit a pipe, and taking a good puff, passed it in a friendly fashion
across to Tom.

"Opium," he said. "Pure as the night air."

Tom thought it the best wisdom to assent to this friendly overture. Having taken a puff himself, he made to pass the pipe to Brutus in the upper bunk. After some hesitation, Brutus declined, so he passed it back to Vincenzo, who said, "I've seen you've a way of tossing a coin. What if I was to wager a coin myself. Would you take a chance on it?"

Tom had no interest in gambling. Especially with Vincenzo. "That wasn't my intent. You'll find I'm not a betting man."

"Just a small bet. Between friends . . . Might as well have a little bit of fun."

"If you're desperate for a wager of course we'll have one. What shall it be?"

Brutus broke in, "That smell you're putting under my nostrils gives me some unease. Either you will stop smoking or I will leave this place."

"Then I think you're bound to leave, as it looks the odds on that are two to one, eh, friend Tom?"

"And why are you always calling me friend Tom? Plain Tom will do."

"Alright, plain Tom, so you'd not be my friend?"

"Pass that up here. I find my legs are too heavy to be moving just now."

"Yes, Brutus," said Tom.

Brutus took a deep puff. "Ah, this is a good pipe. Here, Tom."

Vincenzo stood. His face, now it was higher than the light, took on a queer expression. "I'll wager my dollar against yours."

"Are you putting the pipe away then?" asked Brutus.

"Enough for tonight. Here's my dollar. I'll claim tails. Toss your coin, plain Tom."

"Not plain Tom. Just Tom. Simple Tom."

"That's the way of naming you then: simple Tom. Toss your coin, simple Tom."

Tom wanted nothing to do with this. He started to say no, but he looked at the expression on Vincenzo's face and what he said instead was, "All right. One toss." He tossed.

"No, no, you've caught it in the air. Let it fall to the floor so all can see for themselves if it's heads or tails."

"It makes no difference if I catch it. It's just this way I'm less like to lose it."

"Let it fall to the floor I say."

Tom bit back his irritation and tossed again. "Now it's rolled under the chair."

"Well let's have a look."

It was proven to the satisfaction of all that the coin had come up heads. Vincenzo was crestfallen, but he passed his dollar over to Tom.

"There. I hope you're content now you've had your bit of fun."

"You've got to give me a chance to get it back."

"Here, I'll give it back to you."

"No, no, you won. It's yours, man."

"I'm sorry we started this."

"I'll double the wager. My last two dollars."

"I'd hold onto them if I was you."

Mr. Chips put his head in the room. "It looks to be smooth sailing tonight. There's a light breeze from the east, and the skies are clear. Thought you'd want to know."

"Thanks, friend Chippie, but here below the sailing is naught so smooth as all that. Luck has turned her back on me."

"Is it a wager you're having?"

"Vincenzo just wanted to toss a coin," said Tom.

"Might another join in?"

"No. Now he's lost his dollar I'm thinking that'll be the end of it."

"Here, simple Tom, I've two dollars more."

"Keep your last dollars. I've a stash of dollars of my own." This unguarded phrase echoed in the chambers of Vincenzo's mind. He shared a look with Mr. Chips.

Mr. Chips said, "There's room in my cabin for a table, if you've a mind to a game of cards like a civilized soul."

"Perhaps another night," said Vincenzo as Mr. Chips, with a tip of his hat, moved on. "I'll claim tails again. It's due to come up tails so I'm doubling the wager."

"I trust you're aware the logic of that is unsound. Each toss the chance is the same. If it was heads ten times in a row, still the chance that it will be tails is only one in two."

"Is that right, friend Brutus, do you agree with that?"

"I'd agree with another pipe," said Brutus.

"Another pipe it'll be. Now toss, simple Tom."

Tom tossed again. "It seems luck is not with you tonight."

"Here. Take it. My last dollars. And you'll take my opium too. Clearly I'll have nothing left, dealing with the two of you."

"And you've no one to thank but yourself. It was your constant notion to toss."

"Here, Brutus, sit up." Vincenzo handed him the pipe.

Brutus took a puff.

"You'll have to give me one more chance to win it all back. One more toss. It can't come up heads forever."

"I've told you the logic of that is wrong."

Vincenzo was taking the earring from his ear. "Here. I'll wager my earring against the four dollars you have in your possession."

Tom didn't answer. Noticing it was getting dark he checked the oil in the lamp.

"What do you say? My earring against your four dollars."

"I've had enough wagering. Now," trimming the wick and adding a bit more oil, "we're casting a little more light on the situation."

"What if our words were coins?" said Vincenzo.

"What's this you're saying?"

"I'm just minded of a story I think we were told when we were young ones. I think me Mam told me. That the words came out their mouths like solid things that fell to the ground. Have you no memory of such a story?"

"Not at all."

"Maybe they could be coins, or a lucky earring such as this, that's brought me a great deal of good luck."

"Lucky earring?"

Brutus intoned, "The thieving children of Slothikay played a game. They'd steal a coin and place it beneath the tongue to elude detection."

"I don't want your earring. Have you ever seen me with an earring? Next you'll be cutting off your mustache to wager that, calling it your lucky whisker."

"That must be it. Your young child makes your best thief." Then to Tom, "You want my mustache too? Would you like a wager for my nose also? You'll be wanting my whole face next."

"If I wanted a face I'd wager with Brutus. His is worth winning."

"My earring is gold, it is worth more than your four dollars, but I'd not ask you to wager more. I'm so certain I'll win I'll call it even odds."

"Gold, is it?"

"Bite it, but gentle." Vincenzo handed Tom his earring.

"Yes, soft it is, like gold."

"It is gold. So will you toss then?"

"It's unlike you to propose a wager unfair to yourself."

"Just a bit of fun as I said at first. We're all friends here."

"You'll take tails again?"

"Yes yes."

Tom tossed again.

"Oh, it's a foul night for me!"

"I'll just hold onto this earring then. Not that I've a use for it."

"Luck's turned against me, but my strategy's a good one. Always bet the same and double the wager each time, sooner or later I'm sure to win it all back."

"There seems to be a fault with your strategy."

"The only fault is I've nothing left to wager."

"Here, take your lucky earring. I wouldn't be cursed with the luck it's brought you."

"No, it's yours now. But fortune won't always run with you. I'll win it back. It's a long voyage." He put his hands behind his head. "That's an honest coin, is it?"

"I won it from you. You can best answer that yourself."

"Beaten, and by my own coin . . . But I'll win it back. There's never a tide that doesn't turn. No, no, keep it. You won it."

Tom, with some little discomfort, pocketed the earring. He was unaccustomed to winning, and though he knew in the logic of the cosmos all chances were even, he couldn't escape knowing that good fortune was certain to be repaid with bad. Also, Vincenzo seemed to be making a point of taking his loss lightly, which gave him further cause for concern. But the night had been a good one for him. When finally he drifted off, he dreamt of the mermaids in their coral city at the bottom of the sea, and their seahorse chariots, their wild kisses, and their tangled hair.

CHAPTER FIVE
WITCHCRAFT IN THE WOODS

FORT ESTAMOR had hardly been a fort. It had been little more than a bivouac really. Half Moon's braves had little difficulty surrounding it and killing the soldiers it housed. Their bodies and equipment were built into a towering pile as a monument to the bloody triumph, and the wooden walls were burnt to the ground. Half Moon was certain none had escaped, so it would be several weeks at least before the army headquarters learned of their loss.

The triumphal potlatch had been held last night in the large clearing at the center of the settlement. This was the tribe's permanent home. Here their longhouses were built, and in the center stood the tribe's totem pole. Last night the clearing had been filled with dancing figures, and many tables had been piled high with fresh venison and withy baskets heaped with succulent vegetables. The number of braves assembled here was unparalleled. Never before had so many tribes gathered together under one man. Storm Panther had come with his hundred braves on horseback. They were camped a small distance away but had arrived last night to join the dancing. The nearly finished siege tower had been brought forward on its massive wheels of cedar to be celebrated and praised. It was necessary to complete it quickly and then they would strike. They must strike soon; already some were wondering when they could return to complete their spring planting. Half Moon had given gifts of horses, whiskey and guns to the most courageous warriors, and at the height of the ceremonial dances his totem, the great black bear, had come and spoken to him directly, promising victory and a glorious death. Half Moon knew it would be only a matter of days before Port Jay lay under his heel, and the white man was turned away forever from this land. In the late hours of the night, the throng had slowly drifted away to the longhouses that lay in a ring around the central plot, or to the wickiups under the branches of the surrounding trees, there to swear oaths binding them to magnificent achievements in the up-coming campaign, and to couple in frenzied acts of lust.

This morning Half Moon was standing before his longhouse, taking joy in the light and warmth given freely by his noble ancestor the sun. Several braves, and not a few maidens, were still asleep, prostrate at the feet of the enormous totem pole, where they had dropped during the course of last night's festivity. He took delight in observing the birds, how they danced and bobbed, sweeping through the branches of the pines and hemlocks. Birdsong was returning to the woods. The starlings and blackbirds were back, and the finches would be arriving soon. There were several gulls this morning, more than usual, doubtless a reminder that his path lay in the direction of the sea. One of the gulls had dropped a feather, which lay near his feet. He picked it up, a token to knot among the charms he wore about his neck. His grandfather, Sudden Lightning, had fought a campaign along the same piece of ground on which he would be fighting, but his enemy had been the Indians of the Red Hawk Lodge, whom Half Moon now numbered among his friends. The tale of his grandfather's campaign was told often when Half Moon was growing up. Sudden Lightning drove his enemy into the sea, just as Half Moon would soon be doing, and when he arrived at the shore he was granted a message from the Great Spirit. An eagle flew over-head and led him to the bower of Dappled Doe, whom he took as his squaw. Half Moon wondered if he would also be vouchsafed a sign.

Wild Otter and his nephew Barking Dog were fletching arrows nearby. Wild Otter was rather stout and had a broken nose. Barking Dog was tall and his features were such that he played a role in many day dreams of the younger maidens. Seeing Half Moon, Wild Otter held up the arrow he was working on and said, "We will have use for these soon."

Half Moon walked to where the two men stood. "Yes, we will, but I had rather we had more muskets."

"When we kill the soldiers we will take their muskets," said Bark-ing Dog. "But now they are bringing something more deadly even than muskets. Now they have rifles, that fire bullets, not just lumps of lead. You can load them and take many shots before reloading."

"Yes, I've seen these rifles," said Half Moon. "We even have a few. Storm Panther has been practicing with his, using it when he rides his horse. We will use these rifles when we besiege Port Jay. You see, the soldiers will sally forth like this. Imagine the soldiers are attacking. Imagine they are coming from here." He indicated a direction close to the path where the racks stood for drying the salmon. "They will not see Storm Panther and his horses hidden behind these rocks over here."

"Why do they not see Storm Panther? Don't they send out scouts?" asked Wild Otter.

"Yes, but the scouts that see Storm Panther are killed, probably by these arrows, so when they come to attack us they have no suspicion that any is in their rear. They see us and they attack. And what do we do?"

"I don't know," said Barking Dog. "And wouldn't the death of the scouts make the soldiers suspicious?"

"You have no concept of strategy. When they attack, we retreat."

"What about Storm Panther?" asked Wild Otter.

"Not yet," said Half Moon. "First we retreat and draw the soldiers on, then when –"

"This I've seen before, luring them into a trap where they are surrounded," said Barking Dog, with a look of disdain, as if this were all something he'd known since he was a child.

"But always it works," said Half Moon. "What is different this time is that Storm Panther has horses and rifles, so when we suddenly stand up to them and they see they are in our snare, Storm Panther will let loose with many bullets. This is how the white men will die."

Half Moon had passed many afternoons discussing tactics such as these with his fellow braves. It was one of the things he enjoyed the most. The men returned to their task and he left them and went to stand before his longhouse.

Breezy Woodchuck, his number one squaw, had waited for a chance to talk to him. Once she saw he was no longer in the company of men, she drew near. Her eyes were deep like mountain pools, rinsed clear in the last runoff from the winter snows. She smiled gravely, placing her cheek next his shoulder, and asked why he had cried out and left her side in the early hours of the morning.

He told her solemnly of the great work that was in hand, to drive the white man back into the ocean from which he had come. "We are the children of the promise. The Great Spirit promised this land would be ours. These others are interlopers. I know because I have spent time amongst them, in their city of crooked streets, and I have learned who they are and what they do. They have brought desires and shames we knew nothing of."

"You paint them almost as a different kind of man, one outside the natural order of things."

"Yes, this is the enemy we confront. I have united all our tribes to break their hold and we will succeed. This is my purpose. And once my purpose is achieved, I will lay down my weapons. This is the beauty of the life and the eternal destiny that is ours. You see the snake shed his glorious skin when he needs a new one. I will be the discarded skin. Others will come to lead our people to future triumphs as we are guided by each successive revelation of the incessant soul. I know this will come to pass."

"But you have not come to me as you were used, to play bump-the-frog, and other games of man and woman. What am I to make of this?"

"This is not the time for bump-the-frog. The destiny of nations hangs in the balance, and I have been selected to play a role. I am searching for guidance through the giddy masquerade of cause and consequence, and almost I am certain such guidance will be given."

As he spoke, he saw approaching from the distance three antelopes. They held his attention because they were not native to this place, and because they walked in a manner showing they had a purpose in mind. He also thought it curious that one was smoking a cigarette. All three were female. It was clear this was a visitation, and likely to be one of some importance. When the lead antelope drew near, Half Moon bowed his head in acknowledgement of the honor he was being given. In reply, the antelope took off the skin she wore and stood before him as a woman, wearing an antelope fur.

"Miss Deirdre," he said, "it has been some time since you have made use of the privilege I granted you to travel freely through my lands. I had thought your stratagems, unfolding as they were in extern regions, precluded any involvement in our affairs."

"You are the rightful master of these lands. Nothing happens here that is not your affair."

"My sister the owl informs me of a great light that has recently been put out, and I think by your agency. Was this truly your doing?"

"Aye. I've paid the meddler in the coin he deserved. Now the aftermath is upon us. Many things are afoot, and I've come to assure myself I can trust you to play your part."

"This word trust, what does it mean . . . ? I will tell you. To know someone's motives is to trust him. That is all. You know my motives. My enemies they also know my motives. So you and they and all can trust me. I will act as I must. I am simple and I am true. I am like the arrow you shoot, and you trust it will hit its target." Then, turning to the other two antelopes, "Who are these?"

"I bring a brace of mocking harlots, plucked from an emperor's bed. Their names are Issoria and Vanessa. I hope they will amuse." The other two antelopes took off their skins and turned into young girls wearing antelope furs. Issoria was the one smoking a cigarette. She gave Half Moon a mischievous smile before sitting obediently at his feet.

"I am glad of their company, yet I think there was little need for the assurance you thought these would give. I tell you we are on the move. Already we have taken Fort Estamor."

"It is too sudden. There are plots you know not of."

"Always you plot. Your plots are so thick that you dream up other plots to thwart the plots you planned before. You always think there is some outside encumbrance, and mostly there is not. Always you think there is another thing, a thing outside you with motives you cannot know, so you trust no one. This is your tragedy. Even inside yourself there is another voice you hear that whispers when all else is still, and this other voice has a motive you do not know, so you do not trust even yourself. I am not like you. My spirit is like the fish, that has no need of arms and legs to go where it will. Where it wants to be, there it is."

"There is a munitions depot on Lost Bastard Island."

"I have heard of this."

"And recently much enlarged. Reinforced with massive guns, and the walls strengthened. There are guns that shoot a shell more than a mile, and shells that explode when they land. Drive these soldiers into the sea, still they will sit on that island and bombard the Coast. They know they can never be defeated so long as they hold Lost Bastard Island, because they now have guns that are to their old guns what a real cannon is to a child's toy. I know you are cunning and very brave, but bullets don't care."

Deirdre, as she spoke, had unfolded a map of the Coast, from Port Jay in the east to Kashahar in the west. Much of the map was shaded with pictures of trees, denoting the Forgotten Forest. "So now you sit here like a nut in a nutcracker. One jaw of the nutcracker is Port Jay, the other is Lost Bastard Island. And you are so satisfied with yourself because you have killed a few soldiers."

One of the braves lying prostrate at the foot of the totem pole rolled over and put his head up, blinking his eyes. Issoria stood and surveyed the longhouses and the wickiups beyond. There were people stirring. Deirdre pointed to the map before her. "Here is Port Jay," she said. "This is where the General has his men, with his fresh recruits. So long as he sits here, you can do nothing to him."

"That is what he thinks. But I will be marching on Port Jay."

"That is no good. Others will take care of Port Jay. The soldiers in that fort of stone you could never defeat. However, soon they will be putting themselves where you can do them harm. They will be marching into the Forgotten Forest, their aim being to put you down. This time is coming very soon. And once in the Forest, you will fall on the army and destroy it. You will march to the Coast, pushing these soldiers into the sea."

Half Moon fingered the gull's feather he had added to his necklace this morning.

"So I am coming to tell you this is not the time to attack Port Jay. Sometimes you must wait. You must wait for your enemy to place his neck in your jaw. And that will happen. For now, make sure the horses are curried and dressed, their blankets prepared. And then wait."

"You do not know me if you think I will wait. I will be taking Port Jay. You must tie me down if you want to stop me."

At this she gave him her witchiest look, her face sly, her glittering eyes ancient, but what she said was, "General Hobsbawm's soldiers will have many advantages over your poorly armed braves." Half Moon started to object again; she held up her hand to forestall him. "They are poorly armed. You will come to know this. But you can defeat him if you can choose the place at which you will fight, and you will need the element of surprise. Here," pointing to a spot on the map, "in this narrow passage between the Great Bog and Wind-swept Hill, here is where you will fall on them."

"This is a narrow pathway with many obstacles. It would be foolhardy of them to come this way."

"There are many obstacles, and you must make more. You will build a wall along one side of the passage from here to here."

"More than two miles." Half Moon had spent some time in Port Jay and was familiar with white men's maps.

"Its base will be made of sod. You can remove the sod from the other side of the passageway, so the distance between the Hill and the Great Bog will be much less. Here the army's march will be forced to only double or single file, and here you will fall on them from behind the wall. All this must be done before you leave this place."

"You expect me to dig in the ground like a mole? I say once more, you do not know me."

A man from the further side of the settlement came running, shouting something.

Deirdre went on, "You must understand the urgency. We've dealt a blow to the powers of light. All the law and sanity on which they pride themselves is only a candle in a windy night and the winds will soon be howling. Once put that candle out and paradise is ours. No words will come from our mouths, only sounds, and all signs will be erased. We will exist in the vast darkness, skyclad, uncaged and wholly free!"

It is questionable if Half Moon took this in. There was the sound of a shot and the man who'd been running stumbled. Then all at once a crowd of Indians, many only half dressed, erupted into the large open area in the settlement's center. Half Moon leapt toward the disturbance shouting curses, just as the first line of infantry came out of the woods. The Indians were letting out a continuous babble of confused shouts, and in the relentless noise the soldiers were eerily silent. Their feet floated just above the ground, like ghosts. They advanced in three rank rotation: one line knelt and fired their muskets and then stood and immediately commenced reloading, while the next stepped forward, stood, knelt and fired, then the next. By the time the third group had fired, the first had finished reloading and stepped forward to fire again. They brought a cannon out of the woods and planted it among the outer longhouses. When they fired the cannon, though it made not a sound, the ground shuddered and a cannon ball hit the totem pole, which shook and slowly swayed, toppling with a great sound of rending timber. The Indians, unorganized and unarmed, were quickly being killed. Breezy Woodchuck ran away wailing. The nearly completed siege engine burst into flame. Some braves on horseback attempted a defense, but many were shot down. Through the haze of gunsmoke the soldiers wavered and coalesced, as though under water. Deirdre and the two other witches dropped their antelope furs and sprang naked into a circle. Half Moon lowered himself to hide behind the fallen totem pole. Barking Dog took his bow and the arrow he'd just made, and shot it at the advancing troops.

"How can they be here so soon?" wailed Half Moon. He wanted to run, but his braves sought to impress him with their bravery, and so long as they were fighting he couldn't flee. Wild Otter had some pistols. He lowered himself behind the toppled totem pole near Half Moon and took potshots at the advancing troops. Half Moon saw the flashes of the soldiers' rifles, still ominously silent, and suddenly the pole he hid behind exploded and bit him on the cheek; splinters slashed the turbulent air. Wild Otter took a bullet in the head and rolled to the side. Half Moon ran to him, but a soldier with saber drawn jumped in front and planted his feet preparatory to knocking him down. Half Moon battled with him, seeing Barking Dog take a bayonet in the back out of the corner of his eye. Just as Half Moon fell backward it was as if a curtain was raised and the scene of bloody carnage faded out of sight. In its place was the summer sun in the clearing and a light breeze, bird song and the casual chat of two men fletching arrows. Half Moon looked about himself in wonder.

"That attack was not real," said Deirdre. "But when it comes, that is how it will unfold, if you are not ready. Wait. Make yourself ready. Prepare. And be brave. These soldiers are more merciless than you can imagine and their guns are terrible. And I leave two who can help."

With that, she was gone, an antelope vanishing in the shadows under the trees. When Half Moon returned to his longhouse, Issoria and Vanessa laid their hands on his shoulders.

"We are your sisters," said Issoria.

"We will lead you to your destiny," said Vanessa.

He made to answer, but no words came from his lips, as he slipped, lost, into their terrible gray eyes.

Chapter Six
Something Saved and Something Lost

It was a part of town Katie hadn't visited before and the narrow, twisting alleyways were difficult to navigate. She met few others, and when she did they'd look away and keep their errands to themselves. She'd been given good directions however, so she found the door she sought. It was a crooked door in a squalid house and it bore an enamel plaque which read 'Madam Fortunata' in an intricate, ornate script. She walked the twisted path through the sad, little garden in front, full of dead plants and withered blossoms, and hesitated before knocking at the door. She'd rather have passed this house by and returned home, but the errand that brought her was a desperate and a powerful one, and she hadn't forced herself to come all this way only to turn back now. She knocked and waited a silent minute, her heart almost giving way. She knocked again, harder this time, and was answered by a croaking, squawking voice, "Come again. Come again." *What does that mean,* she thought to herself, *I should come again another time?* "Please, is anyone at home?" she called. She was almost ready to give up and leave when the door was opened by an elderly woman in a faded gown. Her black hair was streaked with gray, and she wore it in a scarf. Something green and orange rested on her shoulder which it took Katie a moment to recognize as a parrot.

"Is this the house of Madam Fortunata?" she asked, knowing full well it was.

"Aye. Come in, girl. But that," pointing to Tommy Dog, "will wait outside."

"He's trained in the house. Must he stay out?"

"He'll trouble my cats."

"Come again," squawked the parrot.

"He won't. He's tame and he'll sit at my knee."

"Suit yourself. You can go, or you can come in, but I'll not have a dog in my house."

Ever since the day he'd been rescued, Tommy Dog had held close to Katie. She knew he'd be skittish if left on his own, remembering the treatment he'd endured before, but Katie saw nothing for it. She told him to be a good dog and tied him to a post, promising to be out as soon as she could.

Once inside, Fortunata proffered a chair in the parlor and then parked herself on a settee. The interior of the house was cluttered with furniture, and the walls were taken up with shelves. There were a multitude of plants in pots of all sizes on the shelves, the window-sills and the floor. Leaves, tendrils and vines were everywhere in a confusion of greenery. There were also many small bottles, alembics and retorts, several with fly-specked labels, and some left open, sit-ting on the various shelves and objects of furniture. Katie was struck by the contrast between the flourishing flora in the house and the dead plants in the garden without.

"I've heard it said you can make up a simple, such as a barrenwort or a mayapple, that a woman can take when she's a need." She felt her resolution wilting under the older woman's coolly assessing gaze.

"There be many such. What have you a need for?" And she took up her fan, which she fluttered in front of her face. Then she stopped, and looking straight at Katie's belly she whispered, "Oh, there's another one inside."

"Is it spelled out on my forehead then?" She smiled uncomfort-ably. "I hadn't thought it was yet so obvious as that."

"Oh, it isn't, it isn't." Fortunata placed her head near Katie's belly and stroked it very gently with her cold, skeletal hand, saying, "Hush now, hush now . . . Its little heart is beating. Yes it is . . ."

"That's what brings me here. I've the need to do away with what's in my belly."

"Come again," squawked the parrot.

"Can he say nothing else?"

"Times he curses me. Come, Henry, on your perch." Evidently

48

Henry was the parrot. Katie saw now he was wearing a pair of spectacles. Fortunata rose and maneuvered him onto a swinging rod where he sat happily clucking to himself. "It's a distressing need."

"That it is. I've a few coppers I can pay."

"This isn't a shop. I'm not a shopkeeper. I'll give you, if I can, what it is you're asking. Then in return you'll give me its worth to you. It's an exchange of gifts. That's not a method would work in a shop, but it's how it's always done. It's not old, this little one. Good you didn't wait. The tiny heart just started beating. But we'll put a stop to it . . ." Fortunata stepped away. Katie began absent-mindedly stroking her tummy, carrying on what Fortunata had begun, soothing herself with soft, gentle strokes.

Fortunata was fanning herself while she examined the bottles on the shelves. "Let me see . . . An admixture of your common buttercup I think. With a little of the goldthread. You haven't put one of these away before, have you?"

"No. Never."

"It will be a bit of an ordeal. Always the first is the worst."

"Will I drink it and then it will just flush away the little one? I've an understanding that's how it's done."

"Yes, yes . . . I have something here . . ." She had retreated to a darkened corner, running her eyes across the shelves. "Perhaps a few drops of this," she said, picking up a small bottle with a crimson label that read 'winter heartbreak.' "No," she changed her mind and returned the bottle to the shelf and stood musing, as if looking for something that should have been there, but wasn't. Katie thought the way the bottles were lined up was a little disorderly, and she saw not all of them had labels.

"Bones and ashes . . . Bones and ashes," said the parrot.

She saw one of the little labels had fallen off and was lying near her foot. While Fortunata was looking through her shelves she picked it up. It said 'sinful memories.' At that moment Fortunata took two vials from the shelves and placed them on a table. Then she turned to Katie and said, "That dog is scratching the paint on my door. Can you not hear?"

"I am sorry. I should have clipped his nails. I'll just go and tighten his leash." Katie stepped outside and saw a mop of black hair and shoes with buckles she remembered from before. "Down, boy."

"Thought I recognized my dog. That is my dog, you know."

"Have you nothing better to do than to follow a dog through the lanes of the city?" She meant it for a sharp rebuke, but the sharpness seemed to have gone out of it once the words left her mouth.

"Oh, aye, much better. As I'm sure you'll come to see. You're a right one, you are, but you won't always have your dog at your foot and your stick in your hand."

"So you're saying he is my dog." She put a knot in the leash to make it shorter.

"I haven't time to quibble. This whole town's changing. You and that old lady you work for are just about done. You'll see. Anyway I don't want that dog. I'd want a better dog than that. One to bite your throat, that's the one I'll have."

"I'm just for a bit of business with the woman inside, and I'll be out again shortly. If you try anything I'll see at once and I'll have the constabulary on to you. So there's no reason to you standing there."

"I'll stand where I damn well please."

"Tommy, if he puts a hand on you, bite it off." She gave the lad a sharp look. "He will too." Then she went back into Fortunata's cottage. The air smelled strange. The old lady was holding a small bottle containing a repulsive looking gray-green liquid which she was staring at intently as she swirled it round. She was humming something to herself, but Katie couldn't make out any words. "Is that it then?"

"You must drink it down, every drop. Don't spill, or cough it up. But don't drink it here. Drink it when you've a bed and a chamber pot near. And a sink would be good too. And when you're not wearing such fine clothes as those. The first is the worst. I've warned you. It'll be a fierce grip you'll feel in the belly. That's the little one letting go. Once that's done you'll feel like all of you is emptying out. Then you'll know it's done." She placed the vial in Katie's hand.

"Thank you," said Katie. She was in a bit of a hurry to get back to Tommy Dog. "I'll just be —"

"Now as to the coppers you were speaking of."

"Oh aye." Katie quickly emptied out her purse. There were three copper pennies and a brass dodkin.

Fortunata threw it to the floor. "Is that all you've got?"

"It's all I've –"

"A girl like you, working in a good house. This is all you bring me? It's an insult!"

"How do you know where I work?"

Fortunata leaned forward and said, "I know all about you." It had an almost unearthly ring and set Katie's knees trembling.

"I'm sorry. I'll return tomorrow with more."

"Oh you're sorry are you."

"I'm sorry I said. I'll get more. Here, do you want this back?"

"Keep it. You with your head in the clouds. You think to show me disrespect. I have to take what you give me."

"I wish it was more like a shop. You should put your prices – "

"Shut up! You think this is a pub? I'll put up a bill of fare? We're two people we are. We should know what we're worth."

"I'll bring more tomorrow. I promise I will."

There was a pause as the two women regarded one another. "Come again," said the parrot.

"Yes, I will come again," said Katie.

Fortunata resumed fanning herself. "See that you do. I want a shilling. A shilling, at least. But I'll not put much weight on your promise. You're a tramp in every sense. Go now."

Katie took a quick look out the window to see Tommy was alright, but she didn't see the front garden. Instead, there were rows of poplars and elms laid out with gravel paths between, and marble fountains spraying jets of crystal water into bright, sunlit air.

"Shall I take it tonight?"

"Take it soon, you mustn't wait. Take it when you're home. Then sit. In an hour, maybe less, you'll feel its grip."

"Thank you. I'm very grateful . . . I'm sorry. The others I talked to, them it was said that's what to pay you. I didn't know." She backed out of the cottage, Madam Fortunata closing the door in her face.

The lad she'd been expecting was gone, and Tommy, as always, was happy to see her. She returned home. It was now late in the day and the lamp lighter was out, and to her relief there was no sign of any wanting to give her trouble. When she got to the mansion she climbed the stairs to her room, where she took down her hair and unbuttoned her blouse and took out the small vial Fortunata had given her. She opened it and held it to her nose. The smell was wretched, but her duties for the day were done and the night was her own. She swallowed the contents. Immediately she choked and had to stand to keep from vomiting the vile stuff up. She reached for the chamber pot and held her face over it, but she was able to keep it down. Just barely. She had a small, cracked mirror above the chest of drawers that held her clothes, and she looked at herself. The person looking back wasn't the person she was accustomed to. More than just being tired, which she was, the person looking at her had no confidence in who she was. Nor did she seem to like being stared at.

At that moment there was a knock at the door. It was the maid Agnes. She'd been sent to ask if Katie could join Madam Lanchester in the garden.

"What is it concerning?" Katie asked. "I'm a bit indisposed, and it is my night off."

"I don't know. She's all a-tremble like she gets. I think she just wants a word."

"It's the drink. Go back. Tell her I'm asleep. She's already forgotten she sent you."

"She saw your light come on just now. She'll not like to be hearing that from me." Agnes was that unhappy with her task, but she'd not return alone.

"Very well, if it's just a word." She did up her blouse. "Best make it quick." Katie followed Agnes down the stairs and into the open air garden at the heart of the mansion. Madam Lanchester was seated at a round iron table at the center of the garden with a glass of brandy in front of her. The night was warm. There was just the hint of a breeze, and the stars twinkled brightly in the summer sky. Katie sat across from her mistress with Agnes standing behind her. There was a pause.

"Madam . . .? I've brought Katie. It was you that asked for her."

Madam Lanchester seemed to wait till some scene in the reverie she was witnessing had finished, then turned her head, slowly becoming aware of Katie's presence. "So you have. Thank you, you can go now."

"Yes'm." Agnes curtsied and left.

Katie spoke up. "I'm not meaning to be rude or any sort of bother, but it is my night off and I've matters to attend to. Is there something that you're wanting?"

"There's much that I'm wanting . . . " She smiled. "Often I've thought of you as a daughter. Did you know? I never had a daughter . . ." She seemed to drift again, then caught herself and fixed Katie with a gaze. "Sometimes I feel there's so much I have to say. But the words I know are inadequate."

"Yes, it's a problem that torments many of us."

"I've had the feeling lately you're unhappy. More than that really. I don't know what's given me that feeling . . . Actually, I do know . . . "

"I'm fine, really I am —"

"You no longer smile in the mornings as once you did. Is there a worry, or some trouble that's come into your life? I don't mean to pry, and I apologize I just realized I've been extremely impolite. Would you like some brandy?"

Now there wasn't much Katie would have liked more at that moment than a tot of brandy, but she'd already consumed goody Fortunata's concoction and the woman had told her in an hour, maybe less, she'd feel the cramp. A clock was ticking desperately in her head as she attempted a computation of how much of that hour had passed, so she felt compelled to turn the offer down, since she just wanted to be done and out of the garden and back in her room. "I hope I've not been a laggard, or lacking in the service I perform. If I'd known it was smiles you wanted perhaps I'd have given you more. But a woman can't be always smiling. They think them daft that are. I'm sorry. My words seem sharp."

"No . . . You're quite right. I shouldn't pry . . . "

There was another lengthy pause as Katie's clock continued to tick. "Is that it then?"

"I've been thinking of how it was when Master Pinehurst Lanchester was still alive. How active, and how . . . active it all was . . ." She looked vaguely into the distance over Katie's shoulder, as if searching for a sight of the activity she remembered, and it struck Katie that here was a soul that had come unmoored, a woman as unattached to the ascertainable realities of daily existence as Katie felt she herself had become. She'd been now with two older women, both with some instinctive bond to another plane of existence, women she felt she'd insulted and deceived, while she herself was bound on a different course, one that had been determined for her by some inscrutable assemblage of circumstance. Her contacts with others were meaningless figments, scattered, filled with delay and deceit, necessary to get through in order to arrive at . . . what? At this moment she suffered an uncomfortable and aggravating contraction of her bowels. She tried to hold onto the situation, but realized she'd totally lost the thread of what Madam Lanchester was talking about. She tried to pay attention. "There used to be parties," she was saying. "People from the town, and from the country, military people, all sorts would come. There was music. There was dancing here, in this very garden, where we're sitting now. Why did I let all that go when he died? I was a sudden widow, and tenacious in my grief. My heart held no location dear, and I allowed this place to crumble. It was —"

"Please, Madam, I told you I've matters to attend to. Is there any point at all to this converse, or can we talk of this some other time?"

Madam Lanchester gave her an austere look, and finished her brandy. "Good night, Katie Jean. I'm sorry I've kept you. Please don't let me detain you any further from these other matters that are so pressing . . . I do think, however, perhaps we'll revive this old custom of entertaining guests. It would be . . . Well, we'll discuss this at a time more appropriate. Thank you again. You've been very patient. You can go."

"I'm sorry, Madam." She would have said more, but a relentless and difficult cramping came on her as she stood, and she felt a little wetness leaking down her leg. She walked back to the stairs to her room, holding herself as upright as possible and not allowing her feet to wobble. She was just able to get through the door to the stairwell before she collapsed in pain, falling face first onto the floor, moaning, and leaving a little puddle of urine. *I'll have that to clean up in the morning,* she thought to herself.

"Katie, girl, what's wrong?" Suddenly Tavish was at her side.

"Oh get lost, Tavish. This is not the night for you."

"And when is it ever the night for me?"

"I'm so sick. To deal with you on top of it all is more than a woman should have to endure."

"When did this come on?" He was holding her as they climbed the stairs.

"Just now. Just sudden like. Oh, it hurts." There was a biting and a tearing cramp in her vitals.

"Let me carry you."

"You'll not be carrying me while yet I have my own two feet to put underneath me. Stop it; take your hand away."

"Then I'll get behind and push."

"There's the gallant gentleman. I'm not certain that's the place any man would want to be."

Eventually they arrived at her door. They let themselves in and she heaved herself onto the bed. Tavish lit a candle.

"Oh, that's good, Tavish. That's good . . . I'm alright. Leave me now." The room was spinning about, but she was lying on her own cramped mattress in her own brass bedstead. Now she just wanted to be left alone. "Go. Go away. Do not think of staying. I'm alright I say."

"Oh, I don't think you are. Here, if you'll not think it indecent of me, allow me to unbutton your blouse and loosen your corset."

"Take your hands away. You're a filthy man, Tavish."

"Oh, you know I'm not. But what if I were, I cannot leave you in such sore distress, whether I'm filthy or clean. What is it that you've got? Should I run for the doctor?"

"No! Certain there will be no doctor."

"Katie – you're in a bad way. Why would you not be wanting to see the doctor?"

"I don't want to answer your questions. I only want you to be leaving me alone . . . Oh, what have I done?" She was crying.

Tavish stood in a perplex, uncertain if he'd done too much, or not enough. He knew the smart thing would be to leave, but since he was not a smart man he knew he would not be doing that. He saw the object of his affection in need of help and though his help was not wanted, he could not turn away. Putting his arm around her, he attempted to give her some degree of consolation for he knew not what. Katie was throwing up vehemently into the chamber pot with a firmness of purpose and a determination he'd not often seen in her. Then, forcing Tavish to turn his back while she disrobed, she shat into the pot as well. She then wrapped herself in a comforter and applied a small cotton pillow to her stomach and told Tavish he could turn around again.

"I don't know what you're looking at," she said. "But if you're too stupid to leave, I've not enough strength to kick you out. You're a dirty, lecherous man, Tavish, I've always known that about you."

"I can't leave you. You're not well enough to take care of yourself."

"Isn't that always their excuse. I've done a bloody good job taking care of myself up till now, haven't I? Oh, I feel it's coming."

"What's coming?"

"The baby." Katie strained, but all that came was urine and some watery movements of her bowels. "Oh God, Tavish, just kill me. Will you do that? Put me down, like you'd do a horse. It's all I'm fit for."

"Katie, what is it? It's a baby you say?" He waited a minute, then he asked, "What've you done?"

And Katie told him. So long she'd held it all to herself alone, now she lacked the strength to hold him out. She told him how she'd found she was with child, and of goody Fortunata and the simple she'd been given.

"Oh, Katie," he muttered. "The old hag's a fraud. You must be the only one in the town hasn't learned that already."

"Am I that?"

"I think you must be."

Katie groaned. "And how did you learn? Have you been to see her yourself?"

"I must have been." He said it shamefacedly. "She's taken my money also. I asked a philter of her, a potion to turn the heart of the one I love. Not a bit of good it's done me. I've applied it as liberal as I was directed, but little more she's ever given me than a curse from the side of her lip, or maybe a harsh kick on the knee."

"Tavish, I've the feeling the one your heart's set on is hardly worthy of your regard. But isn't that the way of the world." She groaned then and threw up some more.

That night gave the impression it went on and on forever, but that could not have been the case. It was a summer night, and so shorter than most, and well before midnight it was clear the only effect the potion would work was to make Katie that ill that she lay like a distempered dog and threw up her belly and shat out her guts, but the child she had, that stayed with her. After she was done, and Tavish had emptied the chamber pot for the last time and bid her good night, she settled into a dull melancholy, and following an altogether unpleasant evening she was yearning for the oblivion her bed seemed to promise, but she found herself still too roused up to sleep, so she left her room and took the stairs to her spot on the roof where she hoped to catch a glimpse of that sovereign of our enigmatical slumberous depths, the sea, but a heavy fog had set in and there was nothing to be seen, so she walked back down to her room where Tommy Dog was waiting. As she settled into her bed and pulled her comforter over her shoulders, Tommy snuffled his wet nose into her ear and whispered, "All life comes from love." Katie was on the point of saying, "Tommy, I never knew you could talk," when she drifted off to sleep.

That same night a game of cards was being played in Mr. Chips' cabin aboard the Queen of Bel Harbor. Tom had been relieved to find the opportunity to allow Vincenzo to win back his earring and the dollars he'd lost. Society in the cramped little cabin had been becoming strained. Tom had even been glad to let Vincenzo win a few of his dollars off him, feeling somehow that that helped make things even. Of course he should have stopped after losing two or three dollars, but it was really all in fun, and he was still restless, not ready yet for bed, Diego and Mr. Chips were both in good cheer, and there was a hope that the bottle of rum, which had made an appearance earlier, might reappear. At the moment the bottle was nowhere to be seen, and Tom was missing its presence, so when Diego dealt another round he anted up rather than head back to his cabin where he was most likely to have only the company of Brutus, snoring in the upper berth. He had to remind himself that the game was no longer play. He reflected that he had thirty silver dollars – well, at the moment it was something less than thirty because a few of them were sitting in front of Vincenzo – but nearly thirty silver dollars that were his base, the foundation of what he would be bringing home to Katie. That, along with his share of the gelt that would be coming to him from the sea voyage and he'd have enough. What enough meant was he would never have to go to sea again. He was comfortable with his accounting. But he shouldn't feel like this was play, even though his companions thought of it that way. He had to approach his cards with serious intent, which he was fully capable of doing, and he was now playing with his money, not Vincenzo's.

Unfortunately, try as he would, luck was not with him tonight. Vincenzo was steadily winning, folding when he had to, but the pile in front of him was growing steadily greater, and Tom was unable to turn the tide. Now the bottle of rum came by again, but Tom was down fifteen dollars. His attention was riveted on the cards. He looked across the table at Vincenzo's smiling face and cursed himself for a fool.

"Another hand, simple Tom?"

"I'm certain this game will be the ruin of me."

"A yes if ever I heard one." He dealt the cards and did so with some harshness. They slapped the top of the table as he laid them down.

Tom's hand was good, so he bet and raised in the first round with some abandon. Diego and Chips folded, but not Vincenzo. The draw did not strengthen Tom's hand, and after the draw Vincenzo proffered a large raise. Of course Tom could not fold and give away what he'd already bet, so he saw Vincenzo's wager. However, Tom's two pair of jacks and eights lost to Vincenzo's three sevens. It was a pattern he recognized. If he held three of a kind he'd never draw the fourth, and somehow Vincenzo always held a straight. He made an earnest effort to follow Vincenzo's hands closely, but he never saw a cheat, and he was convinced by the many hands Vincenzo folded early that he was not sharping the cards. Nevertheless, Vincenzo's pile continued to grow larger while Tom's was dwindling to a precious few.

So it angered him and he was almost brought to tears when Vincenzo raised and he was at the point where he was about to place the last of the thirty silver dollars he'd had from Mr. X onto the table. He looked at his cards. He was holding a straight. He looked at Vincenzo. There was nothing to be read in those eyes. He looked again at his cards. He was holding a straight, damn it, and in a moment of blank terror he knew, knew it with the same certainty that he knew his own name, that Vincenzo was holding a full house.

"Will you see my cards, simple Tom?"

Tom fingered his last silver dollar. He lifted his hand to toss it on the table. He looked again at Vincenzo. And he folded.

"No . . . I'll not see them."

"Always a wise decision." And Vincenzo swept the coins in the center of the table into the pile in front of him. There was a whiff of finality in the air, as though a difficult proof in mathematics had just been conclusively demonstrated. Or as though the party was now over.

"Go, Tom," said Diego. "Go back to your cabin. We're closed for tonight."

"No, I don't want to go."

"It's late," said Mr. Chips.

"I think my luck, my luck is going to turn. In fact I'm certain of it."

"Not at this late stage of the evening, simple Tom. Please, can we say it's enough? Can we go to bed now?"

"I haven't much left with which to wager."

"Then it's time we stopped." Diego took his hand.

"No . . . I'll get more. I'm never without resource. You mustn't think that."

Vincenzo asked, "What is it, this more you speak of?" A wink to Mr. Chips.

"I will get it. I'll show you." Now what had he done? He knew he wasn't thinking straight but he had to make things right.

He walked back to his cabin. Brutus was lying in his upper bunk and heard him clanking about below.

"What is it, Tom?"

"I seem to have had the worst of it in a simple game of chance. Nothing to worry yourself."

"If you're talking of playing cards with Vincenzo, I'd not call that a game of chance."

"Think you he cheats?"

"Does he wear his jacket still?"

"It's certain he does."

"He has the cards all up his sleeve. Take that jacket off him. Why's he wear that jacket down below and the night's so mild?" Brutus put his tattooed face over the edge of his bunk.

"It's the same jacket he wears always," said Tom.

"That's what I say."

Tom had to think about that. "Well, it'll not be doing him the good he hoped for then when we play with this new deck." He stood on the lower bunk to hold up the new deck of cards he had and to show them to Brutus. He saw Brutus lying in his bunk, and he saw that Brutus had a bottle in his hand. "I've a feeling this will turn the luck my way."

"Don't go back. Your luck will not change."

"Of course I'm going back. I have all my silver to retrieve. You'd not think I'd be leaving it behind?" Tom bounced out of his cabin, leaving Brutus rising from his berth. He was back to Mr. Chips' cabin with the new deck of cards in his hand. Diego was passed out, snoring in his berth, but Vincenzo and Mr. Chips were both good for another round, so they sat at the table while Tom shuffled the cards.

The first hand Tom bet heavy on a simple pair of sevens, and everyone else folded, so he was getting a bit of his own back. The next hand he folded, but then the hand after that he was dealt two pair, queens and jacks. He ran the stakes up and at the draw drew a third queen. Just as he'd said, his luck had turned. In the next round of betting he threw in everything he had. Mr. Chips folded with a curse and a black look, but Vincenzo saw his bet and raised him yet again. This Tom had not expected.

"I've nowt. That was my last coin," he said.

"Oh, simple Tom, your last coin? Really? I thought I heard you speak of more."

And there was more. On his visit to his cabin he'd retrieved more than just his deck of cards. Slowly he pulled out and placed on the table a watch with a chain. The outside bore a design of knots and tangles, and on the inside lid was engraved, "From your own darling Katie." He placed it there and looked at it, goods to back his wager. He knew it didn't belong there, but he was damned if he would fold when he was holding a full house. And it was his deck of cards.

"A bit of frippery to put against solid honest coin. What do you think, Mr. Chips, should I accept?"

"Dunno why you're asking me."

"It's silver. Solid, not plate," said Tom.

Vincenzo appeared to think this over. "I think I'd like a watch. It would look good on me. Very well. So you'll see my cards?"

"Certain it is that I will."

Vincenzo smiled. "Behold. Four eights." He laid down his cards.

It was a hard and a crushing hand of ice that closed round Tom's heart.

"This is turning into a profitable evening. A very profitable evening . . . Are you up for another hand? Any other odds and ends you'd like to be giving me? Maybe the gold in your teeth?" He laughed. "Let's see what I have here. 'From your own darling Katie.' This Katie must be a wild and a wanton wench, eh simple Tom? Giving a watch away."

"She's – " Tom could say no more. He stood.

"Well she's nothing to me. I'll be scratching her out."

"Give it back."

"The watch? You want it back?"

"Give it."

"Oh, I'll not give it. Most certainly I will not be giving this back. I might sell it. In fact I think I will sell it. Have you aught to pay?"

Tom could only stare.

"No . . .? Ask your friend Brutus. He strikes me as a man with hidden depths."

"You scum."

Vincenzo laughed uproariously.

"Give it back. You cheated me."

"That's a hard and a vicious word you're speaking. If I thought you meant it I would have to do something injurious. But it's late, and you're in your cups, and I'm a forgiving man."

Singing was heard from the hallway outside. It was Brutus's baritone, raised in song:

> "I'll flout the masters
>> And chew off their ears
> They'll know they were punished by me.
> I'll settle the debts
>> That have rankled for years,
> For always my thoughts, and only my thoughts are free."

Brutus was standing in the door, taking in the scene, observing Tom's ruin, written on his face.

"Who's gotten *you* moving tonight?" asked Vincenzo.

"I've lost everything," said Tom. "Everything I had and all I was given. What sort of fool am I?"

"It was robbery, nothing less," said Brutus. "And I'm here to wring their rotten necks, either that or I've killed a good bottle of rum for naught."

Diego stirred and sat up, "Who's here?"

"A fool and a drunk says he'll break our necks," said Vincenzo.

"I've said no more cards here. It's too much. And now it's late. Get out, all of you." Diego tried to stand, but Brutus pushed him down and then punched him in the face. As he fell he put his hand out to grab his bag of surgeon's implements, but Brutus caught it and hurled it against the wall. Knives and tongs and other instruments clattered to the floor.

"Stop it. Stop it, all of you," said Tom, bewildered by the turn of events. "Don't fight." But already everything was happening at once. Mr. Chips was shouting something, and Vincenzo was trying to gather in all his winnings and cram them in his pockets, while Brutus just went berserk, overturning the table, and ripping off one leg. At the same moment, Tom suddenly came to life, and grabbing a scalpel that had fallen from Diego's bag he held it to Vincenzo's throat. "You cheated me," he said.

"I did not. Put that down before I hurt you."

"You've got cards up your sleeves. Brutus saw you."

"Brutus sees things that aren't there. I never did."

Brutus slammed the leg of the table against the wall next to Vincenzo's head. "Take off your jacket," he said.

"Give me room to breathe and I'll take it off."

Mr. Chips was trying to pull Brutus off Vincenzo, and Diego was writhing on the floor, cursing and fumbling at his face where he'd been hit.

"Take off your jacket!" shouted Brutus.

Vincenzo didn't back down. "You're a mad, stupid man, Brutus, and I've no respect for the friend you keep."

"Empty your pockets, " said Tom.

"I will not."

"Then I'll do it for you." Brutus tried to pull the jacket off Vincenzo. Coins spilled onto the floor, and in the scuffle Tom's scalpel carved a gash in Vincenzo's cheek. Vincenzo howled in pain, but held on to his jacket. Outside the cabin there were sounds of stirring as men were roused by the disturbance.

Tom was stunned by the sudden blood on his blade and backed away from Vincenzo, who tried to bolt out the door as soon as he had a little room. He got it part way open before Brutus slammed it shut.

"You'll pay for this," said Vincenzo.

"Take off that jacket," said Tom. "Let's see what's in the sleeves."

"Only my arms."

All this time Brutus had been fighting Mr. Chips, who was clinging to his shoulders and trying to clout the side of his head. With one violent movement Vincenzo took off the jacket, and in the act of pushing it at Tom, grabbed the blade away from him. Tom fell.

There came a knocking at the door. Someone outside shouted "Open up!" Brutus stood against the door, holding it closed, but now Mr. Chips was in front of him where he could pummel him in the stomach, and Vincenzo was holding the knife on Tom.

"Alright, shall I carve your cheek?" He grabbed Tom, whose arms of a sudden had turned to water. "What say, shall I cut you up, or maybe I should let you go. Which'll it be? Eh? Shall we toss a coin?" He gave a great cackle.

The door behind Brutus gave way and four or five half-dressed men burst into the cabin. Everyone was shouting and the uproar was tremendous. Brutus was mauling Mr. Chips with blows of his massive fists. He grabbed him by the arm and turned it viciously. There was a sound of cracking bone and Mr. Chips fell to the floor, trying to wrench his arm away while still wrestling with his attacker.

In the melee Tom escaped from Vincenzo's grasp and somehow squirmed into the hallway, where Ramsey and the First Mate were now arriving. Brutus, meanwhile, in a rampage was smiting all and sundry. Several men were battered by him as they attempted to bear him down and, when finally he was overborne, it took four of the brawniest to restrain him.

Finally the Master strode in with a loud command, challenging any to continue the brawl. "Halt and hold fast! No one move!" he shouted. The general hubbub diminished. He looked about, a fierce anger burning in his eyes. "What is the meaning of this disturbance in the still hours of the night? We should be abed, not at one another's throats. Who is the man that started this?"

There was a general shuffling and looking about, as most of those involved were unaware of the cause of the commotion or rightly understood why they'd been fighting. Vincenzo's gashed cheek and Mr. Chips's broken arm gave evidence they had been in the thick of the fray, and Diego was still nursing his bruised cheek. Most eyes turned to Brutus as the center and focus of the action.

The Master stood before him and did his best to stare him down. "I've had my eye on you since first we left port. You have comported yourself in a sullen and morose manner, begrudging any slightest respect to those above you, and this is what comes of it. In a drunken rage you have battered and assaulted your fellow seamen, here where most they should look for some civility from their mates. Have you nothing to say for yourself?"

Brutus stood silent as a post, but his eyes were lit by a smoldering hatred and an undisguised anger at the unprincipled indifference of power.

One man had found the bloody scalpel and he gave it to the Master who took it and turned it in his hand as he examined it. "Is this your blade?"

Still stubborn silence.

"I think it is, the bloody witness of your guilt. You're one of those who thinks himself a better man than his superiors, are you not? One who is so rubbed and chafed by this perceived inequity that any act of defiance is justified. I know your kind. How well I know it. Also, you are drunk, a drunken disgrace to this vessel. I shall not tolerate this loose and troublesome conduct to continue. You shall be made an example, before all the men. Ramsey, place this man in irons."

The word was spoken and Ramsey stepped forward to signal the men holding Brutus they should lead him toward the brig. "Have you still nothing to say?" the Master asked. In his heart, Tom pleaded with Brutus to speak, just a word, but he himself had not the courage to utter even one syllable. Brutus was led away in silence. As he passed Tom their eyes met.

The Master departed, and the men dispersed in muttering groups. Vincenzo's face was still bleeding, but he busied himself with collecting the pieces of silver scattered on the cabin floor, casting dark looks in Tom's direction till Diego took him in hand and led him along with Mr. Chips in the direction of the surgery.

Tom walked back to his empty cabin. Looking in the upper bunk he saw Brutus's little wooden idol of Maddibimbo lying ineffectually on its side. He couldn't stay in that room. Wandering blankly in the unforgiving desolation of his heart he at last found himself on deck. A fog was setting in. He walked to the rail and looked over. If he disappeared in the waves below nothing would be lost, only his anguish and all his stupid craziness, and the pointless futility of trying to go on being worth something in the world. He stepped onto the rail, his mind made up to finish himself. It wasn't even a tragedy, it was the punch line to a bad joke. He tensed to spring, and then . . . he stayed where he was. The ship bore on, its course unaffected by this terrible night's events, uncaring, steadily breasting the waves that broke below, and he stood on the rail, poised to leap, one hand holding a line, dangling for that moment over an act of dreadful consequence, and as he did so the knowledge came to him that he would not do it. That his life would go on. That the unhappy events of this night were only that, events, and that they could be undone and made right. He knew that tomorrow – no, to-night – he would speak to the Master, he would tell him that Brutus was not to blame, and he would start the long effort to recover his goods. It would be long and hard, but it could be done. And he almost laughed to think how close he had come to death, and how hopeful he now understood everything to be. And at just that moment the ship encountered a sudden blustery squall and the line he'd been holding was snatched from his grasp. The fog-slicked rail he was standing on gave a sudden lurch, unbalancing him. His hands fluttered uselessly, stretching for the line that was now far beyond his flailing fingertips, and in a moment he was tossed, like a coin, into the rippling surface of the sea.

CHAPTER SEVEN
A DANCE BY MOONLIGHT

GENERAL HOBSBAWM was short and stout, with something of a globular appearance. He shaved every day and kept his red face as smooth as a baby's bottom. This morning he was reflecting on the notion that it was redundant for any imperial power to have both an army and a church. So far as he could tell, the two institutions fulfilled much the same purpose: they kept the natives subdued, which was necessary to guarantee the safety of the goods that were expropriated and to provide protection and comfort to the settlers who were rapidly populating what would otherwise be empty waste. The church did it by espousing the doctrines of love and mercy. The army employed other methods.

Furthermore, the two institutions embodied the same organizational principles. There was something innately pleasing about a good solid hierarchy. From day one the initiates had a well-laid path to follow, from cadet to lieutenant, to captain, and so forth. You could start at the bottom and already project your arrival at the top. Not that General Hobsbawm had started at the bottom. Conversely, he had once seen a list of religious titles and he was convinced that it was a similar hierarchy that kept the deacons and bishops and archbishops and such in order, all striving for the next tier.

The similarities went on and on. Both insisted on uniforms. One valued morale, the other morality. In fact, the faith and the military thought so much alike, the corresponding members of each could probably be replaced pretty much interchangeably without causing the least disturbance. The idea amused the General. He turned to Colonel Snivel and asked, "If you could be in the church, what do you think your rank would be? Archbishop perhaps, or maybe even cardinal?"

"I wouldn't be in the church," he answered. "Don't like churches. They're drafty – dusty, cold and musty."

"They are? You'd think God could do something about that."

"God's a useless bugger. He doesn't do anything."

Ordinarily the General would have allowed the conversation to end there. Snivel was given to these far-reaching observations. However, this morning the General felt like prodding him a bit, if only to see what other nuggets of conversational wisdom might be lurking in the mental seam the Colonel was mining.

"Those are harsh words. God doesn't do anything? What about the Creation? He made the sky, and the oceans, and the land. Surely that's something."

"You ask me, the Creation's over-rated. Especially the sky. Sky's a wasted opportunity. It's huge. Wherever you stand, it covers half of what you see. You'd think He'd want to make it worth looking at. But what did He do? Blue. That's it. Wherever you look, blue. Nothing but blue. I'm not impressed."

"But it's a remarkable blue, don't you think?" Snivel scowled. The General went on, "Staring at it, one gets a feeling of vast distance, a sublime expanse that contradicts everything ever said in any humdrum house of business."

"Blue is a color. It doesn't contradict anything."

"You have such a mundane soul. Anyway there's more than just blue. There are clouds. Sometimes there are sunsets."

"Oh my God, you'll be going on about butterflies next. Look, I'm not letting the Creator off the hook just on account of some clouds and a few sunsets. The fact is, the whole Creation's a botch job. That's why you need the army to keep patching things up. I've spent my entire adult life killing people and blowing things to bits, and the result is always an improvement. What does that tell you?"

They were talking as they walked through the hallways of the massive fort of Port Jay. Having arrived at the door to his office, General Hobsbawm bid Colonel Snivel good day and entered, pondering as he did the meaning the word office held in this context and that of religious service. It was a hobby-horse of his, but at some point he thought he might put pen to paper and produce an essay demonstrating the many linkages between war and religion, which were after all, on the most fundamental level, the same thing.

Lieutenant Lovejoy stood to attention behind his desk as the General entered.

"As you were," the General said. He sauntered over to his own desk, where he sat and cast an eye at the pile of dispatches that had arrived this morning. He shuffled through a few.

"There is still nothing from Fort Estamor," said the Lieutenant. "It's as if they've vanished."

"Vanished . . . The scout we sent yesterday should be back in a week. But the absence of any word is more than mysterious."

"Perhaps they were involved somehow in this escaped slave business."

"It's unlikely. And if they were, still they'd have sent word. No. I'm entirely baffled . . . It's enough to make me wonder if we shouldn't give some credence to this witchcraft talk that's been circulating in the town." Lovejoy snorted contemptuously. "I'm serious. An entire fort can't just . . . disappear." He leafed through the latest update from Indradoon. A band of escaped slaves had fallen on the slave market at the height of auction day and routed the auctioneers and all their defenders. The slave pens had been rifled and thrown down. Many guards had been shot and killed. The center of the city had been burned, and there had been extensive looting. The slaves, armed with a few rifles, and many other weapons such as swords, long metal lances, picks, axes, and garden implements, had escaped and were believed to be camped in the woods nearby. There were disputed estimates as to the number of escaped slaves, some sources placing the number at over a thousand, men, women, and children of all ages. The General had little doubt that the actual number was far less. He put the dispatch down. "The news gets worse and worse." He stood and walked to the window. Port Jay lay spread out below. He followed the line of the River of Tears, from its emergence out of the woods to the south, through the heart of the city, to its terminus in the sea. The docks were busy today, like all days, many ships of all sizes being loaded and unloaded. The HMS Nemesis, chief ship of the line, could be seen at drydock. Here was the beating heart of the city, the wellspring and fountainhead of its prosperity. There were no slaves here in Port Jay. They weren't needed. Or rather, all the citizens of Port Jay were slaves, slaves to commerce, to the dream of material success. They worked as hard as slaves, in most cases harder. And, so far at least, they hadn't mutinied and formed a dangerous mob bent on despoiling the powers that be.

Something would have to be done about these slaves. They couldn't be counted on to fall apart on their own. Pleas for protection would soon be pouring in from the large landowners; it would be best to be able to tell them steps were already being taken when that happened. The General determined to put this in the hands of Snivel. He himself would focus his efforts on the campaign against the Indians. There would have to be a sizable deployment from the forces currently on Lost Bastard Island. These men would be convoyed across the Sound. From there they could march into the Forgotten Forest and the heart of Indian country. The recent recruiting efforts had been more successful than had been anticipated, so the absence of the force under Snivel's command would pose no difficulty. All these thoughts flashed through his mind as he surveyed the city. Then, turning to Lieutenant Lovejoy, he said, "Lieutenant, there is a delicate matter concerning which I would welcome your insight."

"Yessir?"

The General picked up a card that was lying on his desk. "I have received an invitation, what do you think of that? An invitation to a formal dance from Madam Arabella Lanchester. It has been some time since I have last been a party to such an affair. I was hoping perhaps your memories of these occasions are of a more recent vintage than mine."

"Yessir. I suspect they are." Lieutenant Lovejoy was a dapper and a gallant young man. His mustache, his brilliant blue eyes, and his gentlemanly demeanor had not been lost on the young women of Port Jay.

"Good. A formal dance. That's what it says. You can see for yourself." He held the card out to the Lieutenant.

"To be held in four days' time," said Lovejoy.

"Quite."

"In the Lanchester Mansion. I don't believe I know where that is."

"It's in the old city. A walled mansion. At one time the Lanchesters were quite a power in these parts, so I've been made to understand. I seem to recall encountering Madam Lanchester, it must have been a couple of years ago, I can't recollect the exact occasion."

"Do you plan to attend?"

"I think that would be the correct course to pursue. It's best to cement any ties one can in this city. Also I was hoping you would accompany me. Your knowledge of the intricacies in the decorum involved would be of value to me, and you are acquainted with a wider circle of the locals."

The Lieutenant nodded deferentially. "Although I'm sure the decorum will be far from intricate, and the dance will be far from formal. That is generally the case in these colonial ports. The conversations are mostly strained and inconclusive. There is only one thing on everyone's mind, and it is the one thing not spoken of."

"Why do you think I was invited?"

"I don't know. I'm not familiar with the Lanchesters. They must move outside the social set with which I'm conversant."

"Well I suppose I'll find out in four days' time."

"I suppose you will. Sir, if that's all concerning the invitation, might I bring up another matter?"

"Of course. What's on your mind?"

"The local constabulary have asked if we can serve in an unofficial capacity as backup when needed."

"I thought we already did that."

"We already do it in an official capacity. Would you like some tea?"

"Yes please. And that's not sufficient?"

"The official channels can be slow and difficult to navigate."

"Of course they are. That's why they're the official channels. These people want us to be quick and efficient? Ready to help them at a moment's notice?"

"My word, no. I don't think they regard such a state of affairs as being in the bounds of possibility. They would be satisfied if we were responsive."

"You mean when they ask for assistance if we say no, instead of just ignoring them."

"Precisely."

"Well, perhaps we could accommodate that. I presume this is coming from Chief Constable Fragonard?"

"Yessir."

"Why does he go through you, instead of coming directly to me?"

"Because you refuse to speak to him."

"Oh, right. How is the old fellow holding up? Has he gone insane yet?"

"No, not yet. He drinks too much."

"So he's pretty much as crazy as always?"

"It's hard to say."

"What has triggered this request? Has there been a change in the number or the nature of the incidents the constabulary is called to respond to?"

"Apparently there has been. As Fragonard puts it, things are going to Hell. An uptick in cases of arson and domestic brutality, rabble in parts of the city going on destructive binges, that sort of thing. He seems most alarmed."

"Hardly strikes me as anything to worry about."

"My opinion entirely."

"How is that tea coming along?"

"There isn't any tea. I should have checked before making the offer. I'm dreadfully sorry."

"No tea?"

"I'm afraid not."

"Things really are going to Hell."

The next few days were very busy ones in the Lanchester Mansion. Invitations had gone out to all and sundry, all being the neighbors in the old city, and sundry running to such as the parish priest, the more reputable merchants, and even the military in their fort by the river. So now years of neglect were being scrubbed from the walls and floors in a matter of days and the staff was being worked off their feet. Katie had recovered from her bout of illness and had been industriously scrubbing away in the main hall, her hands becoming red and roughened from the hardness of the water. The day before the affair Madam Lanchester, who had spent countless hours ransacking her wardrobe in search of the perfect gown, suddenly realized she should also do something for her staff. At a moment's notice Katie and Tavish, along with Agnes, Fancy and Maria, were bundled off to Cornheiser's Fancy Dress Emporium where they were promptly done up in knock offs of the latest fashions. Katie was given a gown that felt much too snug. Looking herself over in the mirror, she was struck by the ludicrous contrast the formal evening gown made with her chapped hands and tousled hair. She looked like a tramp who'd pillaged the belle of the ball. But mostly she was concerned that the tight-fitting bodice made the slight bump in her belly visible to a close inspection. Well, she'd have to make sure no one had a chance to give her a close inspection. It shouldn't be hard; as a servant she was accustomed to making herself unobtrusive and negligible. Still, she couldn't help practicing different ways to stand, and making note of how she looked.

On the day that had been set for the dance the band arrived and set up at a bandstand at one end of the interior garden. There was a reflecting pool that had stood empty and drained for many years, but was now full of water. Madam Lanchester had hoped to stock it with some decorative fish, but this plan had fallen through at the last moment. There was a large paved area in front of the bandstand suitable for dancing, and the interior of the great hall had been freshened up almost beyond recognition. The hall now held numerous tables and chairs. Buffets and sideboards spread with a variety of food and drink were set along the walls. Katie had spent the afternoon doing some last minute cleaning up and then had bathed and put on her gown. She'd then come down to the main hall where she'd collapsed into one of the chairs, taking the chance for a brief respite before the arrival of the first guests. As she looked around she was struck by how everyone else seemed to know just what they were doing, and seemed so comfortable doing it; how suitable everyone was for their situation. Their placid eyes seemed to look out onto a world that was just what they expected. She, on the other hand, felt herself the victim of an explosive inner turmoil she could neither comprehend nor reckon with, an inner life which she kept hidden from view as she danced through her days, careful never to fall out of step or let drop an unguarded word. And she wondered if this was what all the others were feeling too, if they were likewise looking out from their own emotional foxholes, dazed by their encounters with others, looking at her and seeing just another young woman tidying her hair or drifting insouciant on thoughts of nothing at all, and thinking how fit, how suited she was. And she wondered if everyone wasn't secretly insane and the whole fabric of social intercourse wasn't just a sham and a charade being acted out by marionettes whose strings were being pulled by an unseen madman bent on God knows what. A feeling of irrevocable and unconquerable loneliness came over her as she regarded the world in this light, and she unconsciously started stroking her belly as though to comfort the flickering flame of life she bore within.

"Why so dejected?" Madam Lanchester stood at her shoulder.

"I'm sorry, Madam. It's not dejection. Simple fatigue, if you must know."

"I know I've worked you hard, but try to put that behind you. Perk up. Tonight is a night for gaiety. I hope you'll enjoy yourself." Madam Lanchester was attired in a striking green ball gown, with flounces round the waist, and a sweeping train she dragged behind her. Her hair was colored and done up and her face had been beautified with every embellishment of the cosmetician's art. Tarted up was the epithet Katie's disrespectful mind supplied.

"I'm here to serve the food and the wine. I'm sure I'll be enjoying that."

Madam Lanchester took Katie's face between her hands and stared at her intently. Katie wondered what she was doing, if there was something she was looking for. Her eyes ran all over Katie's face and then she said, "There's something missing. I'll be right back." With that she left.

Katie sat for a minute, a bit puzzled by the exchange that had just taken place. She wondered what she was waiting for. She did her best not to revisit the thoughts she'd been harboring just before Madam Lanchester's arrival. Best just to put one foot in front of the other and keep her mind on the task immediately ahead. There was a desperate problem that was going to be resolved one way or another in the near future, but she'd not think of that. There was a scrub brush left in a corner of one of the window sills. She went to put that away. Just then Madam Lanchester returned with a pair of pendant diamond earrings.

"Here," she said. "Put these on."

"Oh, Madam, I couldn't."

"Of course you can. You must. It's a shame to let these gather dust. Pinehurst gave them to me as a birthday gift. But of course tonight I've got my sapphires; they go with the gown . . . Please. Wear them."

"Madam please, they'll think me one of the guests the way I'm dressed. I'm only here to serve."

"Do it as a favor to me. I'll brook no denial." So Katie let her hang the earrings on her ears.

"Come look." Madam Lanchester led her to a mirror. She regarded herself in the glass. Her face was drawn and tired. Her eyes were red and held a look of guarded wariness. The diamonds glittered unabashedly on each ear. "You look beautiful."

"Thank you," she said. So much for being unobtrusive. *I'll look like a tinseled vixen on the make*, she thought to herself. After Madam Lanchester left she stood for some time looking at herself, the forgotten scrub brush still in her hand.

When the first guests arrived they were met at the door by Tavish in tails and black tie. He took their coats and led them into the main hall of the mansion where they could seat themselves and be helped to food and drink. Agnes, Katie, Fancy and Maria were all decked out in their best and were busily moving from table to sideboard and circulating throughout the hall. The chandeliers were crammed with candles that blanketed the gathering crowd in a gentle glow. When the guests, having fed, wandered into the garden they encountered the moonlight and the euphonious sounds of the band, an ensemble of strings and piano. The weather had cooperated; it was a clear night.

There had been some disturbances in parts of the city during the day. Packs of boys had been active, throwing rocks and breaking into shops. There had been more of this sort of thing lately, but today's outburst was the worst yet. This was the topic on most people's lips as they sipped their wine or danced gravely round the paved area in front of the band. Madam Lanchester was flitting deftly from group to group, making introductions and carrying out the many duties of a hostess. When Father Clumphy, the parish priest, arrived he was greeted in a festive manner by Fancy and Maria, who were two of his most dependable pupils at the scripture readings he gave every Sunday. Ignatius Garner, a banker of some repute, came with his wife and his sons, the eldest of whom, once he'd seen Katie, managed to keep her always in view without ever actually looking at her. They spent some time sampling the buffet and conversing with the local shopkeepers in a corner of the hall. There was a tall, dark-haired lady Katie didn't recognize who was looking at her from across the hall. Their eyes met and Katie stood silently waiting, perfectly still, till someone beside her said something and the moment passed. General Hobsbawm and Lieutenant Lovejoy, after Tavish had taken their coats, were received gushingly by Madam Lanchester in the great hall. She complimented them on their uniforms, and inquired as to the condition of the streets on their way from the fort.

"The streets were crowded," the General replied. "There's been some looting and one or two of the larger boulevards had to be closed. The constables were out in force, maintaining order."

"Who are these gangs doing the looting?"

"No one seems to know. At first they put it down to a few urchins doing a bit of vandalism. But there seems to be something larger behind it all. These outbursts have the appearance of being coordinated. I'm certain Chief Constable Fragonard will get to the bottom of it."

"Well, for tonight put all thoughts of that to one side. I am attempting to revive a custom of my late husband Pinehurst's. These formal balls were a great success in years gone by."

"Yes, so I've heard."

"I used to enjoy them so much. There was always such a steady flow of conversation, and wine, and dancing, and good times, or so it seemed. Those were different days. Do you know what Pinehurst's word for me was? Playful. I was his playful young wife. You'd hardly think so now, would you? You can be frank."

"Yes, Madam, I – "

"Well, maybe we can bring back a little of the fun from those days. But you haven't eaten yet. You must be famished. Here's Katie Jean. She'll get you something." And with that she handed them off to Katie and moved on to another guest.

"Well, officers, can I get you something to eat?" asked Katie.

"Nothing for me," said the General. "Lieutenant?"

Suddenly there was a loud crash from outside. Everyone froze. Then there was shouting and some banging that sounded like it was coming from just outside the mansion's front door.

"Tavish," said Madam Lanchester, "would you be so kind as to go see who's being murdered at our front door?" She was doing her best to keep up an imaginary reputation for playfulness.

Tavish looked at her with something of a grim smile, then cast some side glances at the two military men.

There was a loud knock at the door and Tavish went to answer.

It was an ensign from the fort. He'd been sent out for General Hobsbawm by a very nervous adjutant shortly after the General had left. He'd been hot on the General's heels, and would have caught him up sooner except he'd gotten turned around by the General's tortuous detours. As he'd drawn close to the mansion he'd seen a crowd of ten or twelve, shadowed in hoods, their faces obscured, standing near the door. They'd been shouting and banging sticks on the ground, but they'd disbanded and slipped into the shadows as he approached. He now handed the General a letter. The General excused himself and walked aside with the ensign as he read the contents.

Lovejoy and Katie looked at one another.

The Lieutenant smiled. "Did you ask me something?"

"I was asking if you wanted something to eat, or maybe a drink."

"My throat is awfully parched. Is that a flagon of pomegranate juice?"

"Yes, sir, it is. Can I get you some?"

"Yes, please. And you needn't call me sir. My name is Stuart."

Handing him the glass, "Yes, Stuart, pleased to meet you."

"And you are?"

"Katie Jean."

"What do you suppose that loud crash was?"

"I was rather hoping you'd know."

"I don't think I'll go out and look. Not unless the General orders me to." He gave her a large smile and ate a radish.

Father Clumphy, as if magnetized, drew near. "I see the General is closeted with one who bears some recent information."

"Information has been reaching us at such a rapid pace, it's a wonder the events don't trip each others' heels. The city's like a pot nearing the boil, each bubble's burst announces the next."

"Prettily said. Are we in any danger?"

"We are always in danger. If the – "

"Apart from the accustomed danger which we are always in, is there any new cause for apprehension, any other danger that threatens us?"

"Yes, I believe there is. It is my personal opinion that these are not just spontaneous eruptions of civil disturbance, but that the city is actually coming under attack from within."

"A coordinated attack?"

"Precisely."

"Who would do such a thing?"

"I'm sure I have no idea." The Lieutenant gave a sidelong look to Katie as though entreating her somehow to rescue him from this conversation.

"Father Clumphy," she said, "how have the scripture lessons been proceeding? Are Fancy and Maria keeping up their schoolwork?"

"Oh, they are the best students one could ask for. Very attentive they are. Yes indeed. Here's Fancy now."

"Yes, Father," said Fancy as she approached. "Have you been out to see the dancing?"

"Not yet. Perhaps you would care to lead me there."

"Oh, la, I'm just serving at the tables here. I've no feet for dancing."

The Lieutenant was keeping an eye on the General, where he still stood deep in conversation with the ensign. Katie thought perhaps Fancy needed a little more encouragement to lead Father Clumphy into the garden, so she said, "The good father's just been telling us how you've profited from your lessons, and the readings from the sacred texts."

78

"Oh yes, that's true," said Fancy. "Those sacred texts have struck me sore right to my heart, that they have." Father Clumphy smiled at this. "Especially the parts where God is smiting them that needs smiting, although there's not as many of those as you might expect. There's some chapters in the gospels and the prophets, la, I can't make heads or tails, but it's all very instructive, and it's a blessing to read."

The Father asked, "Have you been able to apply your lessons in practical theology, and has that helped you in the avoidance of sin?"

"The avoidance of what?"

"The avoidance of sin . . . You do know what I am speaking of?"

"Oh yes. I avoid it like the plague. It disagrees with my stomach. I'll have none of that sin."

"Sin disagrees with your stomach?"

"Yes. Especially if I indulge in the evening."

The Father gave her a blank look.

At that moment, breaking away from the adjutant, the General took the Lieutenant's arm and told him he was sending for reinforcements. "I'm very much afraid we will be targeted for further attacks here, tonight."

"So you are responding to the constabulary's request for assistance?"

"They're attacking us. Do you expect me to rely on the local constables for protection?"

They strode off as the Father was asking Fancy, "Do you know what sin is?"

"Oh, Father, I should hope we all know what sin is, though some of us think better of ourselves than to speak of it." She raised an eyebrow in arch amusement and drifted away. Clumphy was mystified as to what to make of this. He'd never known her to take flight on wings of irony, and yet . . . Oh well, she was probably just drunk.

Katie, finding herself unattended, wandered out to the garden, where there were several couples dancing. The night felt giddy with the moonlight and the music. Her eye was caught once again by the woman she'd noticed earlier, the tall lady with dark hair who held her regard a moment longer than necessary. Some tables had been set up around the grounds and Katie thought to ask those seated if they wanted any food or drink from the hall, so she was moving back and forth in the crowd, but somehow felt the eyes of that woman always on her. Lieutenant Lovejoy swooped in and asked for a dance. She couldn't turn him down, and she allowed him to hold her in his arms.

"Well, Stuart, your General seems to have a lot on his hands tonight."

"He does indeed, as always. But matters now seem to be coming to a head. And you, Miss," he'd observed she wore no wedding ring, "I don't recall ever seeing you before. Are you an inhabitant of this quarter of the city?"

"I'm employed by Madam Lanchester. Like Fancy, and the others. We're here to serve."

"Then I hope I have not committed some minor impropriety by dancing with the staff."

Katie laughed. "I think dancing with the staff is permitted."

The music came to an end. They stood looking at one another, he with one hand still on her shoulder and the other round her waist. "Have you . . ." he said. "I mean you look so . . ."

"Yes I know."

"Elegant," he said with a smile.

"Thank you. That was a nice dance." He bowed. And was that a kiss he placed on her finger?

They parted, and she looked at the other couples as the music started up again. She was standing idly, enjoying the night and the music.

"If you have no other partners, maybe you'll have this dance with me?" Suddenly the woman she'd noticed earlier was at her side.

"A dance with you? Who would lead?"

"I will," and with that the woman took Katie's hand and led her onto the floor. She was nimble-footed and sure of her steps. She looked Katie square in the eye, and Katie had the feeling she'd been seen through clear to the bottom, and there weren't any secrets she had, and wasn't that a strange feeling to have with someone she'd only just met? And this woman said, "I've been watching you."

Katie's first thought was to flip that one away, but she said, "I know. I've felt your eye upon me."

"You've the unhappy knack of being the one left out, the one left behind, the one that saw where the others were blind, haven't you?"

80

"Is that what you saw?"

"All that, and a little more."

Katie thought she was being joked with. "I'd not have put it that way, but if it's unhappiness you're speaking of, I've seemed to have my fill." Now why did she say that?

They danced some more. Somehow they seemed to know the steps and how to move together. The woman said, "You might be a sister of mine."

"I think I might not. I know who my parents were and I've no sister at all."

"Yet my sisterhood has legions that aren't sisters by blood. Or not yet. Step right."

"What sort of a sisterhood is it you're speaking of?"

"I might be speaking of them that are daughters of a mighty wicked man."

"Then you may be speaking a great truth, or maybe you're speaking a terrible lie, but I declare by God's gospel I've no notion of what you're speaking of."

"I think you might know what it is if you were to think of a naked girl in an empty place and wanting to run as far as she can and her father there to watch her. And now step left."

"I think you're speaking by cyphers. I've no idea what it is you're meaning."

"I'm meaning we may have more kinship than you know of."

"I'm sure we're all daughters of Eve and so we've that kinship that's common with all and that makes pat that phrase all men are brothers. So also all women may be sisters. But what of that?"

The woman just looked at her and danced a few more steps. Then she did something surprising. She leaned over and placed her lips next to Katie's ear. Katie heard her quickly whisper something, but it couldn't be made out. Then the woman stepped away. "My name is Deirdre," she said. "We shall meet again." She turned and was lost in the throng.

That's a queer one, thought Katie. She saw there were empty glasses and plates and she went about picking them up till she encountered Madam Lanchester and General Hobsbawm chatting with their heads down.

"Madam, General, is there anything you need?"

The General, who took her in with one grave glance, seemed on the point of saying something when Madam Lanchester, evidently agitated, burst in with, "Why don't you help Agnes in the hall, I think she's feeling overwhelmed."

Katie hastened in that direction, as Lieutenant Lovejoy joined the conversation between Madam Lanchester and the General. Just as she entered the hall a squadron of soldiers was arriving at the front door, armed and equipped with rifles. These were not party guests. Their captain approached her, "Do not be alarmed. We are here to offer protection. Do you know where I could find General Hobsbawm?"

Katie gestured towards the garden and looked round the hall full of startled partygoers. She picked out Tavish's unhappy, stolid face and that of Agnes, looking forlornly bewildered. Suddenly there were several loud explosions that seemed to come from outside, or in the direction of the garden. Katie looked that way and thought she saw some sparkling lights like fireworks coming over the top of the wall and into the garden.

"They're rockets!" a man's voice shouted.

There was a wail of anger and confusion, and the music broke off abruptly. People were running into the hall. There were sounds of shooting from outside. Someone shouted, "Don't panic!" and all at once everyone panicked. General Hobsbawm strode to the bandstand and waving his arms called out to everyone to stay where they were. "There is no cause for fear," he said. "The army is actively engaged and has everything under control!" There were a few screams and other outcries, but the general turmoil seemed to decrease. "We have been attacked here, at Lanchester Mansion, by a mob of cutthroats. Their motives and organization are unclear. But we have matters under control." Just at this moment there was a volley of shots from outside. Everyone jumped and looked about, eyes lit with fear. "Those were our troops, dispersing the evil doers. I say again, matters are under control!" He looked around and appeared satisfied by the relative calm his remarks had engendered. Lieutenant Lovejoy brought him a document of some sort and whispered in his ear. There was a brief *sotto voce* conversation between the two, then the General held up his hands and said, "We are at this moment organizing troops to escort all of you to your homes. The streets are not safe. A curfew is in place and the city is under a state of martial law as of this moment." He then stepped down from the bandstand and proceeded towards the hall. There was some scattered applause. A few inebriated guests looked around as though they approved of the interlude, and were now awaiting the resumption of the music.

However, at the front door of the mansion the serious work of setting up the escorts for the guests was underway. General Hobsbawm called Madam Lanchester to assist in organizing them by the quarter of the town in which their homes lay, and then assigning them to the soldiers directed to take them there. It was an involved process, and certainly not one that she had been expecting to perform, but the partygoers were for the most part cooperative, and with the appropriate farewells and polite leave-takings, she saw to it that everyone got where they were supposed to. Katie, Agnes and Tavish had duty at the front door and sent everyone off, catching glimpses of the street, now patrolled by soldiers in armor with rifles and some with large, ferocious-looking dogs.

General Hobsbawm and Lieutenant Lovejoy, with a few soldiers, were the last remaining. Madam Lanchester had collapsed exhausted into a chair. She took the General's hand and said, "Thank God I invited you."

"Yes," said the General. "It turns out to have been a stroke of good fortune that we were here. And you could hardly have anticipated that this would happen."

"No. Hardly."

"When I received the invitation I wondered why you had invited us." The General crossed to the table where Lieutenant Lovejoy was seated. "You remember, Lieutenant, I asked you that very question."

"I invited you because I thought it was the thing Pinehurst would have done. He was always eager to be as inclusive as possible, to bring together all sorts. Oh, how I miss him. I was a young bride, you know, and very devoted."

Lieutenant Lovejoy smiled and spoke in an undertone to the General, "I rather think I know what her motives were."

"Oh?" he asked.

"Oh yes," said the Lieutenant, continuing the whispered exchange, "An alliance with the military would be seen as a step up for a house down on its fortunes."

"How so?"

"She practically thrust that one on me," he said, indicating Katie, who at this moment was resting in a chair at the other end of the hall. "After she'd dolled her up. Diamond earrings. My God." He winked.

"Lieutenant, perhaps you are reading too much into what most likely is nothing at all."

"I have my reputation as a ladies' man, you know. And that one is what we call enceinte."

"She is?"

"Most certainly."

The two men chuckled. "I can follow your chain of thought."

"What are you two laughing about?" asked Madam Lanchester.

"Oh, nothing. Nothing at all," said the General.

"No, please, tell me."

"Well it was only that the Lieutenant was amusing himself with the idea that you wanted to marry him off to your pregnant housekeeper, or whatever she is."

"What?"

"Yes, just a joke."

Madam Lanchester sat for a moment, not comprehending what the men found amusing, feeling somehow there was an important point she was missing. "No. Really. I don't see. What is it?" she asked.

The General felt confounded, having to explain the nature of a joke he didn't find quite that funny. He looked at the Lieutenant.

The Lieutenant did his best. "Your waiting woman, Katie Jean?" He wasn't sure how to proceed.

"Yes?" said Madam Lanchester. There was a pause. "She's pregnant?" It dawned on her now what they were laughing about. How cruel.

"Yes . . . You didn't know?"

Madam Lanchester walked the length of the hall to where Katie was seated. Katie, at this point, was near a drowse, worn out from the day's work and then the night's excitement. She was as startled by Madam Lanchester's abrupt interrogation as if one of the upholstered chairs had suddenly risen to confront her.

"Katie?"

"Yes, Madam?"

"Stand up."

Katie stood. Madam Lanchester looked her over.

"Have I spilled something on the dress?"

"Are you pregnant?"

There was no reply.

"You've humiliated me."

"No."

"Yes you have . . . You have no idea. You have no idea what you're doing. Dancing with Lieutenant Lovejoy? What were you thinking?"

"You said to enjoy my –"

"Is that what you thought I meant?"

Katie couldn't think. None of this made any sense.

"Oh, Katie. What have you done?"

"I don't know."

The two women stood there, neither one knowing what to do. Finally Madam Lanchester said, "You'll have to go. Get your things and get out . . . You've stabbed me to the heart." She walked away, then turned back and said, "You don't have to do it this minute. First thing in the morning. I want you out of this house." Then she walked away. She thought she ought to cry, but couldn't remember how.

Katie burst into tears. There was only so much she could take, but it seemed she just kept taking more and more. With no idea of where she was going to go, what she was going to do, she walked slowly to the stairs to her room. She climbed the stairs and opened the door and Tommy was there bouncing up and down.

"Oh, Tommy, I forgot to walk you." She put him on the leash and took him downstairs and out onto the now deserted street. It was funny to think that not too long ago there had been shooting going on here, and now Tommy was doing his business. She felt totally bleak, and blind to what was happening around her. She walked a little way and saw somebody lying in the gutter. It was a boy, probably not even twenty years old. She went to wake him up and when she did, she saw he'd been shot in the head. Apparently nobody'd seen him or bothered about him and here he was, lying on his back, his wide open astonished eyes reflecting the last of the moonlight. She wanted to tell him get up and go home. She looked at the body and imagined it was herself lying there and she shivered, and with that thought she realized she'd forgotten to take her stick with her like she always did, but somehow she didn't think she'd need it, or if she did need it, she didn't think it'd be any use. Then she led Tommy back to her room and on the way happened to encounter Tavish, who'd changed out of his tails and black tie and into his threadbare doublet and hose.

"I heard," he said. "Don't worry, she'll change her mind by the morning.

"No she won't."

"She will. You of all people should know her moods by now."

"Don't care if she does. I'm going." She closed the door in his face.

"Please open the door. I'm not leaving," he said, standing outside in the hall.

She looked at her image in the mirror. *Well these'll just have to go,* she said to herself. She took off the diamond earrings. Then opening the door she handed them to a surprised Tavish, said, "Give these to Madam Lanchester," and closed the door again. A moment later she opened the door once more to shout after him, "Tell her I'm keeping the dress." *Not that it'll fit me much longer,* she thought to herself.

She got her old suitcase out and laid it open before her. She started going through the chest of drawers, taking things one by one and putting them in the case or throwing them away. But that was all she could do that night. She broke down then and cried herself to sleep, and was haunted in her dreams by the thought that she was searching for something in her room, something she needed, but she couldn't say why, and everything she looked at wasn't what she was looking for, but it didn't matter anyway because she'd forgotten what it was.

CHAPTER EIGHT
IN THE BELLY OF THE BEAST

THE FLOWERS the Master grew in a box outside his sashed cabin window had opened to catch the sun. Tawny orange, garish blue, their hues were the visible refutation of the ship's muted palette of gray and silver. This morning it occurred to the Master to wonder what these flowers were thinking. That is, if flowers could think, perhaps their thoughts were along the lines of, 'Oh really, here comes that annoying sun again. Just when I was having a rest.'

The Master left his cabin and climbed the stairs to the poop deck. Here he saw Brutus tied to the rail on the weather side in his role as defendant in the trial to be held this morning. His posture declared him proud and disdainful, but he was committed to a course of judicious penitence, and had already agreed with himself that it was time once again to accept — not punishment – but the consequence of what he had done. He was not contrite, but he allowed as how in the course of life a man must now and again give the world a knock, and it was not a startling affair when the world chose to give the knock back.

Ramsey and the Master stood before him on the lee side of the poop deck in their roles of judge and assessor. The men of the craft stood below, as was proper.

Bringing down his gavel, the Master declared the trial in session.

"Brutus, you are charged with assaulting your fellow seamen and inflicting powerful damage on their persons, to the effect that Signor Vincenzo has a signal gash carved in his right cheek, Signor Diego has a chip to his tooth and a face that's all one bruise, and my carpenter Mr. Chips will not be the carpenter he has been for some time now due to his left arm being thoroughly broken up, and it'll likely be in a sling many a day. What have you to say to this?"

"I flung them about because they was cheating at cards."

"Cheating at cards." Here he gave a sorrowful look and a great shake of his head, as if those three words recalled to him all the great history of human iniquity. "Are you certain they were cheating? Did they cheat you?"

"Yes, I am certain. No, it was not me they cheated."

"Whom did they cheat?"

"My cabin mate Tom."

"And where is your cabin mate to confirm your story?"

A long pause, then, "I don't know."

The Master turned to the First Mate. "Can you bring forward this man Tom?"

The First Mate said, "I cannot. Search was made, but he has not been found."

"So either he is hidden, or he is lost." There passed a moment for all to reflect on this. "Perhaps there's more than a beating needs looking into. Mayhap a man's been murdered. That's a crime for which a man would hang, but lacking a body what are we to make of this?"

"It could be that man Brutus threw the body overboard in his drunk," said Ramsey. "And perhaps the story of a cheat at cards is just to throw a muddle in our way. Now there's a thought comes to me."

"And a good thought it is."

Brutus said, "I threw no man overboard."

"Have you proof of that?"

"How can a man prove what he hasn't done? But you had me in chains soon as the fight was over. How could I have done it?"

"Eh, Ramsey, there's a thought. How could he have done it?"

"I don't know how. I have naught but my suspicions. Suspicions what'd hang over the head of a drunken battling sailor in anyone's mind."

The Master turned and held up the bloodstained blade that had been found the night before. He held it in front of Brutus's face. "Is this yours?" he asked.

"It is not."

Diego raised his hand to interject. "Please sir, that is my blade. It was among the instruments I make use of in a bag this man snatched and hurtled in his fury. It is called a catling, this blade, one used in amputations, a sharp and a dangerous blade if not wielded with care."

88

"I see," said the Master. Then, turning again to Brutus, he asked, "Did you use this blade on the face of your fellow seaman Signor Vincenzo?"

"I did not," spoke Brutus. "I never handled that blade, nor any blade last night. All the work I did was with my fists, like an honest man would fight."

"But someone cut his face."

Brutus remained silent, a question not having been put.

"Do you know who cut his face?"

"I do not."

"Signor Vincenzo."

Vincenzo stood, his cheek wrapped in a bloody bandage.

"Who cut your face?" the Master asked.

"It was that same fellow Tom. A scurvy fellow. The one that cannot be found."

"The one you cheated at cards."

"There was cards, yes, by your honor, but there was no cheat."

"Cards without a cheat? Now there's a novelty." There was a pause as the Master looked Vincenzo over. "I've half a mind to put you in the dock as author of this last night's affray. But lacking this Tom to point the finger I've not the shadow of a right to do so. Was it you who hustled this Tom away?"

"Nossir."

"Put him to bed, did you?"

"Nossir."

A silence. "We'll see." Then he stood and addressed the assembled sailors and crew. "Is there any here know where this man Tom can be found?"

There was no answer save the wind and a creak in the rigging.

"No . . . ? I've known this leg of the voyage to be a hard errand, though perhaps never so hard as you've made it this time. We'll be putting ashore in Kashahar tomorrow ere sundown, and a rest in port will do us all good. But on board I'll not have any scuffles or fisticuffs. I make no exceptions, and I'll brook no excuses. A man raises his fists to another man, let you know that man will be punished for it. Brutus," and now he turned his attention full on the man tied to the rail before him, "I find you guilty of assault on your fellow seamen for no justifiable reason. I find you guilty on the count of battering Signor Diego and breaking the arm of Mr. Chips. You shall be punished." Then he turned back to the assembled seamen. "And let this punishment stand as a warning to any who would foment fighting and brawling aboard the Queen of Bel Harbor. Should you do so, this punishment will fall on your heads as well." Here he paused. "In the matter of this seaman Tom, further investigation is called for." He was in a grand, satisfied mood. He felt he had borne himself well, and things could have gone worse. He now gestured to Ramsey. "Ramsey, as the boatswain, I leave it to you to pronounce the punishment," and he sat as Ramsey rose.

Ramsey now looked over the crew, and pulling himself back from the inner controversy he ever carried on with himself, fidgeted a bit and then turned his eyes on Brutus. "Brutus," he said, "the crime of which you have been found guilty is one that we look on with great – ah – displeasure. Yes. Great displeasure. And it must be punished so. The severity – the punishment must be the most severe."

Brutus turned his face up to him with a wistful look in his mild eyes, as if seeking elucidation of a matter ambiguous to his intelligence.

Ramsey went on, "You will be punished by eighty lashes of the cat. And I will see to it that the sentence is carried out forthwith."

There was a sound of indrawn breath. Eighty lashes? Had they heard right? The cat was a tangled whip with bits of sharp metal on the end of each lash. For most trivial offenses one lash or two was given. For the more severe as many as five or six. Several of the men carried on their backs the scars of such lashings. For the greatest crimes it had been recorded that eight lashes could be given. Surely that was what he had meant. It must be. More than that was a sentence of death. Eighty lashes?

The Master, from his seat, asked gently, "Eighty lashes? Are you certain?"

Ramsey, afraid to be seen as weak or capable of a mistake, insisted on his eighty. "Yes. Eighty," he said. "To be administered here, forthwith, before the assembled crew."

The Master remained seated, his face a mask of rigid determination. The one who was to give the flogging came forward with the cat. Brutus, after a struggle, was positioned with his naked back turned to the flogger. Ramsey stood, observing the procedure, but whether his eyes were on what was in front of him or not could not be said. In truth, he was wishing someone would overrule him, or maybe God would supply a substitute, as in the case of Abraham and Isaac, but he was not a man to admit to a mistake.

The Master spoke once again. "Mister Ramsey, in your role as boatswain you are the assessor of punishments, and I will not overrule you. We are all servants of a power greater than ourselves, the power of the law, and it were better that a man should die than that the law should suffer even the slightest harm. Law is that which stands between us and the animals. But are you certain that the law proscribes a punishment of eighty lashes in this case?"

Ramsey answered, "Are you implying I have made a mistake?"

What an odd thing to ask, thought the Master. Of course this was what he was implying. He had thought the implication must be clear to all. "I must insist – " he began, but then thought better of it. "As I said before, I will not overrule you. Please proceed."

So, when all was ready, "One," said Ramsey.

The flogger lifted the cat and let it down gently on Brutus's back, barely scratching the skin.

"Oh, come on, man," said Ramsey. "Will you make a mock of it? Give it a lash. Dole it out as it must be done. Hard, man. A hard lash."

The flogger looked back at him.

"We start again," said Ramsey. "One."

The flogger administered the lash. Brutus writhed in pain. Runnels of blood bore down his back and he cursed them with a most vehement and a bloody curse, because they had forgotten to gag him as they ought. He cursed them all and he damned them, both Ramsey and the Master and all their progenitors and all their generations that were to come, with a loud and a clamant oath.

"Two." Again the lash. Brutus writhed again, the blood now pouring freely. There were tears of unendurable pain in his eyes and the curses that he cursed were a woe to be heard. The Master and the men looked on, observing in grim silence, seeing to it that justice was done.

"Three." And again.

After ten, Brutus stopped moaning.

After fifteen, the Master retired to his cabin.

We'll turn our eyes away. But what of Tom? They'd searched for him diligently over the entire vessel, but nowhere was he to be found.

Tom, when he'd spluttered to the surface of the frigid waters, saw the ship being borne away into the night. He tried to shout, but there was none to hear him, and his voice didn't carry over the squalling of the waves and the wind's suspiration. The last he saw of the ship was the yellow twinkle of the Master's cabin light disappearing in the fog. He did his best to stay afloat, but the water was cold, so cold, with an aching freezing chill that got into his bones and wouldn't get back out again. He found his head was dipping below the waves more and more, and he was having a harder time fighting his way to the surface, where he'd take in great gulps of the icy salt water. He was just on the point of giving up the ghost, and of letting his self drift down for the last time, when looking below, he never knew quite how, but he saw a great fish – the speckled back of a great fish he was certain it was, darker than the dark waters beneath it – swimming up towards him where he waited treading water. He saw it turn and pass just under him. But it didn't pass, it kept going, and going, and going some more. The breadth of it was enormous, and there seemed to be no end to the length of it. He counted several intervals till he got tired of counting before the great tail of the beast finally passed below him and he smacked his lips together almost with glee that here, at the very end of his life, he'd been granted a sight of that great marvel he'd heard so many seamen speak of, the monstrous leviathan that sits at the sea's bottom and gnaws at the edge of the world. And as he went down for the last time the great fish turned again and opening its cavernous mouth it took Tom in and swallowed him whole.

Tom was grappled as it were with a shoal of rough fishes and being engulfed down the gorge of the brute found himself slipping over the lip of a waterfall and into a pool of salt water, where gasping and spluttering he was able to catch his breath. He was floating in what resembled a lagoon filled with fish, or bits of fish, swirling in gentle currents around and through a series of troughs marked out by innumerable cartilaginous membranes visible in a hazy pearlescent glow that was diffused by the walls. He sat up in astonishment. Surely he had passed safe and alive into the gullet of the enormous fish he had seen swimming beneath him.

He staggered to his feet and looked around. His first thought was could he survive here? He tried to get a sense of directions. He was looking down a long ribbed tunnel. The walls of the tunnel were a dingy sort of red, and they were alive, heaving rhythmically in huge, shuddering gasps, in and out and in and out again. When he turned around he could see the waterfall over which he had passed. The water descended down a vertical wall perhaps fifteen feet in height. It came gushing in torrents, falling into the pool at his feet and then passing down the long membranous tunnel. If he could somehow ascend that wall, fighting upward against the water's flow, he might then be in a position to reach the creature's mouth and perhaps escape, although escape would almost certainly mean death by drowning in the ocean's depths.

The water in the pool in which he stood came almost to his waist. There were a number of fish of various sorts swimming in it, and there were also fish heads and tails and other parts that might have been torn or chewed by the monster's teeth. He proceeded down the tunnel. From time to time he was flooded by an inundation of water from the giant's mouth which would sweep his feet from under him; but mostly he was able to plowter along in his waterlogged shoes. His passage was illuminated by the pearly luminescence he'd seen at first that seemed to be exuded by the walls, or what he thought of as walls, which were likely the lining of the fish's intestines or stomach or some other internal organ. As he proceeded he found that the tunnel divided and was full of elaborate passageways culminating in caverns or grottoes of one sort or another. He was overcome with wonder at the vast hugeness he'd discovered in the leviathan's bowels, and felt as if he was an explorer descending into caves in the deepnesses of the earth except that the walls were constantly shuddering and quivering, and he was almost always walking in water up to his waist filled with fish and crabs and other crustaceans. If he had to spend any time here he'd certainly not lack for food, though many of the fish were kinds he'd never seen before, with odd colors and queer mouths. But he'd likely die first from lack of water, as he could not drink the brine sloshing all around him. Seeing no point in descending further he turned back and attempted to retrace his steps, but found himself lost in a bewildering confusion of canals and tunnels, and finally, exhausted, he lay down on a patch of relatively dry seaweed and went to sleep.

When he awoke he was confounded for several moments by the complete unfamiliarity of his surroundings. Gradually returning to consciousness he recalled being swallowed by the fish and his subsequent explorations of the halls and corridors in its vast belly. He also came to the slow realization that amidst the various swishing and whistling sounds that seemed to surround him there were other muffled tones carried faintly from somewhere far below that were unmistakably musical. As he listened, he could make out a melody accompanied by a bass continuo, as if being played on the pipes of a mysterious organ. At times the music would halt and then start up again, repeating the same passage, as if the keyboardist was practicing his fingering. As best he could, Tom tried to identify the direction from which the sound was coming and then follow it to its source. He was led down a long and juddering tunnel past innumerable branching passageways, finally debouching into a large enclosed space which as best he could determine was the fish's stomach. He was amazed to see that this space contained several large wooden boxes, hogsheads, barrels and other containers, things which the leviathan must have swallowed at one time or another and which, being indigestible, had ended up here. But the most amazing sight of all was a man seated on a keg at the keyboard of a small pipe organ who was playing the music. He was a chubby man with enormous buttocks. As soon as he saw Tom he stopped playing and jumped off the keg, evidently as astounded to see Tom as Tom was to see him.

"You've arrived," said the man.

"Have I now?"

"I've been expecting you." Tom thought there was nothing more remarkable this man could have said. He went on, "I summoned you, and here you are. I am Colophus of Demarest. No doubt you've heard of me."

"Certain it is I have not."

"Well, you know of Demarest, of course."

"No."

"No . . .? The Torpentine Seaboard . . .? The Capitols of Upper Toravia . . .? None of these mean anything to you?"

"No, I'm afraid I've no knowledge of any of them." Tom considered that the fish he was in must have traversed considerable distances and was familiar with geographies that were well and away beyond any seas he'd ever known.

"Well, you are astoundingly ignorant. Perhaps that was to be expected. At any rate it is no matter."

Tom looked about. The large and enclosed space in which he found himself was filled with the most varied and disparate sorts of objects. There were crates crammed with merchandise of all sorts, glassware, furniture, objets d'art; a fantastic confusion of all sorts had been set adrift here in the bowels of the leviathan. He must have swallowed argosies, great galleons full of all the artifacts of human merchandise, that now, having been consumed by this monster of the deep, had jumbled themselves together, as in a huge storehouse of a fabulous museum, all the odds and ends, the old bits that no longer fit anywhere else, jam packed and put away till their final disposition could be determined. It was no wonder at all that Colophus had found an organ and been able to put it up and get use from it. There were contraptions even odder, for many of which he could not even imagine a purpose, unless perhaps for some arcane torments or plea-sures of which he had no conception. He was so rapt in amazement he realized that Colophus had been speaking for some time and he had not been paying attention.

"So I've been whiling my time away, toiling here in the land of the dead, all alone, but my time has been my own and I assure you it has not been wasted. I've been pursuing investigations into a diverse array of philosophical questions relating to the purpose of existence and of nonexistence, as well as putting the final touches on my memoirs."

"So you're writing your memoirs, are you?"

"Oh yes. In death I've finally found the time I needed. Never could do it when I was alive, there was just too much going on."

"In death you say?"

"Yes. Oh I am sorry but I assure you we are both dead. I have been here alone in the land of the dead for some time. It's impossible to know how long, there are no days or nights here, there is only eternity. But in my loneliness I longed for a companion. I have prayed for one devoutly, and my prayers have been answered. You have arrived, another dead soul with whom I can share this everlasting Purgatory. Welcome."

"I'm disinclined to believe I'm dead."

"Perhaps this comes as a shock."

"I'm not dead at all. I can see I'm breathing, and I feel my heart beating. Surely those would be alarming symptoms in a dead man."

"It is all an illusion. Your dead soul has disguised itself in the trappings of a living body. The air you appear to breathe, the blood that appears to be pumping through your veins, these are all phantasms. Where else could this be, but Purgatory?"

"We're not in Purgatory at all. This is the belly of a very great fish. We've been swallowed and we're at the bottom of the sea."

"The belly of a fish? Did you say we're in the belly of a fish?" Colophus broke out in laughter. "Why that's ridiculous. Do you have any idea how large such a fish would have to be to carry us around in its belly? Why that's – " he broke off, nearly crying with laughter.

"Yes, I fell off a ship, and – "

"Why that's ludicrous!" Colophus was now rolling on the floor, unable to contain his mirth.

"I fell off a ship and saw a great fish, the mighty leviathan, swimming from the depths, and I saw it open its powerful jaws and swallow me down as easy as a man would swallow a crumb. Then I was consumed along with several schools of fish and bolted down into his gullet where I wandered around a bit and fell asleep. Then hearing your music I climbed down to where we are now, which I believe to be the leviathan's enormous stomach. Why, how did you come to be here?"

"Well, I certainly wasn't swallowed by a fish."

"No?"

"No. I was poisoned by my enemies. They had it in for me. It was a nasty plot and one I should have seen through, but I've always been of too trusting a nature. I was very close to the Emperor, you see, I was in his inmost counsels, and my plans were on the point of being put into effect. Naturally, my enemies could not allow that to happen.

"So they invited me to a luncheon on a pleasure barge belonging to Duke Onorio. I ought to have known the Duke had been suborned, he was always of a weak and vacillating temperament, and that's where the dirty deed was done. I am uncertain which dish it was, although I suspect it was the snails in a peacock relish, they knew of my fondness for it, it would have been just like them to select such a choice viand as the means of my demise, but it might have been – oh, who knows – anyway, where was I?"

"You were meeting your death by poison."

"Oh yes. How regrettable. So the last thing I can recall is consuming those snails and then being overcome by drowsiness. The next time I opened my eyes I was here. This is clearly Purgatory, where I have been placed so that I can undertake the completion of certain worthy tasks that were left undone while I was still alive. Upon the completion of my penitential labors I shall be taken into Paradise where I will bask in the love of God almighty for all eternity. But while I was here I was lonely, so I prayed devoutly for a companion, and the presiding powers have sent you. Admittedly you are an oaf, in complete ignorance of the civilized world, prone to rustic conjectures such as being in the belly of –" here he broke off, unable to contain his laughter, "the belly of a fish!" He laughed for several minutes, looking at Tom and shaking his head the whole time. When he was finally able to speak again he concluded by remarking that the benefits of companionship, no matter how lame-brained, outweighed the dreariness of a lonely existence.

"Certain I am you are right," said Tom. "I am an oaf. It would not astonish me if I was the stupidest man ever to walk the face of the earth. I had the love of a fine woman, a kind and a smart woman who looked on me as her sweet boy, her lover, and her one and only for now and forever. The sun rose in her eyes when she saw me and for me it was just the same. I loved her and I love her still with my whole heart, and all my senses would be pleased and perfected if they could just behold her here before me now. And for some reason I took it into my head to go to sea and leave her far behind, hoping for a pot of gold that would make everything good, when everything already was better than any pot of gold could ever make it. Yes, I'm a stupid man. I've no argument with that at all. But for all that, still I say we're both alive, you and I, and we're being carried hither and thither in the belly of a great fish." And just as Tom said that, a tremendous wave of water came through the space where they sat, washing all the odd bits of flotsam and jetsam about, rearranging the furniture as it were.

When things had settled down again, "I imagine," said Tom, "when they thought they'd poisoned you they probably threw you overboard, and then the fish swallowed you. You were unconscious the whole time and when you came to you were already in the fish's stomach."

"Well, we'll see. This fish must be one of the folk legends of the primitive tribe you come from. I'd guess you can't conceive of the world without it. Anyway . . . what was I talking about?"

"I've no idea."

"Nor have I. You see, this is what happens. I've a great chain of thought, but if I get off it I never know where to get back on again. I think I was calling you stupid. Oh, but that's no use. Anyway, I've been at work on a great treatise on the purposes of existence. Seemed like the thing to do here in Purgatory."

"How do you survive here? I can see there's plenty of fish to eat, but what do you drink?"

"Oh, there's gallons to drink. Here," and he found a goblet, which he handed to Tom, and then led him to a cask with a bung and a spigot. "There's sherry. Huge amounts. Seems like the perfect drink for Purgatory. Glorious sherry, fill your glass."

Tom did so and took a deep draft. "That was refreshing," he said. "My mouth was becoming sadly parched."

"For food there's an abundance of fish. I don't know why fish exactly, possibly some religious symbolism there, but an abundance I assure you. Unfortunately you'll have to get used to eating it raw. I tried once lighting a fire. I've flint and iron, and there's plenty of paper, but the walls started palpitating and the water came sluicing through something awful. There was no way to get that fire going and I assure you I've not wanted to repeat the experiment."

"No, fire in his innards'd give this fish quite a vexation I should think."

"You and your fish. Well, as I was saying, I've been at work on a dissertation intended to expound all the possible purposes of existence. Don't you think that's the sort of thing God would want to see completed? Now that I've got eternity to diddle around in, might as well get at it. By the way, don't you think that's the worst tasting sherry you've ever had a mouthful of?"

"Actually I was thinking it's not that bad at all."

"It tastes like the urine of a diseased camel. How would I know what the urine of a diseased camel tastes like, no doubt that's the question you're pondering, am I right? Well, I've had a life just full of experiences. You'd know that if you'd ever read my memoirs. Do you know how to read?"

"Certain it is that I do."

"Well, that's a fine thing. Because I've written just volumes and volumes of my memoirs. Thank God now there's someone to read them. You see, there's no shortage of paper here, nor of ink. We've an ample supply," he indicated several boxes which were filled with blank pieces of paper. "An ignorant, stupid man like yourself naturally you'll have nothing to write down, but you can read all that I have written and you can learn."

"Well, that's something to look forward to. Something to fill the idle hours I'd say."

"Yes, and this is in the truest sense a posthumous work. I have observed that death has often tended to slow the output of even the most prolific authors. You'll be happy and amazed to learn that this is not true in my case. My memoirs may well be the first work ever to have been written entirely after the author had passed away."

"Well, that's a marvel."

"You don't know the half of it." And Colophus proceeded to burden Tom with pages of his memoirs. "I've written other things too, you know. There's my dissertation on the purposes of existence. I also at one time had written a dissertation on the purposes of non-existence, but sad to say it no longer exists."

So Tom set about reading Colophus's memoirs, and other works of a like nature. There was plenty of time in this timeless region where there were no fixed cycles of night and day. He grew accustomed to the taste of the sherry they drank, and actually acquired a taste for it, though Colophus assured him that once Tom had drunk as much of it as he had he'd come to see how vile it truly was. Also he found that when he hungered, he could subsist on raw fish, and one time they stumbled on a round of cheese, which made for a welcome change of diet.

Colophus spent all his time in this large enclosed space which Tom felt certain was the stomach. Tom also spent much of his time there, in reading or in discussion with Colophus on any number of abstruse matters. Colophus considered himself an accomplished philosopher and was at pains to show off to Tom the solutions he'd arrived at for a number of philosophical enigmas. For instance, they debated as to whether happiness and wisdom were two words for the same thing. Tom thought they were, but Colophus differed, saying if you had happiness, why would you want wisdom too? Another time they attempted to unravel the question of free will versus fixed fate. Here Colophus dilated on the idea that God, when He'd created the universe, had set everything in motion, and that there was an inevitable chain of cause and consequence that could account for every single action of every single atom throughout the entire universe. And since every event was the result of the events which had preceded it, every event was, as it were, cast in stone at the first moment of creation and there was no possibility that anything could have happened differently. Yet at the same time, any individual could consult his own thoughts, and knowing he was making choices based on what would content or discontent him and that his choices were entirely free, would know he had free will. How were these two outlooks to be reconciled?

"You see, to simplify the problem – by the way, this is one of the things I love about philosophy; have you ever noticed that every philosopher, without exception, when he explains something begins his explanation with the words 'So, to simplify the problem?' Without exception, having propounded a difficult and complex question he then proceeds to solve a different and simpler problem. It is a metaphysical sleight of hand absolutely indispensable to those of us of the philosophical persuasion. To comprehend the answer you must understand that the greatest natural philosophers of the current day have deduced that the world originated in what they call a Big Bang at the creation of time. The particles which make up the universe have ever since been dispersed and are growing ever fainter and farther away from one another until eventually everything will terminate in a great whimper of silent emptiness. However, as anyone who has ever composed a symphony will tell you, the silence comes at the beginning and the big bang comes at the end. The root of our tragedy lies in the fact that we move through time in the direction opposed to time's flow. This is why we don't always grow younger and happier. The period behind us, which we cannot see and which we call the future, is fixed and unchangeable and subject to fate. This is what we have clumsily apprehended and tried to express by saying it is predetermined by cause and effect. Whereas the period before us, which we call the past, is unformed and changeable and subject to free will."

"You mean everything I remember hasn't happened yet?"

"Yes. However these events are forever beyond our grasp because we are moving through time in the wrong direction. Or perhaps the truth is that past and future are just two different ways of looking at the same thing, like two sides of a coin."

"I must say that seems to fail the test of common sense."

"Yes, but all our science and civilization fails that test. Did you realize that mathematics, that tool which seems most precisely to explain the nature of reality and the universe, is in fact founded on a delusion? It is. All our mathematical knowledge is based on the assumption that there is such a thing as zero. Without zero it all falls apart. And yet zero is nothing, and nothing is that which doesn't exist. So all our knowledge and science is founded on an absurd flaw, the assumption that nothing exists."

From time to time, Tom would take excursions into other parts of the fish's anatomy, looking to see what else he could find, or if perhaps he could retrace his steps and return to the fish's gullet, from which, if there were ever opportunity, he might escape back into the world. However, he never found his way back to that pool under the waterfall where his body had been lodged after he'd first been swallowed. His jaunts invariably ended with a return to the large enclosed space of the stomach. There were times when he thought he could feel the fish moving through the ocean's waters; he had feelings of great distances being traversed. It was hard to say how these feelings were conveyed to him since he had no way of seeing what was passing outside. Sometimes he felt the floor rocking under him and he saw the walls of the tunnels straining and then releasing as the fish exercised its mighty muscles. One time, discovering a route not traversed before, he wandered in mazy passages, hearing what sounded like the rhythmic beating of a vast and mighty drum. Following the sound, he found himself drawn towards a chamber from which he could look out and view a solemn and awe-inspiring spectacle. He saw a gigantic, gleaming muscle of the darkest crimson slowly gathering itself together, drawing what resembled a syrup of viscous dark liquid into itself, and then with a mighty throb, producing the sound he'd heard, dispersing the fluids through what looked like huge chasms that must have been the animal's arteries. He was witnessing the action of the heart of the leviathan as it slowly extended and distended itself and then with a powerful resounding hug compressed itself again, drawing the blood in and forcing it out again. He gazed, rapt, for a long time, spellbound by this awesome display of the terror and magnificence of life.

Apart from the time he spent in these outings most of his time was spent in the company of Colophus, either reading his memoirs or engaged in discussions of his various philosophical theories. One subject Colophus frequently reverted to was his theory of the best government. As a close confidant of the Emperor he had often spoken of it and had taken some steps to seeing it put into effect. He thought this was probably why his enemies had acted when they had, to forestall the instauration of this much to be desired and broadly beneficial regime. He noted that many forms of government had been attempted, at various times during man's march through history. "There was autocracy, rule by a single monarch; aristocracy, rule by those who are most noble; democracy, rule by the people; gerontocracy, rule by those who are oldest; gynecocracy, rule by women; mobocracy, rule by a mob; plutocracy, rule by those who are wealthiest; technocracy, rule by the most scientific; theocracy, rule by God; and so forth. All of these forms of government may be found to be workable for a while, but eventually they founder and have to be replaced because someone totally unfit to govern is elevated to the highest post and the system collapses. Why is it that there has never been found any form of government that assures us of being administered competently? You would think that somewhere in the course of human history someone would have stumbled on a system that put the reins of government into the hands of the most sensible ruler. So many things have been tried, but inevitably we find ourselves governed by venal self-serving blockheads who deserve to be shot. Why does this happen?"

"I'm sure I don't know."

"You'll be glad to learn that I have given the matter a great deal of thought, and I have arrived at a solution. But to understand my solution, it is necessary first to be disabused of a common error that many make in assuming that the seat of man's cogitative faculties resides in the skull. It does not."

"No?"

"Absolutely not. Many people think that the brain, which lies inside the skull, is the engine of cognition. However, my researches indicate that this is not the case. Oh, it's an easy error to make. Just because so many of the major sense organs are all bundled in the head, it's convenient to think of the head as the center of reason. There resides the brain, with his attendant senses, sight, hearing, smell and taste near to hand, am I right?"

"I can see the logic of it."

"Yes, and that's exactly where you go wrong. Now, look at the body of a man. Where is the central point?"

"The stomach?"

"Close . . . When it's necessary to apply all of a man's strength, where is the foundation for it? Where is the biggest muscle to be found? Is it in the upper body? No, of course not. Where is it?"

"In the thighs?"

"Close."

"In the butt?"

"Of course. In the glorious gluteus maximus, the largest muscle of them all. And let me ask you, if you were to create an organ responsible for all the intellectual work a man would find it necessary to perform, you would want that organ to be able to expand and to grow and to become ever more powerful, would you not?"

"Yes, I think you would."

"So if you were a benevolent creator you wouldn't put such an organ into a space where it is confined by a hard bony skull so it can't grow any larger, would you? Of course not, it wouldn't be natural. Where would you put it? You'd put it where there were no limits to how large it could grow. And you'd put it in that very spot that's nearest to where the generative functions reside, wouldn't you? You'd put it in the buttocks! Wouldn't you?"

"In the buttocks?"

"Of course!"

"So you think the seat of man's cogitative faculties is in his buttocks?"

"Precisely. The seat is in the seat, as it were. Could there be anything more sensible?"

"So what's the brain for then?"

"Who knows? The brain's of no account. Nothing it does matters. It's just a silly sponge. On the other hand, I'm sure you've observed that the smartest people are always those who have the largest buttocks."

"Actually I haven't observed this rule to be of an infallible nature."

"Well of course *you* haven't. But look at your buttocks. Hardly the size of a withered old apple. What are your observations worth?

Not much I'd say. Now, compare them to my buttocks. My buttocks, I'm sad to say, are not what they once were." Here he rolled over to give Tom a good view. "Once they were rotund, they were fabulously fleshy," he stroked them lovingly. "They have shriveled somewhat. The diet here is not the best for them. But still, you can see they have a hugeness and a very appealing roundness, do they not?"

"As you say, fat as can be."

"Ah – so my observations would naturally be superior to those of an unintelligent, ignorant man such as yourself, with buttocks like a shriveled pea. Don't take it personally. It's just a scientific fact."

"But what's all this got to do with the best form of government?"

"Oh yes. To resume where I left off, the ideal form of government, the one that would inevitably put the best man in charge, after all those other ocracies have been left in the dust, would be what I call buttockracy, rule by those with the largest buttocks. You see? Rule by the most intelligent, the most benevolent, and the most far-seeing. What could be better?"

"Well, I must say no matter what system people put in place, whether they pick the one who can waggle his ears the best, or the one that can sneeze the loudest, still it always seems like it's the biggest ass that always comes out on top."

"You see, it's nature's law."

Colophus was very satisfied with this proof of the legitimate authenticity of his theory of buttockracy. But despite the fact that he believed the faculties of thought resided in the buttocks, and that his buttocks were a good example of this rule, there were other times when his confidence in the operations of thought was altogether diminished. Sometimes he would be overcome by a feeling that there was no purpose to existence and that absolutely nothing made any sense, or he would become frightened at the idea that all around him malevolent forces were at work and that he was guided by an illusory and deceitful will-o'-the-wisp called reason which had no foundation to rest on, that thought itself was a flawed and dangerous activity. These times seemed to correspond with his most copious tipples of sherry, although it must be said that the constant consumption of this beverage, morning, noon and night, particularly considering there was neither morning, noon nor night in this timeless limbo, gave a certain tipsy outlook to everything that went on. He would sometimes bemoan the inadequacies of human reason, pointing out that it played no role in the most important operations a person performed, those that the body was conditioned to undertake automatically, such as breathing, or pumping blood. "You notice you don't let your mind take charge of those things. Oh no, you need those to keep you alive. So you're quite content to let your body go about doing everything that matters while your mind can play with things like morality and justice and truth and honor and all the stuff that makes us like the angels but which we really know isn't worth a whistle, otherwise we'd let instinct or some more primitive faculty sort them out, like the animals do. We place so much reliance on our bodies to do all the important work that we are even content to go to sleep, and let the mind loose to wander in irrational absurdities, confident that the body's taking care of everything that needs doing." As a demonstration of how little reliance we actually place on rational thought, as opposed to the instinctive actions of the nerves and muscles, Colophus proposed to try walking across the room while attempting to control his muscles entirely by means of conscious ratiocination. Unfortunately his ability to walk across the room had already been considerably compromised by the volume of sherry he'd consumed, so the demonstration was held to have been inconclusive. But there were many discussions of this nature that Tom found himself getting involved in, while drifting in a pearl-gray twilight, where nothing changed and no time seemed to pass, always half intoxicated, listening to the banter of a melancholy philosopher from beyond the grave, and more and more, the longer he was here, he had the curious feeling that time had ground to a halt and was no longer passing. Without cyclical change the whole concept of time began to seem meaningless. His ideas of how and when he could make his escape took on an air of unreality. The very thought of escape seemed incredible. How could he ever get away from here and back to the world of men? And when? He looked forward to it, but couldn't imagine it actually happening. When there's no end in view, there's no sense of direction to draw one on. He realized all his life he'd kept going by having something to look forward to, and now what he looked forward to was nothing. He was waiting for nothing. And it seemed as if the longer he waited, the less there was to wait for.

CHAPTER NINE
PIRACY AND PILLAGE

A TATTERED RAG OF CLOUD hung before a gibbous moon waxing towards the full as the Seahawk, three weeks out from San Luno Bay, captained by Crazy Dog Talbot and crewed by his band of heartless renegadoes, swooped down on the Queen of Bel Harbor in Cutthroat Bay, as she approached the port of Kashahar. Crazy Dog was a remarkably ugly man, missing one ear, his face weatherstormed to the complexion of antique parchment, a scar cut slantwise along one temple and cheek, his beard painted blue and his teeth all awry. He was bound to Kashahar where he expected to seize the great emerald that for untold ages had sat in the eye of Slothikay's one-eyed monkey god Maddibimbo, and he was late. But he couldn't help but plunder this heavy-laden galleon he'd found thrown in his way.

"All hands! Put all sheets up," he ordered, and walked towards the forecastle where he could get a better look at his prey. "What do you think?" he asked his First Mate, Barnacle Jack.

"We have the tide and she's a huge and a clumsy craft. She can't sail close to the wind and I don't think she's even making two knots. She'll not get to port before we have her. I'd ready the carronades on the port side."

And so it was done. They brought the Seahawk alongside the Queen and then unfurling the skull and crossbones and taking the canvas off the ship's figurehead, a skeleton holding a knife in its teeth, they ran the guns out. Once they lay half a cable off they gave a broadside that brought down some spars and killed a few of the Queen's crew. After that the pirates boarded. Crazy Dog was first, with a lantern and a cutlass. Barnacle Jack was right behind him. The Master chose that moment to stride out of his cabin, wearing a long shirt and nothing else. Barnacle Jack raised his pistol and without a flinch shot him through the eye. Suddenly the pirates were everywhere, carrying lanterns and cutlasses and muskets, and they set about rounding up the crew.

When they had them all up on deck, Crazy Dog took a walk around so they could see who he was. The night was overcast, and the moon just peeping through the clouds. There was a little swell to the sea, and Crazy Dog was rolling to it. A few lanterns were lit, one run halfway up the mainmast and another on the quarterdeck railing. Their tawny glow illuminated the flapping sails and the scared faces of the men.

"Now you've led me a merry chase," said Crazy Dog. "But the chase is over, and you'll find I've an enmity for you that's a lot like love. There's many a one would cut your throats, but you've been lucky. Very lucky. You've fallen into the compassionate hands of Crazy Dog Talbot. Any man who lies to me, or any who disobeys, will lose his life far more swiftly than any court could devise. But the ones who obey, and the ones who tell me the truth, they will prosper, and some may even get a chance to grow rich, and they may even get a chance to grow rich while they're still young enough to enjoy it."

He pointed to the Master's body, lying face down in the bilge. "This was your captain. What other officers are there on this ship?"

The First Mate was scared enough almost to faint, but he took a step forward. "I am one," he said.

Barnacle Jack pointed his pistol at the First Mate's head and said, "You'd best call him captain."

"Aye, aye. I am one, Captain," he said.

"Who else?" said Crazy Dog.

It took a few moments, but with some shuffling and some pushing, Ramsey was shoved forward.

"You two. Can you navigate?"

"Yessir," they both said.

"Yessir?"

"Yessir, Captain."

"Good." Then he turned to the crew, his eyes a candid gray. "Now I want every married man to raise his hand. And remember what happens to those that lie to me. Every married man."

Most hands went up, including the First Mate's.

"I see. You married men, stay where you are. Single men, over to the starboard rail and sit down."

They did as they were told. There were only four single men, Vincenzo, Diego, Mr. Chips and Ramsey. Two pirates watched them. While they sat there, the other pirates were getting the long-boat into the water and getting the married men into it, with a keg of water and a string of onions. When the boat pulled away, it was just a darker shadow on the water, but it was jammed full of men and like to sink the first rough wave that hit it. There must have been twenty men packed into a boat that couldn't hold more than a dozen.

Then Captain Crazy Dog came over to the four men remaining. "Listen to me and listen sharp. You may join my crew if you wish. We're the Free Brethren of the Coast. If you do, each of you will take an oath, and your lives will be forfeit should you break it. Once you've taken that oath, you'll share in our gains just as these others do. You'll eat with us and drink with us and be accounted a full member of the crew. If you don't, I'll put you ashore on the next deserted coast or scorching marl I reach. Now every man willing to join us should stand."

They all stood and took the oath. Then Crazy Dog said to Ramsey, "You that can navigate, I'll make you captain of this vessel. Your first task is to take her and all her cargo into Kashahar, where you're to sell the cargo and sell the ship as well, and deliver your earnings up to me at an appointed time and place to be distributed among the Free Brethren. You've got three for your crew, but I see one has a broken arm, so I'll give you four more from the Seahawk. That should be enough. And Barnacle Jack will be at your shoulder to make sure you do not break your oath."

"Aye, aye," said Ramsey. "I mean aye, aye, Captain."

Then Crazy Dog went into the Master's cabin and he went through the desk, and the items on the table. He found a mirror that had been given to the Master on the occasion of his birthday. It had a silver frame with a design of laurel leaves and ribbons. He decided to keep it but he'd no sooner looked in it than his countenance broke the glass, so he cast it aside with a curse. He then sent for Ramsey to join him and when the man entered he put on a pleased expression and said, "You're an honest man now, and you work for the King."

"The King?"

"Yes, that same king we all owe allegiance to back in the old country. It's he I work for. None of these jack-a-nape merchants."

"Does the King know that?"

"It matters not a whistle what the King knows. But General Hobsbawm, his sworn minister here in this land, is apprised of it, and so now are you."

"Oh. I thought you were a pirate."

"The merchants call me a pirate. But what call I them? I dare say peddling shoddy cloth and watered wine in fake measures makes one a merchant. We're all robbing someone. Do you have any idea how long I'd be able to keep this up if General Hobsbawm and his men took the notion to clap me in irons? What would be your guess how long I could keep it up?"

"I don't know."

"Not long."

"I mean, I don't know, Captain."

"You can dispense with that when we're alone. Hear me now. Pay attention. Look at me. The money I'll make from this cargo is money I've stolen from some gang of fat, greedy guts merchants, is it not? And can you tell me, what is the difference between a pirate and a merchant . . .? Eh . . .? Can you tell me?"

"I don't know. I mean, I don't know, Cap – I mean, I don't know." He was really starting to fidget by this time.

"Well neither do I." And he smiled with his great misshapen teeth. "And, for that matter, neither does the King. So, when the merchants come to General Hobsbawm in his great fort in Port Jay and they complain to him of the depredations of Crazy Dog and his Free Brethren, what do you suppose the General does? Eh?"

"I'm sure I have no idea."

"Well, he tells them, I'm going to put a stop to that piracy, just you watch me. That's what he tells them."

"And a good thing he does, too." The fidgeting was really starting to get out of control.

"You think that's a good thing, do you?"

"Oh, no, I don't."

"Changed your mind. I see. Well, in any case, as soon as those merchants leave his fort, what do you suppose General Hobsbawm does?"

"I really don't know. Please don't send me out on this ship with those other three men. They'll kill me. I'm certain of it."

"Oh, for God's sake, control yourself. You're ruining my story."

"I'm sorry. Well as soon as the men leave I'm sure General Hosbawm does something magnificent. He probably writes a lot of orders and sends them off to the captains of the fleet. I don't know. What does he do?"

"Nothing."

"Oh."

"Do you see my point?"

"No."

"I'm not getting much satisfaction out of talking to you."

"If you send me off on this ship, please don't include those other three men in the crew. They hate me. It's because of a mistake I made. I said eighty lashes when I only meant eight."

"You'll have to explain this to me some other time." Crazy Dog stood to leave. "You're in command here." He walked out.

Back on deck he barked his shins against a long wooden box. "What's this?" he roared. The talk with Ramsey had spoiled his mood and he felt like slitting someone's throat.

Mr. Chips, still huddled against the rail, answered. "It's a coffin. Spent the better part of the day I did building it one-handed."

"That's bad luck, a coffin. Toss it overboard."

"We were going to give the body a decent burial, in the Potter's Field in Kashahar."

"No time for it. Toss it in the drink. Do it now."

Diego and Vincenzo dragged the heavy coffin to the rail and lifted it up, grunting with the effort. "Ashes to ashes," said Vincenzo.

"Dust to dust," said Diego. "If God won't take you, the devil must." They dropped the coffin overboard. Then, looking over the rail they were surprised to see the heavy box, that had caused them such pains to lift, did not sink, but was floating on the water's surface. They watched as the lazy swells slowly bore it away from the ship.

"Never saw the like of that before," said Vincenzo. "Must be cursed."

Meanwhile, Crazy Dog selected four old tars from the Seahawk to stay on the Queen. Then he filled Barnacle Jack in on the plan, letting him know he should keep Ramsey on a short leash. Fortunately, they would make Kashahar the next day so it wouldn't be for long.

Then he returned with the rest of his men to the Seahawk. Once in his cabin he unrolled his map of Kashahar and ran his finger along the winding, tortuous streets of the city in search of the inn where the emerald was held. He was two days late.

Kashahar, at this time, was a city of open piazzas and lush gardens. Formerly, it had been a site of religious significance to the Indian civilization that had lived in this part of the world several centuries ago, but they were long gone, leaving behind many enigmatical limestone obelisks and heathen icons slowly crumbling to dust. The explorer Horatio Castro had found it a desert spot, where grasses grew over fallen statues and raindrops dripped and the steps were green with moss and vast weeds flourished in the flower beds. When he first stumbled on the spot he had commemorated it in poetry, comparing the decaying Indian relics to the fading beauty of his paramour. Here is a sample:

> No birds now sing in the gardens of the dead,
> No fountains plash, no words are said.
> Who walked these streets now turned to dust?
> Oh, Kashahar, oh, Kashahar, your secrets hushed
> By silent eons still await
> The masters of a new estate
> Who in time will build anew
> A city by the sea, both tall and true.
> I recognize and call to mind
> The beauty that my memories find
> When, Clementine, your withered face
> Reminds me of a time and place

When youthful loving laughter
Was the rule, not what's come after.
Just so it is with Kashahar:
Whose ancient grandeur lies not far
In sunken gardens of the dead
Where silence reigns and ghosts now tread.

History has failed to record Clementine's opinion of the piece.

No one knew what had become of those who dwelled here long ago. There were obscure legends of a great wave from the sea that had toppled the city, or perhaps it had been a gigantic serpent that, angered by some act of disrespect on the part of the citizens, had come by night to destroy it and make prey of its inhabitants. In any case, its roofs now sheltered mostly settlers from the old country who had come in the expectation of wealth. They employed many of the natives as servants and laborers, and the countryside surrounding the city was rapidly being deforested and put into cultivation.

The part of town by the harbor was the oldest and most densely peopled. There were many inns, taverns and brothels that sought custom from the ships that were constantly putting in and the merchants who traveled great distances to meet them. The inn that Crazy Dog located on his map was one of these establishments. It was in this inn that Stampour and his two fellow bandits were at this very moment waiting impatiently.

Stampour was looking out from beneath the hood of his jellaba at the rafters upholding the roof of the inn. He had been pondering these same rafters for two days now. Was there some message he should read in them? He knew there was not, yet his deepset, roving eyes had memorized their appearance.

This inn had been constructed in a manner common to Kashahar. There was a central courtyard open to all the floors that rose above it, and the rooms on each floor were entered through doors placed around the walls. Guests, when they exited from their rooms, could look down into the bottom floor courtyard before descending the stairs. Also, those in the bottom floor courtyard, such as Stampour at present, could look up to the roof five floors above. At this moment Stampour reached into his sabretache and retrieved the much-folded missive that had led him here. Was he certain this was the spot, he wondered. This deal should already have been consummated two days ago but here he still sat, waiting for the buyer, as the cagey priests he was running from drew ever closer. Almost he felt their eyes were upon him.

All about the stool on which he was perched there were genteel young men watching with awed fascination the various dancing harlots and courtesans who frequented this inn. The innkeeper was busy renting rooms for their trysts, and imparting suggestions as to the sexual favors to be enjoyed. Stampour sat in the midst of this swirling frivolity, unmoving, eyeing the door and waiting.

"Bring me wine," he said to the innkeeper.

The innkeeper placed a bottle of wine in front of his most sullen customer. "Here, drink yourself drunk."

Stampour moved not a muscle.

Outside the inn were three watchers. There was one standing across from its front door at all times. He was watched in turn by two others on the inn's roof. Sometimes these three traded positions. These were the vanguard of the priests of Slothikay. They had been afraid they would arrive too late to intercept the sale of the emerald, however that had not been the case. The remainder of the priests, led by Kanbold the Lame, High Priest of Maddibimbo, were only a day away. Kanbold, mounted on his mighty steed Tessephon, was accompanied by four acolytes carrying the sacred sacrificial blades, whose edges were whetted to a keenness twice that of any razor. Kanbold had not set foot outside the mountain fastness of Tambay, deep in the heart of Slothikay, where the temple housing the great idol of Maddibimbo was located, in over three decades. But he had ridden out on this quest, to make certain that the emerald would be recovered, and to scourge the infamous villains who had tampered with it. When he left Tambay there was a wailing of women, and a clashing of many gongs. After they had departed, there was a rumbling heard in the temple, and many attributed this to the wrath of Maddibimbo.

Stampour was not aware of all this, but his highly sensitive nerves were alerting him to the fact that danger was near and was closing in. All his instincts, instincts which had been honed and sharpened during a lengthy career of thievery, were telling him to move. Yet here he sat, and here he had sat for the past two days. He sipped the wine the innkeeper brought him and looked once again at the rafters upholding the roof of the inn. And he came to a decision. He would wait no longer for the shady gentleman who had promised him such a rich price for the gem. No. He snapped his fingers. Instantly Clovis and Demetrio were at his side. "We are leaving," he said. "This is a trap." At the very moment he said the words he knew them to be true.

Clovis was up the stairs to their room. Demetrio was to the stables for their horses. Stampour approached the innkeeper for a reckoning and after a final tally went out front to meet the other two.

Clovis, however, was being detained by the serving wench Portia. As he attempted to leave his room, bearing the possessions of the three thieves and carrying the emerald eye of Maddibimbo in a leather satchel hanging from his waist, Portia had her arms around him and was imploring him to stay. He told her he would stay later, but at this moment he must leave. Demetrio was just leading the three horses up to the front of the inn when one of the watchers on the roof, under the mistaken impression that the gem was changing hands, leapt onto his back, his priestly robes flapping furiously as he descended. Demetrio fell to the ground with a cry, and Stampour rushed to his aid only to find that the watcher at the front of the inn had him by the throat. Clovis, having escaped from Portia, neared the front door just in time to see both his companions being wrestled to the ground. Not knowing how many attackers were involved, he immediately turned about, rushing into Portia's waiting arms, and then ensconced himself with her inside their room on the third floor.

While this was taking place, the third watcher descended from the roof and assisted his colleagues in binding and gagging Stampour and Demetrio. Once they had been thoroughly trussed, the lead priest undertook a thorough search of their belongings but was unable to find the gem he sought. He removed their gags.

"Where is the eye of Maddibimbo?" he asked of Demetrio.

Demetrio merely spat in disgust.

"The fabulous emerald? Where is it?" he demanded of Stampour.

"I know nothing of any emerald," said Stampour. "I am a simple camel herder. You have made a terrible mistake. Release me."

"This inn will be searched, and we will find what we seek. Once we have found it we will return and you will be killed. If you do not tell me where to find the gem, you will die slowly and in great pain. However, if you tell us where it is, I promise you a quick and a painless death."

"Your promises aren't worth the turds my camels crush beneath their hooves – aaghie!" said Stampour as his hair was wrenched viciously from behind.

"Tell me where it is, or must I roast your testicles over an open flame?"

"I piss on your open flame – aaghie!" Once again his hair was wrenched.

There was a great deal more of this, but in the end the three watchers learned nothing, so they conducted a thorough search of the inn. When they came to the room where Clovis was hidden, Portia chastely raised the sheet to hide her breasts, also concealing Clovis and the satchel containing the emerald. The searchers apologized and left.

So in the end, not having the jewel and uncertain of where it could have gotten to, they decided their best course was to await the arrival of Kanbold the Lame and his retinue, which was expected the following day.

CHAPTER TEN
TWO VAGABONDS

WHEN KATIE OPENED her eyes, the sun was already up and shining brightly into her bedroom. Her first thought was that she was late to lay out Madam Lanchester's bath and prepare her breakfast. Her second thought was that she would never be doing either of those things again. The events of last night tumbled back into her mind and she sat up, seeing the open suitcase where she'd laid it beside her bed. Then, seeing all her scattered belongings on the floor, she sat for one long moment, hoping to summon the strength she needed. She felt as if these jumbled clothes were the memories of her life, now discharged, dispersed and atomized. How would she ever put them where they belonged, and put herself back together again? It was a dangerous step she was taking but a deliberate one. She knew that, and she wasn't lacking in courage. She looked out her window at the interior garden, and at the rest of the mansion, thinking this was the last time she'd have this view. It had become familiar, so familiar she hadn't seen it really in years. The garden was just starting to come into bloom this summer. Well, she'd not see it at its peak. And gardens, what was it Father Clumphy had said about gardens? There was something there. Well, it wasn't coming to her just now.

She went through her chest of drawers, deciding what to keep, what to give away. The things she was keeping she put in her case. All the rest she divided into three piles. After she was done she took a piece of paper ripped in three parts, put one on each pile. Agnes, Fancy, Maria. Something for Tavish? No, nothing for him. She smiled at that.

The picture on the wall, that time she'd tried watercolors, would anyone want it? What Fancy said, "What is it, a fish?" "No, a woman." Well, she'd leave it hanging there, a little bit of herself for someone else to take down. The wall itself she'd stared at so long till it had become a part of her. The stains and the cracks she made out to be a face. What did the man in the wall think of this journey she was starting on? Couldn't quite make out the face this morning, something with the light, she just wasn't seeing it. The face was clearer when the light was dim, candle light was best. Goodbye to him. She opened the door and walked out, and Tommy Dog beside her.

Tavish was at the foot of the stairs. "You don't have to go, you know. She's over it by now. Best thing would be just to go on like nothing happened. Run her bath. Poach her egg."

"Goodbye, Tavish. I've a feeling I really have more words to say to you than that, but those'll do."

"Why . . .? Why are you leaving . . .? Why now . . .?"

"I don't owe you why, but I'll tell you anyway. I can't stay here. I can't stay in this place. I can't take what it's doing to me. I tried to kill my baby. My very own baby, who'll be my flesh and blood after I'm gone, and that's whom I tried to kill. You see what a wicked woman this place is making me? I wanted to kill my baby so I could stay here. Oh, I know she would come around. Of course she would. Coming around is what she does best. She'd let me have the baby here, but it'd be on her terms, and I don't rightly know what those terms would be, but I do rightly know that I wouldn't like them. No, there's nothing for me here. If I stay here I'm the shamed woman, the ghost of someone who was once a person. I'd be safer here, I know that. But safety isn't always the best thing. So I'm leaving. I've thought it up and down and there's no mistaking the path I have to take."

"But where are you going?"

"I'm going to find Tom."

"Are you right in the head? He's off on a sailing voyage. Two long years he'll be gone. Where are you going to be finding him?"

"I'm going to look in Kashahar. That was the first port they were bound to make. Mayhap there'll be some word of him there."

"Katie, you're a mad woman. There's no way you'll get to Kashahar on your own. Stay here in Port Jay. That's the only thing makes any sense."

"No."

"Yes, I'll find you a place where you can stay. I'll help you."

"I don't need your help. If I'm –"

"I will. I can be a help to you. You've friends here in the mansion, you know that. To go to Kashahar, that's – no. You're staying here. And you'll need help when it comes time to have your baby. Don't you see it now?"

"I can only tell you what I must, that I've thought of all these things, and I'm going to Kashahar." Tavish was silent, so she went on. "If I was to stay here I'd be less than. Less than you, less than the rest of them, needing charity. There's boys in town that'd beat me blue if they could, and they'll find a time when they can do it too. I'm no safer here than on the road . . . I'll take the Coast road to Kashahar, it's the shortest. I've seen maps."

"What are you going to live on? Moonberries? Will you join the gypsies? A woman on that road alone is just the victim of every thieving villain and cutthroat and Indian from here to Slothikay. You cannot travel alone."

"I can and I will. I think you've no idea of the strength of me. And I've the strangest feeling this morning that I'm being called to do this. If I don't leave now something – I cannot say what it is – something that I trust and cherish will be torn away from me. I've a feeling a power that's greater than myself is watching over me and that my steps are guided, and my travel assured of success. It's not just my longing that's speaking; it's something more. I know it. So farewell, Tavish, to you and your good sense both. I'll have none of either."

She took one last look around. Oh yes, the first thing God did, he planted a garden. Now it came to her. There will always be a garden. Then out the gate and down the road. She had her stick in one hand, and the case in the other. Tommy Dog was at her feet, his tongue hanging out, running off to sniff the juniper bushes, then back to trip her up again. No, it wasn't the bushes he'd sniffed. It was the spot she'd seen the young man. Had she really seen him? Was that really just last night? He wasn't there now. Someone must have carried the poor lad away.

The morning was a warm one, and the flies were out. And if that wasn't enough to be bothered with, it wasn't long before she knew she was being followed. She'd come to the outskirts of the city, where the houses weren't all close together, but had patches of green between them, and the roads were dirt, and nothing cobbled. Although the day was coming on warm, the sun wasn't yet high and there were shadows. When she looked to her side she saw her shadow, and then also she saw the shadows that were trailing behind. They were exactly keeping stride, so she knew it wasn't just by chance. She didn't look back; didn't want them to see her scared. She wondered how many they were, and how big. She wanted to take a quick peek. No. She would just keep her way. Maybe they would turn back. They were cowards. She knew them to be so.

"Excuse me, miss, can I ask a question?"

She halted and turned. It was a boy, couldn't have been more than twelve, dressed in black. Behind him six others. So, seven in all. And one just a girl. Another, she saw the one with the black mop of hair, had a big dog. *Oh no.*

"So what's your question?"

"Where are you going?"

"And why is that the least business or interest of yours?" She turned again and started walking more quickly. Her case was feeling very heavy, but she held herself straight.

"I thought you might like some help. I could give you some help. You know, some assistance to get there."

"To get where?"

"To where you're going."

"And where would that be?"

"I don't know. You wouldn't say. But wherever it is, I might take you part of the way."

"In what?" she asked. "Have you a cart?"

"I've a wagon. Shall I get it?"

She stopped to look at him. What was he playing at?

"Wait here, while I get it." He ran off between two houses at the side of the road. She looked at the others.

"You I've seen before," she said to the black mop with buckles on his shoes.

121

"Yes, darling, I've come to show you my dog." And the big hound he held barked and strained against its leash. Tommy growled.

Then the boy who'd spoken to her before came onto the road ahead of her, hauling a big wagon. He dragged it over the berm and placed it squarely in the roadbed, blocking her way. She saw now she'd been tricked so they could surround her. "Do you want to get in?" the boy shouted. And then they jumped her.

"You should be ashamed." Katie shouted at the girl, "helping them." She swung her stick at the dog and tried to back away towards the wagon, but the other boy was waiting for her there. He grabbed her from behind but let go when Tommy bit his leg. She managed to get herself underneath the wagon where she could poke at them with her stick, but she was quickly surrounded under there and found herself having to look out all ways and jab at whoever tried to get close.

Black Mop was enjoying himself. They were going to kill the dog and go through her things, see if there was anything they could use, then take her down by the River to a spot they knew and strip her and have their way. Oh yes, there would be payback for the heads she'd knocked. But he wanted to take his time. He had the urge to gloat.

"So, darling, are you scared now?" He let his slavering dog charge at her, then pulled back on its leash.

"What is it you're wanting from me?"

"I want you to tell me you're scared."

"You're a sick excuse for a human being if that's something you're wanting. Does your mother know how you're spending your time?"

"My mother? Is it my mother you're asking about?"

"Or who is it that washes your clothes and kisses you on the nose?"

Black mop laughed. "You think I've a mother, who tucks me in at night?"

"No, no, I think you've a mother who gives you a spanking and sends you to bed."

He laughed again, but the lad next to him said, "Hey, Jock, what's with the talk? Can we not get her?"

"I was just having some fun. Course you can. Go and get her," and he took his dog off the leash. At the same time one of the boys came around behind her and when she turned to hit him with her stick, another boy grabbed her leg from in front. Once he had her leg he pulled her out, like an eater getting the best part of the lobster. She was exposed now. She tightened all her muscles, expecting to get hit. And for a second she knew she was going to die. But the thought didn't fill her with horror or a lot of sadness; truth is, she just hoped she wouldn't suffer. Then she thought, *Oh, what a shame about the baby. Though I'm sure I would've made a rotten mother.*

Just then there was a musket shot and the lad who was pulling her fell. Tavish was standing on a small hill to one side of the road. He was busy pouring some more powder into his musket and he shouted, "Get off and away, you scum, before I shoot the lot of you!"

"You shot Pongo!" said one of the boys. "He's bleeding!"

"I'll shoot you next. Would you like that? I'm just the man to do it. You may think you're tough, but I've got a gun." And he raised and aimed his musket. "I'll shoot any one of you who lays a finger on her. I mean it . . . Come on, Katie, come over here."

Katie walked to the base of the hill where Tavish stood. Her knees and her calves were skinned from the roughness of the road, and she was still wary of the hound, but the boys were standing back, measuring Tavish's intentions.

"You can't shoot people in the street," said Jock, the one with the black mop. "We were just playing a game."

"Then find a constable and tell him to put me behind bars. There's no law in this town anymore."

"Pongo, he's dead," said one of the boys. Then he looked at Tavish. "You killed him."

Tavish pointed his musket at this new interruption. "I told you to get out. I'll shoot the rest of you if I have to. Now get!"

They scattered like chaff in a strong wind.

Tavish walked down the hill and took Katie's trembling hand. "There's a power greater than yourself that's watching over you, lass, you said it yourself, and its name is Tavish. If I wasn't here you'd never have gotten out of the city. Don't say thank you, I'm sure the words would dirty your mouth." She could only stare at him. "That's Neddy," he said, pointing to a pony he'd brought with him. "His saddlebags are full. There's food and supplies."

"Where did you get them?"

"I robbed Madam Lanchester. It was the quickest way. You gave me no time to do anything else, you were in such a hurry to get out and get killed. I had to rob the woman I worked for. Her diamonds were of the finest water, her spoons solid silver and everything was hallmarked. There was remarkable little fuss turning it into cash."

"But what will you tell her?"

"I've naught to tell. I'm not going back. My bridges are burned far more fully than yours. You could return, you know, she'd take you in, even now, but not me. Now where are you headed?"

Katie stood, amazed. "What are you doing?" she asked.

"I'm coming with you. What does it look like I'm doing? Now I ask you again, where are you headed?"

"To Kashahar. By the Coast road. I told you . . . You've no right to do this for me. I never asked you. I never wanted you."

"That's a stupid thing you're saying. I'll forget it. Now mount your pony. You can't walk to Kashahar, miss I've seen the maps. The world is a sight bigger than you think."

"I'm never taking you with me."

"Then where am I to go? Where on the face of this blasted earth am I to go?! I've no job anymore; I'm a thief and a murderer all to look after you. You see what I've done? This day I've stolen from the woman I worked for my entire life. I've killed a boy I don't even know who wasn't doing me harm. I'm out of my mind, I am. I'm cursing myself for a crazy man, it's what I've become. And why? Because there's a lass I can't stop thinking of who has no idea how to take care of herself and who has as much regard for me as for an old boot. But crazy as I am, I still brought a musket that she'll need if she's to stay alive, and I still brought her food, which I'm sure she never thought of, and other gear, and I even thought well she'll need an umbrella for when it rains and I stopped on my way to get her one," he showed her the umbrella, "and still was in time to save her from them that would murder her. So tell me, if I don't go with you, where am I to go?" And he was cursing her but he was crying at the same time.

And she cried too. "I'm sorry, Tavish. I'm so sorry. I was doing just for myself, but you've insisted on mixing with me and I've a feeling – no, I'm knowing for sure – you're a stupid man for doing it."

"There's no question I'm a stupid man," he said. "I expect I'm the stupidest man ever walked the face of the earth, giving up a post where I was set and comfortable, to become a thief and a murderer living on the road all for a brainless woman who doesn't have a kind word for me. Yes, I'm a stupid man. I've no argument with that at all." As he spoke, with his knife he'd dug his ball out of Pongo's back. It had gone between the ribs, into his lungs and his heart, and it was a struggle to get out. Lots of blood came with it. "We must preserve our ammunition. I don't know where we'll find more of these," meaning the lump of gory lead he was holding.

They rolled Pongo over onto his back so they could look at him. He couldn't have been more than fifteen. He had blue eyes and black hair. In a pocket over his heart was a little blue flower from someone who'd had a friendly thought for him. *This is the second dead lad in as many days*, thought Katie. *Looks to be a trail I'm leaving.* "What shall we do with him?" she asked.

"There's naught we can do. We'll leave him for his friends." They straightened him out and laid him with his arms at his sides. Katie wrote 'Pongo' on a piece of paper and laid it under his hand. *That'll do for a headstone.* A breeze blew the scrap away.

The two of them looked at each other; glum and angry they were. Then they laughed, what else could they do? There was no mistaking the joke, and the joke was on them, and they knew it.

"Last night I was a high flown lady with diamonds at my ears and you were the man of the house. Today we're a couple of tramps. Can't wait to see what tomorrow'll bring." She put her foot into the stirrup and mounted the pony. They made an odd pair, she mounted on the stolid gray pony, with the musket and umbrella hooked onto the saddle, and the saddlebags full, he standing beside, wearing a hat to keep the sun off and carrying her case, with Tommy trotting along sniffing the puddles and chasing after birds. With not a glance backwards, they headed down the road towards Kashahar.

It would be nice to say that Katie had a song in her heart, but it would not be true. She was filled with a fear and an alarm and a dread of what awaited her. Looking ahead she saw naught but peril and consequences that were not to be considered. Yet she had hope. For all stories are bound to end with happiness; it's all we can conceive. As to Tavish, who knows what was in his mind? He was a dark and a hidden man, and he held himself close, and his own thoughts shivered with the loneliness the wind brought in every time the door was opened. Tommy could smell his mistress's fear, but he smelled something else as well, and if he'd been able he'd have told her that the worst was well behind so long as he was there. And Neddy? He was the newest to this gang, just getting acquainted as it were. At this time his deepest ruminant meditation was on the subject of carrots, and it was a symphony of satisfaction in itself, and he was content to let the world take its course so long as he was left in the blissful peace of purest contemplation.

PART TWO

MIDDLE GAME

CHAPTER ELEVEN
THE EYE OF MADDIBIMBO

FERGUS WAS SINGING a song, and the words he sang were these:

Who do I see through the long grass going
 A short shift wearing and locks blowing free
As the last wind ere moonrise now sets about blowing,
 Is it the one that looketh for me?
  With a hey and a ho, and a nonny nonny no,
  The rain doth rain and the wind doth blow.

Bright shines the moon, I see her more clear
 She's come to the hazels to meet one she knows,
Full shapely her feet as she treads the ground near
 And oh, as she comes, the more my love grows.
  With a hey and a ho . . .

We lie 'neath the lindens, o'erloathe to awake
 Resting at noon-tide till roused from our sleep
I gaze unmoving, held for love's sake,
 Whilst wand'ring the fowls and restless the sheep.
  With a hey and a ho . . .

O friend of my soul than which none can come nigher
 Thou art the sun's kiss and the sweetness of May,
I'll follow thee o'er all the rocks and the fire
 For thou art my love till Earth waneth away.
  With a hey and a ho, and a nonny nonny no,
  My song is done, now must I go.

He stopped singing and put his banjo down at the base of the masonry wall he was seated on. For a brief spell he contemplated the tumbling waves of Lost Bastard Sound. The strangely curious traveling man he associated with had deposited him here in the morning with instructions to await his return and had then mounted his pale horse and ridden into Kashahar. Fergus wondered, as he often had in the past, what that man's name was. Names didn't seem to stick to him. Fergus just called him Stranger, but there was still a problem.

As they'd ridden the road to Kashahar the traffic had been very sparse, and it was like that again today, even this close to the city. There were tinkers and some small merchants on their ponies, or with donkeys pulling carts. Out on the Sound a few fishing boats were straining in the stiff breeze, and in the distance he saw gulls circling over Lost Bastard Island. He didn't know what business had brought the traveling man here, or why he'd been dragged along. He'd been thinking of stealing off, heading back to Port Jay, but he had a funny feeling the black stallion he'd been riding was keeping an eye on him. So he sat there turning things over in his mind.

He figured if the stranger had had a Ma and a Pa, then he'd have had a name; they'd have called him something. But maybe he'd never had a Ma and a Pa. For sure there was something strange about him, why he was called Stranger. But what other method was there of coming into the world, other than being born? That seemed to raise a number of difficulties. Maybe he should try to sneak up on him some night, see if he has a belly button . . .

As he was thinking this a singular feeling came over him, like a shiver of ice dropping in the middle of the warm summer day. All at once he knew someone else was with him, just behind maybe, or maybe over there, but there was someone watching him, and from somewhere nearby.

"Stranger?" he called. "You there?"

It felt like the silence was angry he'd spoken, but no answer came back. Some of the shadows the trees were casting didn't look quite right. Something rustled in the brush.

"What are you doing here?" The stranger stood beside him.

"You told me to wait."

"You do what I say?"

"I guess."

"You're stupid, Fergus, you know that?"

"That's what you keep telling me."

"Anybody with any brains would've run off. I have to work with fools because they're the only ones aren't smart enough to keep away from me."

"I knew I was right for this job."

"We may be in for some dangerous work today. I'm warning you ahead of time. There's some desperate customers in town and they've got a jewel of great price. I had Crazy Dog's pirates set to snatch it but he hasn't shown. So maybe it'll be up to us to stick our fingers in the hornet's nest. All I know is, we wait much longer and the priests'll show up and take it back. Where's the fun in that?" He inhaled a good pinch of snuff and looked at Fergus. "Any questions?"

"You bet."

"What's your question?"

"Have you got a belly button?"

The stranger had to think about that one, it wasn't an inquiry he'd been expecting. At length he said, "Depends on the day of the week." He spat. "Now get on your horse, and let's get into town."

At that same moment Barnacle Jack was concluding the sale of the Queen of Bel Harbor. Things had gone better than expected. He'd found merchants with ready cash who were willing to make a deal and who didn't ask too many questions as to the ship's provenance. The transaction was to his liking, selling her in such short order for more than half what she was worth, and he was counting the silver and gold and tying up the money bags he and Ramsey would be bringing back to Crazy Dog. To his mind, the only fly in this otherwise gratifying ointment was Ramsey himself. Barnacle Jack had taken a dislike to him the first instant he'd looked on him, and being unable to form a conception of an unreciprocated distaste, he assumed Ramsey held him in the like disfavor. So at this point, being in the mood for a bit of a frolic, and thinking he ought to test the man's mettle, he took Ramsey to one side, and giving him a real hard stare, said, "There's a deal here over what Crazy Dog expects."

130

"Well then, he'll be jolly glad to get it," said Ramsey.

"That he will," said Barnacle Jack and stared him down again. Then he said, "Perhaps you weren't fully understanding me. I was thinking if he didn't get all of it, why, how would he know? So long as what he did get was what he'd thought might come his way."

"But he's going to get all of it . . . I'm new to this pirate business, but the merchants I worked for were men of their word. And so was I."

"I see."

"I've always found it's best to be honest. Especially with people I don't trust."

"You don't trust me?"

"I trust you well enough."

"Then you'd not be honest with me, is that what you're saying?"

"You've a way of twisting a man's words. I never said I'd not be honest. Not with you, or not with any."

"You'll not be honest."

"I will be honest!"

"Well it took you long enough to say it."

"It's taken you long enough to understand it."

"Maybe you'll make a pirate yet." He laughed. "I was only joking with you."

"Yes, I thought that."

They returned to the others and the bags of money. There were seven bags, so they distributed them among the men, each taking one except Mr. Chips, whose arm was broke, and Barnacle Jack, because he was in charge. Then they trudged off to make their rendezvous with Crazy Dog.

It ought to have been a simple task to get there, but walking down the next hill one of the seamen saw Vincenzo wasn't carrying a bag, and he stopped him and asked where his bag was, and after some discussion and dispute the bags were counted and it was found there were only six. Barnacle Jack said this was a queer thing, and how could one of the bags have disappeared just as they'd turned a corner and walked down a hill? Vincenzo said no one ever gave him a bag. There must have been six to start with, or who was doing the counting? "Well I know for certain a bag of money could not vanish into the air between here and where we started," says Ramsey with a tremble and a quiver. "So let's retrace our steps and I'm as certain as can be we will find it." So they went back the way they'd come and were careful to look at every paving stone and every plot of grass along the way, but there was nothing for it. The missing bag was not to be found.

So Barnacle Jack said, "Alright, maybe one of us thinks to play a joke. But I know of a joke or two myself. Now here's what we'll do. We'll put all the bags again together like they were, and distribute them as we did before, and maybe the joker that's joking with us will have thought better of his joke and there will be seven bags again." So every man put his bag in and they counted them, and there were five. Well Barnacle Jack's face got as black as could be and he looked at all the men and he said, "Alright. Who's the whoreson clown not putting his bag in with the rest?" He searched them all, Vincenzo, Mr. Chips with his sling — and his sling also was inspected — Diego, the four other seamen, Ramsey, all were searched, but nowhere could the missing bags be found.

So at this Barnacle Jack takes Ramsey aside once again, and he says, "Alright, you're having it out of me, are you? About being an honest man?"

And Ramsey says, "No I'm not. I thought you might have a joke with me, but never would I joke with you."

"Then where are the two other bags of money?"

"I cannot tell you."

And here Barnacle Jack gave him his grimmest look, because he was certain now Ramsey had a trick and was trying to steal from him, and he said, "I promise you, you will hang from the yardarm if you are stealing from me and Crazy Dog. We are not the men who will forgive you."

And here the tears ran from Ramsey's eyes and he could not endure any more. He said, "I've done everything you told me. I navigated the ship into the harbor. I unloaded the goods. I helped you sell her. I added many lies to make her worth more than she was. I counted the money. I hid nothing. I have been honest. I don't know who's taking the money." And he broke down and fell to the ground. "It's the ghost of Brutus. It's him that's haunting me. His spirit walks beside me and tortures me still."

"Oh, what are you going on about? Just give me the money!" yelled Barnacle Jack, punching and kicking him into the ground. Ramsey kept saying, "I didn't take it," while Barnacle Jack kept insisting, "Yes you did. I know you did." After Ramsey had been reduced to a whimpering, puking ruin, Barnacle Jack returned to where he'd left the men, only to find the four seamen from the Seahawk sitting with knives in their backs, and Vincenzo, Mr. Chips and Diego gone, and the bags of money with them. He let out a roar and set off in pursuit, leaving Ramsey moaning over his broken ribs.

Not far away Crazy Dog was trying to remember how the light had fallen on his mother's face the last time he'd seen her. Although a psychotic cutthroat, he was yet a man of great sentiment and he treasured the memories of his youth in the old country. He would cheerfully castrate a man while looking him straight in the eye, yet he harbored a soft spot for orphans and other unfortunates. This unevenness in his temper had frequently led others to misread his intentions in ways that had resulted in regrettable outcomes. The memory he was treasuring at this moment was that of his mother's last words to him before he departed on the road to his fortune, the very road that had eventually led him to where he sat now. Her words were, "My son, if there is one lesson I would instill in you, it is this. It's a lesson your unfortunate father never learned. Many philosophers tell us the ultimate force that governs the world, that sets the stars in motion and drives the hearts of men, is love. They are mistaken. The ultimate force is fear. Fear will overcome love every time. A man loves at his own discretion, but fears at yours. So as you go forth, remember this: put no faith in the power of love, it is weak and fickle. Put some faith, but just a little, in things that are more lasting, such as wealth and power. However, if you place all your faith in the generation and the constant maintenance of fear, you will never lack for success. You will find that those who fear you will place their wealth and their power at your disposal, something those who love you will never do. Those who fear you will perform the most dreadful and the most humiliating acts, acts which those who love you would never dare contemplate. I am proud to say I have lived my entire life without ever having been loved by any, except, perhaps, for a little, by you, and you hardly count. I have watched those women who sought to be loved. I have seen what becomes of them and I rejoice that I have never shared in their delusion. So go forth and take my words to heart." When she had concluded her remarks Crazy Dog strangled her and made off with the silver she'd kept in a box under the floor of her kitchen. Never looking back he'd found employment as a cabin boy and gone to sea. Now he was awaiting the return of Barnacle Jack with the proceeds of the sale of the Queen of Bel Harbor before proceeding to the brothel where he expected to consummate the seizure of the eye of Maddibimbo. Returning his thoughts to the present moment, he looked at his second mate Ruby, who was seated at his side. Now it was not a common thing for a woman to be a second mate aboard a pirate vessel. There have been more than a few, but practically all have gone under disguise as men. Ruby, however, was openly female, in fact she flaunted it. Crazy Dog himself had lain beside her, though he had not allowed others the privilege. But now he asked her would she await the arrival of Barnacle Jack while he went to gather the holy gem of Slothikay?

"I will await you here," she said. "But be not too long. The tide is like to turn."

So Crazy Dog picked six of his best to go with him and went down to the inn where he'd been told Stampour was waiting with the gem.

At that same moment Kanbold the Lame, mounted on his powerful steed Tessephon, was drawing near to Kashahar. As he jogged along in the pleasant summer sunlight, he was preoccupied with his inner contemplations. His religion taught that the greatest moments, those that composed the very summit of existence, were those moments completely devoid of thought, when the soul was totally vacant, empty of all desires, and that the only goal of meditation was to bring the soul closer to those moments. And as he thought this, he reflected that he must have experienced many such moments, although since these moments were altogether void of any mental content, they could not be remembered. They were the moments that did not exist; that never existed. So long as one could still say be here now, one was not there yet. And he rejoiced in this understanding since it expressed so perfectly the nature of happiness and the constant striving to achieve it, that the struggle was a constant one because when one reached the goal one would be unaware of having reached it, since the goal was a state of unawareness. He considered the many parables and conundrums he'd employed in his attempts to impart this wisdom to his devotees, and how all of them seemed to fall short, and how his disciples constantly appeared to learn something else, something just a little different from that which he taught. They said such things as, the goal is the voyage not the arrival, not realizing that it is precisely the voyage that is not the goal, and will never be the goal, and that at every single moment of the voyage the goal had been reached already, but that it was impossible to state this fact because, by its very nature, it was not a fact, it was only something that could be known. He was interrupted in the midst of these contemplations by an acolyte who tapped him on the leg and said, "We have arrived."

Dismounting he found that the inn was a hive of bustling activity. There were several groups of gentlemen amusing themselves with watching a harem of young harlots, many dressed in velvet and wearing masks, who danced with lascivious abandon atop the cluttered tables. Another gaggle of buccaneers was busy knocking on doors and breaking into rooms. These were Crazy Dog and his men, who'd arrived shortly before the priests and were now searching for the thieves who held the jewel. One of the gentlemen in a room on the ground floor had taken objection to being disturbed and was engaged in swordplay with the pirate who had interrupted him. Meanwhile on the second floor a scuffle had broken out in one of the rooms the pirates had barged into and Kanbold's attention was drawn to this affray when one of the fighters, garbed in priestly robes, leaned over the railing and shouted to him the sacred words "Oloye! Ufthay!"

Not tarrying to await the arrival of the rest of his retinue, Kanbold immediately hustled his acolytes up the stairs to the rescue of this priest, whom he recognized as one of those that had been sent ahead to retrieve the gem. Limping, he followed his men and watched as they attacked Crazy Dog and his pirates who, having disposed of the two other priests in the room, now turned to meet these new assailants.

"Halt!" shouted Kanbold. His acolytes paused, swords in mid-air. Crazy Dog's men froze with their sabers held in attitudes portending menace. Stampour, still bound to his chair, looked cannily about. Demetrio, unfortunately, looked nowhere, having succumbed during the priests' intense interrogation.

"Who are you?" asked Kanbold.

"I might ask the same of you," said Crazy Dog.

"I am Kanbold the Lame, high priest of Maddibimbo, come to reclaim a sacred and a holy gem which was stolen from our temple by this verminous dog." Here he indicated Stampour. "The gem is mine by right. It is sacred to the worship of the great monkey god Maddibimbo. And now I will repeat my question, who are you?"

"I am Crazy Dog Talbot, leader of the Free Brethren of the Coast. I am here to take possession of that gem of which you speak in the name of the King. It is my duty as a loyal subject of that –"

"You are a thief! Just like him," indicating Stampour. "The gem is the eye of Maddibimbo. However, I will show mercy, and I will allow you to depart. I will not even ask for the recompense to which I am entitled for the lives of these my two brethren whom you have slain," indicating the bodies of the two dead priests. "But go now and leave me this one," here he pointed to Stampour.

"I'm afraid I can't do that. I'd advise you to return to wherever it is you came from. All the riches of this land belong to the King and I have with me five strong men who will enforce the King's will. Don't trifle with me. I'm a dangerous man."

"I also have five strong men," said Kanbold, indicating his four acolytes and the surviving priest. "Also, I have my entire retinue who have traveled here with me and who are now entering this inn. So in a matter of minutes you will be outnumbered. You have dallied too long in converse with me and if you do not immediately yield you will be crushed. I said I would show mercy, but the time of my mercilessness will be soon."

Crazy Dog had noticed that the one seaman that had been left behind on the ground floor fighting a duel had escaped out the front door of the inn during this conversation, so he hoped to stretch their talk a little longer yet, to allow time for that one to get to Ruby and the rest of his men. "You don't scare me," he said to Kanbold.

"Then you are a fool. Kill them!" he ordered his acolytes. At once the blades, which had been still, flashed back into action and the fight was renewed, Crazy Dog's pirates against the priests of Slothikay. Kanbold and Crazy Dog engaged each other, their swords almost flickering with the speed of their cutting and thrusting blows.

"Is the gem in this room?" asked Kanbold.

"Would I tell you if it were?" replied Crazy Dog.

"It is not here," said Stampour, who had been ungagged.

"Where is it?" demanded Kanbold.

"I do not know," said Stampour.

"Keep silent!" said Crazy Dog.

"You could not have lost it," said Kanbold.

"I could," said Stampour.

"You insect! You stupid insect! Aaaiee!" said Kanbold, who had allowed the attention he was paying to Crazy Dog's thrusts to waver.

At this point a new host of priests surged into the room, and Crazy Dog's pirates were getting the worst of it. Crazy Dog himself was being pressed against the wall by Kanbold when he saw an open window and leapt for it. Just as his feet hit the sill, he saw Ruby in the street below leading a charge by the rest of his pirates.

"Halt!" he shouted. His shout was not so effective as Kanbold's had been earlier, but it did cause Kanbold to pause and look up at him perched in the window. "You are surrounded. If you look down you will see that your retinue of priests is being savagely attacked from the rear. I must ask you to surrender the gem to me."

"I do not have the gem!" cried Kanbold in mounting frustration. "Stampour stole it from me and now he declares he has lost it!"

"So who has it?"

"I do not know."

"Then why are we killing one another?"

"This also I do not know."

"Neither do I. However, since you are now outnumbered, you are the ones who will die!" He waved to Ruby below, and she waved back. "For the Free Brethren!" he shouted and the massacre resumed. The gallants who had come for an afternoon of pleasure were fighting the pirates who had interrupted their assignations. The pirates with Crazy Dog were fighting the priests, and the priests were fighting them, as well as the new pirates from the Seahawk who, tide be damned, had just arrived to rescue Crazy Dog.

It was then, as the fighting reached a crescendo of savagery, that a sound like thunder was heard, a series of deafening rumbling thumps coming from the hills in the direction of Slothikay. The traveling man, who had just arrived and was seated across the street from the inn, looked up in that direction and saw appearing over the city's rooftops a dark and hairy face. It was the face of Maddibimbo himself, come to recover his eye. He stood, towering over the town, a huge, hideous and hirsute figure, his face grimacing in rage, his mouth wide, with teeth like boulders, his nostrils distended, and above his nose, where his one monstrous eye should have been, a gaping hole. He turned his head about, as though trying to see, his chin tilted towards the sky. Then, turning down, he seemed to become cognizant of the inn, and recognized it as the destination he sought. He leaned down and grasped the roof in his mighty hands. Contorting his face with the effort, he lifted the roof off the top of the building, held it in his hands for a moment as though in wonderment at what he had found, and then tossed it to the ground, where it crushed several carts and a few unlucky bystanders.

The embattled denizens of the courtyard broke off their fighting and looked up in amazement at the enraged, blinded face of the huge monkey god that seemed as if regarding them from above. Maddibimbo turned his face about, one way and then another, almost as though he could see. He reached down with his hands and felt about in the courtyard, his great fingers knocking the chairs and tables around, as people scattered out of the way. His hands found the walls and then gradually walked up them on their fingertips, until he'd found the third floor. Feeling the doors, as if counting them, he found the door he sought and pushed it open. Inside, Clovis and

Portia cowered on a bed, the bedclothes strewn across the floor. It was evident that while the rest of the inn had been the scene of desperate searches and the clash of arms, these two had been entirely consumed with one another. Their idyll was now brought to an end as the left hand of Maddibimbo violently pushed aside first Clovis and then Portia, and finally overturned their bed to reveal a leather satchel. The left hand was then joined by the right and the two hands together opened the satchel, divulging the enormous emerald it had contained. The fighting, meanwhile, had come to a halt as the combatants watched the monkey god lift the emerald and place it in the gaping hole in his forehead. Having done so, he looked about and located Stampour, still tied to his chair. He picked up the chair and placed it in the courtyard. Then, with a sound like mountains falling in, he put his foot on poor Stampour and ground him into the earth. Bellowing defiantly the holy words, "Oloye! Ufthay! Ufthay! Olo-o-oye!" he withdrew his foot and then turned back to the hills, his stamping feet making thunderous rumbling thumps, as he receded into the distance.

Crazy Dog and Kanbold regarded the carnage around them, looking at the many bodies of priests cut down in their robes, pirates disemboweled by the sacred blades, and others, gallants and whores, lying where they were slain. There were moans coming from the wounded and the dying. Kanbold went limping among the remaining priests, helping those that were hurt, and saying prayers over those past hurting. Crazy Dog tried to gather his pirates together. Ruby's right arm had been almost severed, but fortunately the ship's surgeon was there and he managed to save it, though it was almost useless to her after that night. She could barely move the muscles and there was little feeling along most of its length. Crazy Dog told his men to gather their dead, they would take them to the Seahawk and give them burial at sea. It had been a bitter and a sorrowful exploit altogether, many good men killed, and no gem to show for it. At least he'd taken the Queen of Bel Harbor, that was pure profit, but it would be awhile before the Free Brethren would recover from this dismal episode.

It was now late in the day. It had been a hot one, and the shadows were lengthening as Crazy Dog and his pirates in a sullen mood went walking away from the inn to meet Barnacle Jack. Crazy Dog thought he saw a figure he recognized, a short man with a broad-brimmed hat, rambling along on the other side of the street. He approached him, but as he did so he felt a crackling under his feet and smelled something burning in the air. It startled him so much he looked about and when he looked up again he'd lost sight of the man.

"You came three days late and you're a sorry fool." It was the stranger now who had him by the shoulder. "What did you expect?"

"I expected I'd pull a great success out of a murky mess, the way I always do. And how did you sneak up on me?"

"Had you come when I told you you'd have found just three thieves and a priceless jewel, but you chose to wait till the priests walked in. Well, you'll not be laying the blame for that at my door."

Crazy Dog, however, was not resigned to being found in the wrong. He told the stranger just what he thought of all his crafty schemes, and added that an honest pirate like himself would not be listening to the likes of him again.

"Now if you want to make up for your losses," the traveling man went on as though Crazy Dog hadn't spoken, "perhaps there are some escaped slaves you could round up."

"No, no, I'll none of that business, thank you. I will happily embrace robbery, kidnapping, murder and the blackest blasted treachery and I'll do it in the name of the King, but I'll not stoop to being a slave master. I'm the leader of the Free Brethren, and it's freedom I embrace in all its forms and always have." Ruby leaned on him just then, she was having trouble walking and the pain in her arm was something fierce. "Ruby, my love, what have we done to you?"

"I'll not be the sweetest thing in your bed tonight. That I can promise you."

"Many's the night you've not been a sweet morsel, but you're a good woman still, for all that." And the two of them looked at each other and laughed, though when she laughed Ruby was squeezing out some tears also, it hurt that bad.

"So where's Barnacle Jack then?" asked Crazy Dog. They'd come to where they were to meet, but Jack was nowhere around.

"He's likely gone for a pint, don't you think?" said Ruby.

Crazy Dog looked about. No, he'd not gone for a pint. Jack was not the man to go for a pint when business was appointed to be done. It was a black feeling he had inside himself. "Ruby," he said, "we'll wait here a bit. But Barnacle Jack's not the man to miss an appointment, not one he swore he'd make. Not unless he'd a marlin-spike up his nostril that killed him dead . . . Now I've said it I hope I've not made it true."

Crazy Dog wiped his brow and looked about himself. The day was turning far worse than he could have imagined. He could almost hear the good fortune he'd always kept in his back pocket skittering away down the Coast. He needed to hurt somebody. Pointing to the man standing next to him he snarled angrily, "You! What good's your God damn ear?!" Grabbing him Crazy Dog wrestled him down, took out his knife and cut off his ear. There was a howl of pain and great gouts of blood pouring on the man's face. Crazy Dog himself was covered in it.

"Ah, that makes a man feel better." His earless comrade was cursing him steadily with a rant of furious oaths. Crazy Dog put the ear between his teeth and tore it in half. Then he grinned and said, "We'd best find him. I'll kill someone if I've no profit from the Queen of Bel Harbor."

Across the street, the short man with a broad-brimmed hat watched as Crazy Dog led his loyal and very tired pirates up the road. The moon, almost full, cast them in silhouette as it rose in the east. It was a fine sight. *Almost . . . Almost . . . Almost* he howled silently. He turned to Fergus, "Let's find a place to stay the night."

"Alright. I don't think that inn's in any shape to –"

"I seem to remember I lived around here once. Turn left here . . ." and he led him away into a part of town that was just a bit shadier, a bit older it seemed than most of the rest. The street wound down to an old manse that stood alone, apart from the buildings around it. It looked like it hadn't been lived in in years. The roof was sunk in in places, and there were many shingles missing. The grounds around the house were grown out in weeds, but as they drew near a sickly yellow light came on in a crazy, cracked window high up in a turret in back. "Yes, this is the place. Just like I remember it."

But the last image of that night belongs to Kanbold, standing with his dead acolytes laid at his feet, their lifeless hands still clutching the disgraced blades. As he raised his voice in the traditional threnody for the dead there was a glitter of awe in his eye. His was the face of a man who, having endured much, has at last seen the face of his god.

Chapter Twelve
Once More under the Sun

"Have you ever noticed that the simpler something is, the more difficult it is to understand?"

"Under no circumstances can that be true," answered Tom. He sat holding a portion of Colophus' memoirs. "Unless you'd be playing games with the meanings of your words, because the word simple has no other meaning than easy to understand."

"Not in my dictionary."

"You have a dictionary now?"

"I'm compiling one. A dictionary is indispensable for an author such as myself. After all, author is just short for authority. I should have done this long ago."

"You have to make sure of the meanings of your words, is that it?"

"Oh, no, couldn't care less about that. But without a dictionary how do I know if my spelling is correct?"

"It's spelling that worries you, is it? Well I'd not waste the tiniest trace of thought in that direction. There's no one ever likely to read your writing, unless it be myself, and in the matter of spelling I am generally clueless."

"I don't care about you. It's God I care about. After all, He's the one who put me here to perform this task. And He can be such a niggler. Hate to get it all done and arrive at the pearly gates and He says, 'Not so quick there. Here on page seven, don't you know how to spell onomatopoeia? Afraid it's back to Purgatory for a few eons till you get it right.'"

"You really believe God cares about your spelling? With the affairs of the entire universe to attend to, He's concerned with that?"

"I would think so. You know what it says in the gospel, 'In the beginning was the Word: And the Word was with God: And the Word was God.'"

"And what word was that?"

"Well . . . the word God I suppose."

"And you're needing a dictionary so you'll know the spelling of the word God?"

"No, of course not. I need a dictionary to know how to spell onomatopoeia. Anyway, do you want to know the definition of simple in my dictionary?"

"I'm certain I do not. Perhaps then the gospel should be saying, 'In the beginning was the Word: And the Word was with God: And the Word was onomatopoeia: And God needed a dictionary.'"

"Now you're having fun with me."

"Not at all, but it strikes me as presumptuous to assume that all words have a meaning, which is what you do when you make a dictionary."

"A word without a meaning wouldn't be a word. It would be no more than a sound."

"So every word has its meaning. Has every meaning its word?"

"It's difficult to say. If there were a meaning that didn't have a word I wouldn't be able to tell you what it was."

"So maybe there are meanings out there just waiting for their words to come into existence."

"Maybe so. Maybe my problem is that all my meanings don't have words, and the words I'm using mean something different from what I mean to say."

"In that case maybe we mean to talk about something else."

"Yes. To get back to what I was saying, it's the simplest things that are the most difficult to understand. Take stories, for instance, narratives. There are all kinds of plots, some of extreme complexity, but at their core they're all the same. There are some where a man overcomes a monster to save a woman, or overcomes some other difficulty, and once again whatever difficulty he overcomes the reward seems to be he wins a woman. Or there are stories of rags to riches, a person of humble origin rises to become someone of some esteem and once again invariably he seems to marry a princess. There are comedies in which the young lovers outsmart their curmudgeonly parents and marry at the end, and tragedies which are tragical precisely because the young lovers are thwarted and end up dead instead of in bed. These are the general sorts of stories we encounter, and perhaps you can see a pattern emerging. In some cases the plots are highly elaborate, involving letters that are lost and then found at precisely the right moment, or twins that are recognized or not recognized as the case may be, shipwrecks and so forth, all the implements in the diligent plotter's tool chest, but they only serve to disguise a basic template, the fundamental story which is constantly being re-enacted. The hero and the heroine are the archetypal stand-ins for the man and the woman who unite so that a new life can come into the world. This is really the only story we ever tell ourselves. And there, having seen through all the narrative complexities, we come to the very core of story which is shrouded in a fundamental and impenetrable mystery, and that is how do a man and a woman unite to create a new life? Do you see what I'm getting at?"

"Oh, well that's alright then. That has all been explained to me by a philosophical gentleman of Slothikay. It has something to do with active and passive blood."

"Active and passive blood?"

"Yes. And a sponge comes into it."

Colophus pondered this in silence. Then he asked, "Are you sure you got that right?"

"Oh, absolutely. I couldn't be mistaken."

Colophus reflected on this some more. Eventually he said, "Your friend must be just a staggering intellect. Absolutely among the forefront of the greatest philosophers, because I must say his explanation doesn't cast the slightest light on anything."

"I seem to have a knack for engaging in conversation with gentlemen of great philosophical acumen."

"Referring to myself do you mean? Thank you for the kind word."

"Though it's turning into a bit of a slog getting through your memoirs."

"Of course it is. I would not have it any other way. But you know I had to live through it all first. Talk about a slog. All you're doing is reading it. You have no grounds for complaint. And let me make it clear that I do not welcome criticism, nor do I take suggestions. The writing is punishment enough."

"But it just seems to be the most pointless chronicle. There are catalogs of how often you pissed, and how often you shat, and how loudly you belched and various idiotic and trivial thoughts you had. Things like cutting your toenails. You know in most memoirs that sort of thing is omitted; they aren't really the sorts of events I would expect to see recorded." Tom took a sip of the sherry, the flavor of which he had grown remarkably fond.

"But these are precisely the sorts of things that need to be recorded. Otherwise they would be forgotten. That's the whole reason writing was invented. There was a need to write down all the things that people kept forgetting, the things that weren't worth remembering. There's no point in recording memorable events. They would be remembered in any case."

"So you record the things that aren't worth remembering?"

"Precisely. Like this conversation we're having now for instance. Who would ever want to remember this later? That's why I need to write it down." Colophus looked around himself, searching through the various papers that lay scattered about. "Now where did I put my pen?"

"I'm certain I haven't any idea."

"This is why I need more pockets. You know apart from writing, pockets are probably mankind's most useful invention. In fact mankind's need for pockets predates even his need for pants, as witness the quiver, or the pouches in marsupials, such as the wallaby. Wallabies do have pouches don't they?"

"I wouldn't know, and in any case I'm disinclined to believe that wallabies are human."

"I can see you've never met my wife."

"You have a wife?"

"Yes. Although actually I suppose I don't anymore. The marriage vows state 'till death do us part,' so I would presume we're no longer married."

"Oh, right, I keep forgetting you're deceased. Still it comes as a surprise that you were ever married."

"Why is that?"

"I've been reading your memoirs, and there is no mention whatsoever of your ever having a wife. It strikes me as a surprising omission."

"In that case you will be amazed to learn that my life has been crammed full of startling and remarkable events, countless instructive occurrences, actions of the most outstanding consequence, all of which I have omitted."

"That is a novel and I would say almost an inexplicable authorial strategy."

"I have my reasons."

"And I dare say they're the very reasons you've been elaborating. Since those events are worth remembering, why would you write them down?"

"I wouldn't, of course. It would be a waste of paper."

"Although unlike the events you have recorded in your memoirs, I think your marriage to a wallaby would have made for some interesting reading."

"What are you talking about? Why would I marry a wallaby?"

"I'm certain you said your wife was a wallaby. My memory could not be that undependable. It's hardly been five minutes since you said it."

"No, I brought her up by analogy as it were. She's just reminiscent of a wallaby. If my wife was human, and there's good reason to think she was, it's possible wallabies are also. Ah, here's my pen. Now I can record all these ideas we're having that aren't worth remembering."

"I don't see the need for even having ideas that aren't worth remembering, much less recording them."

"I rarely have any other kind. My God, can you imagine if I had to remember every idea I'd ever had? There's a terrifying thought, best put that one right out of my mind."

"I see what you mean. You know, I'm starting to see the value of these sort of Socratic dialogues we have."

"Socrates. Now there was a philosopher worth emulating. He never wrote anything down. Probably saw what was coming though.

I mean my god, there was Plato staring him in the face. Probably why he drank the hemlock when he did. Said an unexamined life wasn't worth living; next thing you know he killed himself. If only all the philosophers since his time had possessed his wisdom. This whole enterprise of civilization would likely never have gotten off the ground. A couple of chaps, chaps like us, sitting around shooting the breeze one day, they start to get ideas, you know, like agriculture, geometry, domesticating animals, the square of the hypotenuse, what not, they take a pause to eat their raw buffalo, one chap says what were we talking about? No one can remember – poof – there it goes. Civilization never gets started. It was writing was at the root of it all."

"I'm beginning to be of the opinion that I have been here far too long, because the things you're saying are starting to make sense."

"You mean up until now you never thought the things I said made sense?"

"Well . . . No . . . Not really."

"That's discouraging. But now I've said a sensible thing?"

"Yes, I think you have."

"What was it?"

Tom paused to think. "I can't recall."

"Should've written it down."

"Maybe it was when you were saying you wouldn't marry a wallaby."

"Oh, that was sensible?"

"I thought so."

"Let's get it down then." Here Colophus took a fresh piece of paper and wrote. "I will not marry – how many l's in wallaby?"

"Two I think."

"I will not marry a wallaby. There. At least we've preserved that gem for posterity."

"At first I thought all the things you said were just childish mistakes, but I'm starting to believe you've actually acquired a certain amount of wisdom."

"That's the curse of being a philosopher. You read the works of the really great ones and from time to time you can't help but wonder 'My God, what was he thinking?' Take Socrates, for example, whom we were just talking about. He believed that the things of this world are not real, because they are imperfect. A strange idea when you first consider it, is it not?"

"Where are the perfect things?"

"He believed that they existed in the real world. In the real world were all the ideals of which the things in this world were but imperfect copies . . . From what we know about him I'm convinced this idea must have come to him one day when he was complaining about his marriage, and all that allegory of the cave rubbish was just something Plato dreamed up to put some meat on the philosophical bone. Which just goes to show that the path to acquiring wisdom is often one which a wise man might choose not to follow."

Tom returned to his reading. After a moment he said, "And there's another question I'm having about your memoirs. From time to time I come across all these blank pages. What's the meaning of these?"

"They're just in there by mistake. They got included when I was gathering the pages together to give you. You can ignore those."

"Actually I thought they were the best part."

"Thought they were the best part," and he laughed. "You're having me on of course. You liked the blank pages best?"

"They're certainly to be preferred over the other bits. I've come to look forward to them, these passages where nothing is written."

"The passages where nothing is written . . . Well . . . Their blank perfection makes a mockery of the drivel that's on the other pages, is that so? You'd probably like it better if the whole thing were blank."

"I can't help but think that would be an improvement."

At this Colophus was very crestfallen. He stood and walked about awhile, kicking some of the small fish heads and other debris in his way. Then he sat down again. He put his head in his hands. He said, "At a stationer's they'll sell you blank paper, so many pence for so many sheets. Of course they couldn't sell it to you if it had been written on, could they? You wouldn't want to buy that. At the end of the day, when a writer concludes his work, he discards the pages he's written that he no longer needs. He wouldn't throw away his blank paper, that would be senseless. The dust man picks up the discarded newspapers and throws them away. If he found any blank paper, he would doubtless hoard that for a future day. And you prefer the blank pages to the pages I've actually written. So what am I doing, senselessly defacing blank pieces of paper? It seems this whole literary endeavor amounts to nothing more than taking a valuable commodity like paper and turning it into worthless rubbish by writing on it."

"Don't take it so hard now."

"But of course I take it hard. This whole time I've been industriously scribbling away, and what have I accomplished? Nothing. It's been a complete waste of time. The paper would be of more value had I never written anything on it." He stood up again and knocked over the keg he'd been sitting on. "Why am I doing this? There's no reason. There's nothing I'll ever achieve." He set about bashing the various machines and cases in his way. He picked up stacks of his memoirs and was tearing them to bits. Tom tried to intervene, but he gave him a whack and shoved him away. "This is all pointless!" he shouted. "A complete waste of time!" Then he took his flint and iron and tried to strike a flame.

"Don't do that!" Tom shouted in alarm.

"No, there's nothing for it. Waste, all waste!" And he set fire to the pile of manuscripts at his side. Several of the pages caught alight, and he took these and threw them around, starting small fires in other parts of the enclosure. The walls began to shudder and the pearly glow, which up until then had shown at a fairly steady level, was flickering abruptly, sometimes illuminating the space in a blinding light and then throwing everything into darkness. Tom tried to stamp out the flames, but he could not keep up with Colophus who kept setting more things ablaze in his desperate abandon. Water came sluicing up from the various canals and tunnels and was swirling about the two, but the fires once set were finding more and more tinder to consume. There was a sound like an angry wailing and the walls of the space were rippled and tossed. A huge wave of briny water came in, sweeping everything before it and Tom was knocked off his feet and submerged. Trying to catch his breath, he lost sight of Colophus and felt himself being doused and ducked and plunged into violent criss-crossing currents of water. All the contraptions and cases and furniture and bric-a-brac that had been in the enormous space were being heaved around and past his head, and all the while the luminescence was flickering unsteadily. Finally, his lungs bursting, he felt himself propelled upward and through a series of ducts and conduits like a fish in a millrace until he was expelled with the utmost turbulence into airy space where he gulped down huge breaths, filling his exhausted lungs, and then, feeling the water's force diminishing, the wave broke downward with himself on the surface and he saw he was floating on the sea, amidst a mass of other objects, boards, large pieces of wood and papers, many of them partially burnt, all floating in the spume. Suddenly he was slapped upward again by the tail of the mighty leviathan as it turned its back and set its course once more for the bottom of the sea. And then, the violence over, save for a few small whirlpools quickly subsiding into the substance of the sea, he looked up and saw the sky, blessed blue that he'd never thought to see again. And on the horizon, not too far, he saw the green of vegetation. Freeing himself from his shoes and his pants he struck out for the shore. It took longer than he'd expected – there was a current running strong across his way – but after much swimming finally a great landward rolling billow took him in and he felt the ground beneath his feet again. He staggered, the muscles in his legs trembling with exhaustion, past the wash of ripples onto a sandy beach where he collapsed, with no idea of where he was, or how much time had passed since he'd fallen off the ship, knowing only that against all odds he'd returned to land again at last.

CHAPTER THIRTEEN
FREEDOM AND ITS DISCONTENTS

DEEP IN THE FORGOTTEN FOREST a large band of slaves who had freed themselves from their masters sought to create a community of people living together, founded on the common good. These were people from many disparate families, men, women and a few children who were attempting to join together in their mutual interest. It was a chance for a fresh start. They all knew that valuables and responsibilities would have to be shared around the group. Famularis, who took the role of leader of these people, said they must put their property and possessions into the common pot, that there would no longer be any property except the property that was owned by all. He also laid down three rules that all must live by. He thought three was the right number. Fewer than three would not be enough to cover all situations. More than three and the rules were likely to conflict. So there were to be three rules. The first rule was: all are equal. There would be no hierarchy. The second rule was: the group cannot grow so large that all the individuals who make it up do not know one another. If it were ever to become that large, it must divide itself in two. And for the third rule he was uncertain. After some thought he said the third rule was: whatever the group decides to accomplish, it will put all its will and might into the effort to accomplish it. After some reflection he thought perhaps the third rule was a bit more rhetorical than the first two, and of course there was some question as to how it could be enforced, but the sentiment it gave expression to was a true one, so he let it stand.

This group of freed slaves lived and worked together. All things were held in common. When decisions had to be made, they were made by the consensus of the group. The few children in the group were the children of all the adults. There was no money. Since these people had been brought to this place with a total absence of specie of any kind, at first this was simply a bare statement of fact. But in Famularis's mind it took on a greater significance. They would build a society that did not use money. In truth, there was no need for money. In fact, Famularis realized, money did not even exist. It was simply an idea, with no more reality than other ideas like truth, and justice. And Famularis realized that the bits of paper and the golden coins that people made such a fuss over were only counters in a game. It amused him to think of the measures men took to dress up these toys with laurels, portraits and lofty slogans he couldn't read, when what put 'money' into them was only the imaginations of men, and they were only worth what men agreed to think they were worth, no more and no less. He also saw it was a game played with great intensity, because it was this game that separated those who had power from those they had power over. In the society he envisioned there would be no need for any such game. Surely human society must be more than just a game.

Having put paid to money, Famularis went on to conquer mankind's other ills. They all committed themselves to live without alcohol, tobacco or gambling. That third was easy, since without money there was nothing to gamble for. The first two, however, drew complaints from some adherents of those substances. When Famularis went to round up all the rum and tobacco which some had been hoarding they entreated him earnestly not to waste it, so the supplies of these banned substances were placed under a large pile of banana leaves outside the central clearing where they all lived, on the side opposite the latrines. Just two problems were found with this. The first was immediately apparent and that was that these substances were under no circumstances ever to be consumed, which meant that from time to time the pile of banana leaves had to be moved. The second problem became evident after some time had passed, and that was that the supply of these substances could not be refreshed by the hunters in their daily forays in search of food, but rather required that a raid be made on the local town, which occasioned some trouble with the outside world they would rather not have undertaken, to say nothing of the loss this entailed to the group's dwindling supply of ammunition.

Men and women were equal in the group, this was fundamental. However, their talents, and as a consequence their tasks, were not the same. Famularis could not see his way past this. The men must be the hunters and trappers of food and the warriors who defended the group from their old masters. The women must do the housework. This way the tasks were fairly distributed. And when it came time to perform certain tasks such as digging and maintaining the latrines, or cleaning the clothes, Famularis observed there were certain individuals who were slow to undertake these and who cast animadversions on those of the warrior class who felt justly that these tasks should not fall to them. There were even some who grumbled to the effect that being free wasn't much different from being a slave, except their clothes were more ragged and the meals weren't so regular. These disorderly grumblers were a tribulation to Famularis. However, he observed that these disorderly individuals who would argue and stamp and hold their ground no matter how clearly he explained the theory underlying the distribution of tasks, would be much more agreeable and show little inclination to protest when he gave them an abbreviated version of the theory, while holding a rifle in his right hand. Therefore he decided that although in theory all property was held in common, in practice it was best to make sure that the limited number of guns the group held were in the hands of those he could trust. And when he made an honest effort to determine whether his idealism had been compromised by his practice, he was happy to find that in fact this was not so, and that he must have had some arrangement such as this in mind when he had framed the third rule, the one he had at first suspected of being mere wind, because otherwise nothing was ever going to get done.

Nero was a member of this band. He'd formerly been a house slave on the plantation of Master Andrew Merriwether in Trento, where he'd been brought up to be cheerful and well-spoken, and to carry himself with pride as befitted his master's place in society. He'd had buckles on the knees of his breeches, and his hair had been regularly oiled and powdered. He was accustomed to being treated as a thing of value. Though he never admitted this to others, he was coming to see freedom, with its attendant worries and sacrifices, to be a harsh and demeaning disappointment. There were times when he regretted his spur of the moment decision to join Famularis in his hare-brained revolt, particularly since, as he recalled the events of that day, it was clear the revolt could never have succeeded without his involvement. In his former state, when he had imagined himself a free man, he had always envisaged himself as holding possession of the chief and foremost perquisite of freedom, namely some slaves of his own. He saw now that being a free man had placed him in an unnatural state relative to the rest of the world. He was owner only of himself, and with no one to put him in his place, he understood now why his masters had so often seemed to hold the world in a sort of belligerent contempt, something he had formerly attributed to the effects of hard liquor, or misadventures with the other sex. It was this very liberty they extolled that was the root of their trouble. With every free breath they drew they came to expect more from the world than a man could reasonably expect, and this made them unhappy, and caused them to treat themselves as things of no value, going on binges and engaging in duels and carrying on like the eternally discontented and reckless children they were. Nero thought the world would be a far better place if all men were slaves, or at least acted as though they were slaves, regarding themselves as being worth something, and knowing their place. This whole experiment with freedom was bound to come to no good. Heavens, what was the point of telling people all were equal when anyone could see with their own eyes that was not the case? What sort of nonsense would they expect you to believe next? There was a reason only free men went mad.

When Famularis first informed the group of his plan to attack the slave markets in Indradoon, Nero had joined willingly, largely because it meant he was given a rifle. Also, he had secretly hoped it might offer an opportunity to be recaptured. When the attack had taken place, however, he had found that his person was placed in jeopardy by the reckless exuberance of the trigger-happy slave traders, and any attempt to be recaptured in a sensible fashion had to be set aside.

After the attack, as they were fleeing Indradoon, one of the female slaves caught Nero's eye. Her name was Akoko. She wore a tight-fitting dress, and as the newly freed slaves marched back to Famularis's camp Nero had ample opportunity to note from behind that there was a bottom in that dress that moved back and forth in the way a bottom should. Also, when she turned around, he discovered there was a dimple in the front of her dress where her belly button would be. These were the traits he liked in a woman. So, laying his plans in place, he decided he would begin by teaching her how to speak in a civilized manner. This was something he had been accustomed to doing when new slaves were brought to the Merriwether plantation, and by doing this he would have the opportunity to spend some time in her company, which would lead naturally by degrees to a mutuality of affection.

Akoko had other ideas. In her native land, she had been the daughter of a king, and she had acquired many of the habits of royalty, which she was loath to forsake. In her new surroundings she took pains to watch the men of the group very attentively, and she noticed that even though all were equal, when Famularis gave an order, people obeyed. Now, this was the trait she liked in a man. It bothered her that Nero kept coming around trying to be likable. She had little patience for the hand gestures he made accompanied by appropriate sounds in this new language. And when he attempted to point out the various parts of her arm and leg and give them names, he was rewarded with a kick from a leg he'd gotten a little too close to. And she had absolutely no use for the little piles of sticks and pebbles he assembled to teach the numbers from one to ten. She was certain her vocabulary was sufficient to let Famularis know how things stood. In fact, she found that that required little more than removing the upper part of her dress and allowing the beautiful orbs which depended from her chest to bobble and gyrate freely. Famularis agreed that words, no matter how poetic, would only have spoiled the moment.

Nero was oblivious to these developments, supposing only that Akoko was a naturally gifted, if inattentive, pupil who was bound to come around in time. Akoko for her part felt that Nero was a little slow in getting the drift. So she went to Famularis and told him – well, by told him it is to be understood that fully more than half of what she said was conveyed by gestures of the hands and face – but could she have given utterance to her statement it would have been something to this effect, "That guy Nero keeps coming around. I get a creepy skin-crawly kind of feeling every time that man comes near me. If I was you I'd do something about it."

As this conversation was taking place, Nero was lying in his tent formulating a scheme. Actually, it was nothing that overt; it would be more accurate to say he was allowing himself to daydream. In his daydream he imagined a time when he crept stealthily out of the slaves' camp and into the surrounding woods. There had been stories given out about slaves wandering away and being eaten by bears, or being recaptured by the heartless slave traders, but he put no stock in those. He knew what was going on. People were escaping and going back to their old masters. And that's what he dreamed of doing. Once on his own, as his daydream proceeded, he found his way through the woods back to Trento. He wasn't sure exactly where the slaves' camp was situated, but he had a feeling Trento was somewhere to the southeast. So he would head in that direction, guided by the sun. Once he struck a road he would be able to follow that and as soon as he got to the outskirts of Trento he would know his way. He would return to the plantation of Master Andrew Merriwether, where he would be welcomed with open arms and where he would immediately start setting to rights everything that had gone awry in his absence.

He was jolted out of this reverie by a young boy who smacked him on the knee and said, "Famularis wants to see you. He says you'd best come now."

"What's he want me for?"

"Didn't say."

This summons coming just as he was imagining his happy return to slavery gave Nero a bit of a guilty shock. But he quickly recovered. There was of course no way Famularis could know what he was thinking, and the front he'd put on for so long of being an ardent advocate of freedom surely had them all fooled. In fact, as he reflected further, it became clear to him that was the reason Famularis wanted to see him. He was going to be rewarded for his loyal support. So, making an effort to brush his tangled hair into some sort of decent condition, he set off for Famularis's tent.

When he came there he found Famularis seated in front. It was that time of day, when the sun had just set and the shadows seem to creep upwards from the bushes and the roots of the trees. The fire flies were out in number. The moon would be up soon and this night it would be full. Famularis was scratching the scar on his right hand, token of the oath of blood he'd shared with the traveling man. It had been bothering him lately and this evening was particularly troublesome. He wondered if he had an infection. He rose when Nero approached and the two men embraced. Famularis then led Nero into his tent and motioned him to sit.

"Nero, it's been too long since we spent some time together," he said.

"I feel the same," said Nero, "but I know you have much to occupy yourself with, keeping everyone here at peace and things running smoothly."

"Freedom has proven to be a burden, there ain't no mistaking that. But it be one I'm happy to take up."

"You know I've always supported you. Was that what you wanted to talk about?"

"You've always been a help when help was needed."

"Remember how I came through in our moment of glory, when we made the attack on Indradoon? That was something, wasn' it?"

Famularis put on a thoughtful look and replied, "You know it, brother. What you did that day will not be soon forgotten." When Famularis had first imagined this conversation, he had thought that somewhere around this point he would introduce Nero to one of his friends, who would lead him a little way into the woods and then shoot him in the back of the head. It was a method he'd used recently to deal with a few trouble makers. He'd put about stories of slaves wandering away and being eaten by bears, or recaptured by the villainous slave traders, so these disappearances hadn't aroused any suspicion. However, he now decided this would be a waste of precious ammunition. It was a secret known to only a few but there was a serious shortage of bullets. So he settled on a different plan. Patting Nero sociably on the shoulder he said, "I would like to enroll you among the group of warriors we has here. What do you think of that?"

"I am honored, of course." Nero thought a little more, and added, "I'll be glad to pick up a rifle again, I can tell you that."

Famularis did not look at him. His gaze was directed elsewhere, into the middle distance, as though he was thinking through a knotty problem. The truth was his thoughts were becoming muddled with other things. A substratum of darkness was rising into his consciousness. He scratched the scar on his hand again. "A troop of soldiers is entered the forest and camped nearby," he said. "Be prepared to fight." He then picked up a hoe lying close at hand and gave it to Nero, saying "There's no more rifles. Here. Practice what you can do with this."

"A hoe?" A rich smile spread itself across Nero's face. "Now I know you're taking it out of me. What is Nero going to do against General Hobsbawm's soldiers with a hoe?"

"In the right hands, your everyday garden hoe be a mos' grievous an' deadly weapon."

"Deadly to potatoes, I'm sure. Am I not even worthy of a sword?"

"We hasn't enough rifles and swords for all. You's shown yourself to be superlatively valiant. Why do you need a rifle?" And at this point Famularis felt an unfamiliar urge to bare his fangs and bite this stupid clown. He growled a little, and said, "You can do more damage with a hoe than a lesser man could do with a gun."

Here Nero made another of those impulsive decisions he so often regretted later, and he said, "Famularis, let us speak frankly to one another. I can see through you like a barn with its two doors wide open. You do not fool me. In fact, I've been able to see through you ever since the first time your cotton picking scrawny black ass came whining for a glass of water at Massah Merriwether's back door. You have your eye on Akoko and are jealous of the attention she shows me, so you've decided to let General Hobsbawm's soldiers do your dirty work for you. You're going to put me in the forefront of the battle where I will have no defense, and if the soldiers' bullets don' do me in, you'll do the job yourself, am I right?"

Famularis hadn't followed Nero's little oration through to its conclusion. He was still attempting to digest the bits about the scrawny black ass and Akoko showing attention to Nero, while another part of his mind registered the challenge he had received from that very same sanctimonious just as good as a white man house slave that had refused him a glass of water when he was a boy picking cotton. In his immediate necessity the hoe flew to his hand. The two men engaged in fisticuffs to the extent that they rolled on the ground as Famularis sought to do what damage he could with the business end of the hoe, and the blade on that thing was a good deal sharper than you might have thought. Nero dodged around the tent picking up objects and throwing them, but a berserk fury possessed Famularis, and he was not deterred. After some moments of tussle, Nero, seeing he was getting the worst of it, broke away and went running into the night, his heart pounding and his mind racing. With no conscious consideration of what he was doing, he set out to find Akoko.

CHAPTER FOURTEEN
THE FULL OF THE MOON

"I CAN'T LIVE without you. I'm not a man when you're not with me. I'm nothing. Can't you see what you've done?" The words gushed forth.

She ignored him, picking up her rawhide shirt and putting her arms through the arm holes. He reached for her and laid his head against her back.

"I've neglected all others, turning them away time and again. Any time I am not with you is torment."

Making a small moue of disdain, she rose and left the teepee. Outside, the full moon climbed slowly through the sky in the east. Joining hands with her sister, they turned towards one another. Their nipples touched, then their lips, sealing unspoken vows. Then, donning robes of antelope fur, they ran under the eaves of the Forgotten Forest, two savage animals chasing the eternal heartbeat of the night.

The trail they followed became a path, transforming before their racing feet into a glade where there were others of their kind, a coven culled from tree and plain, from mighty sycamores and humble junipers, from all about, the living roots and tangled branches of the living web that inhabited these darkened spots, brought to brimming life in the fullness of the moon. At the glade's center stood a willful malevolence, a dissension, a conflict of all with all, and it took on the appearance of a man. What followed it were women, wailing and prancing in many forms and many voices, driven by eruptions of obscene desire, prickling with drunken terror. The man who led them tumbled them, coupled with them, testing them, trying them, turning them to implements of destructive venom, poisonous agents of rank devastation. And they danced in twining circles, reveling in their power and their need, till all about them the night and the forest and the whole of creation were made instruments of loss and savage desolation.

Woken by a whisper in her ear Katie lifted her head, but no one was there. She looked about. Her bedroom window was etched in moonlight. A stray beam bounced off the sacred tipstaff lying at her side. On the ground next her bed the aged king reposed in slumber. She rose, and stepping over him made her way to the window, which opened onto a balcony overlooking the fortress keep, from which a stair wound downward. She paused. She looked about. All was still. Then, exposing her naked majesty to the night, she descended the cold stony stairs. A marble pathway lay at the stairway's foot, glowing in the moonlight. She ran along the path, through towering groves of cedar and pine. The untouched primeval woodland spread about her, dark and gloomy in the glimmering light. Coming to the sacred glen in the heart of the woods, she threw her glance upward, trembling in expectant ecstasy.

Akoko was startled when Nero, bloodied by his confrontation with Famularis and the hoe, his clothes torn and rumpled, came charging into her tent. He tried to communicate to her the plan he had hastily evolved. The two of them were to leave the slaves' encampment that very night and make their way to the estate of Master Merriwether, where Nero would be taken in and returned to his rightful place, and where she would be his honored consort. However, his unkempt appearance and his wild gestures, accompanied by loud repetitions of the simplest words, caused Akoko to conjecture that Nero had gone insane and that she was on the point of being assaulted and raped. Her screams brought others running to her assistance, among them Famularis. As he burst into the tent, bearing the bloody hoe, blood also oozing from the long-healed cut on his hand, he had a feral look in his eyes and was starting to rave, issuing loud and thundering curses interspersed with threats to kill any who stood in his way. At this moment all he knew was anger. All he wanted was to attack, and the crumbling remnants of his rationality found a hook to hang this on.

"Listen to me!" he shouted. "We's tried to live in friendship with our fellows. We's tried to live as nature made us here in the forest where there be provision for all. But our enemies is everywhere and they won't allow this. They's come to put us in chains again and return us to our masters. We will not permit this! It will not happen!" People came from all over the encampment, running and shouting in the belief they were under attack. "The white men think we's weak and they can subdue us! But our cause is just! We cannot be overcome!" He felt the ability to kill pounding in his veins. "We will turn on them! We will assault them with destruction and with fury!" The negro slaves, many only half dressed, were quickly arming and setting torches alight beneath the mossy branches of the ancient trees. Under an evil moon, things were stirring everywhere, like a pot coming to the boil. Famularis was becoming a fearsome and hitherto unknown being. Men were shouting and clashing their weapons. Famularis howled. "We will attack them tonight! On the move! At once!" All his flesh, and every limb and joint and point and articulation of him quivered. His skin was rough and hairy. His shins and knees shifted themselves and were behind him. His teeth were long and sharp. The frontal sinews of his head were dragged to the back of his neck. His eyes were rabid pits of focused malice. Falling to all fours he loped ahead of his flabbergasted followers, holding up his right hand – no, his right forepaw. It had been cut, and blood dripped from it. He snapped it forward and with a great rush like a mighty wind he was off through the trees.

The slaves burst on the camp of their enemy in a ragged wave, led by a huge, slavering beast of a wolf. Caught off guard, the soldiers had no opportunity to coordinate themselves. They hadn't anticipated the slaves' recklessness, and their hurriedly formed outer ring was quickly penetrated by an onslaught of maddened negroes wielding swords and lances and picks and any number of other implements. But once inside the outer ring, the slaves' attack dissolved into chaos. They found themselves under heavy, if badly directed, fire and were now engaged in what was little more than a vast brawl.

Famularis, in the form of a wolf, was in the midst of the battle, but his rude crew of followers melted away rapidly behind him. So far as he'd had a battle plan, it had just been to hit and run, but now retreat was going to be a matter of considerable difficulty, and many slaves were bound to lose their lives before they could get away.

The slaves could have been mercilessly mowed down, but Snivel ordered the soldiers to hold back, as they ran a great risk of hitting their own men if they engaged in indiscriminate shooting. He went about instructing his men to hold their fire, unless they were absolutely certain they were firing at a slave, something that was difficult to determine in the moonlight when masses of men, very few in uniform, were rampaging about. Famularis attempted to find some cover from a low but steep bank of earth, and discovered that quite a few of his followers had had the same idea. However, most of them, seeing the werewolf diving into their midst, broke and ran for safety elsewhere and were quickly cut down.

Famularis's muddied mind was now thinking more of retreat than of attack. He saw a band of slaves who were trying to get back to the shelter of the woods, but he also saw they had no chance, they were heading directly towards a squadron of soldiers with rifles who at this very moment were preparing to shoot. Quickly he dashed into the open, drawing the soldiers' fire away from the escaping slaves. Just at this moment the moon was obscured by a passing cloud and the soldiers lost sight of him. He got away as quickly as he could, with the soldiers in frenzied pursuit.

Elsewhere, in an abandoned house, a short man in a broad-brimmed hat roared in fury. He had Fergus tied up and Fergus's terrified eyes were watching as he grew and dissolved at the same time, re-arranging his physiognomy in ways both disturbing and subtle. One eye became engulfed in his head, while the other eye protruded suddenly and rested on his cheek. His mouth was twisted awry till it met his ears. Then his eyes moved back into new sockets, for what he was growing into was nothing less than a fearsome wolf, sharp of claw and fang. Fergus witnessed the transformation with wonder and dismay.

A crowd had gathered in the plaza that fronted Kashahar's lush and fragrant central gardens. These were theatergoers just leaving a production of the latest drama from the old country which had been performed that night at the Tragi-comique, a tragedy in three acts, depicting a student of natural philosophy who sold his immortal soul to the Devil in return for those worthless baubles, knowledge and power. The audience had been transfixed by the squibs the demons had set off as the unfortunate philosopher was being dragged through the mouth of Hell. It was absolutely the latest thing in theatrical effects. The actors had been abundantly applauded by a well turned out crowd who were now taking the night air and discussing the play's moral purport.

"Why are these baubles the Devil's to dispense?" asked Gervaise. The night was fragrant with the scent of lilac, and he was in a mood to challenge the most abstruse philosophies. "And what, if anything, does that imply about God?"

"I think it isn't the knowledge and the power themselves that are sinful," replied Apollinaire. "After all, these are things men strive every day to attain; how can such striving be sinful? I think it is asking the Devil to supply them that is blasphemous."

"So if I were to request a pedagogue to provide me the knowledge I wanted there would be no sin in that – after all, God helps those who help themselves – but if I were to ask the Devil to provide the same knowledge that would be sinful? Seems a bit of a niggle to me."

"Perhaps it's the type of knowledge, knowing how to bring beauties from ages past back to life to make love to them, forbidden fruit you know."

"Personally, I would be satisfied if I could make love to the many beauties of the current age. I'm just having trouble seeing how the Devil comes into it."

"Speaking of which, what's that disturbance there at the corner?"

"And why would God care anyway? Amazing the things God seems to care about. What disturbance? – Oh, I see."

"That wolf has just ripped that old woman to pieces," said Apollinaire.

"I must take issue with the premise on which you found your observation. That is no wolf. That's a loup-garou."

"How droll you are, Gervaise, of course it's a wolf. The loup-garou is a figment of legend."

"Perhaps when the sun is shining it is a figment, but tonight, when the moon is full, it is a living, breathing reality."

"Whatever it is, don't you think we should remove ourselves from its presence? That is now, I think, the third person it has disemboweled."

"There is no need for haste. It has not yet looked in our direction. But its presence here gives me cause to believe that the rumors we've been hearing are true. The Son of Light is dead, and there is nothing shielding us from the wrath of Satan."

"Surely the wrath of Satan is a boogy to scare naughty children, like the demons in that most entertaining play we were just discussing. Also it is now looking in our direction."

"Fortunately, Apollinaire, it has been my fixed habit for several years now to carry a pistol and silver bullets on nights when the moon is full. I foresaw, you understand, that something of this nature was bound to occur eventually. Here is the pistol of which I speak."

"Gervaise, your sang-froid amazes me. Do you realize while you have been idly talking to me you have allowed that creature to kill four – no, five – of your fellow citizens when you could have saved them by simply loading your pistol and shooting the beast?"

"The discharge of firearms in a crowded public setting is fraught with hazards."

"This setting is rapidly becoming less crowded."

"It would be rash to undertake such a step when other methods of quelling the threat are still viable. The use of deadly ballistics must always be regarded as a final recourse. Now, where did I put those bullets?"

"Gervaise, would you think it terribly impolite if I were to take to my heels at once? Aighee!"

"*Alors!* You have dropped your cane. Allow me to retrieve it for you."

"Please, there are other matters requiring your attention. For the love of God, could you just load your pistol and shoot this hellish beast?! His teeth are planted firmly in my calf."

"I am attempting to do so, but I am not so adroit as some, particularly with this monster snapping at my wrists – oh, confound it, look at that, he's scattered the bullets all across the pavement. What an infernal nuisance."

"Gervaise, you fuck – Bluaghzzarbaab!"

"There's no call for that language. I think I will have to beat this bloody brute to death with your cane. Where did you find such a fascinating finial? Is it a foliated fleur-de-lis?"

"Foliated?! How could you think such a thing of me. It is solid silver – Ahgiee khrazzurh!! – Or else I have been swindled."

"In that case, this will do nicely." And with that, Gervaise brought the heavy cane down onto the cranium of his elemental adversary. This had more of an effect than one might have anticipated due to the fact that the finial was, as Apollinaire had been assured, composed of solid silver. The slavering brute whimpered in pain and backed off to lick its wounds. Apollinaire looked up hopefully, but he winced when he tried moving his ruined leg. Gervaise asked, "Do you think you could hand me those two bullets lying next your ankle?"

Apollinaire handed them over.

Holding the cane in his left hand and the pistol in his right, Gervaise attempted to load the two bullets into his gun. He hoped two bullets would suffice. The rest had rolled into the gutter. The werewolf was watching him the whole time with uncanny attentiveness and at one point lunged towards him, but he delivered a devastating back hand with the cane. However, in order to hold the gun steady, he was going to have to drop the cane so he could put both hands on the revolver. He deftly flung the cane into the monster's face and then using both hands fired a bullet that ripped through its right ear. The bullet discharged with so much force the recoil threw Gervaise to the pavement, and the creature leaped backward in pain. Then, falling to all fours it paced back and forth, keeping a wary distance, eyes on the pistol. Gervaise kept the beast in the revolver's sights, preparing to shoot it through the heart. At the very moment he was ready to pull the trigger, the brute turned tail and ran, disappearing round the corner.

Once Tom had struggled up the strand past tidal pools and the untidy line on the beach that marked the high point of the tide, he'd thrown himself down. Sleep overcame him and he lay prostrate, shuddering gasps shaking his frame, as the last light leaked from the sky. The moon rose in the east, round and luminous, and traversed the heavens.

Now descending, it lay just above a bank of clouds, casting a glimmering pathway across the tireless waves, to the yellow sands where he lay. Had he looked up at that moment he would have seen its mottled surface shift as a figure stepped from it onto the stairway of clouds, down to the pathway painted on the ocean's surface. The distant figure walked along the path of moonlight towards where he lay, gradually taking on the appearance of Melinda, Mistress of the Shuddering Moon. As she drew near she shook her head, loosing her lustrous silver locks. Her gown of pure white samite moved and shimmered beneath a lace of amethysts, pearls and moonstones. She stepped onto the sand and approached, placing a hand on his shoulder. He looked up only to be mesmerized, haunted and spellbound by the unexpected glory in her eyes; the pupils were pure white, hardly to be distinguished from the iris. All thoughts were swept away. She spoke to him and afterwards he never knew if her words were sounded in the air, or in his mind alone, and the words she spoke were these: "Despair not. True love's journey ends in gladness. Chaos, fear and death are illusions to the heart that truly sees and never wavers. The world was created and is redeemed by love. Love is everything. All else is the mind's phantasm. Love is everything." She held his gaze a moment longer and for that moment he felt his heart pumped joy, not blood. Then, just as she had come she passed back along the watery pathway, gradually losing distinction as the distance grew greater, up the stairway of clouds and back into the moon. Then the moon resumed its descent, and as it did, the first rosy gleams of dawn appeared in the east above a dirty smudge of cloud.

Fergus felt as if the discomfort of the knots had almost become part of him. Long ago his left leg had gone to sleep, the rope holding that limb being particularly efficacious in cutting off the flow of blood. His mind had wandered from one thing to another. He'd tried to sing, but his reedy voice sounded naked in such a big, empty house, so he stopped. He'd gotten tired of looking at the chairs with their old-fashioned richness, the wall clock with its gilded case, the broad, cumbersome mirror. Everything had the gloomy appearance of long forgotten splendor, shrouded in ancient spiderwebs. He'd counted the nails in the wall, and the cracks in the ceiling. He wished he could sleep, but couldn't quite get there. When he closed his eyes he heard the house settling slowly in its long concession to decay, making the resonant little creaks and knockings of an ancestral abode at night. He'd been left completely alone, his only visitor the occasional draft that whimpered through the wainscoting. After a time when his thoughts had seemed to drift lazily back and forth to no purpose, he suddenly came fully awake to the realization that he was being watched. There was nothing he could hear, there was nothing he could smell, he didn't know which sense it was that told him, but he knew he was being watched. He was being watched by someone or something behind him. He couldn't turn around, he could only move his head so far. "Hello?" He waited for an answer. None came, but the space around him felt tighter somehow, more uneasy, as if whatever it was had just moved a little closer. The air suddenly became colder. He imagined eyes opening, and looking at him. He imagined their unfriendly glare. He imagined hungry lips. He imagined teeth. "Stranger, is that you?" In an instant he was panicking, struggling against the ropes, trying to break free. He wrenched and wrenched his arms, he twisted, but he was caught, he couldn't get away and it was now only inches from his back. He felt its touch and he screamed. The stranger had a grip on him and was trying to settle him down.

"Stop that!" the stranger said. "Stop! Lord knows who you'll wake up here."

Fergus was panting and blubbering. "You didn't have to tie me up!"

"You'd have run away if I hadn't. It was for your own good."

"The only person I want doing things for my good is me."

"Calm down. Stop all that thrashing . . . I'm going to untie you. Don't waggle, you're just making the knots tighter."

Fergus watched the stranger patiently untying the knots. He saw he was bruised and limping, and there was an ugly oozing wound on the right side of his head where he'd lost his ear. Something really mean had gotten to him. "What are we doing?" he asked. "All this riding around the country, stirring people up. What's the point? And who are we fighting? If we're fighting someone I want to know who it is so I can keep a lookout."

The old man just laughed.

"It looks like you should've kept a lookout tonight. Something bit your ear off."

"Oh, Fergus —"

"And turning into a wolf, that's not natural. And this house gives me the creeps. Lights always coming on just before I walk into a room, what's that about? And how come you don't have a name? I want to know what I've gotten into and why I have to be tied up to keep me from getting out of it."

The stranger just looked at him a moment, an amused smile on his face. "I tied you up to protect you. There were some malicious characters on the prowl. I had to keep you someplace safe."

"You call this someplace safe?"

"And I do have a name. I just don't give it out." He leaned back, removed his snuffbox from his waistcoat pocket and took a good snort. "It's long. I have thirty-seven middle names. And you know something . . . ? I once met someone with the exact same name as me. All thirty-seven middle names, in the same order, spelt just the same. Course he wasn't related, just sort of a coincidence." Fergus was flexing his legs, now the ropes were off him. "Come here," the stranger went on, "I want to show you something." He led Fergus outside. Dawn's first light was leaking into the sky from the east. It rested on the lines around the stranger's eyes and mouth. To Fergus he looked old, very old, an old man probing past mistakes and revelations. The full moon was in the west, just on the point of disappearing below the horizon. Afterwards when Fergus thought about what came next he wasn't sure if it'd really happened, or maybe he'd dreamed it. The old man reached for the moon in the west and took it out of the sky and held it in the palm of his hand. "See this? It's just a small thing really." Fergus looked at it where it sat in the man's hand. The stranger turned it over, showing both sides, the dark and the light. It looked like one of those silver dollars he always had about him. "The whole universe is just a cockeyed toy." He tossed the moon and it twirled in the air before falling back into his palm. "We just pretend it's big enough to matter, but I could sweep up all the stars in the sky and they'd barely fill my pockets." He put the moon in his back pocket. "Think I'll go spend it."

"Wait. You can't —"

"You're right. I better put it back." He put it back just above the horizon where he'd taken it from. "Don't think anyone noticed, do you? . . . Anyway it won't matter much longer. Everything's falling apart. Soon we won't even recognize the words that come out of our mouths. It'll be Paradise again, like when all were animals. What man is now isn't right. Man's not an animal. He's more savage, more cruel. He's got this veneer of civilization, but what's inside him? What's waiting inside, that he can't understand? "

"I don't know."

"No, you don't, because there's nothing. You can't see what's inside you . . . Now get your rest. You're going to need it. Today we sleep, but when the sun goes down we'll head out. We're on our way to the Forgotten Forest. And then we'll light up that munitions depot on Lost Bastard Island."

Captain Jasper Squeak, the quartermaster, was seated in front of his tent, polishing the ornamental saber he always wore on his right hip. His thoughts were far away, on the distant downs of his beloved home in the old country. Soon he would throw off the mantle of this stale old military life and actually become the person he'd always been. Where shall a man find happiness to surpass his own old home? He'd not live in a house of gold in this God forsaken land.

He'd kept his distance from the disturbances of the night. There'd been wild talk of a wolf, or a wolfman, or something of that sort. He heard a sound and looked up apprehensively at the dense, shaggy pines surrounding the camp. They cast a dark curtain of impenetrable shadow. *God knows, there could be anything in that forest. The sooner we're out of it, the better.*

He was suddenly brought to his feet by the appearance of a bedraggled, tattered negro who shambled cautiously out of the woods. His face was bloody and his clothes were torn. Squeak held the saber in front of himself while attempting to retreat into his tent. "Hold it," he shouted. "Stay right there."

The negro put his hands up. "I surrender," he said.

They stood there for a moment. Squeak didn't know what to do. "Throw down your arms," he said.

The negro lowered his hands.

"No! Keep your hands up, but lay down your arms!"

"I don' see how tha's possible, but if you mean my weapons, I don' got any. They wouldn' trust me with a hatpin ovah theah."

Squeak was seriously perplexed.

Nero could see this white man, like most, was a dummy and would have to be taught. "I'm your prisoner," he explained. "You've captured me."

"I have?"

"Yes. These are the fortunes of war." He smiled.

"I see. Well, in that case —"

"An' this is your lucky day. There's a big reward offered for my capture by Massah Andrew Merriwether of Trento . . . You're sup-pose' to ask me to identify myself."

"Identify yourself."

"My name is Nero."

"You're Nero the negro." Squeak smiled.

"No one calls me that."

"Oh."

"Tha's alright. I was a slave on the Merriwether Plantation. You're gonna get a big reward. You betcha."

"Oh yeah?"

"Yes. Just take me to your commanding officer and throw me in chains. It's all I deserve."

Squeak was having a hard time taking this in. He'd avoided all the fighting, but somehow he'd captured a prisoner. He hoped there wouldn't be a medal involved, or anything that would complicate his retirement.

"And you know what else? I can lead you right to the head man of these no good slaves. Tha's what I'll do. Where is your command-ing officer?"

"That's Colonel Snivel. I'll take you to him. Am I supposed to put you in handcuffs or something?"

"You probably are, but I don' think that will be necessary. I am not a troublesome prisoner." And he actually gave Squeak a wink. Nero told himself, *Oh, what a clever man I am.*

When Katie looked about herself she was disheartened to see that in the first light of dawn the sacred god-haunted glen was nothing more than a clear patch of sandy soil in the midst of some scrubby oaks and twisted, thrawny pines. The godhead whose overpowering

172

call had summoned her was diminished to the twittering of birds waking to greet the sunrise, and she was standing naked in front of a large mossy rock somewhere near the inn where they'd lodged for the night. She turned around. She retraced the rarely trodden path she'd used in the night. It led her to the apple tree outside the inn and she climbed the tree and crept out onto the branch that touched the window of her room. As she climbed back into her room she saw Tavish just rolling over and opening his eyes.

"Hello," he said. "You're up early."

"Turn your eyes away. I'll not have a man regard me so." She quickly grabbed a blanket to cover her nakedness.

"Oh, Katie, you'd think I'd never seen a woman before. Your shyness is silly." He stood and scratched himself before the mirror. He made no effort to be modest, and she felt she had to turn her head away. She was very self-conscious. Mornings had been proving especially difficult, as the cramped conditions on the road often compelled them to sleep close together, but always when they slept she kept her stick between herself and Tavish.

"Look away please," she said as she crossed the room with the blanket around herself to where she'd left her clothes the night before.

"I am turned away."

She dropped the blanket and dressed. She saw he was turned away, but then she saw he still stood before the mirror, and wasn't she the foolish girl, she was putting on a show for him. An angry blush rose to her cheeks. "Close your eyes," she said.

"They're closed."

"Keep them closed," though she was dressed now, there was no point.

"If you'll allow me to open my eyes, so I won't be stumbling over my own feet, I'll go down to the stable. I'll settle our reckoning and see Neddy gets some oats and put the saddle on him."

"Do that," she said.

As he was going out the door he turned to say, "I'll settle things with the innkeeper and the ostler. I think that latter is a bit of a thief but I'll not let him swindle us. Don't bother to say thank you, I think the words would probably knock a couple teeth loose trying to get out your mouth."

"Oh that's a hard way to talk. You feel so sorry for yourself go find someone who'll treat you better. I never asked you to come." But he was already out the door and down the stairs. Why was she so angry this morning? Was it just him, or was there something inside herself that was stirring her up? She looked out the window and counted to ten, forcing herself to feel calm. Then she followed him out the door and down the stairs.

Tavish was already outdoors when she got to the room below. There was only one other person in the room, or rather there were two. It was a woman giving suck to a very young infant. She looked up when Katie walked in and smiled, but said not a word. The baby was sucking intently on the woman's left nipple. Katie watched as the woman used one finger to gently release its mouth and then shifted it to her right teat. She smiled at Katie and said, "She's a girl. Just seven weeks today." Katie came closer and watched. The little girl had her eyes closed, but her lips and cheeks were busy drawing forth the milk. Occasionally a little would escape and dribble down her chin for her mother to wipe away with a soft cloth.

"Might I hold her, just a minute?" said Katie.

The woman looked at Katie and saw the small bump in her belly. They smiled, knowing what they shared. She handed the infant to Katie, and as the baby drifted off to sleep, Katie rocked her gently, humming a soothing cradle song, one she remembered from her mother.

"When are you due?"

"I don't rightly know." She put the baby down in a carrier the woman held. She placed her on her stomach, her face to the side, two fingers in her mouth, her little tush in the air. She thought, *Why does a woman love the baby to whom she's given birth? It's no longer part of her. It's another person that's come into the world with only one purpose and that's to steal her life away, another person she's condemned to care for and to nurture day after day, year after year, for the rest of her life. And yet she loves it. Why?*

Half Moon spent the night in his teepee, shivering with loss. Since the arrival of Issoria and Vanessa he'd fallen hopelessly under their spell. He felt as if he'd been initiated into the truth of life's purpose, the entire world holding significance only in so far as it bore witness to the hopelessness of ever loving them enough. And now they'd left him. He stepped outside, but they were not there. He looked to the east, where a towering column of billowing smoke was now taking shape, the visible sign of an awful conflagration. Almost the greatest of the flames could be seen, lighting the sky with a brilliance greater than the sun's. He didn't understand then what he was seeing, so unexpected and almost incomprehensible was the sight of Port Jay burning.

CHAPTER FIFTEEN
A MAN MUST HAVE A PURPOSE

CASPER CLUMPHY had felt the call to enter the priesthood at an early age. Some of his tenderest and most prized memories were of the services at the local church where his family had worshipped. The incense, the sacred music and the light through the stained glass windows had combined with the words read from the sacred books to create an overwhelming awareness of the spiritual presence of a loving God.

When he was still young his mother and a younger sister had fallen prey to an attack from the death birds, after which his father fled the old country with the rest of the family and resettled in Port Jay. All he'd known prior to coming to the Coast had been the tales he'd read in an old book about savage Indians living in the woods, their faces blazoned with terrifying paint, and the harsh lives the settlers endured. There was also a story of the holy hermit Trogle, who'd entered the Forgotten Forest where he'd slept for fifty-seven years, and when he woke had spoken to the birds and the beasts. Many hours he gazed at his picture, hollow-eyed and stooped, his Druidical robes damp from the maddened waters of the sacred spring. The actuality he encountered in the bustling city of Port Jay was far different, but as he grew older he never entirely forgot the romantic images he'd formed of the natives, whom he was told could still be found living deep in the surrounding forests.

From the start he involved himself in his local parish. He joined the church choir and assisted during services. The first close attachments he made were to the deacons and monks he met in the church. He diligently sought these men out and joined them in their various tasks, such as visiting those members of the church who had fallen ill, and assisting at the altar. Finding himself much in their company he sought out their advice as to the path he should follow.

One suggestion he was given was that of the missionary priesthood, and in this connection he imagined himself bringing the word of God to those savages whose warlike faces and exotic demeanor had held such terror and fascination for him as a boy. He envisaged himself holding the hand of a noble but spiritually empty Indian chief and leading him and all his tribe in prayer. It was a scene that frequently played itself out in the most intense moments of his inner vision. However, when he was finally ordained he put all such fancies aside and, taking on the role of a parish priest, settled into a comfortable routine of officiating at the sacramental table, performing baptisms, presiding at weddings and funerals and in general assuaging and salving the immortal souls of his parishioners.

Lately, however, his spirit had come to be troubled. More and more, while sitting solitary at night or in the confessional, the feeling came to him that he was no longer in touch with a credible source of moral principles. The spiritual presence he'd known in the church as a boy was now only a passing recollection, removed from his daily rounds. He watched the trivial feuds that seemed to inflame and animate so many of his parishioners, but saw no sense in them, and as he tried to reconcile their disputes he came to see that the whole basis for the golden rule was far from being self-evident. He couldn't pin down where these notions came from or when he had begun to feel this way, but he was increasingly certain he could identify a similar malaise in the people of his parish, and in the city as a whole. He was struck by the fear that there was no cosmic order, that that had all been some sort of old wives' tale or childish nonsense that could comfort him no more, and this fear was echoed and reinforced by the growing disorder and chaos in the streets around him. He felt as though he had turned away from the light and a shadow was now cast before him. When people and objects were seen in this shadow he saw them as they really were, and he was resolved to see truly in this way. He would not say he saw beauty where there was no beauty to be seen. And if he knew now that he lived in a wasteland and not a paradise at least he knew where he lived.

There were days when he would wander directionless, without any goal, one way seeming as good as another, and it struck him this was true of his spiritual life as well. There were no ideals anymore, and so far as he could tell there hadn't been for quite some time. When had that happened, and how had he not noticed? Even the words yes and no became muddled and in some lights he could no longer distinguish between them, and the mass, which in the past had been a solemn mystery radiant with sacred significance, now seemed like a hollow ritual drained of all meaning. Despite these inner misgivings he did his best to carry on as though nothing was amiss. As he spoke his sermons he looked around his cozy church lit with candles, the precious stained glass seeming to glow, the parishioners for one moment of the week bowed together in spiritual awe. He tried to take comfort from this homely scene. But what of the world outside? His fevered mind entertained fancies that the church had been submerged beneath a thousand feet of water. Outside the windows swam the ravening kraken and other terrible beasts of the deep, many-tentacled, their monstrous incomprehending eyes pressed to the glass. And he was startled to find his congregation rising from the service as contented as on Sundays past.

On the morning of the day that was to culminate in the great fire, Father Clumphy found himself on an errand for which he had little stomach. The Deacon had come to him a few days earlier with rumors of a troublesome young girl. The things that were said struck Clumphy as unexceptional – lewd dancing, linen stolen from a washerwoman, and various people complaining of aches and pains after she'd looked at them – but it was enough to elicit whispers of witchcraft. There were times when he wanted to tell the Deacon enough is enough. If you go about constantly telling people they are at the mercy of demons, eventually they will point the demons out to you. But this was not the time. So he'd promised to investigate.

The family had made him welcome when he'd shown up at their house. It was little more than a hovel really, like too many in this part of town. But they'd done their best to be hospitable, inviting him to their table, sharing their scant repast, smiling and calling him sir. Her parents accepted what he'd said about a philanthropic errand, outreach to the poor, without question, although there'd been nothing spoken of any sort of relief, only handing out some cards with schedules of services and some conventional prayers. Their affectless, dead-pan faces were giving nothing away if they had any misgivings about his uninvited presence. In the afternoon there'd been one occasion when the girl ran up to him, as though there was something she wanted to show, but after touching him on the knee and backing off she'd paid him no further attention. When they'd asked if he was staying for the evening meal he'd said yes, intending to leave as soon as it was over. But now, seated at their table, he realized that had been a mistake. Their invitation had been only perfunctory and he should have declined it. He felt like a fool, taking from them food they could hardly afford to dole out, seated in a room obscured more than illumined by rushlight, occasionally rubbing soot out of his eye, and spooning a ghastly bowl of soup into his mouth. There was no conversation, and just to break the nerve-wracking silence he'd thought to show off a little of his learning, sharing with them something the day had put him in mind of that he'd read in a book a few nights before. He said, "You know, there's a place in the old country way up north I've heard of, in the Riphean Mountains maybe, you know where that is?"

His host nodded. The daughter looked a little blank. It seemed like the mother gave Clumphy a glance of withering hatred, he couldn't have read that right, but they were all paying attention, so he went on. "Anyway what they say about the people up there is when a stranger comes visiting the first three things they tell him are lies. Then the fourth thing they say's the truth."

As soon as the words were out of his mouth he realized it was probably the most idiotic remark he could have made under the circumstances. However, it didn't seem to have made much of an impression, so he added lamely, "I just thought it was kind of amusing."

The husband slowly put his spoon down by his bowl of soup and said, "You think that's what we've been doing to you? We've been filling you up with lies to take back with you, and you were hoping now the truth's going to come out?"

He said it so softly, and with such an open look on his face, at first Clumphy was blind to the man's hostility, as though seeing a dagger, but one still in its sheath. He sat and thought a minute before he answered, "No, I don't think so . . . This is right good food you've given me, and I don't want to impose on you, so I think it's time I left."

"Well I think we've been repaid in kind," the man said. "Because that's three lies you just told us, before you told us the truth.

"First, you said you didn't think we'd lied to you. That's number one. Then, you said we'd given you right good food. That's number two. What we ate tonight is slop, barely fit for humans, it's a sign what this city's come to, people have to eat like this. I expect you don't eat like this when you're with your other priests up at the church."

"No, that's true. I don't. I'm sorry. You've caught me out. But normal people don't call those lies. It's just polite conversation."

"And the third was when you said you didn't want to impose on us, because of course you think it's your God given right to impose on the likes of us. It's all you've done all day. But after three lies you told the truth. You said it was time for you to leave."

Father Clumphy was roused by a sudden impulse of anger, but he forced himself to keep a lid on it. A hot flush rose to his face. "I can see I'm not welcome here, so the social courtesies can be dispensed with."

"You were the one brought up lying and telling the truth," the daughter said. She'd been standing and watching while they talked.

Clumphy rounded on her. "Do you think that's a decent way to talk to people? Telling the truth?" He continued to horrify himself with the words that came out of his mouth seemingly before he thought of them.

"Maybe so," said the mother, who'd remained silent up till now. "No more 'Good day to you, Father, what brings you here, and how can I be of assistance?' Maybe instead it should be, 'Hah, you're here to check up on us, heard our girl was getting uppity, didn't you, well get the hell out.' Maybe that's the way we should talk."

"I was going to return with word that your daughter's innocent of any taint of witchcraft, if you must know. But maybe, I'm thinking, that's not the right thing to say; not if we're going to be telling the truth. Your daughter has a way of looking at a man that makes him convict himself out of his own mouth of ignorance, fear and sinfulness. It's not right, what she does." There'd been a crackling, spattering, hissing sort of noise building up outside the house, and he had to raise his voice to be heard.

180

"My 'Becca's untainted by witchcraft," said the man. "She's no more a witch than you are, or that mouse in the corner."

Clumphy looked and there was a small mouse in the corner of the room. He was sure it hadn't been there before. "How did that mouse get there?" he asked, edging his way towards the door.

"There is no mouse," 'Becca said.

Clumphy couldn't make out her words over the noise from outside, which was now quite loud. "What did you say?"

"I said, there is no mouse," she shouted back. The mouse was gone.

"I'm getting out of this house," said Clumphy, bolting for the front door.

"Men invented words so they could tell lies to one another," 'Becca shouted after him. "Animals don't need words. They don't lie."

But as Clumphy got outside the last words she said were drowned out by the huge sizzling roaring wall of noise that had been muffled indoors, and he found there was something far more terrible waiting for him. His first thought was that the mouth of Hell had opened to swallow him up. A wall of fire was marching down the street, devouring the small huts and buildings in monstrous gouts of flame. People were stampeding, running in desperation to get away from it. It was a scene of such chaos and destruction as he had never before imagined and it was heading in his direction. All thoughts save escape were driven from his mind. He didn't stop to think of his own house and his possessions and the people he lived with. None of that existed anymore. He turned and joined the panicked crowd running, running anywhere to stay ahead of the flames.

That night was filled with the roar of combustion and its intense, all-consuming heat. Clumphy had never conceived of heat such as he felt that night. It was all around him and in everything he touched. Everywhere he looked there were flames, and in the fires he thought he saw all the riotous fiends of Hell on holiday, laughing, shouting and burning. When he remembered it afterwards what he recalled was the whistling of the descending clinkers, the ash and smoke everywhere, and the screams of people and animals in their anguish and their dying. It was a nightmare world of pain, death and demolishment. He joined groups of strangers fleeing to the bridge across the River of Tears, to the fields and the Forest where the fire couldn't come. He took little note of who he was with, and they took less of him.

The morning found him deep in the woods. He'd lost all sense of direction; all he knew was that fire was his deadliest enemy, and he'd escaped its touch. He felt drained and relieved and after what he'd come through, finding himself at last in a place where the flames couldn't get him, where he could rest and think about something other than putting one foot in front of another, for an instant he felt a touch of hope, and it was almost as if nothing in his life before had prepared him for it. It was a blessing descending on him, all un-worthy, that he had found life and safety, here in the serenity of the pathless woods. He looked about himself and at the others who were with him, who had shared his nightmare and were now awakened to this new day, even as many of them in their exhaustion closed their eyes and slept. He felt carried back in spirit to the days of his youth, inhabited by an emotion he'd forgotten, the simple love of God he'd known as the words of praise and the incense rose up through the lights to Heaven. He lived again his dreams of boyhood, everything intervening – the journey to Port Jay, the struggle to become a priest, the life of his parish – all of this obliterated now by the fire, wiped away, as though it had never been, and once again he imagined the Indians as he'd thought of them in his youth, terrible with a longing for life, and him bringing the word of God. So it was with little sur-prise, almost as if it had been expected, that he now saw there were actually Indians, slipping with their light tread into the glen where he lay.

These Indians seemed at first part of the Forest, as if the trees had grown more branches, or new flocks of birds had arrived. But as they stepped from the shadows it could be seen they were dressed in the hides of animals, not the tan of tree-bark, and the feathers they wore were decorations. One of them looked around at the bedraggled ref-ugees as though she were searching for someone, someone she knew would be there. At length she appeared to settle on one that suited her. She tapped Clumphy on the shoulder, and he looked up. It was a woman – a squaw they were called – with brown eyes and dark hair. Moved by what impulse he didn't know, perhaps thinking he was continuing the conversation of the night before, he said, "Why do we tell lies to one another? The way to God's kingdom is the path of truth."

Half Moon, in his hopelessness and despair, had dispatched these to find the witches, as he paced restlessly round his teepee giving the orders to go, to search all the Forest round about, they must be close, he thought. "Find them and bring them to me." Now Breezy Woodchuck smiled back at Father Clumphy. "Surely the holy power has led us to you," she said. She rose and Clumphy followed. He was never able to explain to himself why. He felt like a piece in a game being subtly maneuvered to where he would be most useful.

Half Moon now sat alone in his teepee and his eyes were closed. He sought to remember the faces of Issoria and Vanessa, but found he could not fix an image of them in his mind. It worried him that they could leave and he could forget what they looked like so quickly. Would he recognize them when they returned? Surely he would. But he felt uncertain. As if tracking an animal, but one whose footprints subtly changed, from bear to marmoset, to raccoon, and then to bear again, he knew not what he sought. But Breezy Woodchuck was bringing to him the lost one she had found. In the desperate hope that he could guide Half Moon back from the land of the lost, she was leading Father Clumphy to the high chief's wigwam. The trail she followed led through many winding culverts and along the sides of shady streams. Many birds were singing and sometimes Clumphy thought he caught the sound of distant music carried on the wind, like the singing of bells, if bells could sing. They came to a clearing where there was a large teepee and several braves standing around as if on guard. Breezy Woodchuck made signs to the braves, who bowed and allowed her admittance into the teepee.

Inside was dark and warm. A hole high up admitted a slender shaft of light, but the interior of the teepee was cast in gloom. Coming from the brightly lit outdoors immediately into the shadowed interior was like walking into a darkened closet. It took Clumphy some time to make out the man seated inside. He was wrapped in a blanket, his head hanging down as though he were asleep. Breezy Woodchuck approached this man gently and whispered some words into his ear. He looked up slowly and eyed Clumphy, who all at once remembered the dreams of his lost youth, of converting the hollowed, unhappy chief of the Indians, and he knew suddenly this was why he had come here. His steps could have taken him in no other direction. His whole life had been prelude to this moment. And he wondered why God, in His craftily negligent way, had brought him here at the very moment when his faith had left him and he felt most weak.

Thinking it was moments such as this that later were preserved in song and memorialized in art, he gave some thought to what he must look like. His cassock was dusty and covered with ash. His face, customarily clean shaven, had a slight stubble and was ruddy from the exertions of the past day and night. His hair was unkempt and disordered. He smiled, but under the circumstances was uncertain of the effect.

Half Moon did not smile back. Father Clumphy thought he'd never seen eyes so lost, as though all they looked on was ruin. Half Moon was a shell of the man he had been. The soul that had grown fat on good luck and sated itself the night of the potlatch had been snatched from him, stolen by those two enchantresses. They had taken it from him and now they had left him. Their antelope skins no longer hung from the rack outside his teepee. In this time of the year, when the days were at their longest, in his world all was darkness. "Who are you?" he said.

"That is of no importance," answered Father Clumphy.

The two looked at one another. It seemed to each that their lives had reached a crux, that the wandering, the loss and the despair were now to come to an end. Each looked to the other for some sign of it, but neither spoke. At last Half Moon said, "You wonder why I do not search for them myself . . .? Because I do not know where they are. So I wait. Perhaps someone will bring them to me. Perhaps they will decide on their own to return. If I am not here, how will they find me? But they would find me anywhere. I am not lost. It is them – they are lost."

Father Clumphy said, "I think not. I think it is us. We are lost . . . Often I feel I am lost, as though all effort is a waste. As though nothing is better than any other thing . . . But we are living men. We must have a purpose. Who will give us the purpose we must find?"

"No one will give it to us. It is ours to find."

"God will give it to us . . . He will . . . That is why He exists."

"You think the Great Spirit, which you call God, needs a reason to exist? I do not think so. The Great Spirit is the one thing that exists for no reason. Everything else has a reason to exist. But if the Great Spirit exists, there is no reason for it."

"He does exist." Father Clumphy knew many proofs of the existence of God, both *a priori* and *a posteriori*, both common sensical and nonsensical, many very convoluted, rife with the striking paradoxes that delighted the intellectuals. But on this occasion he chose the one he'd always found simplest and most satisfying. "Why is there something, and not nothing?" he asked. "Do you know?"

"Because nothing does not exist."

"You grasp the point. God creates things that exist. That is His nature. He cannot create things that don't exist, because once He creates them, they exist. And what does He say? He says, 'I am.' So He created you, and He created me. And we must have a purpose. Though sometimes, in our smallness and our blindness we may not know what that purpose is."

Half Moon thought this over. "You say a man must have a purpose like you would say a knife must have a blade. But a man is not a knife. Why must a man have a purpose? I see no need for this."

Once again Father Clumphy was roused by the hot flash of his temper. He asked Half Moon, "What are you? A man? Or a toad? Because a man must have a purpose. The entire universe is filled with purpose. All creation is set in motion for a purpose. Look about yourself, everywhere you see the endless aspiration of life . . ." Half Moon was looking at him with empty, uncomprehending eyes. Father Clumphy realized his words were having no effect. He was trying to use words to make Half Moon understand something that could not be expressed in words: the feeling of God's boundless love. He felt it, but when he tried to tell others they heard only his words and missed his message. "All men are filled with purpose. Perhaps purpose is not what you call it. Then call it intensity. Call it hunger." *Those words aren't right,* he thought to himself. *There, I've told three lies. Now, to tell the truth.* "Look at His works. Look at the mighty woods. Look at the terror, look at the beauty you sleepwalk through unseeing, look at the restless and constant creation of all the beings who inhabit this vast and splendid gift He has given us! Why are you unhappy? My house has burned down! My city is in ruins! Alleluia! Praise the Lord! I have nothing! And I am happy! Here in the heart of this forest I feel the grace of God that I thought was removed forever!!" He was on his feet now. "Alleluia! God has given me hope! When He has taken away everything I had, He has made me richer!" The Indians were looking askance at this wild man who was almost dancing now. The divine fever had come on him unexpectedly, and he was bellowing his sermon to all who would listen. He grabbed Half Moon and almost pushed him over in his enthusiasm. "All of you, get on your feet and bless the Lord!"

At first Half Moon looked at this crazy man, who was haranguing him, with outrage and alarm, but he could not hold out against Clumphy's infectious exaltation. Soon he also was moving, a glint of intention lighting up his eye. "Yes," he said, "I have a purpose."

"Of course you do. I know you do. How can a man not have a purpose?"

"I had forgotten. How could I have forgotten? All the time they were here it was as if only they existed. But I have a purpose. My purpose is to drive the white man from these shores. The black bear has told me this. He has promised me victory, and then a glorious death."

"Of course he has!" Father Clumphy raised his fists. "Drive the white man into the sea!" He was far gone, raptured out of himself, once again the words coming out of his mouth before he'd thought of them.

"This is my purpose. How could I have forgotten? My brother the gull, I remember where he gave me this feather as sign that I must bring myself to the water's edge where I will bear witness to the key, the revelation, the sacred word. Yes! I see now all the promises lead to this. I will drive the white man into the sea!" He stood and stretched his arms out and looked all around himself in wonder. And then he laughed. "You are right." He embraced Father Clumphy, lifting him off the ground. "A man must have a purpose. And his purpose once achieved, a man has no more use for life." He spun Clumphy around and walked out of the teepee, his arms raised in triumphant salute.

The other Indians in the teepee were also swept into motion. Where before all things had been sunk in torpor, now there was activity and resolve. Breezy Woodchuck kissed Father Clumphy. "You have done it!"

"What have I done?" he asked in sudden wonder.

CHAPTER SIXTEEN
COUNSELS OF WAR

THE ARMY, or at any rate most of it, had watched from the safety of the fort's massive stone walls as Port Jay was consumed by a wildfire so destructive and so rapid it was almost as if the city had been a bomb that had set itself off. Where formerly had stood a provincial town of gracious charm, whose wide boulevards ran at the feet of mansions of mellow hickory and weathered oak that shone in the sunlight, there was now little more than a vast glowing mound of ash, overlooked by here and there a handful of tottering survivors of stone. General Hobsbawm, surveying the desolation from the war room in the fort, had little doubt that when Port Jay was rebuilt it would be resurrected as a city of brick.

He had given orders to his men to remain inside the fort through all the terrible events of the night. They sat there while all around them everything was combusting and burning. Panicked fleeing people pounded at the fort's gates, but at General Hobsbawm's orders the gates remained firmly shut. Soldiers with family and friends in the town could only watch and worry. They sent appeals to General Hobsbawm, who replied by telling them to put their feet up and enjoy an evening beside the open fire.

The war room, where General Hobsbawm was seated the morning following the fire, was near the summit of the fort's tower. Its windows had splendid views of the city as well as the Forest to the south. There was a large table on which was unrolled a detailed map of the Coast and surrounding regions. Numerous small bits of wood painted various cheerful colors were strewn across the table, representing diverse units of armed force. Hobsbawm, with Lieutenant Lovejoy at his side, was seated next to Colonel Dunder. They were smoking cigars as they studied the map, attempting various positions for the little bits of wood, but not evincing much satisfaction with the results. Dunder was a short man. He was observing the map keenly with his bright eyes, which were nestled underneath a pair of white eyebrows.

"Do you suppose it was an accident, or do you think it was deliberately set?" the General asked Lovejoy, knocking the ash from the end of his cigar.

"I haven't the slightest doubt it was set deliberately," replied the Lieutenant. "Fires burst out simultaneously in different parts of the city. That could hardly have been an accident."

"So you suspect a cabal of arsonists, acting in unison, were responsible for this disaster."

"Just so."

"And yet we seem to have had not so much as a hint that such a group existed."

"I wouldn't go that far. The attacks by mobs of boys, such as the one we endured at that ghastly dance, were surely more than a hint."

"What do you think, Dunder?"

"Not the army's concern." Dunder scratched his ear. "Surely Fragonard can –"

"Fragonard is an incompetent, bumbling wretch. If such a group exists, we're the ones who have to deal with it." He turned back to Lovejoy. "How would we go about identifying the culprits?"

Lovejoy grew pensive. "It would be a matter requiring some delicate detective work. It would have to be conducted by someone with a feel for the local populace, someone with contacts in a wide range of social milieus."

"Someone like you perhaps."

"I was not making that suggestion."

"It would be a post of some importance. Surely the one in charge would have to carry at least the rank of major." He gave his cigar another puff. "But there remains the question of motive. Who would stand to gain from doing such a thing?"

"You mean setting the fire?"

"That is what we're discussing."

"I suspect it was not a means to an end, but rather an end in itself."

The General cleared his throat. "Explain yourself." He moved a red bit of wood next to a green one the Colonel had just placed.

"That was only if we set out today," said the Colonel, referring to the move the General had made.

"Are you saying whoever set this fire had no motivation other than taking delight in seeing things burn?"

"Yes, their only desire was to create a huge bonfire so they could dance round it. That's exactly what I mean," said Lovejoy.

"And as you know," Dunder continued his chain of thought, "this depends entirely on the seaworthiness of the Nemesis, which I believe departed for Lost Bastard Island two days ago. Where is Lieutenant Eliot? Eliot!" he called.

"Well that puts things in an interesting perspective. So you'd say these people were just insane, and they weren't motivated by political goals, assuming there's a difference."

"Insane might be too strong a word."

"Really? To set a fire that would kill hundreds and leave thousands homeless, to meticulously plan and carry out a scheme designed to leave the populace of this city with no way to get the food, the shelter and the clothing they require, to ruin their lives and utterly destroy their pastimes, to say nothing of destroying their own homes along with everyone else's, and all just so they can see the merry dancing of the fires – oh yes, I'd say insane covers it. You're saying –"

"And what of a man who could have saved the lives of hundreds who were burning to death and chose not to, who chose to play it safe and not make an effort to put out the fires or allow even a single person into the safety of a stone fort. Would he also be insane?" There was a fraught silence. "I'm sorry, probably I'm the one who's insane. I withdraw my question."

"Yes, and perhaps a promotion to major is something we need to reconsider . . . We were talking about the motives of the arsonists. You were saying their motives were aesthetic, they were like artists, inspired by their rotten imaginations, and not to be judged by anything so mundane as morality."

"*I* would judge them by the moral code, but *they* would not. Yes, I think they would see themselves as artists."

There was a pause as Hobsbawm and Lovejoy appraised the wreckage of the city. Colonel Dunder continued moving bits of wood around the map. "And here's the fleet," he said, indicating some red pieces of wood. The other two paid him no attention.

General Hobsbawm puffed on his cigar and continued, "Why do artists create works of art, do you suppose?"

"To communicate their ideas," interjected Dunder from the table, "express themselves, make money, that sort of rot."

"Well, making money would seem to be out of the question for our arsonists. And to express themselves . . . That's rather vague, isn't it? What action could not be thought of as self expression?"

"Things one is ordered to do," said Lovejoy.

"Or maybe all that self expression stuff is a lot of malarkey. Perhaps those aren't the things that really motivate an artist. What do you think?" the General asked.

"The motives of artists," said Lovejoy. "There's a cesspool I never thought I'd be climbing into this morning. If I had to judge on the basis of the few artists I have actually known, I would say they probably thought being an artist was a good way to get women into bed."

Dunder smiled and started to say something, then said something else. "Where is that man?" He walked to the door and shouted into the hall, "Eliot?!"

"Well I doubt that was the motive of our arsonists. Unless they're acquainted with women a good deal stranger than I've encountered. But you're talking about being an artist. No doubt many want to be artists because of the gaudy life their imagination paints. But that's different from actually making art. Let me back up. Perhaps we should ask what is the purpose of a work of art?"

He was interrupted by the arrival of Lieutenant Eliot. Eliot was a tall, spare man. He was going bald and his face was disfigured by a bushy mustache which his wife claimed to adore. Both she and their young son had last been seen in the city the day before. Eliot had spent many sleepless hours writhing in inner torment and cursing the General's orders. "Lieutenant Eliot reporting for duty."

"I would posit that the only purpose of a work of art," the General continued, speaking to the room, "as opposed to something actually useful, is to be just what it is. So on the one hand we have utility, and on the other we have . . . well, what have we?"

"Beg pardon?" said Eliot, believing a question had been addressed to him.

"Oh." The General focused on Eliot. "I was saying what is the purpose of a work of art? As opposed to something useful, such as this gun." He placed his revolver on the table. Eliot eyed it warily. "On the one hand we have utility, and on the other hand we have . . . Hmm . . .?"

"I don't know . . . . Truth . . . Beauty . . . ? Neurosis . . .?"

"I think necessity."

"Necessity?" said Lovejoy. "I don't see that."

"A gun is useful, but art is necessary. Why does a man exist? I know, to get a woman into bed." Here Eliot and Dunder both cast quick glances at Lovejoy. "But apart from that? He exists to create art. He exists to create something that has no other purpose than to be what it is. And I think, when we judge a work of art, we judge it on that basis. If we detect in its making anything other than a striving to make it be what it is, we feel it is a failed effort. If we suspect the artist of distorting the truth he sees because he wants to please us, we are displeased. He must make it be what it is and if he tries for anything else he is not an artist. And all this going on about the impression it makes on us and the artist's technical skill and so forth is entirely beside the point. Don't you agree?"

Dunder applauded. "You make a very good point and a very striking one too! I've always thought, ever since I was a boy you know, but I never said anything, but I've always thought it, that it must bother every artist, after he's painted his masterpiece, that he has to put that one disfiguring thumbprint on it somewhere in the corner, his signature. It's the one part of the artwork that's not part of the picture. But it's exactly that little smudge that the connoisseurs scrutinize. Otherwise they wouldn't know good art from bad."

"I'm not sure that is the point I'm making and you've detoured into the business of art, which is something else altogether."

"In any case, I don't agree with anything you've said," said Lovejoy. "We judge the artist by his intention."

"A seven year old may have a laudable intention, but he has no skill. We judge the artist by his skill."

"The skill he needs," the General replied, "is the skill to make his intention known. And the intentions of seven year olds are never laudable." Dunder suppressed a chuckle. Eliot grimaced.

"So he does need skill."

"Of course. But it is folly – no – it is obscene to judge an artist successful because of his technique when he is dishonest about his intentions, which is why most art is crap. Would you rather watch someone crawl, or would you rather watch someone run, even though the runner is more likely to stumble?"

At this Dunder broke in. "Yes again I see what you're saying. Why do people watch tight rope walkers? To see if they'll fall."

"And why would someone set a fire? To see if he can burn the whole city down. Which brings us back to this splendid fire we've had which was set, according to Lieutenant Lovejoy, by people whose intentions were just to see things burn. So from the artist's point of view, the fire was a brilliant success."

There followed another pause.

"Frankly," said Lieutenant Eliot, "I think it's high time we stopped all this foolish chatter. There are people suffering."

"Always there are people suffering. I think all this brings up my plans for the army. But before we discuss that I'd just like to say that I don't think it was deliberate. It was an accident, a very sorry, very disastrous accident. I choose not to believe there could actually be an individual so fiendish that he would deliberately set off such a conflagration. I refuse to believe in the existence of such a person . . . Now," and he turned back to the table, where he recommended moving the bits of wood about, "Snivel's force was dispatched two days since to deal with the escaped slaves. I have no intention of calling him back."

"That reminds me," Said Dunder to Eliot, "I wanted to ask you about the Nemesis. I know she's out of dry dock. When did she leave port?"

"Two days ago," Eliot answered. "To convoy the troops on Lost Bastard Island."

"That's what these other red blocks are for. They're the other arm of our pincer."

"Yes," said Hobsbawm, "as you know it had been my plan to set out today with the main body of the army," here he put his hand on a large pile of red wooden blocks, "to crush these Indians." He pointed with his cigar at an impressive pile of green blocks. "Obviously last night's events have put that plan on hold. The question before us is: have the circumstances changed to such a degree that that expedition should not be simply delayed, but should be abandoned altogether, and instead should we remain here and deal with matters closer to hand, to wit, identifying and capturing the arsonists responsible for this fire?"

"But there were no arsonists. You just said so," objected Dunder.

"Why does it matter how the fire was set?" said Eliot. "We have to stay here. You can't be thinking of moving out to attack the Indians. That would be senseless. The people will come to us for help. Thousands have fled, and now they have nowhere to live. They're probably this minute wandering in the Forest, waiting for things to cool down so they can return."

"I'd rather not –" said the General.

Eliot cut him off. "They'll need food, shelter, medicine and I'm sure many other things. Our force is relatively intact, our supplies are whole. Who will these refugees turn to for assistance but to us? And here we are to help them!" He put his foot down with an audible stamp.

"I'd rather not get bogged down doing the work of an humanitarian," said the General. "Besides, we need the supplies ourselves." He stood and strode to a window overlooking the Forest rather than the city. It was starting to rain. "Rain. See that? That's what they need to quench the fires."

The room was silent as the General looked out on the trees. All day the sun had been hidden behind a thick, smoky haze. There was just one tiny patch of blue far off to the south.

Finally Eliot said, "The army is something that was made to be useful. It was not made with no purpose other than to be what it is."

"Don't get cute with me," said the General.

194

"It was made to protect the people of this city and this colony. I may be taking some liberties here –"

The General turned and regarded the three others in the room. "Please, speak freely. We are not on the battlefield."

"I was saying that the people of this city and this colony created this army for their protection. But last night when you ordered us to close the gates, and again this morning, I feel as if I am being told we will not protect them."

"Protect them from what? From the fire? No, I don't think that's what the army's for. We protect them from their enemies. Would we protect them from a hurricane? Of course not. From a volcano? How are those any different?"

"We have food and medical supplies. We have places where people could find shelter –"

"And I don't think the people created this army. Where are you getting your democratical ideas? The King created this army. He created it to protect his people from their enemies. The supplies we have are a necessary part of the army he created. Without those supplies we couldn't do what we must do. I'm sure the people you talk about are all very grateful that now, when they are most vulnerable, they are protected from the onslaught of the wild Indians. And that's whom we will attack. I want some men to go out from the fort, find the refugees and the survivors, wherever they're encamped, and tell them that this fire was the work of their long-time bitter enemies, the Indians. Indians set the fire." He looked at the three others. "I know at this point you're probably hitting your foreheads in consternation and saying, 'Of course. It had to be the Indians.'"

Dunder laughed. Eliot looked at the General with something like disbelief.

"Can you say otherwise? For all we know they might have done it. Polluted heathens."

"And what good will this do?" asked Eliot.

"Good? I don't know if it will do any good, but it will have an effect. More recruits. They have nothing else now anyway. Let's get every able-bodied man and sign him up and give him a gun. I know we're going to run out of uniforms, but that's alright. We have plenty of rifles. Get them recruited, get them trained, get them drilled, and then let's go kill those Indians. A week — no, not even that – four days. I can turn a man into a soldier in four days." Here he turned back to the large map and pushed some red blocks into position. "And by that time the Nemesis will have convoyed the force on Lost Bastard Island to the Coast. I'm looking forward to a grand campaign. Why have we not been able to whip these Indians in the past? Why? Because when we attacked, they scattered. As soon as you'd look for them they were no longer there. But now they're preparing for the sort of battle we know how to win. They're massing, and we'll be closing in on them from both sides, through the Forest and from the sea. We'll shatter them. We'll positively demolish them. We'll chase them all the way to the shore. And then, when their backs are to the water's edge, we'll blast them with the guns of Lost Bastard Island." He paused, and took a moment to imagine the sight. "This will be a feather in all our caps." He pushed the red blocks he'd placed earlier, sliding them across the table towards a pile of green blocks, but his aim missed and the blocks went off the table edge, hitting the far wall and falling to the floor with a clatter.

Eliot and Lovejoy looked at him in dismay. Dunder chuckled.

Five days actually is what it took. Five days of drills and exercises. Five days of constant rain. The recruiters who'd been sent amongst the bedraggled survivors of the fire had painted the soldier's life in the glowing lights of a perpetual holiday, and as Hobsbawm had foreseen, many young men flocked to their banners. Of the remainder, some left, taking the road to Indradoon, and a few set out on the road to Kashahar, though army intelligence told of a large massing of Indians in the Forest near that road. The River of Tears ran past the ramshackle encampment of those that remained, and it was used for both washing and drinking water. There were a few cases of cholera, but the settlers were a sturdy lot, and a barter economy came into being with the farmers who lived along the riverside.

Also some returned to the burnt-out shell of the city. There they set about scavenging for what remained, living wherever a few walls, a chimney or a roof still stood to provide something in the way of shelter. Gangs of looters roamed the abandoned streets, terrorizing the few shopkeepers or merchants who'd gone back to salvage what they could. There were outbreaks of fighting when some rich trove or other was uncovered amidst the ash and other debris.

Lieutenant Eliot spent much of those five days wandering through the tents and campfires looking for word of his wife and son, but found none. On the fourth day there was a desultory mutiny, many of the soldiers who'd lost family in the fire rising against General Hobsbawm, but this was put down, the leading mutineers were hung, and their places were taken by fresh recruits. Lieutenant Eliot deserted and fled into the woods. Those who pursued him quickly lost his trail.

Meanwhile, the new recruits were drilled, marched up and down and pronounced soldiers. There were no uniforms, it was the raggedest army ever seen, but six days after the fire that burnt Port Jay to the ground it marched out of what was left of the city, and into the Forest.

The sisters, mothers, wives and daughters they were leaving behind stood and watched them go. There were no flags waved or cheers shouted. It was an altogether dismal occasion, made even more so when the rain turned to hail shortly after the last of the infantry had marched away.

CHAPTER SEVENTEEN
COLDBLOOD FARM

JOSH STUDIED THE FARMHOUSE from where he stood on the side of the road. His Mom was still indoors. This was her day for laundry and she usually took her time about it. It looked as though he'd have the morning to himself so he went out on the sand to where the wind was blowing in his face and the waves pounded the shore. The beach was empty. A lone gull watched him with baleful yellow eyes. He waved to scare it, but it just stuck its head up and gave a haughty stare. He spread his arms and ran, lunging at it. As it took to the air it cast its cawing curse down on his head. He gave back a right salute, and in a flash he was the captain of a naval frigate bound for points west. The waters here were treacherous. Monsters prowled the shore. He directed the first mate to go in close and get a good look. Sails were struck; the canvas on the foremast was lowered. They were cruising at a slow pace past the strand. They saw the large, hairy brutes beating their chests and roaring their fury. Some had the bodies of men and the heads and horns of cattle. Others sat in the trees like birds, with the faces of hideous, howling women.

"Cannons out!" He gave the order.

There was an explosion and a cloud of gunpowder in the air. He looked over his shoulder and saw King Neptune walking down the road. He was covered with sand and he had no shoes or pants. He had a ragged beard full of seaweed and what looked like one or two dead mollusks. Josh went closer and saw he was wearing a wet raggedy shirt and was walking pretty fast. What really struck him though when he got close was the smell. He smelled like a two day old fish, and there was a powerful briny stench all over him. When he saw Josh he waved to him and asked him if he knew who lived in the house.

"Yes I do know," said Josh.

"And who is it, my good man, if I may make so bold?"

"Me and my mother. This is our house."

"Your house?"

"Yes."

"Well you've got a fine house. Do you think it might be possible I could impose on your hospitality? I'm that tired and worn to flinders I think I could just about kill someone to get a bath, and there's no telling how many I would massacre to get a bed to sleep in. I haven't any money, but I'd be happy to make myself useful any way I could."

"Where'd you come from?"

"From the ocean."

Josh thought that one over. "I didn't see any ships come in."

"Didn't come on a ship. What land is this?"

"How'd you come then?"

"In a fish. You didn't answer my question."

"No. You didn't come in a fish."

"You're right. I dropped out of the sky. I ask you again, what land is this?"

"This is the Coast, and this here road is the road into Kashahar."

"Kashahar . . . ? And which way's Kashahar?" Josh pointed, and the man looked up towards the sun and said, "So if Kashahar's in the west, Port Jay must be that way," pointing back the way he'd come.

"Yeah, but it's pretty far. And why won't you tell me how you got here?"

"You think it would be alright if I talked to your mother?"

"You wouldn't want to talk to my mother."

"And why wouldn't I?"

"She's a fierce woman and when she meets a man she doesn't like she turns him into a pig."

"You're thinking I'm one she wouldn't like?"

"She wouldn't like you a bit."

"Why would that be? A tall good looking lad the likes of me."

"Because you smell like a fish."

"There's worse things to smell than a fish. Is she in the house?"

"I expect, but she's doing laundry."

"I think I'll have a word with her. My name's Tom by the way."

"Oh. I'm Josh."

"Pleased to meet you, Josh. What's your mother's name?"

"Her name's Agata. Come on, I'll introduce you."

"Ach, you smell like a fish," said Agata, wiping suds out of her eyes when Josh confronted her with the tall strange-looking man he'd met on the road.

"That would not be surprising, seeing as I've spent some time in the belly of the leviathan," said Tom. "If anyone ever tells you the stories about that beast aren't true, they're a liar. It's the greatest fish in the world, and it swallowed me and I lived in its stomach till it disgorged me not far offshore. I swam to the beach and laid there overnight. When the day came I got up and found this road. I walked along it till I came to the first house, and it was yours."

"You know that's actually not the craziest story I've ever been told, but it's close."

"It's not much I'd ask of you. Just to take a bath and give me a bed for the night. Or if a bed's too much I can curl up in a corner in the hay. I've no money but I'd be happy to make myself useful anyway I could so as to repay you. I'll leave tomorrow. I promise."

She gave him an appraising look. She'd been startled when Josh first brought him in. She'd taught him not to mess with the drifters on the road, too often they were just looking for a handout or something to steal, but this one was by a long sight stranger than most. Anyway, she made up her mind.

"Josh, show him the tub outside and get some water from the well. This man needs a bath."

"Thanks so much, ma'am. You don't know what this means to me."

Tom cleaned himself up, but he didn't know what to do for clothes. Agata said she'd wash his shirt, and Tom of course had no choice but to let her. However, he possessed neither pants nor shoes. Josh offered him some of his old clothes but they were a good deal too small. Tom said he would be happy to work on the farm for a bit so he could get some money, and then he figured he could get in touch with a tailor or someone in town and get something to wear, but his immediate necessity was for a pair of pants, so Agata had no choice but to give Josh some change and send him in to town to get something Tom could wear.

That evening he tried to settle into a bed they'd made him in a second floor room. It had a window and he could see fields and trees. He was facing west, not towards the ocean. The sun was setting behind a bank of clouds. There was little wind and the smoke from a campfire in the woods trailed straight into the sky. It made for a scene of rural peace and contentment of a sort that Tom had thought he'd probably not be seeing again. Josh was back from town, and he'd brought with him two pairs of pants and a pair of boots. They were dingy and dirty and had seen a good deal of hard use, but Tom figured they were about his size.

"Where'd you get these?" he'd asked.

"There's a rag and bone shop on Mortimer Street where you can get just about anything if you don't mind how dirty and foul it is. The man who owns it has an eye patch and his name's Scruto. He picks up all the odd leavings when people die or get killed. There's always tramps and drifters there, sorting through the trash, seeing what they can get."

"Sounds like a lively place."

"It is. And you never know what you'll find. But even as strange as the things there are the people that come in. All sorts like you wouldn't see collected in one spot anywhere else."

"Did any think it odd you looking for pants for a man? They're a good deal too big for you."

"It did get a little laugh from Scruto. He knows Agata and you could see he thought maybe she'd got herself a man. But I told him it was just for a strange seaman that had dropped in."

"Did he ask you where the strange seaman came from?"

"He didn't. And if he had I couldn't have told him, because you never told me. There was another gentleman though, seemed to take an interest. Asked me who the man was and where I lived."

"And what did you tell him?"

"Nothing. First place I don't know nothing about you. You could be King Neptune himself for all I know, and with your green beard you did bear a resemblance. Second place my Mom told me never to tell strangers nothing."

"You told me where you live."

"There's some I trust and others I don't. I knew I could trust you but this other one was one of the ones I don't."

"So you'll trust a man with a green beard and no pants, but this other customer didn't look so dependable as that?"

"No sir," said Josh, scratching a freckle. "But he did give me a piece of licorice and told me he was my friend."

"You may not be the best judge of character, but it's all one now I've got my pants."

"So are you going to hang around and earn the money to pay my Mom back for those clothes?"

"Yes I will, but I won't be staying long. I'm headed back to Port Jay. There's a lassie there who's an ache in my heart. It's a long and a languishing time since last I saw her."

"I've never been to Port Jay. What's it like?"

"It's a big city. The buildings, most of them, are made of wood and they've been aged by the wind and the sun. They look like rows of grand old gray-haired ladies standing out in the weather. In the right light it's a beautiful city, and a busy one too. The port there's never still. There's vessels putting in from all over the world. They load them and unload them in a flash and then they're out again."

"When I'm older I'm going to live in Kashahar. I see how the people live there. It looks like a good life for most of them."

"You don't like living on the farm?"

"Don't see no future in it. I want to get out and live some. Don't tell my Mom I said that."

"Your secret's good with me."

Meanwhile at the campsite in the woods where the little log fire was burning, Vincenzo, Diego and Mr. Chips were having a dispute. Vincenzo and Mr. Chips were in favor of staking out the farmhouse, killing the people there and taking it over. Diego wanted to cut and run; head east and get as far from Barnacle Jack as possible.

Mr. Chips adjusted the sling on his broken arm. "I say let him go. Give him his third. We'll take care of business here." He threw another log on the fire.

"I don't want to scarper on my own," said Diego. "I'd prefer not to. And I agree it's a nice farm. But you're too close to Kashahar. Too close to the sea. You won't last the week. He'll find you, and his friends are close. Anyway I never lived on a farm."

"It's a good point you raise," said Vincenzo, "but we can't be always running. We've run a few days, we've covered some ground for sure, and now I say that's enough. This farmhouse looks like a good setup. Once I'm dug in here no one's going to dig me back out."

"They could come any night. You'll always be looking over your shoulder. If you –"

"I said you raise a good point. You want to leave no footprints. So go. That's not me. I'll set myself up and I'll challenge any man to knock me down. There's not one will do it."

"Then let's divide the bags. These two are mine. We're all agreed to that. It's just this bag we must divide now. One third of it is mine." As he said this he brought one of the money bags forward near the fire, so all could see.

They counted out the doubloons, making three piles. When they'd all been counted Diego clutched his pile and pulled it next to him.

"So those are yours," said Mr. Chips. "What are you going to be carrying them in, because this bag is staying with the two of us."

"There's nothing to worry about there. I've got many pockets in this jacket. I'll just fill them all." And he proceeded to do so. It was a warm night, but he had his jacket bundled around himself. Then he hefted the two bags, one on each shoulder. The weight was something of an impediment but he'd accustomed himself to it the past few days. "How do I look?"

"Like the good country squire, out beating the bounds," said Vincenzo.

Hands were shaken and last farewells said, and Diego was off. Vincenzo and Mr. Chips sat together by the fire. Neither said a word. Finally Vincenzo cocked his eye at Chippy and said, "You didn't think I'd let him go, did you?"

"I don't think he thought you'd let him go."

"He'll likely spend all night looking behind himself, wondering when we'll be creeping up on him. A frail, scared man like that I don't want him around. He made me nervous. Sometimes it's good to be honest." Then a thought came to him. "Think you when we come to the pearly gates we'll get credit for the things we didn't do?"

"That'd be a winner if we did, because we'll not be getting any for the things we did do." They laughed.

"Let's bury the rest of these bags here," said Vincenzo.

"No need to bury them. Just hide them a little out of the way. We'll be back soon enough."

"Are you set for tonight's work?"

"I am and no mistaking. Only one hand's needed to hold a pistol."

"It's just a woman and a boy. They'll make no trouble. They should be grateful to us for taking the farm off their hands. I've got the knife . . . And I was thinking, now I'm turning honest, maybe we'll let the lady live. It'll be nice to have a lassie in the house."

"Not an old biddy the like of that. She's used up."

"You're right."

"She's done in. What are you thinking of?"

"No point in a soft heart. Let's go."

Under cover of darkness, the two set out towards the farmhouse.

Josh had gone out to take care of some chores, closing up for the night. Agata came and knocked on Tom's door, see if he was settled in right. There was still a stench of the fish on him, it'd take a couple of days to wash that off. Maybe he really had been in the belly of a fish. Who can tell? It was strange times now.

"Why's this place called Coldblood Farm?" he asked. The window was open. It was a still night and sounds carried. They could hear the creak of the gate when Josh went out to the henhouse. And always in the distance was the low roar of the surf.

"The story goes when they come here first they brought a dowser to look for a place for a well. He spent three days going up and down and all over, finally found the spot he liked. So they dug there. And when they dug down to where they thought the water'd be, up it came trickling, cold as ice, but red as blood. They thought it was blood at first, thought the land was bleeding. Thought there'd been some sort of grand old crime and the land was suffering. They called it Coldblood and the name stuck. I think it was just some of the red clay like you find around here. It got in the water, gave it a reddish color. But who knows now."

"That's a thought, that the land would bleed like a man. But then I guess there's many things that bleed. Anyway, as I was saying, if there's anything I can do to help out the next couple of days, just tell me. I aim to pay you back for the clothes and the room and the board."

"There's not much really needs doing. It's a big spread but I don't farm but the half of it since Josh's dad left. Just chickens mostly. If there was a man around I think we'd rise to a few cows, there's good pasturage in those fields to the south, you can't really see them so good now. But for just Josh and me chickens are plenty. You ever lived on a farm?"

"No, ma'am, that's not been my fate. Brought up in the dock-yard I was, a fisherman's son. Made the sea my life."

The room didn't hold much furniture, just a small table, a couple chairs and a bed. Tom had been seated on the bed and Agata, decid-ing she'd stay a while, sat down on one of the chairs and made herself comfortable. "How many boats have you been on?" she asked. They could hear Josh taking the little wagon out to move some eggs.

"Too many to count."

"That's the exact same number of chickens I've killed. Exactly the same. A miracle . . . You want to play some cards? It passes the time and I have a pack." She produced a deck of cards from a pocket in her smock.

"That casts a shadow across my heart, to be sure. I've unhappy memories of a game of cards."

"I'm guessing you lost a wager, one maybe you shouldn't have made."

"I'm certain I did."

"You'd think there'd be an even distribution of winners and los-ers. But that's not how it is. All you ever meet are the losers. Where are the winners?"

"The winners know better than to let you know they've won. It's a perilous thing to be a winner. They hide themselves among the losers like myself. It makes for a great confluence of losers."

She placed the little table between the two of them and dealt the cards for a game of Nasty Notions. It was a recreation known commonly up and down the Coast, though the rules are long forgotten. Now a game of cards played between men and a game played between a man and a woman are very different things. When a man and a woman are together their minds need to be occupied, and for them to be occupied properly it is best if there be periods of silence as well as conversation, and this is best allowed for by playing cards. Conversation alone tends to be carried on just to avoid silence, but when playing cards there is no such compulsion. In the conversation that follows little note is taken of the pauses that occurred, but one shouldn't think they did not occur; they did. It was in the silences that perhaps they understood one another the best, and when people understand one another it is natural they smile. And the smiles best understood are those not made by the lips, but by the eyes. But to return to Tom and Agata, as she dealt the cards, she asked, "How long you been traveling?"

"Don't rightly know. I lost all track of the days and weeks when I was in the fish. It seemed like an hour might last a year in there."

"Did you have a deck of cards to while away the time while you were in that fish?"

"I did not."

"Too bad."

"I had a companion, and amazingly we did not slit one another's throats. Had there been a deck of cards, I'm sure matters would have turned out otherwise."

They were playing now.

"A deck of cards is a calendar," said Agata. "Did you know that?"

"I did hear tell of such a thing once on a time."

"There's fifty-two cards in a deck and there's fifty-two weeks of the year. I lay down a seven." She tossed her head to get her curls out of her eyes. "Four suits for the four seasons, and each of them has thirteen cards for the thirteen weeks of each season . . ." She looked at him and could see he was thinking it over. "Can't you imagine the old farmers long ago, watching the sun making her solstices and her equinoxes and then noting them in the cards?"

206

"And the moon also, making her thirteen trips across the sky."

"And that's how many times the blood of a woman is moved. I bet they saw the hand of God in it the way it all worked out . . . And when you add all the pips on all the cards there are exactly three hundred and sixty-four, which is a grand old number that tells the days of the year."

"Yet a year has three hundred sixty-five days."

"There's your joker." She spun the card at him and laughed. She took off her smock. She was wearing a light cotton shirt underneath. "You've played your whole hand. Oh, you're clever at this. You win."

He was enjoying the conversation, so he asked, "Another hand? I'll deal."

"No, it's my deal."

Tom had been tired when first he settled in, but found he wasn't tired now. He felt a little regret about asking for another hand, at least part of him did, but there wasn't much all the parts of him agreed on. "Maybe it's too late," he said.

"We'll stop when Josh comes in." She dealt the cards. "I know you're not asking about his father. Shows you've some sense. Likely you don't want to know what happened, but . . . Are you thirsty?"

"My throat is a little dry."

"I'll get some cider in a minute."

"It's funny like you say, how it all works out. I mean the year. The sun and the moon and the planets, they don't seem to work together but they all get to their appointments on time." She'd finished the deal and was just looking at him. He noticed the contours of her face were more rounded than they'd seemed before. Also her breast was not flat, nor were her hips narrow. "So what did happen?"

"Thought you'd never ask. He decided he wanted to go for a soldier. Couldn't live on a farm –" She broke off. There was a sound downstairs. "Did you hear that?"

Tom nodded yes.

"Josh?" she called. There was no answer. They realized it had been some time since last they'd heard him. "Oh no." They held very still and listened intently. Someone was downstairs, and it wasn't Josh.

Tom stood and moved toward the stairwell. "Have you any weapons?" he asked quietly.

She shook her head no.

When he started down the stairs he saw Josh a few steps below looking up at him. Josh whispered, "In the top drawer in the bedroom in back," and pointed.

Tom waved to Josh to come up the stairs and then stealthily trying to muffle his footsteps, walked to the room in back. He turned at one point to ask who was downstairs, but Josh wasn't there. When he got to the room Josh had pointed him to there was a chest of drawers, and in the top drawer, along with some old broken toys and other oddments there was a knife with a sharp six inch blade. Taking the knife he went back to the stairwell. He passed Agata on the way. She was shaking and almost crying with fear. He whispered to her to stay with Josh, which got him a quizzical look, and then went downstairs.

The ground floor was completely dark except for a little moonlight from the windows. He remembered seeing a candle in a candlestick holder on the dining room table earlier in the day, and he went cautiously down the hall in that direction. The door to the dining room was open and he paused stock still before going through it. Just as he did he heard a footstep from behind, so he went quickly into the dining room and as he reached for the candlestick another hand grabbed his arm and he was spun about. Trying to keep his balance, he grappled with his attacker, and the two of them tumbled noisily over a chair onto the floor. The other man was on top of him, but Tom got onto all fours and rolled over, pinning him to the floor. His right hand was still holding the knife, and he was struggling to get a grip on his assailant's throat when he felt the muzzle of a revolver on the back of his head and a hard, cold voice said, "Hold it right there."

Tom froze, allowing the man beneath him to get up and get to the candle on the table. When he lit the candle there was a round of amazed gasps as those in the scuffle saw one another. Holding a knife in his other hand, Vincenzo lifted the candle up to Tom's face.

"Well, well, well. And isn't this a night full of surprises." Vincenzo laughed. "Of all the people I might run into again it never crossed my mind one of them would be my old cabin mate Tom."

"Vincenzo," said Tom. "Sure there must be a curse on me keeps putting you in my way."

"We thought you'd drowned."

"I did drown. But then I remembered you cheated me, so I've come back to get what you owe."

Mr. Chips laughed.

"I owe you nothing," said Vincenzo. "And I owe your ghost less. Oh, you are a madman. You know what I owe you? I think I know. I owe you a good scar on the face. Then we're even. Give me that knife." Placing the candle on the floor he snatched the knife from Tom's nerveless hand, so now he held two. The scene was all lit from below, giving their faces a queer, otherworldly look.

"I'm thinking your face is much improved since last I saw it," said Tom. "That's a wicked good looking scar you bear."

"That's a bold way to talk. Aren't you the brave one. You like this scar, I'll give you one better. I'll give you a smile for the ladies. But first, where's your old biddy. You've got her upstairs?"

"I'll not tell you." Mr. Chips knocked on his skull with the butt of the gun.

"It comes to me, you're a right one with the ladies." Vincenzo reached into his waistcoat pocket and produced a watch. The outside bore a design of knots and tangles, and when he opened it on the inside of the lid was engraved "From your own darling Katie." Vincenzo read it aloud. "I've not yet had time to scratch her out, already you've another. You're a tom cat, that's what you are, and you set all the bitches in heat."

Tom had nothing to say, albeit tears stood on his cheek.

"Of course she's upstairs. Well then I'll go and grab her." Vincenzo put the watch away and crept up the stairs while Mr. Chips held the gun on Tom.

"If you shout or say one word there's a bullet through your brain."

"I'll not cause trouble," said Tom. He was completely disheartened and knew not what to do.

There was a bit of silence while the two of them attempted to decipher the noises coming from upstairs. Then they heard Agata screaming and Vincenzo shouting, and the two of them came down the stairs, he holding a knife at her neck.

"I tried to get out the window, Tom, I'm sorry I couldn't."

"More candles! I want light," shouted Vincenzo.

"There's some in the sideboard," said Agata.

The candles were obtained and lit and candlesticks were found. Then the four of them sat down and looked at one another.

"The presence of simple Tom makes things a wee bit complicated," said Vincenzo. "I'd thought it'd be just the woman and we could do her and be done."

"We still could do that," said Mr. Chips.

"Still we could. But what shall be done with Tom . . .?" The thought hung in the air. "I'd like to know why he's here, wouldn't you?"

"What are you doing here?" Mr. Chips addressed him over the muzzle of his gun.

"Do you know these men, Tom?" Agata asked.

"That I do," he answered. "In a former time these were my shipmates on the Queen of Bel Harbor."

"And it was a very queer trick you pulled," said Vincenzo, " getting off that ship. Like I said, we thought you'd drowned. Poor Brutus was the one had to take the lashes for it. How did you do it?"

"I fell off the ship. Then I was swallowed by a fish." Tom told them the whole tale, how he'd gone into the fish's belly where he met Colophus, and the time they'd spent together. It was a strange tale, one that suited the surroundings, which were strange as well, with the wind blowing through the house and the candles flickering. It put the queerest feeling into all of them. And as Tom was nearing the end, Vincenzo said, "I don't believe a word of that."

"Believe what you like. It's the truth."

"No. You had a partner. You must have. In a boat. He lay beside us that night and that's how you got off. And I think I know who your confederate was."

"I had no partner. But you were telling me what came of Brutus."

"They killed him," said Mr. Chips.

"Who?"

"The next day. The Master and his flogger. They had a trial, did it right and honorable. Then they lashed him eighty lashes of the cat."

"Eighty?" His voice broke.

"Eighty . . . He died."

"We watched the life go out of his eyes." Vincenzo was only inches from Tom's face. "With his last words he put a curse on you, who left him to take the punishment you didn't get. He cursed you, and your children, and your children's children too. They're all cursed."

Tom hadn't thought of Brutus for many days but now he did. He felt guilt come on him like a heavy cloak, one that bore him down and he'd never be able to take off. "Oh no," he said. "Poor Brutus, what did I do . . . ?" He trailed off. All the events of that night came crowding back into Tom's mind. "Oh, Brutus! Poor Brutus! Eighty lashes!" was all he could say. Then he sat in silent grief a few moments, till he resumed his tale. "One day Colophus started a fire, which so angered the animal he spat me out. When I looked about I saw a shore in the distance, so I went for it with all my strength, and it was a long and a hard swim till I came to land at last. That was just last night. I spent all the night on the beach. Then this morning I got up and came here, where now you've captured me. But what of you? I take it you've jumped ship and have come down in the world, being no longer honest seamen, now you're naught but robbers and house breakers."

Vincenzo hit him on the mouth. "I'll take no lip from you. I'm a better man than you are. You're happy enough to leave your cabin-mate to take your punishment and now you go all tears and crying. And you think I'm so stupid you can just tell me a fairy-tale of being in a fish's abdomen? Well I'm not. Not by a long shot. You went to Crazy Dog that night, didn't you? I see it now. How he knew where we were bound. You sold the lot of us to him. Am I right? Or maybe it was Barnacle Jack."

"I'll not say who it was." Tom's only plan was to keep them talking long enough for Josh to come back with some help.

"You will. You'll tell me everything before this night's out. Where are they?"

"I'll not tell you."

"Shoot him in the foot, Mr. Chips."

"He doesn't know anything," said Chips. "How could he? He's been inside a fish."

"I said shoot him in the foot!"

"Alright!" Mr. Chips shot Tom in the foot. Tom fell to the ground, writhing in agony.

"I should hurt you like they hurt Brutus." Rage surged through Vincenzo's whole body. "Let you know what he felt." He had to take a moment to get under control. Then he turned to Mr. Chips, "You still believe he was in a fish?"

"He sure smells like it. Ah, if he's a liar I'll just shoot him dead and be done."

Agata was mumbling prayers under her breath.

"Our good friend Tom thought he could play us false, didn't you?" He hit Tom again. Tom cursed. "I wish I had some rope, I'd tie you."

"We have rope," said Agata.

"Shut up! I mean, where's the rope?"

"Why waste time tying him up? Out of my way. Surely I'll just shoot him in the head."

"Don't shoot him, I'll get you rope," said Agata. "Sure you can't run a farm without rope. I'm the only one knows where it is." She left to get the rope.

"You just let her go?" said Vincenzo to Mr. Chips. But then she was back, carrying a rope coiled round her upper arm. Vincenzo went on, "I suspect – no, I'm knowing for certain – this scoundrel's in with Crazy Dog." Tom was trying to follow his chain of thought, trying to figure out the names he'd used, Crazy Dog and Barnacle Jack. He was praying he could stick a wicket in his gears, get him more confused. "Or maybe there's a reward he plans to claim. He's been following us. Else how did he come here?"

"Oh . . . I hadn't thought of that," said Mr. Chips.

"No, you hadn't, had you? He was just swimming around inside a fish. Oh, Chippy, you've a brain the size of a walnut." Then, turning to Tom, "So, where is he?"

Tom put on a long face like he was thinking things over. "Well, I –"

On that instant Vincenzo jumped him and put a knife to his throat. "I'll have none of your wells. You'll not drag this out till your friends get here. Tell me where he is or I'll slit your throat this minute!"

"Alright, I'll tell you. Get off me." Vincenzo got off and Tom sat up. "Christ, my foot hurts . . . But if I tell you, I'm a dead man for sure, you'll not have any use for me."

"Oh, and I suppose you thought you'd survive this night?" He laughed, and it was a real laugh, all the way from the belly. A great wind came through the house then and set the candles flickering.

"Let me just shoot him in the head," said Mr. Chips.

"No, that's not the way of it." He turned to Tom. "I'll ask one more time: where is he?"

Tom was silent.

"What color you guess his brains are?" Mr. Chips gave a chortle.

"I will now be counting to five," said Vincenzo. "If I say five before he's told us where Crazy Dog is you'll shoot the woman. Do you understand? The next time I say five this woman is dead. One . . ."

"I knew I'd be shooting someone."

"Oh, Tom," said Agata.

Two . . ."

"Tom, if you know, tell him."

"Three . . ."

"That's not like you, Vincenzo. Don't you want to rape her before you shoot her?"

"That ain't funny," said Agata.

"Four . . ."

"He's waiting in a boat just off the beach," said Tom. "He's been there now a good hour."

"Oh, I knew it," said Vincenzo.

"I was to signal him. Three flashes of the dark lantern meant they was waiting on him, it was no go. One flash, he was to come in."

There was a puzzled pause.

"What?" asked Chips.

"Waiting on him . . . ? Who'd be waiting on him . . .?" asked Vincenzo.

"He won't come in if the . . . Your Crazy Dog's a smuggler, is he not?" said Tom.

There was another pause as a dawning awareness grew on Vincenzo. "Tom . . ." he started to say something, then he laughed.

"I think you're spinning a tale . . . Yes I do. Shall we go down to the beach and meet Crazy Dog? What do you say?"

"Yes, I think we should."

Vincenzo laughed again. "No, I don't think so. You'll not play me for a fool. There's no one there, is there?" Vincenzo gave him a broad smile. There was not a word Tom could say. "Shoot him, Mr. Chips."

Agata gasped. And though there was no wind, at just that moment all the candles went out, and in the sudden darkness the closet door flew open and Josh hurled himself onto the back of Mr. Chips. So surprised was he he did not have time to pull the trigger. As he went down, with Josh on top, he dropped the pistol so he could use his good hand to block his fall. However, he was only partially successful, and his broken arm hit the floor hard. He cried out in pain and rolled over onto his back. As he did so, Tom leapt at Vincenzo. Vincenzo tried to jab him but missed in the dark and Tom got in close under his guard, grabbed him around the chest and wrestled him to the floor. Agata found the pistol Mr. Chips had dropped and picked it up. Mr. Chips was just getting to his feet again and Josh was backing off into the hallway. She held the gun on Mr. Chips and told him to stay down. There was an awful moment when Chips was crouched, staring at Agata, a rictus of pain on his face, and she was standing her ground, both hands holding the pistol. The moment could hardly have lasted a second, but it seemed drawn out as each measured their will against the other's intention. Then Chips pounced, and Agata fired. Mr. Chips fell writhing to the ground, a gaping, bloody hole in his neck.

While this was happening, Vincenzo and Tom were locked in struggle. Vincenzo couldn't get a grip on Tom, as he was holding a knife in each hand, but he did manage to gash the fleshy part of his thigh. Tom, however, got hold of Vincenzo's right arm and gave it a good twist. Vincenzo dropped the knife in that hand and backed away from Tom who let go of his arm and picked up the knife. As soon as he had it, ignoring the pain in his foot, he lunged at Vincenzo's face. Vincenzo knocked the blade down but couldn't deflect it entirely and it penetrated his stomach on the right, just below the ribs. Seeing he was wounded and Mr. Chips was down, Vincenzo made a break for the back door. Tom tried to follow, but was toppled by the pain from his wounds, which were bleeding profusely. Vincenzo was out the door and they quickly lost sight of him in the pitch black night and the shadows of the trees.

Agata turned her attention to Josh, to see he was alright, but when she looked she couldn't find him. "Josh?" she called. She looked through all the rooms on the ground floor. While she was doing this, Tom had a look at Mr. Chips. There was nothing to be done for him as he was clearly dead so Tom turned his attention to his own wounds. There was a gash in his left thigh and a bullet hole in his right foot. There was a good deal of blood also but it appeared no major arteries were cut. He looked up to see Agata had returned and was staring at him.

"It's a good job Josh got me two pairs of pants," he said. "I'm afraid I've ruined this pair altogether."

"I don't know where Josh is."

It didn't seem important, yet it put a weight on his mind.

"And how did he get in the closet?" She rattled the door. "It's locked. I locked it this afternoon when I put the besom away. Here's the key. This door's got but one key and it's stayed in my pocket."

"Josh must've found another . . . Perhaps he's upstairs." Then he thought some more and said, "It would be no surprise and certainly no disgrace if he was scared and found someplace to hide."

"Why's he hiding now . . .? Let's see to you," Agata barely whispered.

"It looks bad, but I think not fatal."

"Take your pants off. Josh . . . ? Where is that boy."

Tom was grunting with the pain as he removed his pants, but outside of that the house was still. The moon was up now and just past full so, even though the candles had gone out, there was light to see by. Nothing stirred. Even the wind was sunk now to less than a murmur.

"I'll bandage your leg and your foot, but then I must find Josh. I don't know what I'm in fear of. My heart misgives me."

"There's no harm could have come to him."

Suddenly she was desperate. Dropping the bandages she sat and shivered for a moment. Tom looked at her, not knowing and not understanding. Then she picked up the bandages again and wrapped Tom's wound. "How did he get in the closet . . .? Hold this."

"How did he get away when Vincenzo caught you upstairs?"

"And where's he gone now? You're not holding it."

"Sorry. I think after he tackled Mr. Chips he went upstairs."

"I hope he hasn't gone to chase that one who got away."

"He didn't. I started to chase him. I didn't see Josh. Josh didn't leave the house . . . How did he get away when Vincenzo brought you down here?"

"You keep asking that." Her hands stopped moving for a minute. Then she cut off the bandage she'd tied around his leg. "Is this tight enough?"

"No. Yes. I left the two of you together when I came downstairs."

"You didn't . . . Josh wasn't upstairs."

"Of course he was."

"No."

"I saw him. I told you to stay with him."

"Was that what you meant? He wasn't with me . . ." The two of them looked at one another. Then she said, "Give me your foot. He must have gone to his bedroom. Why didn't I think of that before? I'll look for him there. Hold this." She tied the bandage round his foot. When she'd done with that, she started upstairs, but something stopped her and she turned around. "But why he'd be upstairs and not with us is something I can't understand . . . Don't you come up; I don't want your blood everywhere. It'll be the devil to clean up."

Tom's wounds were bandaged and the worst of the bleeding was over. He heard Agata for quite a while, moving through the rooms of the house. He wouldn't have thought it would take her as long as it did, but the truth is he wasn't thinking about her. His wounds were throbbing mercilessly and he couldn't think about anything except the pain. When she came back down she was alone. "He's nowhere in the house." There was a little breeze and a sound of footsteps in the hall, and then the door from the kitchen to the back garden was shoved open with a clatter. Agata went to look. Tom found a stick and using it as a cane he followed her. No one was there, but they

216

thought they still heard footsteps in the grass and they followed them to a little ditch behind the hen house. That's where they found him lying on his back. For a dreadful moment the flies made it look like he was still moving. He had a monstrous gash on his throat, from ear to ear. Whoever did it – and Tom, remembering the knife in Vincenzo's hand had little doubt who – had then carried him here and laid him out of the way. He pictured it: stealing up behind him while he was busy with the wagon and then a hand over the mouth, pulling his head back and a quick slash, left to right — Josh must've been dead before he'd realized what had happened — then picking up the body and hiding it out of sight before coming into the house. And all the time he and Agata upstairs playing Nasty Notions.

Then the spirit had played its part. It followed them into the house, directed Tom to the knife and hid in the closet. And after it did what it had to do, it had gone. Where . . .?

They buried him that morning in one of the fields south of the house. Agata was a useless bundle of tears, forever lapsing into a shivering despair, and Tom was hobbled by the wounds he bore, so they had a couple young men from a neighbor's to help with building the coffin and digging the hole and placing the body. They stood round the grave to say a few words, but no one could bring himself to say very much. Agata tried, but she couldn't get a sentence out before it became a long crying sob. Tom looked at the pine box as they threw dirt back on it. *I'm a curse.* His thoughts were dark. *Wherever I go I bring calamity and death. Brutus I left and he died in my place. Colophus must be drowned. And sure it was I drew Vincenzo here to kill Josh. Everything I touch I destroy. Everyone I befriend I kill. I'm a curse. And my children are cursed. And their children too.*

They also buried Mr. Chips, though not with any ceremony, and they didn't build him a coffin. The carpenter he was, for certain he would have taken offense at that. They just laid him in the ground and covered him up. The neighbor lads, respectful as they were, were yet in a stammering hurry to be done and gone. After they left, the silence and the empty sadness came down on Agata and Tom. Agata saw no reason why her useless heart still beat and she leaned hard on Tom. She'd fancied him a bit when first they met, but now she needed him. Without his companionship she'd have sat wailing and staring at the wind, venting her grief in inarticulate sobs. She looked out too for Josh's ghost, sometimes sensing his presence certain moments when things went still. They never heard the footsteps again.

Tom wanted to get on the Road but he knew it'd be several days yet with his wounds not healed. It was a bitter blow the morning one of the neighbor lads brought word of the disaster that befell Port Jay. Tom hung his head, wondering if the Lanchester Mansion had survived the fire and if Katie was safe. Then in the afternoon he and Agata walked to the beach where the wind was tossing the sand about and the great rolling waves were smashing against the rocks and drawing back again in boiling, hissing foam. It was a scene of constant turbulence, one wave following after another. He looked at the jagged, upthrusting masses of rock surrounding the beach and saw the rocks were in combat also, reared up from unknown depths in awful angles and broken off again by forces that were thrusting them up and pulling them down just like the waves, and it was only the smallness of the little bit of time he was looking at them that gave the illusion they were still. He saw that in the little bit of time between one wave's rising and its falling down a kind of scum had crept out and covered all the base and the sides of the wave, and when the wave fell down the scum was washed away like the boiling surf and never seen again. And that scum was man and his works that had covered the earth in so short a time. As he thought these things he said nothing to Agata but only talked of a coop that needed mending and of why she'd worn her green shoes instead of her gray. When he looked at her he saw the question in her eyes she didn't speak of, though it filled the noisy silence and he knew it was a question to be answered. So when they'd walked back to the house and they'd made themselves a pot of tea and Tom had changed the dressing on his foot, which was healing well, though it was still raw, and they were settled in their chairs he asked, "Have you a coin?"

"I know you've been working to earn the money you'll be needing when you go. Sure I'll not cheat you. Must we speak of this now?"

"I think we must."

She looked at him a moment, but his expression told her nothing, so she rose to get her box of coin and opening it she took out a coin and handed it to him. "Here. There's yet what you owe for the clothes but I'll not have you saying you were never paid." She smiled, thinking it was his joke.

"You can keep it. Would you toss it for me?"

" . . . Toss this coin?"

"Yes."

She tossed it and it fell to the floor.

"What's the verdict?"

"Heads."

"I'm sorry, but I must leave you this night. I've a long way to go, and it'll be all the longer for a man lamed as I am. So I'd best get a good start."

She looked at him in disbelief. "So tails you stay and heads you leave?"

"Yes."

"You're not leaving just for the toss of a coin. I'll not believe you'd do that."

"Believe what you wish."

"Wait. Sure it's dark in here and I didn't give as close a look as I should. Now I look closer I see I was mistook. Sure it's tails. You can see for yourself if you'll not believe what I tell you."

"Agata, the coin will never fall right for you and me."

"Then why have me toss?"

"I must be going, and you must stay."

"Sure, you've a cruel way to tell me, saying a woman and all her charms can't get the better of a toss of a coin?"

"I can't explain the why of it but I'm always leaving women and I've never come back to any. But there's one I'm going back to now. I'm sorry I stopped here. I wouldn't have done it if I'd had a choice."

"Wait. We'll toss again. I'll not let you leave. This time sure it's due to come up tails."

"The logic of that is wrong. Each time the chance is the same. If it came up heads a hundred times in a row, still the chance on the next toss is one in two."

"If it came up heads a hundred times in a row, sure that coin has heads on both sides. More fool me, setting my cap for tails."

He had nothing to say to that, so he went to put his things together, but it struck him he had no things, just the stick he used for a cane.

She walked to the door and shut it before he could go out. She took off her shirt and showed him her breasts. They were white and firm like those of a young woman, the nipples hard and red. "I'll give you everything. I just don't want to be alone." Tears stood in her eyes. For a moment Tom thought of a younger woman and of a man beguiled by the glamour that was a soldier's life. Then as gently as he could he took hold of her and moved her out of the way. He opened the door and went out, closing it behind him. He walked to the end of the path and looked back at the farmhouse. The door was still shut. The windows were dark. The night was silent. The moon had risen in the east. He turned his steps towards Port Jay.

Chapter Eighteen
The Devil's Kiss

In the guttering light the hall stretched forever. Plinths were laid out in long rows bearing crates like coffins. Katie paced the endless aisles, stopping from time to time to open one of the crates. She would look in quickly, then move on. She knew what she sought was in one of them, but the ones she opened all bore corpses: women with long, stringy gray hair; men with chiseled faces and beards. They all looked the same. Time was running out, and a terrible destiny would befall her if she did not find that which she sought.

At odd times sounds like muffled footsteps echoed from other parts of the hall. These footsteps — slow, leaden – filled her with dread, but though she looked behind and to the sides she caught not a glimpse of a pursuer. All she saw were the distant walls covered in macabre hieroglyphics, and the endless rows of caskets. Coming to a spot where two aisles intersected, suddenly sharp claws plucked at her from behind and as she screamed she woke to see Tavish looming over her. "Where is . . .? Did something happen?"

"Don't worry. We're safe." He had his arm over her belly and he smiled, but she didn't read friendship in his smile. "Forgive me for waking you."

"Was there a reason?"

"I'm lonesome. I need someone to talk to."

"Must we talk this time of the night . . .? Can it not wait till morning?"

"Many nights I've wanted to talk."

"What is it you've wanted to talk about?"

He took a long time before answering. They heard the forest's small rustlings and nighttime whisperings. "I've wanted to tell you I love you."

"Now you've said it can you sleep?"

He looked at her. "No." He closed his eyes.

"You're a fine man, Tavish. You're good and strong." He opened his eyes again. "But you should not have come with me. I let you come because I needed you, and I'm selfish. But you should not have come. You're not strong enough for the task you set yourself. I think you know that."

"I would be if I'd yet had hope of your kindness. But that's drained out of me. Can you not care for me at all?"

"You know the answer and it's the only answer I'll give. It's not that I've a cold heart or I'm hard to please, but there's another man I love." She took his arm and moved it off herself. "You're a good man, Tavish, and you know you're better than to do whatever it is you're thinking of. I've feared the coming of this moment, and I must ask you to swear one thing for me. Will you swear, for the love you bear me?"

He answered in a low, choked voice, "I will."

"Do you swear you'll go no further but will always be my loyal protector? Be the man you want to be, the man I know you are, and go no further but to love me in your thoughts . . . ? If you swear, that will give you the strength you need. And I'll swear in return never to think you less than the brave, good-hearted man I've always known you to be."

They looked one another in the eye, hers deep and blue, lit by an inner glow none of those who'd loved her had been able to pin a name to, his brown and misshapen with the hurt he'd carried all his life. Finally, in the same low and choking voice he said, "I swear."

"And so do I." She placed her hand on his.

"I worship you. I'd never hurt a hair on your head."

"Thank you, Tavish. You're better than I deserve." She stood and looked about. The night held no answers. She felt no safer and she knew she must hide. "The fire's out and there's a chill in the air."

"I'll get some brush." He smiled at her. Then, with the ghost of a bow he left the little clearing and went to gather some kindling. The moment he was gone Katie fastened on her sandals and with a quick tug at Tommy Dog she ran into the forest in the opposite direction.

She felt she'd come quite close, and it frightened her. She'd tried to see Tavish differently, to like him if she could, but she'd given her heart to Tom, and she had no room for another man. For the rest of this night, at least, she'd put herself where Tavish would not come across her. She looked for a little hidden patch where she could lie low like a squirrel till the sun rose.

As soon as she'd gone a good distance from the campsite she stopped to rest and take in her surroundings. The ground was covered by a thick mat-like grass. Above her the stars twinkled like drops of dew on a frosty morning. The trees at her side stood like spectral sentinels. Almost she remembered this spot. There was a moment of resonance as her mind and her memory became one. She had been here before. Looking about she recognized each twisting branch and every trailing tendril of moss. This was a magic spot. How had she known?

"I said we'd meet again, and it's a fair night you've chosen to resume the acquaintance."

It was the woman from the night of Madam Lanchester's formal dance, the night she now thought of as the last of her old life. She had a new life now and in this new life were many risks and a multitude of uncertainties. Here was one now.

"The dance is just beginning," said Deirdre.

Katie heard soft music borne on the still air. "I've only now put on my sandals." Her feet were moving of their own volition.

"How very fortunate." Deirdre held out her hand. Tommy gave a growl and then laid his head on his twisted limbs. Katie looked at Deirdre's hand. Then, not certain why, she placed her hand in the other woman's. They danced. Much to her surprise, Katie found she knew the steps. Indeed, she found she'd always known them. She could feel other dancers in the pattern. She looked around and there they were, the others, all her sisters, throughout the forest, dancing together. The music, the moonlight and the rhythm of the dance all meshed to make a mystical moment of magic.

But what was this? Something was wrong. There was a disturbance, some roughness in the wood. A man, she thought she knew him, held some kindling for a fire. He looked about, distracted.

His harsh voice rasped, "Katie . . .?" Her name sounded vile in his grating voice. "Where'd you go?" She took the next two steps in the sorcerous gavotte, and turned.

"Pay him no mind," said Deirdre. The man had tossed the kindling to the ground and now was looking intently at the track Katie had left. Katie laughed at the distress written on his face. He muttered something to himself she couldn't make out. But his actions upset the pattern she and her sisters were treading out. He moved violently in her direction. He looked straight at her. She saw how ugly his face was, and the pain written on it made it uglier yet.

"Katie?" he called, and then passed her by. Tommy barked.

"He sees us not. You are invisible to his eye."

The man went thrashing away, desperately searching for something. Deirdre took Katie's hand and led her a little away from the dance. "So where are you off to this night?"

"I don't know."

"Oh, I think you do." They walked a little in silence. "Shall I take you there?"

"Methinks thou art a witch."

"I am a woman, as you are. You could be more."

"Could I now?"

"Obstinate hussy, you must kiss the Devil."

"And why's the Devil in such need of a kiss?"

"It's a little thing. Smaller than that. And you want to do it . . . Look, we've come to a stream. How shall we get across?"

A clear stream of water crossed their path. It was deep, and Katie saw the grass standing in the ground the water was flowing over, like looking through pure crystal.

"Is that a boat?" Katie saw a wooden box, like the coffins she'd been dreaming of, on the bank of the stream not far off.

"I think it may be. Shall we sit in it?" The two women sat in the wooden box. Tommy came in too and curled up at Katie's feet. Deirdre gave a little shove and they were out in the stream.

She said, "This little dog cannot cross." She picked Tommy up and she twisted him and made his legs stick out at odd angles. Then she held his head under the water till he was drowned. And after he was dead Katie saw his body drifting away down the stream, like a broken toy.

When they came to the other side of the stream Deirdre got out first, and then she helped as Katie got out of the boat. There was a great hall, and stairs that led up to it. There were just seven steps in the stairway and when they'd gone up it they could see for miles and miles all around. Katie realized she was looking out at the world and its grandeur, and she could see all the human creatures in their sordid situations. She saw wars being fought, and she saw ill-tempered children throwing tantrums, and she saw many other things, and she saw that a whitewash had been laid over all men, but it had come off now and she could see them clear, the pushing, self-protective, malodorous, carnivorous, lecherous puppets they were. A man came and stood beside her. He was a very fine man and he wore a scarlet coat with silver buttons. Her gown swirled around her feet and it had gold buttons that reflected the man standing next to her. He was an elegant man and all things were contained in him. This was the man she'd been born for. He took Katie's hand, and kissed her fingers, and gave her a deep and a courteous bow. Then he did something she'd not expected. He plucked a pomegranate from a tree at his side and handed it to her. She took the pomegranate and as she did she realized she had a ravenous and a voracious hunger on her, so she opened the pomegranate and put the seeds in her mouth and ate them. Then she took the man's hand. She knew she was making a mistake, but little did she care. She wanted to be all things for this man. There was a power and a passion in him that could not be controlled. She saw this in his eyes, also she saw it in the way he smiled, and it was reflected in the jewels and the buckles that he wore. And he went to kiss her on the lips, but full well she knew what tomfooleries he'd be up to, so she said, "Not at this time. There is no urgency. I think I will withhold my kiss."

The music stopped. She looked in his eyes and she looked at his smile and they weren't what they had been before.

"Then why did you come?" the man said. "You've partaken of my hospitality. Now here you must stay till either you give me your kiss, or else I give you leave to go. And never will I give you leave."

And Katie said, "I came because this woman asked me." Deirdre smiled and curtsied. "But why she'd ask me I cannot say. I'd think she'd rather ask a man than ask me. But she doesn't ask a man and I think I know the reason for it. If she asked a man, the man will have her teach him all her magic tricks and then he'll use them against her to lock her in the closet. He'll want to marry her without the payment of a bride price and when she has a daughter he'll want to marry her too. He'll want her to tell him his future, and then he'll lie with her in many filthy ways and enjoy himself in a manner not becoming. So that's why she'll not ask a man and she'll content herself with you who only wants a kiss. And I haven't even a kiss to give you. Sure I've given my kiss to another and he's taken it with him far across the sea, so I've naught for you."

At this the man disappeared in a nimbus of wrath and a sulphurous flash that left a scorch of pure black where he'd stood. But Katie, sure as he'd said, had to stay. Her fate it was to remain in that shadowy land till he'd give her leave to go, and never would he give her leave. So she watched as day passed after day across the world below, enduring the passing months and wheeling seasons. She saw the people coming and going in their furious errands and their tireless rituals. And all the while the baby grew within her stomach. And when the day came she gave birth, but it was a shrunken, misformed thing with sticks for arms and stones for eyes and she didn't like it at all. So the man, who was the Devil, put the baby in his crocodile jaws she'd not seen before and he ate it all up.

Still Katie withheld her kiss. She'd grown to be a haughty lady and lived many years so. She found she could order the other witches about. She could do this for the simple reason there was nothing she wanted them to do. She told them to dance, and Deirdre and the others danced round her at her will, but truly there was nothing she wanted of them. She was the queen of all evil, and the Devil was her consort, but still she withheld her kiss.

One day she went down the stairway of seven steps and walked in the land below. A knight in foul armor, much rusted, came her way. She said to him, "Whither are you bound, and what is your name?"

"I am bound for the battle that all must lose, and I haven't a name, for I am the child that you bore and never was I granted a christening."

"How can that be? I saw that child eaten and by the Devil."

"The Devil has a womb also and also gives birth. And I am the child that the Devil consumed and gave birth to. You see my armor all dented and rusty for I've been in battle for the worser side. And now my day is done and I am for the defeated dust which is what we all become." And with those words he passed and was gone.

Now she looked and saw that all those round her were old and gray and falling into decay. She also was old and her hair was faded and hoar. So she went down to the stream she'd crossed before, but now it was a mighty river and it was deep and broad and the waves on it were fierce with whitecaps and much spray. She looked for the little wooden boat she'd used before, and after a while she found it, but it was old and fallen apart. She did her best to put it together and then dragged it to the shore and sat in it, just as she had so many years ago, and let it take her across the river. But it was an old boat and the wood was rotten and no one had taken care of it for such a long time and the waves tossed it mercilessly and in the middle of the river it fell apart and Katie went into the water. She sank down and down and down and there was no bottom to the river. And then she saw there was a gap, like a thick black line at the bottom of the river and all the water was flowing out of it and the water started to shake and she heard her name being called, "Katie . . . Katie . . ."

She woke up and Tavish was shaking her. The sun was just peeping over the horizon. The air was filled with the gladsome sound of birdsong. A new day was just beginning.

"Katie, oh thank God I found you." He put his arm around her. "Why did you wander away? It was on account of me, I'm guessing."

"No, Tavish . . ."

"I fear it was."

"I don't know."

"Oh, I'm sorry. All night I've been cursing myself for an idiot. I wouldn't be the cause of any hurt coming to you. I'm the greatest idiot God ever made. You know you're safe with me."

"I'm sorry, Tavish. I forgot."

"Or was there someplace you wanted to go?"

"I don't know . . . I thought there was a place I had to get to. When I got there there was nothing for me after all . . ." Truly she was bewildered.

They broke their fast, then bundled up their few belongings and tied them to Neddy's back. That was when they discovered Tommy Dog was gone. In the night he'd followed Katie out of the camp, but where he'd wandered off to later they had no way of telling. After much calling for him and much time spent looking, eventually they set off, hoping he would find his way to them, and proceeded in the direction of Kashahar.

CHAPTER NINETEEN
LOST BASTARD ISLAND

IT HAD ORIGINALLY been built as a jail, and somewhere deep in its interior there were still a few dank, musty cells, long disused. It was said that on nights when the wind was high, rattling the battlements and howling round the turrets, you could still hear the screams of the inmates, the original lost bastards who had bequeathed the island its name. When the need arose for a munitions depot the spot had been deemed favorable for a number of reasons. Its position on an island made it easily defensible. It would not be subject to attacks from the Indians, since they did not inhabit the isle. The bed of granite that formed the island, and that lay just beneath the windswept grass, occasionally visible in rocky outcrops of moss-covered gray, was ideal for the depot's walls. And finally it was far enough from any human habitation that in case of the ordnance being accidentally ignited the resulting death toll could be tolerated.

The munitions depot had been constructed in two distinct stages. The first stage, shortly after the army was stationed in Port Jay, was the erection of a stronghold to house the arsenal, at least that portion of it the army did not immediately require. The depot was a short distance from the shores of Lost Bastard Sound, where there were boats that could quickly distribute the munitions to any spot along the coast. In addition, a gunnery was built housing artillery which could be used to protect the merchant crafts in the Sound, and to keep the pirates and privateers at a safe distance. Things stood this way for many years.

When General Hobsbawm took command he looked at what had been done and wondered why the army had chosen to place most of its artillery on an uninhabited island far from any sites of strategic significance, where the guns were aimed at open water.

Surveying the landscape round Port Jay his eye fell on Windswept Hill, a high elevation in the midst of the Forgotten Forest, a perfect spot if one wanted to keep an eye on the Indians. So his first order of business upon taking up his command had been to order a road constructed from Port Jay to Windswept Hill and a battery built atop said hill. As his scouts and engineers were taking steps to carry out these orders a letter arrived from the King. The King did not have much reputation as a correspondent, so those instructions he did communicate were felt to be of very high importance indeed. The letter, after much highly polished and unavoidable rodomontade touching on the King's exemplary benevolence and his humble servant Hobsbawm's diligent attention to duty, informed Hobsbawm of a purported breakthrough in the science of ballistics. The engineers in the royal gun works had assured him they were now able to build cannons that could fire shells containing inflammable substances and hit targets more than a mile distant. More than a mile! A few tests had been undertaken in isolated spots so as not to alert the spies that infested the military, and the tests had confirmed what the engineers were saying. It brought back memories of the King's youth when he had fired broadsides from the toy cannon in the Hawksbill Tower clear over the royal bridle trail onto his sister Amberwax's daffodil plot, wreaking untold damage on the unfortunate daffodils. These guns, the King went on to say, would overthrow the existing balance of power in the old country, and he was looking forward to the opportunity to train them on his enemies, the nations that heretofore had held him in check. However, before upending the delicate balance of power that currently held sway, and initiating a war certain to result in millions of fatalities and the complete revision of the borders that had existed for the past few hundred years, he wanted a test of what these guns could accomplish in actual warfare. What he had in mind was a war that could be waged as a trial of the guns' power. So he had searched the globe, scrutinizing all his colonial holdings, in search of the ideal spot for such a war, and at last had found on Lost Bastard Island a gunnery and a munitions depot suitable for his purpose. Indeed, it was as if the site had been prepared with amazing foresight. The Indians were on the mainland, separated from the guns by only a mile of water. It would be possible to lob shells clear across the Sound to where the Indians were known to live. They could be bombarded pitilessly, rather like Amberwax's daffodils. He thought this would serve as an excellent demonstration of the fate that awaited any enemies so benighted as to offer resistance.

So the gunnery on Windswept Hill never got built, and instead the arsenal on Lost Bastard Island ended up being rebuilt much stronger than before in order to house the powerful new cannons that were brought from the old country. They were made of triple-refined steel, with muzzles that could be raised or lowered, depending on the target. They were so massive, they couldn't be deployed with the army like ordinary artillery. They were put in one place, and there they'd stay. These new guns were given the name 'Hercules cannons' out of respect for their range and power. The munitions depot was built up into a sturdy bastion, surrounded by a series of bunkers and entrenchments. A palisade was erected, and within it was the gunnery.

Recently, a large armed force had been raised and was stationed in barracks built at the depot, under the command of Colonel Milquetoast, a renowned veteran of many colonial campaigns. General Hobsbawm had placed this force here in anticipation of the war he planned to conduct against the Indians. When all was ready this force was to be convoyed across the Sound and unleashed against the natives. Pending the arrival of that day the depot was a busy place where the shouted commands of drill sergeants, the staccato crack of rifle fire and the rhythmic stamping of marching feet were heard from first light till long after the fall of darkness.

A few weeks' prior to the date of the anticipated convoy a short man with a broad-brimmed hat had spent some time on Lost Bastard Island. He had befriended a young guard at the postern gate who had a fondness for rum and strong opium. The guard had been unaware of these proclivities prior to the traveling man's arrival but had now acquired a heightened appreciation for the true nature of temptation, and was excited by the role it was to play in his career. It was now understood that the gate would be left unlocked for some hours on a certain morning. The guard swore with great solemnity that this was to be the case and the traveling man, although initially distrustful – after all, how much reliance could be placed on the word of a man who consumed such tremendous quantities of opium — had decided in this case to hope for the best. The young guard had not had the heart to inform him that the key to the gate had found employment as a cheese knife and been irretrievably lost several years earlier, and so, to prevent the gate's accidentally becoming locked it was at all times kept ajar by an empty canister used as a door stop.

So, on the evening prior to the date of the convoy Fergus found himself seated on the back of the black stallion, trotting behind the stranger as he approached Storm Panther's hogan. All the way from Kashahar, Fergus had been thinking over the events he'd been involved in since becoming the stranger's companion. He was fitting it together with what he'd been shown the night of the full moon in that strange house where they'd stayed. It occurred to him that perhaps every man, though he might think himself free, only served for the cruel sport of dark powers, and was unknowingly trapped in a labyrinth of evil intent. But then he decided that had to be the nuttiest idea he'd ever had, so he forgot all about it.

As they drew close they saw a brave standing outside the hogan. The stranger dismounted and spoke with him, then called Fergus to his side. "Storm Panther is within," he said. "He's been smoking the holy mushroom and seeking guidance from his dreams. We come now to a tipping point. I don't know how long I'll be with him, but you stay here. Look after the horses, and no matter what happens, don't go anywhere." Then he went inside.

Fergus sat and looked at the brave who stood outside the hogan's door. The brave stared unwaveringly straight ahead. The silence of the evening and the brave's air of watchful intensity gave Fergus a distinct chill all down his spine. He tried one thing or another to relieve his fretful sense of anxiety, drawing patterns in the dirt with his heels, or gnawing on the end of a stick. Once or twice he thought to start up a conversation, but couldn't think of anything to say. Eventually he asked, "You mind if I sing a little?" The brave didn't move a muscle. So Fergus took out his banjo and resumed where he'd left off on the ballad he was composing. By now it was well over three

thousand verses. He'd forgotten what it had been about to start with.
This was what he sang:

He was strolling down the street
When a splendid angel he chanced to meet
Who told him that was where he'd stay
For seven years and a single day.

"Oh, angel, did you really plan
To halt the travels of this man?
For if —"

At this point the brave, without speaking a word, walked over to
Fergus and took the banjo out of his hands. He broke the neck into
three pieces. He tore the strings with his teeth. He took the body of
the banjo and broke it once, twice over his knee and then threw the
discarded fragments onto the ground.

"Not much of a music lover, huh?"

The brave pissed on the broken fragments of the banjo.

"Nope, didn't think so."

Inside the hogan the traveling man was conferring with Storm
Panther. He was talking about the guns of Lost Bastard Island and
the soldiers lodged there. Storm Panther had only recently acquired
twenty rifles, which he had distributed among his warriors. He had
thought this made a great addition to the might of Half Moon's forces, but he realized now he had been deluded and that his twenty rifles
were as useless as twenty blades of grass against the power General
Hobsbawm could muster. He cursed the great delay that had come
to the Indians' attack, the paralysis that had overtaken Half Moon,
the stupor in which they had sat for so many days, allowing the army
to recruit more men and grow ever stronger. He saw that the Indians were fated to die in great numbers, and that the battle they were
planning would lead inevitably to their undoing.

Yet the stranger held out hope. It was a crazy plan, but the plans
that were not crazy were certain to fail. The stranger laid out his
idea, striding about the hogan, his arms windmilling as he made his

points. Storm Panther remained seated, his arms clasped on his chest before him, a rock in the stranger's rushing stream.

"It must be this instant," said the stranger, "while the soldiers are still there. The blast will destroy the guns, but just as important it will turn near a half of Hobsbawm's troops into dust and flinders."

"Any who go will not be coming back," said Storm Panther. This was the crux. They looked at one another. There was a long silence.

"It must be a stout lad that goes. Whom would you send?"

"You think I am so poor-spirited I would send another to do what I must do? I will go myself."

"It is for you to say."

"Truly it is not. It has been said already by the force that shapes our fates. I cannot say to another, you must die in my place. That would not be me speaking."

"It's a thing leaders often say. They are needed to lead; they must stay alive. Who will look after the tribe if you go?"

"I have brought up Dark Owl ever since he was born to be pre-pared for that task."

"But even so you're the man that does it, I do not think you can do this alone. Perhaps you should take one or two to accompany you. It would be a great misfortune if the quest failed for lack of a second rifle, and I am sure there are those who would go."

"Fleet Cougar would go, but I will not ask this of him. He has still a squaw and a young pup. My only companion will be solitude."

"Truly you know best." The stranger stood very still. An aware-ness hung in the air. Storm Panther came to the realization that he was going to go to Lost Bastard Island and ignite the ammunition that was stored there. There was no other way to save the Indians. Once he had made this decision he was – he had almost said at peace, but it was not peace. Peace would come after. What he felt was a great intensity, a hunger. He knew he was going to die. He had al-ways known this in an abstract way, but now he foresaw exactly how and when it was to occur, and that it was to be the result of what was done by his hand. He knew he had made a decision, that his life would be used for a purpose. His life was a tool he was putting to use to accomplish something great and of an importance far beyond his individual survival. It was not something he was throwing away, like a worn-out plaything. His death was not a nihilistic rejection of life resulting from a personal anomie. This was a necessary step which would allow him to triumph over an enemy he detested. At the same time he felt like a climber on a steep ascent, up the wall of a cliff, or on a tall tree, who pauses and makes the mistake of looking down. He saw that all his life he had taken care to look only straight ahead. But now he had looked down, and he was falling under the enchantment of the swooning temptation that was his death. The distance between his lofty perch and the hard, unyielding ground called to him. He pictured himself letting go and surrendering to the irresistible pull of gravity. Now that he had looked down he was set apart from other men who still lived in the world of looking straight ahead, the very world he was dying to protect. And he realized that this world was a fragile artifact and that the comfortable mask of reason it wore was only visible if one kept one's gaze fixed straight ahead, and that the inhabitants of this world were like men on a high wire flung across a chasmous abyss, sleep walking as they put one foot in front of another, where one wrong glance could lead to madness, derangement and lunacy.

These thoughts led him to consider his son. His last wish, before he destroyed himself, was to set his relationship with his son to rights. "I will say farewell to my son, and then I will go with you." He took a spear decked with feathers that stood nearby and stamped it on the ground. The brave entered from outside, gave a short bow to the traveling man and then kneeled before Storm Panther. "Bring my son Dark Owl. Tell him I would speak with him." The brave departed.

When he returned he brought with him a young man. Dark Owl stood apart, his face dour and brooding. He had been in the act of wooing the maiden Distant Star, but his wooing was not going well. Always he found her flighty and unreasonable, and the more she acted so the greater was his desire. At this moment he was impatient to return to her, since he had little interest in what his father had to say. Of late he had noted a growing feebleness in his father, a decline in both his wits and his strength. He had considered not coming in answer to his call, to make it clear the leash his father held was no longer tied to his collar, but he thought the outward show of deference should be retained at least for the moment.

"My son," said Storm Panther, "the time has come when I must leave you. Always when I brought you up I have prepared you for this moment. I am placing the welfare of the tribe in your hands. This is a signal and a solemn responsibility, but you are equal to the task."

"Wait – you're leaving?"

"Yes. I am going to rejoin the Great Spirit, where I will look down on all that is done from a place beyond space and time."

"Father, I am sure you will be with us for many more years."

"No. Tomorrow you will see a great blow struck against our enemies. That will be the sign I am no longer with you. I am departing from this camp tonight; that is why it is important that we speak . . . I hope you have found me to be a good father. It has been my task to discipline you. I have not always been able to be kind when I would wish to be so. It was needful to make you strong, so that you could follow me and fulfill the duty to which you were born. I believe you understand this."

"Father, since this is the last time we will be speaking, I will not hide from you the truth. I was brought up to be dishonest in your presence, since your self-esteem was a feeble reed that required constant care and was nurtured by my subservience; but the truth is I have always found you to be stubborn, irascible and stupid. The first lesson I learned at your knee was how to find pleasure in my own way and hide it from your view. But now I can tell you bluntly: you are not the man you think you are."

"My son, I had hoped for better from you, but truly I am not surprised. I have witnessed your craven disposition in the past. It is permissible to show it to me, but I would caution you against showing it to others. The tribe has need of you. For their sake you must be strong as I have been strong. I have been a mighty warrior and an indomitable support for our clan. Even today, though I am now in my sixth decade I can outfight any man in this tribe, and in the running of the ponies always I come first. This I accomplish through sheer force of will, since it matters not which pony I mount, I win."

"Father, these things simply are not true."

"They are true. What I say cannot be denied. I can call fire into being with only the sound of my voice, and I can cure the sick by the laying on of my hands."

"Often you have boasted of these things, but I have never seen them performed. Just two days ago some came to you to be healed and you beat them off with a stick."

"You know I cannot summon the powers when I am disrespected. I did not tolerate disrespect from them and I will not tolerate it from you."

"Since we will never speak again, I will not hide from you the truth. I have never respected you. And I am glad for the chance to say this to your face. If you die tomorrow I will always remember you as you are now: angry and indignant to the point of apoplexy. So filled with rage you can barely speak."

Storm Panther grabbed the feathered spear and used it as a club, hitting Dark Owl over the head. "You are not my son," he shouted. Dark Owl pounced on him and knocked him to the ground. The two men wrestled with one another, spitting and kicking in their fury. The traveling man and the brave jumped on them and separated them from one another before they could inflict any serious harm.

"Fleet Cougar," said Storm Panther to the brave who was restraining him, "you should have been my son. My wife must have slept with a weasel and gave birth to this one."

The traveling man was holding back Dark Owl. "You two are more alike than you know."

Eventually Fleet Cougar and the traveling man were able to calm them down. Fleet Cougar then saddled two horses, one for Storm Panther and the other for himself. The two of them mounted and, joined by the traveling man with Fergus, set off for the shore.

They rode through the night, coming to the water's edge under cover of darkness. There was a single canoe waiting, beached on the shore. Once they dismounted, Fleet Cougar knelt at Storm Panther's feet.

"I have shaken off the fancies of the night, and the ride has left my mind clear. I will go with you. Together we will do what must be done." As Storm Panther stood undecided, Fleet Cougar added, "You will need another paddle. It is a far distance you go."

"This task has been decreed for myself alone. I say this not in pride, but in just forbearance. Go home to your squaw and your pup. They yet have need of you."

"My squaw and I have long since said all we have to say to one another, and my pup I do not think is mine. There is no one closer to me than yourself. If I cannot stand beside you I have no place to be."

Storm Panther placed his hand on Fleet Cougar's head and looked for some moments into the distance. Finally he said, "As you say, it is a far distance we go. Your paddle will be welcome." The traveling man then gave Storm Panther some petards and incendiary devices he had prepared. Storm Panther took those he could comfortably carry. Some he gave to Fleet Cougar. They would use these to get through any gates they might find closed against them. Also each had a rifle. Storm Panther intended to use a shot from the rifle to ignite the fatal spark once they arrived at the gunpowder room.

They sat in the canoe, Storm Panther in the stern and Fleet Cougar in the bow, and took their paddles in hand. Then, easing into the Sound, they turned to wave farewell to the traveling man and Fergus, left on shore. As they turned back to put their paddles in the water Storm Panther saw a third figure seated on the thwart in the middle of the canoe. He hadn't seen him arrive, but here he was, his paddle in the water, a figure made of shades of darkness. His face was hidden, one shadow inside another, and at the heart of these shadows were his eyes. They were completely black with no sign of iris or pupil, black orbs that regarded Storm Panther with an uncanny vision incapable of sight. No reflections could be seen on the surface of those orbs. There was nothing, only a blackness that looked out and searched and seeing all, saw that it also was nothing.

"Death," said Storm Panther, "of all the gods, truly you are the most punctual."

Death spoke, but its speech was a nearly silent mumble, a garbled jumble of sounds, hinting of a terrifying threat and signifying nothing.

"Had you far to come, or is all distance the same?"

Again the sad mumble, fading into silence.

So they had a companion unlooked for and the three of them paddled the canoe across the still waters of the Sound, observed by none but the countless stars. As they traveled, Storm Panther spoke softly, letting his words drift into the night. He spoke of the many joys he had known in life and of the many heartaches also and the mysteries he'd left unsolved and the nightmares he'd endured and the romances and the dreams he'd had, all of them making the one great dream that had been the life he'd led. He mourned the ending of this dream and as he did he thought he saw a tear fall and slowly drift down Death's cheek. All this was done as they paddled across the Sound, bringing destruction to Lost Bastard Island.

At one point they saw the lights of a fleet of ships looming out of the night to their left. These ships were going opposite to the direction of Storm Panther's canoe. These were the Nemesis and other ships of the line, convoying the soldiers who had been stationed on Lost Bastard Island across the Sound, the second pincer in General Hobsbawm's grand deployment. As the ships passed in darkness some note, albeit very little, was taken of the canoe off their port side. Two midshipmen sharing a mug of grog were out. Happening to glance in the direction of the canoe, one said, "Look, there's something there."

His companion leaned casually over the rail. "I don't see anything."

"It's a canoe, an Indian canoe. I'm certain of it."

"Oy, Harry, toss that spyglass over here."

"I wonder what it's doing there?"

"Oh, I see . . . That's not a canoe. That's a walrus."

"Don't hit me on the back of the head. I hate it when you do that."

"Well I can't believe you can't recognize a bloody walrus when you see one."

"Are you sure? Give me the spyglass."

"Here."

"Woops!"

"Oh crikey!"

There was the sound of a splash.

"Well now that's in the drink."

"In any event, I'm certain it's a walrus."

"We've gone past it anyhow."

Coming into shore they silently beached their canoe and disembarked. They picked the canoe up and carried it to a nearby sycamore, where they concealed it under the leafy branches. The sun was just rising in the east. They each checked their rifle to make sure a bullet was loaded and ready to fire, then they crossed the field of waving grasses between the Sound and the walls of the depot.

The convoy had already left, so one portion of the traveling man's plan would not be achieved. But they were probably lucky this was the case, since the barracks being now nearly empty there were very few sentinels on patrol, and those that were were exhausted by the exertions of the night, when the troops had been loaded onto the ships. This helped the two of them elude detection till they had nearly reached their goal.

Coming to the postern gate Storm Panther saw it was open, as the traveling man had told him it would be, so they entered and proceeded down a hall with walls of stone, gradually giving way to bricks and mortar. Storm Panther led the way. The traveling man had taught him the path to follow to the gunpowder room, which lay at the very center of the arsenal. It was fortunate Storm Panther had studied this path well, for there were many twists and turns through that stony maze. On either side were corridors leading to unknown places, dark halls and iron doors shut tight against them. Times the light was bright as day, times so dim they barely saw their way. They encountered no one, but imagined watchers in every shadow. Quickly they walked, their moccasins making no sound.

They were nearing their destination when, hastily turning a corner, they saw a guardsman stretched across the floor, his head resting on his right arm. As they cautiously approached he raised his head and gave them a bleary look.

"Hello," he said. "You're dressed funny."

Fleet Cougar raised his rifle to shoot, but Storm Panther, sensing the guardsman posed no threat, stopped him with a hand to his chest. "Are you alone?"

"Course not. You guys are here." He gave a chuckle, then looked around. "The others must have left. Spoil sports."

Storm Panther gave a glance to Fleet Cougar and then pointed his head in the direction they were going.

As they were leaving, the guardsman got to his feet. "Wait. There's another bottle. I'm sure there is."

"Keep your voice down," said Storm Panther.

"You don't understand. I have to get to my wedding." He gave a cockeyed smile. "Won't you help me?"

The request was altogether ludicrous, but the guardsman looked so bereft the Indians had to struggle with their instinctive urge to help. Fleet Cougar asked, "Where do you need to go?"

"I'm not sure. I think it's . . . this way," pointing to a door. "Please help."

"Here." Fleet Cougar helped him towards the door.

Storm Panther clucked impatiently. "We can't. Someone could be coming."

The guardsman looked over his shoulder to where he'd been lying and said, "There's blood. There. On the floor."

Fleet Cougar looked about. "Where?"

"Can't you see it? The floor is slick with blood." He wailed softly in fear and confusion.

"Keep quiet. You'll bring others." He grabbed the guardsman and hustled him to the door. He opened it as the guardsman's wails grew louder and shoved him through, then ran back to Storm Panther.

The guardsman abruptly reemerged through the door with a pistol in his hand. His air of dazed bewilderment had been dropped like a mask. He fired a shot that caught Fleet Cougar in the shoulder, shouting, "Die, you cursed Indians!" Fleet Cougar fell. Storm Panther raised his rifle and got off a shot at the guardsman, but before he could do so the guardsman had fired another shot that hit Fleet Cougar in the head and then disappeared through the doorway shouting, "There's Indians inside the fort!"

Storm Panther knelt beside his fallen companion.

"I am finished," said Fleet Cougar. "I have just a few breaths left. Leave me."

"No, I will not leave you behind."

241

"Already pursuit is forming. I will lie here and slow it down, but you must go ahead."

"I am so sorry, my brother."

"Be glad. You are able to do what you came here to do. Go."

So Storm Panther left him, but it was not very long before he heard voices raised in alarm behind him, and then the sound of shots being exchanged.

He was in a long hallway leading to a flight of stairs down to the gunpowder room. At the foot of the stair stood two sentries who shouted to him to stop. He stopped just long enough to raise his gun and shoot. He saw Death seize one of the sentries. The other fired his gun, and Storm Panther felt the pain of the bullet in his side. He rushed forward and battered the man, knocking his head against the wall. Then, looking back, he saw his pursuers reaching the top of the stair. Before him was the entrance to the gunpowder room, blocked by a stout, metal door. He drew forth a petard the traveling man had given him and placed it at the foot of the door. He lit the fuse. Then, fighting the pain in his side, stepped back far enough to be safe from the blast. He turned to fire at the soldiers streaming down the steps. Putting the rifle to his shoulder, he shot as many as he could, but took two bullets to his legs, and fell to the floor. The petard behind him exploded, sending fragments of stone and mortar blazing towards him. He hadn't gotten far enough from the blast, and he was covered in rubble, but at least the pursuing soldiers were set back on their heels and the door to the gunpowder room was shattered. Looking into the room he saw the massed munitions, kegs of gunpowder, shell after shell filled with inflammable material. He tried to stand, but he no longer had legs, only the unspeakable agony of broken bone and throbbing pain. He saw Death, with not a hint of speculation in those ghastly orbs, holding out a hand.

"Death," he whispered, "once I take your hand I am done. I must do one thing first." He tried to crawl through the shattered remnant of the doorway, but already the first soldier from the stairs was upon him.

Death spoke. This time his words were clear, but only Storm Panther heard them. Then, taking Storm Panther's hand he lifted him up and held the rifle steady. Storm Panther aimed it through the blasted door and fired, but nothing happened. There were no more bullets.

"I can call fire into being with the sound of my voice." Just as the first soldier to reach him grabbed his shoulders and brought him to the floor, he called out the word to ignite the fatal spark.

CHAPTER TWENTY
THE FIGHT IN THE FOREST

THE BLAST WAS HEARD for many miles up and down the Coast. Teeth were rattled and ear drums concussed. Bits and pieces of the guns came raining down on Indians dancing their war dance under the fragrant boughs of the hawthorn trees in the Forgotten Forest; on a very footsore Tom trudging along the Coast Road in an old pair of boots that were giving him blisters; on fishermen trimming their sails and casting their nets in the waters off Lost Bastard Island. All the silver bells in Deirdre's bower deep in the woods were set to ringing. The warriors surrounding Half Moon leapt to their feet with a resounding whoop of triumph. It even woke General Hobsbawm as he slept uncomfortably on his cot in the tent that had been hastily erected the night before to serve as company headquarters.

The adjutant who had been sleeping at the tent's entrance came in, bringing some gritty morning light with him. He lit an oil lamp and hung it on a hook. "A tremor passed through the encampment, sir. I suspect there might have been an earthquake."

"I thought I heard an explosion," said the General.

"You were snoring again."

"You've got some lip. I would advise you . . . Oh the hell with it." He'd get another adjutant. He sat up. A blue kerchief was tied around his head. He'd suffered from a headache all the day before and he'd adopted the cure recommended by his old nurse when he was very young, although he'd never known it to help, a kerchief to provide relief. "I don't snore."

"How do you know? You're asleep. Here's water." The adjutant set a bucket of water down near the General's cot.

"An earthquake, I think, would be a bad omen." The General rose and placed a three-legged stool next the bucket. "I'm going

244

to need the report from Captain Musgrove. And while you're at it could you go round Colonel Dunder's tent and ask him to poke his head in? I have a question for him." The adjutant left as General Hobsbawm sat on the stool and proceeded to shave. As he ran the razor across his face, with his other hand he pulled a deal table with a map of the Forgotten Forest over to his side. The army had many maps of the Forest, no two alike. The Forest's reputation as a place where all paths went astray and all travelers were lost was well established. Everyone knew tales of wanderers who'd entered the Forest and were never seen again. And it was thought that it wasn't always Indians who were responsible for their disappearance. But what other nameless scourge it was that had done away with them none would say. Most of the army's maps dated from a time when the scouts had made an attempt to survey the Indian trails. This was part of a project, later abandoned, to put an artillery post on Windswept Hill. All the maps of the Forest were similar in outline, but differed in countless details. They all showed the glens that were sprinkled through the Forest like a giant's footsteps. Also Windswept Hill was a notable landmark. But there was much less agreement when it came to other topographical features, such as the bogs and various patches of swampy terrain, and many small lakes and streams that seemed to come and go with the seasons. On the map Hobsbawm was looking over, the major Indian paths had been drawn with great clarity in maroon-colored ink, like veins of blood superimposed on the green of the Forest. Once he'd concluded his shave, Hobsbawm shifted his attention from the map to a large piece of broken mirror in which he inspected his appearance as the adjutant, returning from his errand, shepherded Colonel Dunder and Captain Musgrove into the tent.

Captain Musgrove's beard was flecked with gray. He gave his report while standing at attention. "Last night the scouts spread out a bit and took in parts of the Forest we'll be passing through. There's nary an Indian between our camp and the Hill. They're all on the other side."

"There are Indians everywhere." The Colonel was in a rare mood. "Everywhere!" He could hardly hold still. He was one of those who actually enjoyed the fighting. He put up with the humdrum and discipline of military life just for the chance to devise martial strategies and inflict them on his wretched opponents. "Today's the day. I can almost smell them."

"With all due respect they aren't between here and the Hill. They're on the other –"

"Yes you said that."

"— side of the Hill and they've been there the better part of two weeks. "

"The other side of the Hill?" The General looked at the map. "That would be to the west? Dunder, where is our precise location?"

"We're in the Forest," he answered with a smile.

"Please, I need specifics. Can you point to the spot on this map?"

"Let me see . . . If I'd known this was to be an exercise in geography I'd have brought my sextant to get a good reading on the latitude."

"You have a sextant?" asked Musgrove.

"If they've been there the better part of two weeks," asked the General, "what have they been doing? Making preparations obviously, but what?"

"Last night, as we were pitching camp, I saw the last light of the sun as it set just behind the bluff of Windswept Hill," said the Colonel.

"Don't know," said Musgrove. "They had been building some machines like they were – "

"That would make us east nor'east, or, for all practical purposes, practically due east of the Hill. Can't do better without my sextant."

"But they seem to have abandoned that and gone on to do some excavating."

"By the way, did you hear that explosion this morning?"

"I've been informed," the General gave a look at his adjutant, "it was just my snoring."

"Then I'm damn glad I'm not sharing your tent."

"I thought it came from the direction of the sea," said Musgrove. "The Hercules guns was my passing thought, though I'm surprised we can hear them from this distance."

"That would depend on just what this distance is," said Hobsbawm. "I'm attempting to ascertain our exact location."

The Colonel joined him at the map. "Well, given the position of Windswept Hill, I would think we've been following this trail leading west, hmmm? And it has taken us to the spot we currently occupy, which would be this spot here."

"I see."

"So . . . if we continue on this trail we'll come to a fork. Do you agree, Captain Musgrove?"

"That's what the map says." The Captain removed his hat and rubbed his brow.

"At that point we will have the choice of this narrow path to the north side of the Hill, around the curve of the bluffs, beside this swampy terrain here, or we can take this other much wider trail which leads clear round the south side of the Hill. It's six of one half a dozen of the other in the end since both paths join up on the west side over here."

"Where the Indians are."

"They'll be waiting for us with their machines and their excavations – you did say excavations, didn't you?" asked the General.

"That's what it looked like."

"Undoubtedly they've been digging in. They'll have trenches and what not. So we should take the wider trail, even though it looks to be a bit longer."

"Yes," said Dunder. "Also that way we won't come near this swampy area which the mapmakers, surely in a moment of whimsy, have designated the Great Bog."

"It is a bog, I never sent any scouts in there," said Musgrove.

"Whimsical mapmakers, what next?" said General Hosbawm.

"Sir, is it your intention to attack the Indians today?" asked Musgrove.

"Yes."

"What about Colonel Milquetoast's force? Where are his regiments?"

"They should have been convoyed across the Sound during the night. They'll need a day to rest and restore their strength. Tomorrow they'll attack."

"Then shouldn't we wait so we can coordinate our attack with his? Wasn't that the point of this pincer operation?"

"Milquetoast's force is a contingency plan. It's important that we attack the Indians before he does."

"Why?"

"These Indians are going to be crushed. They have no cannons, no firepower, nothing. Bows and arrows. Milquetoast is a cunning little rat, and he's ambitious. He has his eye on chucking me out and putting himself in my position. If he gets any credit for the victory it'll only strengthen his hand."

"But if we attack before he does, the Indians will concentrate all their efforts on us. The fight will be a bloody one and we'll suffer greater casualties than if we wait for Milquetoast's force. Likely it'll be only a day."

"Battles are not fought in order to avoid casualties. I can't quite believe you haven't learned that by now."

"A soldier risks his life when he's on the battlefield. Of course we all know that. But he risks it for a cause. Surely battles are not fought in order to heap honors on the Generals."

"And yet whenever a battle is fought, the soldiers die and the General gets the glory. I'm sure it's just a coincidence." A bright red flush came to Musgrove's face. The General went on, "We have three regiments. That's more than enough to pound these savages into dust. I know what I'm up to; and you'll do what you're told."

"Yessir."

Hobsbawm tossed Dunder a smile as he strode from the tent, glancing at the shard of mirror and straightening his hat on the way out. He was followed by the others.

Outside, the army was coming awake. It was an awe inspiring spectacle. Everywhere was activity, bustle, purpose. A sea of red uniforms was on the move. Here and there were flecks of gray or brown or other homespun colors. These were the most recent recruits who'd joined after the uniforms had run out. But red was the color: a river of scarlet ran right through the woods. Colonel Dunder almost danced for joy.

At that same moment Half Moon, with Father Clumphy at his side, was leading a band of warriors on horseback across a high patch of bare rock near the summit of Windswept Hill. He had posted sentinels to look for signs of the witches as they advanced. He was still heart sore for Issoria and Vanessa, but he had locked all that in a tiny corner of his mind where he didn't always need to look at it. He did not understand how he had allowed that infatuation to possess him and rule his thoughts for so many days. Fortunately, the time he'd spent huddled in despair had not been wasted, as Black Crow and Wild Otter had given spirit to the Indians and led them in the work Deirdre had laid out. Now he was hoping he might encounter her again. He wanted to learn more of her tactics and get some help from her magic. He had received reports all day yesterday and even through the night of skirmishes that had taken place with some outlying forces of the army. These skirmishes were in the form of a volley of shots, a few arrows let fly, and then a quick retreat. There was no meaningful advantage to either side, but the times and places where these skirmishes occurred had established a pattern showing him the army was advancing towards the very place where he had laid his trap. *It is excellent,* he thought, *the way my enemies are lining up to be killed.* From where he stood he could look down on the Forest below as if it were a map, and plot the progress of General Hobsbawm's march. The army had progressed slowly, which was good, as it had allowed him time to make his final preparations.

Black Crow caught Half Moon by the arm and directed his view towards the west, where puffs of smoke were rising into the sky. Indians were using wet blankets to interrupt the flow of smoke from their fire, thus creating smoke signals. It was a language known of old by all the Indians of these woods and Half Moon read the message. "Witches spotted. Come quick."

"I cannot come so quickly as I would like," said Half Moon. "I must first deal with these soldiers in front of me." He knew his reunion with Issoria and Vanessa would be coming soon, and it would be all the sweeter for coming on the heels of his great victory over the white man. He rode his horse to a spot a little lower on the Hill where other warriors awaited him, wearing war paint and softly beating drums. When the braves saw him approach, they formed a semi-circle and awaited his words, and this is what he said:

"Black Crow, Wild Otter, Barking Dog, and all you others, all my brothers from all the tribes of the Forgotten Forest who are gathered here together, welcome! The Great Spirit has called us and we have come. He has entered into each one of us, and to each one of us He has given a purpose. And today we will all bring the purpose each one of us holds sacred inside himself, and we will create a great action – a thunder and lightning that will leave the white man houseless in this land.

"We all know why the white men must be driven out. There is little need to rehearse the litany of troubles they have brought. You recall when first they came, we welcomed them. We thought they were our dead returning to us. We thought they had forgotten language, so they spoke like birds. We embraced them and let them in. We helped them. But even then, helpless as they were, they showed us their scorn. They were never grateful to us for saving them when they arrived here with no food or supplies. They could not have survived the first winter without our help. And then after that more of them came on their gigantic canoes, more again and even more. And they stole from us, from us who had given what we had. When we helped them they showed their gratitude by killing us and driving us deep into the Forest . . . So now the time has come when all that will change. We will strike the white man today. We will strike him to the ground, and he will grovel before us and he will die!" There was a great cheer. "In their pride and their senseless arrogance they are this moment walking into our trap. And we will be there when the moment comes to strike off the heads they parade above us!" There was more cheering. Perhaps some of Half Moon's listeners thought his metaphors were a bit mixed, but they weren't there to nit-pick. "We have waited, all of us, for this moment. We have known it was coming. You all carry in your breasts the cause of this great battle. We will thrust our spears through the white man's chest! Our arrows will pluck out his eyes! He will fall to the ground and be trampled beneath our conquering feet! No trace of him will be left! We will defeat the white man and drive him back into the sea!!" There was another great cheer. When it died down, he went on. "There is, however, one white man who is different, one who in our eyes does good. I refer to my friend Clumphy." He held Clumphy's hand up for all to see. "It was he who came to me in my darkest hour and showed me the way. He has powers unlike those of other men. He is able to leave his body and communicate with spirits in other worlds. He is a prophet. He can foresee the future, and he has told me that today we will achieve our greatest triumph: a complete victory over the white man's army! He is a great shaman and what he says will come to pass. Clumphy, guide us. Show us your wisdom."

Clumphy's mind was blank, and now he awaited inspiration. Ever since he had reawakened Half Moon, Clumphy had been living in an ecstasy of sanctitude. He looked upon the Indians as so many dead souls, which it was his duty to bring to life. The Lord had blessed him by destroying everything he'd possessed. He was well aware that most men would not consider this a blessing, but he knew now what he hadn't known before, that just as he came into the world with nothing, so would he leave it. Everything must be given away and the last and greatest giving would be the gift of himself to God. All the lesser givings preceding that one partook of its holiness. Every taking was a sin and every acquisition a punishment. He thought sometimes of the family he'd been with on the evening of the fire. If they were not yet dead, he was certain the fire must have taken from them everything they'd had – all their possessions and their means of sustenance. They had been blessed as thoroughly as he, but it was a question whether they rejoiced in it as he did. They were probably wishing God would bless somebody else. They were probably wishing God would bless some of these Indians standing in front of him right now. But the truth was so simple it was impossible to understand. The less he had, the more he possessed. His possessions were not of this world. He could not point to them. They were inside him, invisible to everyone except himself. It was his task to bring this state of blessedness to the Indians, and to all men, but he hardly knew how to begin. How do you convince someone to give up everything he has in return for something invisible that no one else will comprehend? Surely he must seem insane to these people. He hoped God would show him the way.

Now there was a great silence as all waited for him to speak. Even the drummers stopped drumming. He looked at the assembled braves, their faces made hideous by garish war paint, wearing war bonnets of eagle feathers and necklaces made from the teeth of their enemies, some with scalps won in previous battles dangling beside their ears, their eyes lit with the fierce lust for blood. He realized he had nothing to say to them. Finally, he said, "The kingdom of Heaven is at work in us. We, who have been afflicted, are blessed by God's grace. Blessed are those who mourn. Blessed are those who have known sorrow for they will be comforted . . ." He trailed off. The Indians were getting restive, and Clumphy himself was tired of what he was saying. As he started to go on, Half Moon raised his arms and took the first two steps of the war dance. Clumphy said, "The earth is ours to inherit —" But none heard him now. The drums had started and the warriors were taking up the rhythm of the dance. Clumphy found himself swept up in the line of sweating, chanting Indians. All around him they stamped their feet and waved their spears and tomahawks in time to the beating of the drums. Half Moon led the warriors down the Hill to the trench they'd dug at the base of the bluff. Here they hid themselves behind mounds of dirt and clumps of bushes so they could not be seen from the trail only a foot or two away. One after another the Indians concealed themselves. There were almost ten thousand Indians lined up along a two and a quarter mile length of the trail, but after they had covered themselves with sod and clumps of brush anyone walking along the path would not have known they were there. Half Moon also distributed almost a thousand braves around the edges of the Great Bog, to trap any soldiers who would try to escape in that direction. His snare was well laid.

As this was going on, General Hobsbawm and Colonel Dunder, having arrived at the fork in the road they'd been contemplating that morning, were staring gloomily at a pair of massive toppled tree trunks blocking the path they had planned to take.

"We need horses and chains to haul those out of the way," said the General.

"There's not much point," said the Colonel. "The trail is little more than a muddy trough. It takes a lower course and it's been swamped by the recent rains." Indeed, it almost looked as though an excavation had been conducted along the course of the path, and the original sod had been removed and replaced by deep trenches that had become quickly flooded and full of brush. "However," he went on, indicating the other track to the right, "this is a good trail. This is higher. It's narrower, but at least the sand is tightly packed and makes for good, sound footing."

"But we won't be able to march nine men across. You won't be able to go more than six at a time. And you'll have to stretch out the baggage train if you want to allow room for the men to guard it."

"If we only go six at a time it'll take us forever to get round this hill."

"Here's what we'll do. We'll speed up by going both ways. You lead the Eighteenth Regiment through that narrow trail. I'll stay with the Seventeenth and Nineteenth and we'll see if we can't make our way through this broader passage. I know at this point it looks like a muddy ditch but it's bound to improve further on. We'll join up on the other side, where the Indians are. Take them from both directions."

Dunder didn't like this plan at all. "I'd advise against dividing the force in two."

"It makes perfect sense. Undoubtedly they're waiting for us and they think the narrowness of the passage will give them an advantage because we'll only be able to fight with the force at the head of the line. Probably what those smoke signals were all about. We won't be able to spread out and outflank them. That's why it's imperative that I force a passage through this other trail so I can come at them from the side and relieve you."

"I suppose you're right."

"They won't be expecting that."

Dunder was slowly being won over. "We'll have the Hill on one side and the Bog on the other so the only way they'll be able to come at us is along the road, either in front or behind. We'll only be able to fight them with a small portion of our strength but at least we won't have to look out for attackers from all sides."

So Hobsbawm gave the order to divide their command, Colonel Dunder leading one regiment round the north side of the Hill, while he led the other two regiments round the south. Hobsbawm's unit first had to deal with the tree trunks that blocked their path. Dunder's regiment had already marched away and disappeared into the Forest before the path was made passable. As Dunder had noted, the path was very muddy, but not so muddy that no progress could be made. The day was hot and over hot; a haze of flies hung in the air. The men did their best to protect themselves from the burning sun and General Hobsbawm was now using his blue kerchief to wipe the sweat from his brow. The caissons were getting stuck quite regularly and the horses were having a hard time pulling the cannons through the mire, so the line of troops moved slowly, with great difficulty and with an enormous amount of profanity and perspiration. All the men were becoming miserable and the horses were hanging their heads, when they heard some popping sounds in the distance, as if they were coming from the other side of the Hill. "What's that?" asked a private.

"Don't know."

Then there was a sustained rat-a-tat-tat. There was no mistaking the sound of rifle fire.

"There's fighting."

The word spread through the ranks. There was a fairly continuous sound of guns being fired now, muffled by the distance. Hobsbawm unloaded a mouthful of curses and dispatched his adjutant on horseback to find out what was going on, but before the adjutant could return a mounted cavalry officer arrived from the Eighteenth Regiment.

"We're ambushed!" shouted the officer. He told a terrible story of how, as the force had been advancing through the narrow passageway between the bluffs and the Great Bog they had been forced to walk only four abreast. The shoulders of the road were slippery and hard to see, and the marchers on the edge were constantly sliding off into the Bog. This had slowed them down and caused all sorts of problems for the cavalry, as the horses could never get a firm footing. Then, as the troops were strung out across a two mile passageway between the Hill and the swamp suddenly the world exploded. At one moment the woods had swayed in the still sunshine of a summer breeze, and at the next they were instinct with the dreadful rage of war. Thousands of Indians appeared as if erupting from the forest floor. Casting off the dirt and sod that had hidden them they emerged with bows and spears and proceeded to wreak terrible damage from behind the wall of branches and brush they had constructed. Other Indians, behind the ones responsible for the initial attack, sent many arrows arcing overhead towards the soldiers' position. The terrified soldiers were unprepared and were cut down in great numbers before they were able to load their guns and return fire. If they tried to run away they found themselves floundering helplessly in the Great Bog, which was thick with water, sinkholes, dense thickets of thorns and other obstacles, so they couldn't escape from the trap once the ambush was launched. The cavalry officer who brought news of this disaster had been near the rear of the march and had galloped as furiously as possible, trampling some of the infantrymen who were slow getting out of his way, to bring word to General Hobsbawm.

This was horrifying news. General Hobsbawm felt as if the fist of God had hammered him in the chest. He ordered the troops under his command to turn around at once and retrace their steps. After a great deal of struggle, late in the afternoon they found themselves back at the fork where they had split up in the morning. A few small detachments, all that was left of the Eighteenth Regiment, were trickling back from the ambush bearing tales of what was coming to be seen as an absolute massacre. With a large portion of the regiment trapped at the foot of the bluffs, the rest of the column had still been marching steadily along, unaware of the trap they were marching into, pressing their comrades further into the fray. Dunder had been in the vanguard and was among the first attacked but he'd been unable to send back word of the Indians' onslaught quickly. He relied on a horseman to deliver the word, but this was all but impossible given the narrowness of the path and the muddy condition of its shoulders, which caused the horse constantly to slip off the side of the road. There was nowhere for a horse to be ridden and the only roadway was clogged with the dead and the dying, so the horseman was unable to make any headway, and it wasn't till the disaster was already well in progress before the cavalry officer who apprised Hobsbawm of the attack was able to get away. At any rate, by the time Dunder realized the extent of the ambush, it was far too late for him to do anything about it. Everywhere he looked he saw more Indians coming from the depths of the Forest. The Indians that had been placed behind the first row of archers came flooding onto the road, smashing whatever resistance remained among the troops.

As the Indians swept ruthlessly into the column, Dunder was desperately attempting to form some sort of defense. But it seemed pointless, as all around he saw the friends and comrades he'd passed most of his life with being killed. Shortly after the start of the ambush he already understood he'd lost, but there was no place to run. With this in mind, and having heard blood-curdling stories of how the Indians tortured their captives, he decided to commit suicide. As the Indians pressed ever closer to the center of his column, he squinted at the summer sun, lingering in its lazy traversal of the afternoon sky, grasped his pistol in his hand, held it to his head and shot himself.

After Dunder was dead several of his men attempted to hide the body to keep it out of the hands of the Indians, but this proved useless. His body was eventually discovered and Half Moon, with a martial salute to his totem the great bear, took his scalp so he could send it round to the other Indian chiefs.

As word of Dunder's suicide was passed to the remaining soldiers, it destroyed the last shreds of their will to resist. Discipline broke completely, and the survivors of the column tried to fight their way out or flee from their attackers. In just about an hour's time the Indians slaughtered a regiment of five thousand soldiers, including those who were mortally wounded and left to die on the road, while suffering only minor casualties themselves.

When Hobsbawm was apprised of the extent of the catastrophe, he ordered the regiments under his command to camp where they were, at the spot where the road forked. Camp fires were started, and a hospital tent was erected to care for the wounded. Hobsbawm sat in his tent in a mood of absolute despair. The adjutant who'd attended him in the morning was nowhere to be found, so he'd enlisted an orderly to take his place, a tall thin clean-shaven man whose regimental tags he couldn't quite place. The General was poring over the map of the Forest he'd been examining in the morning when Lieutenant Lovejoy opened the flap of the tent.

"Stuart?" said the General.

"I heard about Dunder. I'm awfully sorry . . ."

"Dunder?! This whole mess is Dunder's fault! I'll not waste any pity on Dunder and all those other deserters and cowards. Come sit beside me . . . This whole campaign's been a fiasco, but that's going to change." He indicated a point on the map slightly east of their current position. "Do you see this trail?"

"Yes. We crossed that one yesterday."

"Yesterday we didn't take that trail because we wanted to get to the Indians, who were on the west side of Windswept Hill. But now they're here, on the north side. Where do they go from here?"

"I don't know."

"Of course not. It was a rhetorical question . . . Maybe they'll attack us, but a head-on attack they'd lose . . ." He turned to the orderly. "Do you suppose there is anything in the way of a cigar in this tent?" Turning his attention back to the map he went on, "Now what if we were to go back to this trail, the one we crossed yesterday, but this time we take it heading north. You see, it curves round, and there we are, see? North of the Bog and behind the Indian camp."

"I see."

"There was – I think – a box that fell behind a table over here," said the orderly.

"An interesting idea, no? Then what could happen?" asked Hobsbawm.

"Look, one unsmoked cigar."

"Thank God. The battle's been lost, but at least a man can enjoy a cigar."

"It hasn't been lost. This is just the first day of fighting. We have two regiments still at full strength, not to mention Colonel Milquetoast's force." Lovejoy was determined not to give way to defeat.

"We could just fall on them," said Hobsbawm.

"You mean once we're behind their camp."

"Yes."

"But the Bog's in the way."

"Depends on exactly where they are. I imagine they'd be dispersed around the Bog. I suppose . . . " he drifted off uncertainly.

"Will there be anything else?" asked the orderly. "Do you want something to drink?"

"Just – I can't seem to get a spark." The General was having difficulty lighting his cigar.

"Allow me."

"Thanks . . . It's looking like it's all coming down to Milquetoast. We can attack but it'll be a head-on attack. The best case then is we beat them and penetrate their lines and the victory is ours. If Milquetoast can get to them in time he could attack from the rear and then I'm sure we'd have them. But what if we don't win, and Milquetoast doesn't arrive in time. What then?"

"Then every man will do his duty. We fight bravely or we die," said Lovejoy.

"No, that's stupid. What we'd do is we'd retreat. And when we do that, these Indians aren't trained troops, they'll follow us. I'm sure they will. They have no discipline. And then look at this. See where they'd be? Right in the sights of the Hercules cannons."

"Yes. I see."

"Yes. You bloody well can see. This is the maneuver. They'll be so confident after today, we'll pull Half Moon out of his shell . . ." He looked at the orderly. "Were you getting me something to drink?"

"There's only this bucket of water."

"Water will do."

The orderly brought the bucket and set it down next to Hobsbawm.

"I can't drink out of a bucket. Get a goblet or something. But even if we pulled that off, once the guns started firing they'd just go back into the Forest. Damn it, we need Milquetoast again. If he were behind them they'd be trapped on the shore. The guns would just annihilate them."

"So now you're willing to share the credit with Milquetoast?"

"I know, it's disappointing. But it'd be a damn sight more disappointing to take the blame for getting beat by the Indians."

258

"Well he was convoyed across the Sound last night. He's had a day to get ready. In all likelihood tomorrow is the day he'll attack."

"In all likelihood isn't good enough. Not by a long shot. He must attack tomorrow." He turned to Lovejoy. "Here's what I need you to do. Take this trail till it curves around, then cut through the Forest here to San Dorio on the Coast Road. Once you're on the Road head west. You're bound to encounter Milquetoast's men at some point. When you get to Milquetoast give him my orders. Here, I'll write them for you." Hobsbawm took pen and ink and drafted the order to attack. "You must do this tonight."

"Go back till I find this trail. Take it north. Then, when the trail curves –"

"I can't find a goblet anywhere," said the orderly.

"Go off the trail and into the woods? I'm not sure about that."

"It's the only way." Hobsbawm waved his cigar in Lovejoy's face.

"Riding through the woods alone at night; I don't like it. There's Indians everywhere."

"Then take someone with you. Oh Christ." The cigar slipped out of his hand and trying to catch it he knocked it into the bucket of water. "Who put this confounded bucket here?" He turned back to Lovejoy. "And don't delay! You have to get there before dawn."

"But if I –"

The orderly was looking through a cabinet, tossing various unwanted utensils out of his way. "I'm sorry, I'm looking for a goblet."

"What do you want a damned goblet for?" shouted Hobsbawm in a rage. He felt like the whole world was uniting to frustrate him. "Get me another cigar!"

"There are no more cigars."

"There have got to be more. I brought two full boxes."

"Well I can't find them."

Hobsbawm turned and saw Lovejoy. "Are you still here? Go! Go!"

"I'm on my way." Lovejoy snapped off a salute and departed. He strutted angrily in the direction of his horse, muttering to himself. *Of all the idiotic notions, sending me riding through the Forest in the middle of the night. Why didn't he think of this yesterday? And who will my companion be?* Having reached his mount he looked around and realized he might be able to find another rider, but where was he to find another horse? There were none in this part of the camp. The cavalry were bivouacked on the other side of the little ridge they'd camped on. It would take a while to get there and there was no one there he could command anyway being only a lieutenant. He started back towards Hobsbawm's tent, to get the General to write out an authorization, but he wasn't looking forward to confronting him in his enraged state and having to explain the delay.

Meanwhile, in the tent the orderly was still looking through the cabinet he'd opened. "Please stop that racket. You're rattling my nerves," said Hobsbawm.

The orderly stopped what he was doing and looking around saw that Lovejoy had left. "Are you going to be holding any more interviews tonight?"

"No. Actually I have no idea . . . They gave us a good bashing today, but tomorrow it's our turn." He sat and caught his breath. "If there are no more cigars, can I ask you to ramble over to the canteen and get me some dinner?"

"Dining alone?"

"Yes."

"I don't think you'll have any need for dinner."

"What cheek —" Hobsbawm broke off, seeing that the orderly had removed his hat and was holding a pistol pointed in his direction. "What do you think you're doing? Put down that pistol. You're liable to hurt someone."

"You're the one that's liable to get hurt, General Hobsbawm. Do you know who I am?"

"Of course not. And why would I care?"

"Look."

It took a moment. "Eliot. You've shaved."

"Yes."

"I must say you look a damn sight better without the mustache."

"Thank you — I mean, so what. I only grew the mustache for Stephanie. And she's dead."

"You have my condolences."

"You killed her."

"I certainly did not."

"Here's her picture. And my son, Danny."

"I see. A nice looking family."

"You killed him too."

"Will you please get that out of your head."

"No. Don't come any closer. Step back. Look at these pictures."

"Well then I'll have to get closer."

"Stand there. Here, I'll put them on the table. Now go and look at them."

"Oh, for Christ's sake . . . If you want to be excused the court martial for desertion, I'll do that for you. But I'll be no use to you dead."

"You think I'm worried about a court martial? You think that would matter to me at all? I'm going to murder you – no, I'm going to execute you – and then as many other officers as I can. And I'm saving the last bullet for myself."

"Sounds a bit dodgy. If you take my advice you'll shoot yourself first. That's the most important bit. Get that done and then you can take care of the others."

"You think this is a big joke, don't you?"

"No I don't. I understand your sense of despair. But I was not responsible for the deaths of your wife and son."

"Yes you were."

"Blame the arsonists, if you want to blame someone. But from the moment you put on the uniform you pledged yourself to a duty greater than the defense of your family. You pledged yourself to be the King's man and to put his orders first, before everything else. You're a soldier. Or at least you used to be. Killing me will accomplish nothing. Killing yourself will accomplish even less. If you want to do something with your life I can help you. Otherwise shoot yourself and stop interfering with people who have something to do."

"I have something to do."

"Then do it instead of just talking about it . . . Here, give me that pistol."

"No."

"Give it to me so I can shoot you in the head. You can perish the same miserable way my good friend Colonel Dunder did."

"Do you honestly expect me to feel sorry for you?"

"Sorry for me? Why would you feel sorry for me? Feel sorry for Dunder, don't feel sorry for me."

"I'm sorry. There's no point talking about it. I have to do this." Eliot fired the pistol, but his hand was shaking, so the bullet shattered Hobsbawm's knee cap. "Oh Christ, I'm not even a good shot."

Hobsbawm was on the ground writhing in fury and agonizing pain as Lovejoy reentered the tent. His first thought, seeing Hobsbawm at the adjutant's feet, was that they were playing some addle-pated game. Then he looked more closely and saw, "Eliot, is that you? First a deserter, now a murderer?"

"Damn it, Lovejoy, he has to be killed." He shot at Hobsbawm again, this time hitting him in the shoulder.

Lovejoy loaded and fired. There then followed a savage dance as Lovejoy chased Eliot around the tent, both of them dodging the other's bullets.

"The General's gone mad!" shouted Eliot.

"I'm not mad!" shouted Hobsbawm.

"You're the one who's mad," said Lovejoy.

Moving backwards, Eliot stumbled over the bucket of water and fell defenseless to the ground, allowing Lovejoy to shoot him in the chest. He shouted, "The madness has to be st –" before Lovejoy succeeded in killing him with a bullet through the eye.

Hobsbawm was lying on the ground in a puddle of his blood. "Stuart, I'm done for."

"Not yet you aren't." He raised the General's head and found a pillow to rest it on. "I'll get the doctor. Don't go anywhere." Lovejoy rose and left the tent.

"Is that your idea of a joke?" the General shouted after him, but he didn't shout it very loud.

Lovejoy returned almost immediately with some men and a stretcher. Hobsbawm was laid on the stretcher, given a quart of whisky and taken to the hospital tent. He called to Lovejoy to remember his orders as he was borne away. Eliot's body was dragged to a pit which had been dug nearby for a mass grave, and the pictures of Stephanie and Danny were trampled in the muddy grass.

Early next morning, long before the break of day, the Seventeenth and Nineteenth Regiments executed the maneuver General Hobsbawm had ordered and fell on the Indians from the north. The Indians, however, hadn't squandered the opportunity they'd been given yesterday to seize as many rifles and cannons as they could from their defeated adversary. So the colonial army was confronted with a well-armed contingent of braves who returned their fire with redoubled force and succeeded in pushing them back. There were over ten thousand soldiers in the two regiments and approximately the same number of Indians. It was vicious and sanguinary combat. The total number of casualties easily exceeded that of the previous day. As the fighting wore on the advantage turned slowly in the Indians' favor. Hobsbawm himself conducted the army's operations from a jury-rigged hospital bed behind the lines, where he was ensconced with an abundance of pillows and salves and numerous bottles of gin and whiskey to keep down the pain. He was totally drunk by the time late in the day when the Indians finally penetrated the army's lines and the army fell back, the Indians pursuing towards the shore where at last they were in position to be shelled by the guns of Lost Bastard Island. But the guns were silent. Hobsbawm was perplexed by the absence of the artillery on which he had placed so much reliance. This was the whole reason the war was being fought, so the guns could prove their worth. He could not understand why they didn't fire. Whatever the cause he decided it was not his fault. He was drunk and confused and in pain and he just wanted to go to sleep. It was his fervent prayer that when he woke up the problem would be solved.

Late in the afternoon the rout was on. The soldiers were running away. They were being pursued by the Indians north, towards the shore. They burst from the overhanging boughs of the Forgotten Forest onto the marshy plain that separated the Forest from the Coast Road, and when they got to the Road many ran back to Port Jay, but some stumbled onto the beach on the other side of the Road and attempted a defense.

"What shall we do?" asked Half Moon. "Shall we run them down?"

Black Crow just raised the spear he held, from which were hanging scalps he had taken in yesterday's fighting and pointed it north, as much as to say, "Drive them into the sea."

Half Moon turned to Clumphy. Clumphy felt out of place. He was mounted on a large but very tractable mare, as befitted one of Half Moon's inner circle, but he had no spear, no scalps and no war paint. He had been presented with a feathered head dress, but hadn't been able to figure out how to put it on. His head was bare. "Clumphy," said Half Moon, "I feel the time is near when I will see again those enchantresses who tantalize me in my dreaming hours. But perhaps we must finish these soldiers off first. What is your counsel?"

Clumphy looked at Half Moon. He realized the words he spoke to the Indians were not the words they understood him to say. He realized that communication between one person and another was a chancy proposition at best, that people's minds were like stars separated by vast distances twinkling to one another, that anything he said to this man would be creatively misunderstood and applied in ways that no doubt would make his flesh crawl, but that he would be given the credit for having passed on whatever insight it was that Half Moon would be inspired by. He opened his mouth to say these things. "I think that –"

Half Moon cut him off. "Did I ever tell you about my grandfather? He also was given the promise of a great revelation to be made clear after he had finished destroying the last of his enemies. For him it took the form of an eagle that led him to the spot where he found Dappled Doe and made her his squaw. I wonder what form it will take for me? You are right, Clumphy, as always. We must complete the job that is before us. We must drive the remnants of this army into the sea and then we will see what is revealed."

They rode on. The Coast Road came into view. Half Moon rode in triumph across the Road, onto the strand and saw the ocean. Gulls were in the sky. He waved to them, his brothers. He looked all around. The cloud wrack that had hovered over the Sound for most of the day was moving inland, portending rain later in the day. But apart from that there was nothing, no great secret waiting to be unveiled. Just a few Indians whooping it up, a stiff wind from offshore, and a lot of clouds. Not a bad day, but he'd expected something more.

Something in the waves caught Clumphy's eye. It was hard to distinguish amidst the frothy masses of foam the waves were washing onshore, but there seemed to be – no, could it be? – a piece of paper being pulled slightly forward and slightly back, at the sport of the surf. The more he looked the more certain he became that it *was* a piece of paper and, what's more, there was writing on it. "Look," he said and pointed. Half Moon saw what he was pointing at and he dismounted and walked to the water's edge. Clumphy slid off his mare and followed him. Half Moon picked up the piece of paper. The ink had run slightly, but amazingly the words could be made out. There could be no question this was the message he had been promised and which he had come so far to receive. A look of dumbstruck disbelief and dismay came to his face.

"What does it say?" Clumphy asked him.

Half Moon stood, staring at the piece of paper, but said not a word.

"Well, man, don't keep me hanging," said Clumphy.

Half Moon looked at him in perplexity. "It says, 'I will not marry a wallaby.'"

"Alleluia!" shouted Clumphy. "The Lord has spoken!" He danced up and down, sand cascading from his sandaled feet.

"But it is not clear what He means to tell me."

"Of course not. The words of the Lord must be interpreted. You don't expect Him to come right out with what He means, do you?"

"Why not . . .? The black bear spoke clearly. He said I would have a great triumph and a glorious death. I had no need to interpret his words."

"This is different." They had been joined now by Black Crow and some of the other Indians. "The words of the Lord are always subject to interpretation. This is why priests are necessary. Now, let's start with the first phrase. He says, 'I will not.' This is the negative. There is something He will not do. Or, putting yourself in the position of the first person you can interpret it as a commandment directed to you, something you must not do."

"I mustn't marry a wallaby."

"That is the literal meaning of the words, but what is their spiritual meaning? To read the words of the Lord you must always look beyond what the words say to the awesome truth that is being un-covered. Marriage is a joining together. God is telling you there is something you must not join together."

"What?"

"It is a great mystery . . . God is saying you must not join yourself to a wallaby. But what is a wallaby?"

"I don't know."

"I think it's a marsupial," said Black Crow.

"Now if you were to join yourself in marriage to someone, it would be to a woman. So the wallaby in this commandment must stand in place of some sort of woman."

"What sort of woman?"

"That's the question: what sort of woman? A w —, a w — . . . a witch! Of course. They even start with the same letter. Could it be any clearer? You must not join together with the witches!"

"I mustn't?"

"No, of course you mustn't. Don't you see? 'I will not marry a wallaby.' You mustn't join the witches. You see how interpretation makes everything clear."

The upshot was that Half Moon did not lead his Indians to the spot where the witches awaited them. He did not unite with them to sport again with those incomparable beauties Issoria and Vanessa, and to receive the magical help Deirdre could have given him. He turned away instead and, the rain now coming down in earnest, the Indians stayed where they were, where they were encountered by the fresh troops under the command of Colonel Milquetoast that had been convoyed across the Sound. Fatigued after almost a full day's fighting the Indians were cut to pieces by these reinforcements com-ing to Hobsbawm's aid at the eleventh hour. Half Moon was killed leading a charge against the colonial armed cavalry. He fell from his horse shouting his war cry, and his close friend Black Crow fell at his side. So he had his great victory and his glorious death, as promised by the black bear. The day that began in triumph was turned to de-feat by the time darkness fell. Colonel Milquetoast's victorious forces routed the Indians, sending them east along the Coast and south into the Forest, where the great gathering Half Moon had forged into a unified war party dissolved into bands of separate tribes seeking the safety of their individual home grounds. Many warriors returned to crops that had not been harvested, bearing tales of a campaign that had wreaked awful destruction on the white man but which, despite its many triumphs, had ultimately fallen short. The guns of Lost Bastard Island had been demolished and three regiments of the colonial army commanded by General Hobsbawm had been effectively destroyed. But in the end there were just too many soldiers. It was General Hobsbawm's dedication to the recruitment of new soldiers that proved decisive. The white man had made it clear he was here to stay.

But what had become of Stuart Lovejoy?

After leaving General Hobsbawm's tent for the second time the night before, he had stood alone for several moments. Killing his erstwhile friend and companion had given him an irrational feeling of grandeur which he was allowing to rocket through his veins as he realized he'd just outshot a dangerous and unexpected antagonist and perhaps saved the entire campaign. At the same time he had a duty to fulfill but was still without a written warrant authorizing him to enlist another's aid. *Oh well,* he thought, *the sooner I get started the sooner I'll be done.* So he decided to make the ride to San Dorio on his own. This was the first of a string of decisions he made that night that perhaps he should have reconsidered.

He spurred his horse and rode out of camp, galloping to make up time. However, what with his hurried pace and his wandering thoughts, in the dark he missed the path Hobsbawm had told him to take. He kept on for more than an hour, convinced he would come to it soon, before finally deciding he must have gone far past it. Just as he slowed his horse and prepared to turn back, he saw a faint trail entering the path he was on from the left. Of course he knew this was not the turning he'd intended to take, but doing his best to bring to mind the map he'd seen in Hobsbawm's tent, he thought he remembered seeing a trail that intersected their route further to the east and which led to the port of San Dorio. The more he thought about it, the more certain he became that he had seen it on the map, and that this unprepossessing little track must be it. At any rate, if it wasn't, by taking it he would almost certainly be heading in the right direction, and since Hobsbawm had told him he'd have to leave the beaten path anyway, he reasoned that he'd be no worse off than if he'd taken the correct turning to start with. So, to save the time involved in retracing his steps, he decided he'd best take this path. He thought this all through and then laughed at himself because he realized it was all total nonsense, and he wouldn't even have considered doing it if not for his grandiose and giddy mood. Obviously, he should just accept the fact he'd made a mistake and ride back the way he'd come, to the path Hobsbawm had told him to take. His horse already had taken seven steps backwards as he considered this, before he dug in his spurs and headed into the little track.

The little track quickly faded into a porridge of soil, gravel, weeds, bracken. He found himself picking his way between the boles of birch trees and the shadowed shrubbery. He felt confident he was continuing to head north, though in the darkness under the leafy branches he was unable to get a fix on the sky above. As his assurance in his direction slowly waned, he contemplated turning around, but at this point he was certain that doing so would definitely do away with any sense of direction he'd been able to hang onto, so he continued moving ahead. His procedure was to pick out a tree trunk directly in front and move towards it. Once he'd gotten there he would pick out another one, and this way he was satisfied he was going in a reasonably straight line. From time to time he'd tried looking backwards, to identify the trees he'd used as landmarks and assure himself they led directly back the way he'd come. He thought he was able to do this, but the trees looked different when viewed from the other side, so he wasn't sure.

It had been a hot night when he started, but as he went deeper into the woods the air took on a definite chill. He wondered if this was a sign he was approaching the shore. He noticed that the ground was becoming less overgrown, there were fewer small bushes and vines to contend with and his mount was having less trouble with its footing. If he was approaching the shore, this had definitely been a worthwhile short cut and he congratulated himself on having made the right choice, but if that was the case why was he still heading uphill? He didn't remember any high points in this part of the woods, so this was an altogether puzzling development. This was to be only the first of many puzzles. The trees had become corkscrewed, scanty and bare. It wasn't always possible to find one directly ahead, so he now attempted to guide himself by gaps between the tree trunks. In addition, it was becoming much colder. He folded the collar of his coat up to prevent the chill night air from getting to his neck, and he saw his tired horse's exhalations were making plumes of condensation in the frigid gloom. *It never gets this cold here, certainly not in the summer.* He was nearing the summit of the hill and he hoped he would be able to spot some landmarks and make sense of where he was, but when he reached the top and looked around he didn't recognize anything. It was a landscape wholly unfamiliar to him. He wondered if he was still in the Forgotten Forest. Perhaps he had wandered somehow into another forest further north, or into another season, or another year. Where was he? He looked up, and as he did a snowflake landed on his nose. *This is impossible. It never snows here.* But he looked around, and snow was falling. He was on the peak of a high hill somewhere, where only a few scrawny pines were able to establish a foothold, and it was snowing. He must have traveled thousands of miles from his starting point in the Forgotten Forest, but he couldn't have. It couldn't have been more than a few hours since he'd left the army encampment and gotten lost.

He saw the sky now. It was full of stars, but no constellations he could recognize. He stood in his stirrups. He tried looking west to see if he could spot any sign of the army. But . . . which way was west? He'd come completely untethered. He looked about himself and everywhere he saw the pure revelation of an answerless puzzle. He'd left the desperate grinding broken desperation of war, where nameless thousands tossed themselves at death, and in the darkness he'd found a mysterious still solitude here, which was nowhere, somewhere above and away, where snowflakes were falling now with more weight and almost with a purpose, covering the ground in a uniform whiteness, glistening in the starlight, concealing all the bumps and gashes of the wounded ground under a primeval blanket of the purest white.

269

PART THREE

ENDGAME

CHAPTER TWENTY-ONE
DODGY EYEBALLS

WHO CAN SAY where love starts? In a fancy or in the heart? Is it buried within, or a thing apart? Does it start with a look? Or maybe a smile, a laughing eye across a room, a gentle guile persuading us in words we thought were long forgotten. Does it start when two people know something no two people knew before? Or was it there already, before those things could happen? Did it start as a secret in the heart? A secret trapped that couldn't get away, that had one thing to say, that escaped one day when that look, that smile, that guile found the words they had to say? I love you. The love was always there, just the you was lacking.

Thoughts such as these went through Tom's mind as he trudged the dusty Coast Road towards Port Jay. He'd left one trouble behind, and there was sure to be trouble ahead, but this afternoon trouble lay on him lightly. He reasoned if Port Jay had burned, refugees would be streaming towards Kashahar and he thought he might encounter them, but so far he'd seen no one. That puzzled him. There were also very few overtaking him in the direction he was headed. Of course he wouldn't overtake any, he was going slow as a man could go, bar crawling, which he had considered. The pain in his right foot was as agonizing as any pain he'd ever felt and his boots had worn blisters on his heels and toes. Dusky light was stealing across his path and there wasn't a house or building in sight where he'd be able to beg or borrow a roof over his head. It would be a night in the woods beside the road, but the night looked to be a fair one, so he sought a likely spot.

For Tom it had started with a brew, a potion he'd quaffed, and ever since he'd not been able to call his heart his own. It happened the afternoon of the honsung – that was the name they gave the celebration when a merchant ship returned after a profitable voyage – when the Master and the merchants distributed the proceeds to the sailors and the crew. The townspeople came and of course the women came too who were always wanting to help the sailors celebrate. It was a happy day. Tom took his portion as always to his aged father, but when he got to his house he found a stranger at the door who told him if he was looking for the old man who'd lived there he'd died three months ago, and he'd find his old rags, that were all he'd possessed, down at the town hall. He'd tried to learn more but the door had been shut in his face. Coming back to the celebration he hadn't felt like drinking and carousing with his fellows, and the women all repulsed him with their pasted-on smiles and calculating eyes, so he'd gone to sit outside the saloon and ponder what he'd come to. He was sorely distressed, and the little he'd drunk only deepened his gloom, and the jaunty music from inside, where couples were dancing and acting gay, couldn't find the smallest chink in his spirit to get in and give him some cheer.

He was on the point of leaving and losing himself in the streets of the city, when he saw a woman was seated across from him. She bore an air of having sat there awhile, though he hadn't noticed her before. Silent mystery hovered about her, and he realized he was staring at her silver locks, and the way the light seemed softer when it fell on her pale skin. He met her gaze and looking quickly away was on the point of apologizing when she held up her hand.

"Don't speak. I know your sadness well. Today it stings, but sorrow cannot last. Memories of your father's goodness soon will fill your heart. Unhappiness is all illusion."

"How do you know of my father?"

Her eyes rested on him and he felt like an empty vessel seen all the way through. "I watched as you made your way to his house. The firmest foundations on which we rest our lives sometimes turn to water."

"Were you one of the women inside? I don't remember you."

"My daughter is inside. Your throat is dry."

Tom realized he was parched.

"She'll bring you that you thirst for." She rose and disappeared into the saloon.

A moment later Katie came out with a pitcher of wine and two glasses. "Come, my friend, this is not the place to be sad and lonely. I've brought you a drink." She sat beside him.

"It's kind of you to share some time with me. But I'd not be an object of your pity."

"This is pity I'm showing, is it? No. I call it kindness. You can call it what you want. But I believe a kind deed done will come back to the one that did it." She poured them each a glass.

"Then I think you've not much experienced the way of the world. Nothing's rewarded less than a kind deed."

"Oh, aren't you the wise man. Drink up your wine and I'll have no more of your long face and your sorry words. Why must you be the one blister of woe on such a happy day as the honsung?"

"I'm sure your mother told you all the story of my old father's death and how I learned of it."

"My mother? Sure my mother is nowhere near nor has she ever told me aught of your poor father."

"Wasn't it she that sent you out here?"

"I wasn't sent, I came seeing a good man with a silent sorrow, thought he needed cheering. The idea just came upon me powerful and I – well I thought maybe he'd be happy to see me. Anyhow I'd had enough of those sodding twits and their hands that won't let you alone. But I surely don't know what you're talking about my mother."

"Then there's been some mistake."

"Always there's mistakes. So what shall we drink to?"

". . . To the memory of my old Da."

"That's a good thought and no mistaking. And to the mother that bore me, whom you think you've met."

So they drank the wine. Then, putting down the glass Tom had a strange feeling as if he was sitting there with her but also he was up above, and he looked down on the two of them and seeing them that way it was as if a great truth was suddenly revealed. And Tom wondered which one was he truly, the one below or the one above, but he knew who he was truly was contained right in the very center of him and it was something he'd never seen quite so clearly before.

As if when he was born he'd been told there was a secret he was never to know, and he'd understood all his life he'd never know it and then suddenly he looked in Katie's eyes and saw the secret shining out and it was something he'd always known. He came back together and was no longer looking down on himself. It was just him and Katie sitting together and the bottle of wine between them and they were laughing, though neither of them could have said what they were laughing about, or what had just happened. They were happy, and they believed their happiness was something no two people had ever felt before.

As Tom remembered this he was ripping the weeds and bushes out of a little plot he'd found by the side of the road, trying to make a comfortable patch to lie down on for the night. He was on his hands and knees, which took the weight off his aching feet, and he cursed himself heartily and without reservation. It was not the first time he'd cursed himself. He cursed himself for starting out before his foot was healed, before he'd gotten a sensible pair of boots instead of the castoffs he wore, before he had enough money to buy himself a meal. He told himself his heart had been stronger than his head, but there must be more to it than that. He thought there must be something seriously wrong between him and the world he lived in because he couldn't seem to live in it in a way that made any sense. Suddenly in his anger he took the staff he leaned on as he walked and lashed out with it, hitting the trees and the small bushes around him. He was furious and he was hitting the ground with his staff, just to get the feeling of breaking something. How had this suddenly erupted? Any sensible man would have taken Agata and the farm she offered, and the more he considered it the less he understood why he hadn't. Now his sudden tantrum was coming to an end and he saw he'd done for a couple of ferns and fair blasted a patch of daisies, and he stood in the little area he'd cleared, exhausted. Why couldn't he just want the woman he was with? Surely that must be what most men do. He sat and took off the boot on his right foot. His whole foot was swollen and had turned a garish crimson, with the bullet hole a sickly looking green-tinged black at the center of it all. Why couldn't he decide for himself who it was he desired? It felt like someone else had decided for him. And why was he on this futile quest to Port Jay, searching for the love of a woman who probably wasn't even there anymore? But if she wasn't there surely he'd find clues where she'd gone. Oh, it was hopeless. Tossing among these and many other thoughts he slowly passed into a fitful slumber.

At one point in the night he was aroused by the pounding of hooves, hastening from the direction in which he'd come. He rose to see a horseman thundering past who, seeing Tom, brought his horse to a halt and came round back to him. He held the reins in one hand and gestured with the other, which Tom saw was missing and had been replaced by a hook.

"Holla, there. Where are you from?" he asked.

"I'm a native of Port Jay."

"I wasn't asking where you were born. Where are you coming from now?"

Tom limped to the side of the Road. "The whole story were a long one, but most recently I've come from back that-a-ways," he waved his hand in the direction of Kashahar, "and it's Port Jay I'm hoping to return to."

"How far back-a-way?"

"Far enough."

"From Kashahar?"

"Not that far. What's the point of this inquiry if I might ask?"

"It appears you have a wound."

"You've keen eyes. What of it?"

"I'm on the lookout for a wounded man with many pieces of gold on him, that he took from my master."

"I am a wounded man, but you can see from the cut of my clothes, not a rich one."

"For surety of that, might I take a look at that wallet at your waist?" Here the man dismounted. "I'm not a cutthroat nor any that would waylay an honest traveler."

"What would you be looking for?"

"That I'll know when I see it. You ken I've no weapon."

"Other than a hook." Tom thought he might resist, but truly his wallet was as empty as his belly, so he held it out to the man. "There's naught but some crumbs and shells."

"So you've not any doubloons or pieces of eight?"

Tom laughed. "It's been some time since there's been aught there save a copper or two that a widow lady paid me."

"You're not the one I seek. God bless." He mounted his horse and was gone. There was no more disturbance during the night other than the return of this same horseman in the hour before cockcrow. *Someone's found news of what's ahead on the road,* thought Tom.

When he rose the next morning the first thing he did was to get some water from a rill bubbling nearby and wash his wounded foot. The pain was less this morning. He stood and attempted to memorize the height of Windswept Hill so he could track his progress during the day by how the Hill stood over the surrounding trees. Then, putting his wallet at his waist and taking his staff in his left hand, he set off on his daily pilgrimage. He did not put any food in his mouth because he hadn't any. He did not give any thought to his route because the road was there before him. There was nothing more for him to think of, so he bethought himself of the times that followed that drink he'd taken at the honsung. Katie had been his whole world. If she gave him a flower he'd save it till the petals were dead and falling off, or if there were a book or locket she'd fancied he'd hold it close like a talisman. What joy that had given him. One day he'd had the great good fortune to be holding still the scarf she'd worn, after they'd said their good-byes, and he pressed it to his nose all that night and breathed the smell of her. Those were enchanted days and the thought that he could ever experience anything like them again seemed impossible, like a dream he'd gotten into his head and couldn't forget. Still he kept on, one foot after another, the pain throbbing up his leg, one cursed step after another.

There was a tavern ahead, with a sign of a bush. He thought he would reach it and then take a rest. Maybe try his luck if he could do some chores in return for a meal. At the same time he was catching some of the banter from a group of travelers drawing near. He cast a glance over his shoulder and saw they were a motley group, two on horseback and the rest on foot, six or seven altogether, in good spirits and keeping up some lively conversation. He wondered if this was the party that had sent one of their number scouting ahead during the night. He also realized his strength was not what he'd thought and he would have to rest before getting to the tavern. So he spotted a good block of stone by the side of the road and sat on it and waited for the other group to catch him up.

When they did he saw that his friend from last night, the one with the hook, was now on foot. There were two large dark looking men riding the horses and the others seemed to be their servants, or at least they took their orders from them. They were all men and seemed like a bunch accustomed to rough work. Besides the one with a hook, there was another with a peg leg. As they drew even with him the one with a hook said, "Here's the beggar man I told you of that's going to Port Jay."

"Hello," said Tom to his acquaintance of the past night. "Did you learn any news of the Road ahead?"

"Only there's a massive amount of soldiers convoyed to the shore a little ways up the Road. There's like to be some blows I'm sure struck between them and the Indians."

One of the horsemen rode over and asked, "How far back was it you came on this road?" The group had stopped now and he saw they'd ranged themselves around him, eyeing him with what he thought was watchful intent.

"Far back enough." He looked at them and saw a cunning intelligence in their eyes, predators with prey in hand.

"Did you pass a stead hight Coldblood Farm?"

"I did that."

"As did we, and we heard a tale from a widow there. I'd guess you'd have knocked at her door too, to see if there might be a morsel for you."

"I know naught of a widow, nor any tale she may have told."

"Last night you said a widow woman paid you some coppers," said the one with a hook. "What widow woman was that?"

The man on the horse said, "Hush, Elijah, let's not badger the man." Then he reached down his hand to Tom and said, "Sure we haven't introduced ourselves. I'm known as Barnacle Jack." They shook hands. "This fine gentleman," indicating the other horseman, an ugly man with a scar and a rich blue coat, "is Crazy Dog Talbot, known up and down the Coast as a defender of the right and a sterling advocate of freedom. And what might your name be if I could make so bold?"

The names Barnacle Jack and Crazy Dog awakened uneasy echoes in Tom's mind. "I'm called John. Honest a name as there is."

"Oh, it's honesty you're after then, is it?"

"I'd think so. And it's an honor to have met the two of you."

"I can assure you, honest John, the honor is all ours. And often I've heard honesty spoken well of, though people tend to avoid it. Personally, I've never found a use for it." Here he gave a large laugh. "We're on the lookout for a pair of knaves. They sold something that belongs to us but they've not brought the money back. No, they've kept it for themselves for all the world like a dog who takes his master's roast from his table and would hightail it off for his own enjoyment. So we're taking steps, you might say, to find these two so as to clarify the matter."

"I see."

"There was originally a third of their number but him we found lying in the ground at that stead Coldblood Farm which I believe you were just starting to tell us of. Is that right, John?"

Tom stuttered, not knowing which way the wind was blowing nor how much was safe to say. So he shammed a hacking cough while he sought a moment to think.

"Oh, but I can see you've been walking a long way, and the dust of this road must be thick in your throat. I'm sure you'd be better for a good pint of ale," said Barnacle Jack. "It would be an honor if you'd allow me to buy you one at this tavern just ahead."

"No, no, I could not allow myself to take advantage of you."

"Do you find my company that objectionable?"

Tom found there was no way to turn the offer down, so he went with them to the tavern. He had to do a bit of a jog trot to keep pace but when they got there they found the place not too crowded, with just some working men at a couple tables in the back. There was a long table near the door made of some good maple which had room for all of them to sit around it. Barnacle Jack and Crazy Dog took the seats to either side of Tom and after some bread and ale had been set before them Crazy Dog took up the questioning. "These men we're after looking for had acquired a mighty sum of gold, and I'm certain they've put it underground somewhere. Buried it, wouldn't you know? But they'll keep some on their person. They'd have to. Now that's what we know. And this widow woman told us a tale which cast a little light on the matter. I know you said you know naught of that tale, but I was hoping a mug of ale might help your memory. And it seems to me likely you'd have had some dealings with these two, wouldn't you know, John?"

"That widow woman – was she well when you left her?"

"She was not a well woman when we found her, and to speak truth I don't think our visit brought her much comfort. She was kind enough to let us look around a bit, but after what I would call a pretty thorough search we did not find what we were seeking. And this is odd, you see, because we tracked the trail of these three knaves right to her door, and we found that one of them, as I said, had breathed his last and left his remains there, but we've been unable to find their track since. And I've a suspicion that you might be one that could put us on their trail again. If that was the case, you might find there was some reward in it, honest John."

Tom saw he was fairly well cornered and would have to tell them something, but he thought it best not to let on that he knew aught of Vincenzo and his friends. "I'll tell you all my tale," he said. "I'm a fisherman by trade and have been all my life. I was in a boat out of Port Jay when a squall came up and I fell off the boat. Well the next thing I knew I was swallowed by a great fish. When I —"

At this Barnacle Jack gave him a great slap on the back and said, "Alright, John, I see you've not the stomach to tell us the truth. It was not our intent to squeeze lies out of your mouth."

Just at this moment the innkeeper reappeared with some platters of beef, roasted with potatoes and herbs. As he did so, he asked, "Have you heard aught of these rumors that the guns on Lost Bastard Island were exploded?"

"I'm certain I've not," said Crazy Dog. "When did this happen?"

"Early yesterday morning, so they say."

At this a couple men at the other tables came over to see if they could learn more and some general discussion broke out. Tom told of the debris that had fallen from the sky yesterday morning, and others told of the explosions they'd heard. There was disbelief and dismay reflected on everyone's faces. No sooner had they come to grips with the destruction of Port Jay than they were overwhelmed by this fresh news. There seemed no solid ground to stand on. The thought that the colonial government was falling apart was terrifying, but it set Crazy Dog to thinking. He saw an old world ending, and perhaps a new one would be taking its place. Maybe the colonial army and the big landholders no longer had the muscle to keep all under their thumbs. It was times like this, he reasoned, when all was in confusion and the way forward unclear, that a determined man could, with just a little force at his command, tilt the balance in his own direction. He looked about the inn and speculated as to how much force it would take.

As these ideas were running through Crazy Dog's mind, Barnacle Jack turned to Tom to inquire what it was the widow had paid him for.

"I fixed a hen coop that needed mending. Sure I didn't stop there long." He saw Jack had a sly little smile and was looking him in the eye. He tried holding his gaze, but had to look away.

"I see you've a notable limp. P'r'aps you've recently hurt your foot?"

"Certain it is that I did."

"What manner of injury was it you suffered?"

"It makes no matter."

"Tell me. I'd like to know."

"It was a bite."

"A bite?"

"I was bitten by a scorpion. It was while –"

"The sting of a scorpion! Surely few things are more painful. Well, isn't this your lucky day? We've just the remedy you're needing. Haven't we?" He turned to Crazy Dog.

"That's the righto," says Crazy Dog. "Just the item. Elijah!" He called for the man with a hook.

"Yessir?" says Elijah.

"Wasn't it a salve, a salve to heal a scorpion's sting, that you purchased from the gipsy woman on Hebrados Island? Have you it with you?"

"Yessir. I do, sir. As we're making an excursion on land I brought it with me. The scorpions here are said to be most troublesome." He opened the tunic he wore, revealing a small pot held on a string round his waist.

"There's no need," said Tom. "The scorpion was small. Very small. It will heal soon. In fact it's already healed."

"Let's see where that scorpion got you," said Jack.

"Please, don't bother."

"Take off your boot." Elijah was now standing next to him with the pot of salve. It bore a potent stench.

"No. Please don't."

But the sailors were getting into the spirit of the thing, and were chanting in unison, "Take off your boot! Take off your boot!" Finally Jack grabbed his leg and took the boot off, despite Tom's protest. When they saw his foot there was a gasp, and then silence.

Tom knew not what to say.

"Was that scorpion holding a gun, then?" There was a roar of laughter.

"I'm sorry, but what happened was I was so clumsy I shot myself in the foot. I was that embarrassed I didn't want to tell. Now you know my secret."

There was general discussion of this, along with many remarks about the wild life now hunting men with pistols, and what a sad state things had come to, and much laughter. Elijah said, "That's alright then. This salve never did bugger all for a scorpion sting, maybe it'll help a bullet wound." He smeared the foul-smelling stuff on Tom's wound.

Tom thought the joking had covered the situation and he was out of suspicion, but as he put his boot back on Jack said, "This brings me to a perilous question, honest John, because I've a suspicion the good coin I'm paying for the ale you're drinking is not being repaid with the candid coin of truth. What is it you know of a rogue named Vincenzo, and another that goes by the name of Diego? Because I'll not believe it that you've never made their acquaintance."

"As I was telling you, I was swallowed by a fish. And in –"

Barnacle Jack brought his hand down hard on the table. Mugs and platters clattered; other conversation abruptly stopped. In the silence all heard him bellow, "I'll have no more of your fish! . . . You've a queer way of stringing a man along. Now tell me what you did with the widow at Coldblood Farm."

"Easy, Jack, easy," said Crazy Dog. "There's no call to be shouting."

"I'll have no fighting on these premises," said the innkeeper. "If you want to fight I'll have you go outside."

"Perhaps you and me should step outside," said Barnacle Jack. "I've a feeling I'll be needing to beat the truth out of you. Connor, come with. I'll have you hold him while I do it." He grabbed Tom's collar and dragged him to his feet. The man with the wooden leg rose to accompany them. Tom saw his wooden leg was a bit the longer and he walked with an ungainly clump-thump.

Just as they were leaving, a man in a tattered red uniform staggered in, horror written across his face. This was one of the soldiers who'd escaped into the woods in yesterday's fight. Having hidden overnight, he'd found his way to the Road in the morning. He was bloody and covered in dirt. "Help," was the only word he could utter.

"Who are you, man, and what's your story?" asked Barnacle Jack.

"I'm Cuthbert Childress, Captain Childress of the Eighteenth Regiment," he said. "Water, please — ," he tottered into Barnacle Jack, "for the sake of God." Then he collapsed into a nearby chair. "And bandages if you have them."

Jack had been on the point of cursing the man for getting in his way when, recognizing the ragged remnants of the uniform, he quickly understood this was more momentous news. "My God, man, what's happened?"

"We've been massacred. The Indians knew our route and were waiting for us. Some traitor sold us out."

The innkeeper came bustling up with the bandages and the water.

"I've been bleeding pretty bad. I was fearing I'd lose too much blood. Never thought I'd make it this far."

"I'll patch you up," the innkeeper said, applying the bandages. "Are more coming?"

"Can't tell. Haven't seen any others."

Tom sought to get away while Jack's attention was elsewhere. Hobbling as quickly as he could he got out the tavern door and was down the Road in the direction the soldier had come from before anyone knew what he was up to. He was just thinking he'd gotten away when Connor, the peg leg, saw what he was doing and started after him cutlass in hand. It made for a zany chase at first, a lame man run down by a one-legged cripple, and Tom thought his chances of escaping were good, but it didn't take long for him to realize his stamina was so poor and his blisters so bad he was bound to lose even this race, so he ducked out of sight into the woods to his right and tried to find a place to hide. Scrambling through the undergrowth he came on a rock with a tree trunk fallen over it that provided some shelter, so he clambered under and held as still as he could. Connor came blundering around near him, moving in and out of shadow, chopping down vines with his cutlass and cursing, so he just held his breath and prayed for a little luck. But luck wasn't with him. Connor, brandishing his cutlass, pushed the tree trunk to one side and said, "There you are. Stay still. Don't move." Tom prepared to fight, but Connor just lay down next to him and kept still.

After a few moments Tom asked, "What are you doing?"

"What's it look like? I'm giving you the collar."

"But you're —"

"No point going back this quick. We can take the afternoon off. I'll take you back when I get hungry."

"But . . . aren't there things you have to do?"

"Yes. And I've done them. I have to nab you, and now I'm tired. I've been walking all morning, and that's hard on a one-legged man. They ought to let me ride one of the horses, but they don't see it that way."

"Aren't you worried I might beat you up, or steal your cutlass and cut your throat and escape?"

"No."

"Why not?"

"You wouldn't even try."

Tom thought about trying it, but decided to wait for a better opportunity. "Won't Crazy Dog and Jack be angry at you for taking all afternoon to bring me back?"

"Not if that's how long it takes. How long you think it takes a one-legged man to catch a varmint like you? It takes all afternoon."

Tom thought he should be bothered by this, but couldn't think of a reason why. "I don't think you're doing a very good job of catching me if it takes all afternoon."

"I'm doing a great job of catching you. You're just doing a bad job of getting away."

"They'll know you didn't take all afternoon."

"How they going to know that?"

"What if I tell?"

"They won't believe nothing you say. They already know you're a liar. You're no good at telling lies."

Tom thought that over. "That's certainly something I know about myself. I suppose it's because basically I'm an honest person."

"No. It's because your eyeballs go all dodgy."

Meanwhile at the tavern Captain Childress had told everyone what had happened. He'd had a hard time of it after the battle in the Forest. He'd found a place to hide during the day and then when darkness fell he'd fetched a compass through the Forest to stay away from the Indians. The morning had found him approaching the Coast Road and from there he'd walked to the tavern. Since his arrival, the locals had been expressing a good deal of apprehension, and fear of an Indian attack. Crazy Dog and Barnacle Jack were deep in converse, discussing whether it was safe to travel further at present.

"We should make our way back to the city," said Jack. "If they'd come this far, which I doubt they did, not having seen any sign of them, they would not have gone any further."

"But I'm starting to have an idea I might like to wait and see how this dispute between the army and the Indians works out," said Crazy Dog. "I've a feeling I might want to wait around to pick up the pieces."

"In that case you'll want the ship. And the crew. And I've a feeling we might have left them too long on their own. I dislike this land life."

A disheveled looking man with a musket over his shoulder, leading a pony with a young woman mounted on it, came to the door.

They'd been traveling all the morning and had thought this might make a place to stop and rest. If you observed the woman closely, you'd see she had a bit of a bump in her belly. The man took a look inside and reported to her what he saw. She was afraid what might be made of it if she were to enter a tavern full of a very rowdy sort whom they deemed would be rough playmates, so they decided as they were nearing Kashahar they would push on and look for another place to rest, perhaps find a spot beside the Road. Little note was made of them as they did not tarry long.

"This honest fellow John knows something," said Crazy Dog. "I think he knows where they've gone. I'm sure of it. Connor will bring him back."

"I hope he does. He's not been the same since you took his leg," said Jack.

"If he returns alone I'll have his other leg. I hope we're not embarked on a wild goose chase after this gold, but it is a mighty sum, one I'd not like to see lost . . . And then perhaps I'll ask you to return and bring the Seahawk here."

As Crazy Dog and Barnacle Jack were talking, Connor and Tom, the objects of their discussion, were likewise talking of them. Connor was a sturdily built man with broad shoulders and chest. He had abundant hair of a ginger color and thickset features. His mouth was just a straight slit in his bluff face, though when he smiled he gave it a little twist, as though he'd just tasted something bad. "Barnacle Jack's as mean as they come but Crazy Dog he's just flat out not right in the head. He does things for no reason, like when he took off my leg."

"Why do you stay with him?"

"He'd kill me if I left. And hell, who's going to take a man only has one leg?"

"You could find another kind of life."

"This life found me. That's the way of it. You make your plans but the one thing you know for certain is things'll turn out different. So bugger the future. And the one thing you know about the past is it didn't happen the way they say it did. So bugger the past too. I'm a seaman. Never decided to become a pirate, but that's what happened."

"How?"

Connor took on a thoughtful appearance, as though the explanation involved perplexities of a baffling nature. "You ever walk up to a ship being unloaded and see the crate they're unloading the moment you get there? Think about it. Why that crate? There were likely twenty-one other crates they unloaded first, just so they could be unloading that one crate when you got there. Well it's the same way when life decides what to make of you. It's like coincidence, but it isn't, because there's no such thing as coincidence when you know all that's going on."

"Sorry. What's the coincidence?"

"Everything happens for a reason. I became a pirate because pirates took over the ship I was on. It was that or die. Maybe I thought about running off once or twice, but where would I go? Live in the woods and hunt for meat? A man finds his role in life that's what he should stick to. I'm not going to work on a farm. What about you? A man like you's going to stick to begging. Why do what you're not fitted for?"

"I'm not a beggar."

"Course not, and I'm not a pirate."

"I was brought up to be a fisherman, but I became a sailor on the merchant ships because they wore better clothes and there was more money. Well you can see how that's worked out. Maybe I should work on a farm. I've considered it."

"No point giving it much thought. Life's like a book. You read one page and then the next. What happens on page twenty-five is because of what happened on page twenty-four, and so forth, but you can't tell what's on the next page."

"If my life is like that someone must've taken the book and ripped the pages out. Then the wind got at them. Next they were trodden on."

"I don't see how that could be. You ever read the Bible?"

"Do pirates read the Bible?"

"'The stone which the builders rejected, the same is become the head of the corner.' When I first read that I thought it was saying maybe I could be the cornerstone, or anybody. But it says more than that." Connor was getting charged up now, these weren't things he'd ever explained before. "It says people are the stones. The builder's going to build the house we live in. And you look at people and you see how they're all carved and chiseled in certain ways so as to fit together, but nobody's building anything. There's a right way everybody should fit together, that's the plan, but the stones are just lying around, all jumbled like . . . When I take you back there's a chance Crazy Dog'll ask if you want to join his crew. If he does, say no. You'll never make it as a pirate. One day and you'll be shark bait . . . Think there's any way I could sneak back and get a bottle of rum?"

"What are you thinking?"

"I was thinking this is a slow day. It'd go faster if I could creep back, sneak in the back door, steal a bottle and bring it back here."

"Are you crazy? You think I'd wait for you?"

"Well if you wanted some rum." Connor looked at the forest surrounding them. "Where were you planning to go? If I was you I'd think it was a stroke of luck getting captured by Crazy Dog. At least you'll get a meal out of it. Let him think you're trying to escape. Long as he thinks you've got someplace to go maybe he'll keep feeding you."

"But I'm a soft man really and I'm afraid of torture. He'll hurt me, I know he will. I know naught of the gold he's looking for."

"He'll chop something off for sure. Maybe you'll get lucky and it'll just be a couple toes."

" I never get lucky . . . Actually that's not true. I've been very lucky. All my problems I've caused myself. And then when the hammer's come down it's just glanced off me and smashed them that were close to me. I bring nothing but trouble. Connor, if I was you, I'd be extremely careful. You've touched some very bad luck here. Katie, Brutus, Colophus, Agata, Josh, they're all worse off because of me . . . But it's nothing I did. People think I'm good-natured, and I do have a certain frankness – call it simplicity – it earns me goodwill, maybe more from women than from men, but I don't deserve it. When I compare how people think about me with how I think about them I'm crushed by how wicked my thoughts are. If anyone sees any good in me at all it must be some good they find inside themselves; it's not in me. The only worthwhile thing about me is this love I carry for Katie Jean. I'm true to her no matter what. I'm so in love with her it's like nothing else matters. Everything else I've trifled away. She gave me a beautiful watch, it must have cost her a lot, and don't you know I lost it. But I never stopped loving her. This love I have is so unlike me it's almost as if it was put on me somehow."

The wind off the water was blowing a little more fiercely and the clouds that had hovered over the ocean in the afternoon sunshine began piling up, casting a shadow across the countryside. Connor rubbed his brow and put on a serious-minded appearance. "Your problem is you're beaten by life. You don't see it, but everyone else does. You're just waiting for someone like me to tell you, so you can lie down and give up."

"Certainly not, I've got to keep going. I don't know why. I have to get to Port Jay to find a woman who's waiting for me."

"Let me tell you something about women. She's not waiting . . . I was in love once. Prettiest peach you'll ever see. We were crazy together, but she left me for her uncle, a man twenty years older than herself. Her own uncle. It wasn't a natural thing, but you know why? He had money. He was a catch . . . You can figure the rest. He beat her, knocked her black and blue. Inside of a year she was dead. So you ask me, that's what love's good for. It's good for making you see cockeyed and making you feel ripped up inside. That's all it's ever done for me . . ."

Tom thought all that Connor said was true. *Look at me,* he thought. *Penniless, with a wounded foot, hobbling on to Port Jay to find a woman I'll never find, and if I do find her it's inconceivable she'd have waited for me. I'm choosing to die, and this is the straight path to my grave.*

He felt he'd hit bottom and could go no lower. But he'd show them. When Crazy Dog asked if he wanted to join his crew, he'd say yes. He wasn't shark bait. He'd prove to them he was as good as they were. More importantly, he'd prove it to himself. A wind came gusting through the trees, fluttering all the leaves light then dark. There was a pattering sound, and he felt the first raindrops.

Connor got to his feet. "Time to head back." On their way back they were caught by the quick-coming rain. When they got to the tavern they saw that though it had been a warm day, someone had started a fire in the large fireplace, and for all the rowdiness of the men the place had a welcoming and a homely sort of feel.

When Tom walked in Crazy Dog put a hand on his shoulder and said to Connor, "I knew you'd get him."

"He was a right elusive rascal," Connor replied.

"Now, John, you've nothing to be afraid of. We're all friends here. I want you to tell me the whole story of what you did at the widow's farm, and I'll pray you leave nothing out." Crazy Dog sat Tom down at a table and sat himself on the stool next to him. Barnacle Jack was on the other side giving him a deep dark scowl.

"Then I tell you truly, I was on a merchant vessel called the Queen of Bel Harbor, bound for Kashahar."

"We know that vessel well, do we not, Jack?"

"Aye we do," Jack agreed. "But you were not on her when we boarded her."

"I'd guess that was on account of the fact that I fell overboard. I was a dismal sailor. I fell off the ship into the unfathomable, pitch black sea, wouldn't you know."

"And how came it that you were rescued?" asked Crazy Dog.

"Here is where I fear you thought I was spinning a tale because the truth of the matter is very queer. Yet if I'll tell you naught but truth I must tell you I was swallowed by a fish."

"You insist on the fish."

"It is the honest to God's truth."

"Is there perhaps something you brought back with you, something from inside the fish, something would give color to this story?"

"You know, there is not."

"I'd think a man telling a story of being swallowed by a fish would bear some proof, some significant indicator of where he'd been."

"I never gave thought to obtaining such proof. Shows what an empty-headed noodle I've got."

"Might I ask, before you fell off the vessel, did you make the acquaintance of certain men that go by the names of Vincenzo and Diego? For they were also mates on that same ship."

"Certain it is that I did."

"And the ship's carpenter also, who was called Mr. Chips."

"I made acquaintance of all those men." Crazy Dog and Jack threw each other a meaning glance. "And when I was in the belly of the fish I made acquaintance of another named Colophus. I feel I must speak of him. He traveled about in the fish's belly with me. He spoke of many things, such as buttockracy, which he said was the natural way men were meant to be ruled, by the biggest ass."

"I once knew a man named Codfish, said exactly the same. What did you call that fellow?

"The one in the fish?"

"What did you call him?"

"Colophus."

"Codfish. A man with an enormous bum."

"That's him."

"This fish that swallowed you, it swallowed him also?"

"Certain it is that it did."

"Yo, Connor," Crazy Dog's voice boomed across the room. The rain was beating an insistent tattoo on the roof. "Connor, do you remember Codfish?"

"Codfish?" Connor crossed to come closer. "Surely I do."

"What ever became of him?"

"I don't know."

"Jack, do you know?"

"I don't. One night he was there. The next morning he was gone. I never gave the matter much thought. As you'd not notice an insect that's been buzzing round you when it takes its leave."

"I remember him, a comical man. He was on one of the vessels we captured. A rich man's toy or a tutor I'd guess. I kept him because always there'd be some daft remark on his lips to make you laugh. It never failed. I hadn't given him a thought in some time. This gentleman says he was swallowed by a fish."

"Codfish?" asked Connor.

"Yes."

"Swallowed by a fish?"

"So he says."

"I'd have paid good money to see that."

291

"So you were carried around by this fish, and you made the acquaintance of my friend Codfish."

"It appears so," said Tom. "But one day the fish became enraged and spat me out. So I swam to the shore, where I met the widow woman of Coldblood Farm and her young son. And that night my old mates Vincenzo and Mr. Chips came breaking their way in. There was a bit of a dust up. The widow's son was killed. Also Mr. Chips. But I know naught of any gold."

"Did they have any gold on their persons, or did they speak of where they might have put it?"

"They did not."

"And you spoke of only Vincenzo and Mr. Chips. Did you see aught of Diego?" asked Jack.

"Certain I did not."

There was another pause as Crazy Dog sat and pondered, his eyes fixed on Tom. It was the sort of pause that comes after a far off burst of lightning, before the first rumble of thunder.

"This agrees with what the widow told us," said Jack.

"That it does . . ." said Crazy Dog. "But it brings us no closer to the gold." He stood and walked slowly across the room, his hands clasped behind his back. He stirred the fire with a stout iron poker that stood next the hearth. "John, I only met this Vincenzo one time and that was but brief. I believe you've had the opportunity to get to know him a bit, is that not so?"

"We were cabin mates for a few days. I know him to be a cheat at cards."

"Did he ever speak to you of any place on the Coast, any place that might be of particular interest to him, or did you know him to have any family, or perhaps a friend or two?"

"No, he never spoke of his family and the only friends of his I know of were men on that vessel, Diego and Mr. Chips. I know I should have learned more from him about his family and where he was from, but I didn't. I'm afraid it's the old empty noodle again."

"Close mouthed, was he?"

"He was a man who'd not use three words if two would serve his turn."

"Have you ever eaten a sheep's eyeball?"

". . . Sheep's eyeball?"

"There's them considers it a delicacy. They eat them with periwinkle forks. It's said your sheep's eyeball has the consistency of mayonnaise. Did you not know that?"

"I'm certain I did not."

"Is there anything you could tell me that might bring me closer to finding the gold I'm seeking? Did you see aught on him at all that might be of use to me?"

"Not a thing."

"Now you said that pretty quick. Perhaps you want to think about it?" As he spoke, Crazy Dog stirred the logs in the fire again. When he was finished, he stood looking at the red hot end of the poker with an unpleasant smile on his face.

"I wish I could tell you more." Tom gave him an ingratiating smile, almost spaniel-like. "You'll find I can be a valuable man when there's somewhat to be done, but in this instance there was naught that I saw."

"That's what I'll find?"

"Yessir."

"You're sure of that."

There was a pause, as Tom was uncertain if a question had been put. Crazy Dog's eyes screwed him to his chair. Finally, Tom said, "I would not have thought he had any riches at all from the manner in which he was living, which was to break into a widow's farm to rob her, but if you say he had gold, I'm certain he did."

"Kind of you to take my word." He lifted the poker from the fire. "Do you know how they get the eyeball out of the sheep's head?"

"I'd not thought on that. I'd guess they gouge it out."

"That's not how it's done. Hold him, Jack!" Jack grabbed Tom from behind. He wrapped one arm around his shoulders, and with the other he grabbed his hair and pulled back his head. "No, they hold a hot iron up next to the eyeball in the sheep's head like this, till it sizzles and swells up."

"Take that away!" cried Tom.

"The eyeball will swell up to twice its size, that it will. It's a splendid thing to behold. And then it will pop right out of the socket. A much finer method than your gouging, don't you think?"

"My God, what do you want from me?" Tom was scared to struggle. The poker was so close to his eye he was afraid he'd skewer himself.

"I believe you're in league with your old cabin mate, and I want you to tell me where he put my gold."

"If I knew I'd tell you!"

"Is his eyeball swelling, Jack?"

"It's not swelling at all," answered Jack. "You must place the poker closer."

"Pity. I don't think it'll pop out. Oh well, I doubt we've any periwinkle forks in any case." He looked at the innkeeper, who sat on a stool next the kitchen, saying nothing and sucking at his teeth. "If my hand was to tremble I'd poke out your eye. Don't close it. I'd think you'd want to preserve the eyelid, but it's all one to me."

Tom tried to push back against Jack, but it was like pushing against a brick wall.

"Now I want you to think back very carefully," said Crazy Dog. "I'm sure there was something you saw on his person, or on that of Mr. Chips, that would put us on the trail of that gold."

"There wasn't anything." Tom was almost shrieking.

"I believe you were confederate with the other three. They sent you in first to scout the place, as it were. Is that not so?"

"No! No!"

"Well what a shame, honest John, I don't believe you." He jabbed the poker into Tom's eye. The pain was a sharp explosion in Tom's head and he felt his cheek bathed in a warm gush of blood.

"My God! You've put out my eye!" shouted Tom. Jack let go of him and he fell to the floor. "Christ, why'd you do that? Oh, it hurts! It hurts!"

"Stop your crying. You've another eye; that's why God gave you two. You'll wear a patch. There's many good men do." Crazy Dog leaned the poker against the chimney.

"God, it hurts!" Tom was writhing and pounding his fist on the floor. With his other hand he covered his mutilated eye. The pirates were dead silent. The innkeeper had gone into the kitchen. "You didn't have to do that. Why did you do it?"

"I said stop your crying!" He tossed Tom a damp cloth that had been used to mop up some spilled ale. "Put this on the wound and stop your unholy blubbering. You've learned something now. You did not give up your eye for naught. You've learned if you tell me a lie I take out your eye. You've an eye remaining. If you want to keep it you'll tell me the truth."

"I'm telling you the truth!"

"You've not told it to me yet. I've had to figure it out myself. But now I see it all. After you were joined by your three confederates there was an argument over the gold, and I guess Mr. Chips lost, and you took his share for yourself, didn't you?"

"No."

"Where is it?" Tom was blinking his remaining eye. He tried to wipe the tears out of it so he could see Crazy Dog clearly. He was still lying on the floor. "Now we'll try again. What can you tell me about this third one, this Diego? He's a bit of a mystery to me." Crazy Dog was walking in a circle around Tom, the firelight glinting yellow and red on his ale-soddened beard.

"Diego wasn't with them. I never saw him."

"Is he perhaps also in the ground . . . ? John, you must help me. I'm not one who'd leave a man eyeless. A man must have at least one eye to see. The loss of an eye is not such a misfortune, unless it be the only eye one has."

"I can tell you nothing!"

"Oh, I've the feeling you can tell us quite a bit."

"Just look at me. Does it look like I have any gold? If I did I'd give it to you, I swear I would, but I don't have it." He was holding the rag over his eye, rocking back and forth, whimpering in pain. "You son of a bitch."

"Now, that's not satisfactory." He took a dagger from his belt and fingered the blade, all the time looking at Tom. "I don't ask for much." He looked out a window at the steadily falling rain. "Where is my money? No one will tell me." There was no sound except the rattle of the rain on the roof and Tom's low keening moan. Crazy Dog turned to face Tom. "You walked away with Mr. Chips's share and you buried it."

"No."

"Yes, you did. Nothing else makes sense. Why would you leave her, and with your foot not healed? To squirrel away the gold. Hold him, Jack!" Jack put his knee on Tom's back and leaned on him hard, holding his head against the floor.

"No. No."

Crazy Dog kneeled down. "Know what I could do with this knife? Open your eye, look at it . . ." He held the blade an inch from Tom's eye. "I could pluck your eyeball out of your head and hold it over the fire. Roast it nice and slow. Then I could eat it."

"I don't have your gold."

"Do you think I'm stupid?"

"No."

"Where did you put it?!"

"I didn't put it anywhere." Tom felt Jack's breath hot against his ear.

"Do you think I'm stupid?! Say it!"

"No!"

"Say it!"

"No!! No!!"

"Say it!!"

"You're stupid!!"

Crazy Dog slid the point of the knife between Tom's eye and its socket and pressed. Tom screamed. Jack held him while Crazy Dog rocked the blade back and forth, cutting around the edge of the eyeball. Tom's feet were kicking the floor in sheer shock and terror. "You're a sad boyo, you are. You'll not enjoy my gold. You may keep it from me, but I swear you'll be sorry you did." When the eyeball was out he used a corner of Tom's shirt to wipe the blood off his blade and then stood. He looked at Tom and gave a doleful shake of his head. "And you know what else? Your name's not John." Turning to Jack, he said, "I think I'll ask you to run with a couple of the lads to Kashahar, there to take the Seahawk and bring her hither."

"I'll only take one," was Jack's reply. "We'll use the two horses."

"Throw him outside." Connor and another lifted Tom's body and opening the door they tossed him onto the ground outside the tavern.

After he'd fallen, Tom heard the clump-thump draw near and felt a hand on his shoulder. He heard Connor say, "You should've tried harder to get away. But at least now we can't tell when you're lying." Savage laughter was cut short as the door shut.

Tom lay in the pouring rain, making anguished gasps till he staggered to his feet, blinded, knocking into fence posts and tumbling down the steps. But he refused to fall again. If he did he feared he'd never get back up. He heard the splash of galloping hooves in the puddles nearby as Barnacle Jack departed for Kashahar. Turning towards the sound he was seized by sudden fear. What if they took him back inside and hurt him again? What if they weren't done? Blindly, not knowing if he was on the road or on the grass, he ran, his legs straining to get him away, to hide in the darkness. Holding onto nothing, with no way to see, running from the memory of hurt, trying to outrun the pain, out of darkness and into the unknown, he ran.

CHAPTER TWENTY-TWO
THE SPECTER OF THE WOLFMAN

A SPECTER WAS HAUNTING the plantations of the Coast, and that specter was the wolfman Famularis. Where had he come from? No one knew. Who were his parents? The facts were not known. In the absence of facts, the slaves told legends of Famularis's origins as they sat at their humble repasts or worked at their various tasks, and these passed from mouth to mouth, and plantation to plantation. One story ran as follows: he was the illegitimate offspring of one of the masters. He had been conceived in a moment of forbidden passion, his mother a slave. The same day he was born a white son was born to the master's wife. Famularis's slave mother stole the master's baby, boldly putting her own in its place, and when the enraged master, seeking to destroy all trace of his illicit amours, came to his mistress's birthing bed to kill the child born out of wedlock, he unwittingly killed the son he'd sired on his own wife. Matters standing thus, Famularis had been raised as the pampered scion of the household. Many noted that his skin was unusually dusky and his hair remarkably nappy, though few possessed the audacity to point this out.

As he grew, whenever he saw a slave treated unfairly or with disdain, he would take the side of the slave and see that restitution was made. He had a natural affinity for the oppressed, and yearned at all times to overthrow the oppressor. One day, seeing a slave horsewhipped for an infraction of which he was innocent, he took the slave's side. Ripping the whip from the offending arm he turned it against the one doing the whipping. Other slaves joined in, and a melee broke out. This fight would have ended as they always did, with the greater force of the slave drivers overcoming the resistance from the slaves, had not Famularis, at the height of the hostilities, transformed himself into a wolf. Snapping his massive great jaws and howling an awful roar that sent shivers down the spines of all those present, he was a slavering nightmare, ripping the arm from one slave driver and using it to pummel the next. When his enemies fell, he devoured them, feet, shoes, hands and all. The slave drivers fled in disarray. He was left lord of a grateful band of emancipated slaves, whom he then led into the Forest, establishing a community in which there were no masters and no slaves, all were equal, and all could live together by following three simple rules.

It was a tale that merited repetition, and in the heart of the long, hot summer, when the cotton must be harvested and the sun stood overhead and the heat shimmered on the fields, when the calls of the slave drivers were at their harshest, and the snaps of their whips at their most intense, the slaves took heart and slipped away in droves to join the upstart band. In the hottest time of the summer a wildfire dream was burning in the breasts of the underclass.

Famularis watched as his little band grew, becoming an unmanageable mob. New slaves arrived, first in a trickle then in a flood, and he did not know these newcomers. He didn't know their names, where they came from or what work suited them best, but he could see that when they looked at him they were forced to reassess their outsized expectations. He saw the questions in their eyes: Could it be that the specter Famularis was only a man? Was he going to transform? What was the source of his power? And more than anything else, the one question that burned their brains and bothered them the most: was there anything to do here except clean out the damn latrines? They gave him wary looks. He himself was uncertain. When he'd been under the spell he'd felt reborn, recognizing the forest for a living thing and sensing that the sky above, crowded with stars thick as thought, bore messages of a brave beauty he could only hope someday to comprehend. Now, merely human, he felt abandoned and desolate. He wished he could transform at will, but that was not possible. The time and manner of his transfiguration were not his to choose. Why couldn't he be a wolf whenever he wanted? Why couldn't he be a wolf all the time? Why couldn't he be a wolf right now . . .?

It was his power that cut him off from the rest. It made him different and in their eyes dangerous. They feared him and they feared the power he had discovered within himself. They would do away with him if they could, he knew it. He saw it in their eyes when they thought he wasn't watching. He knew his every step was marked and assessed. He remembered when he'd felt safe because of the rule that rifles would only be given to the men he trusted. Now he was stubbing his toe on the corollary to that rule which stated that once you give a man a rifle you can no longer trust him.

But his greatest concern was the desperate game of bait and switch he was playing with Colonel Snivel. On two occasions Snivel had mounted surprise attacks only to find that the slaves' encampment had been abandoned just hours earlier. As the size of his campsite grew, however, Famularis was becoming less nimble, and he knew soon the day would come when he would have no choice but to fight these vexatious soldiers, something he was reluctant to do on account of the relatively small number of rifles in his armory and the lack of discipline among his followers. Always when new slaves arrived he asked, did you bring any rifles, but in all cases the stupid Negroes had brought only themselves. And when he looked in their eyes he saw it wouldn't matter how many rifles he had, because these wouldn't know how to fight, they'd only run.

Colonel Snivel, meanwhile, was experiencing difficulties of his own. After the most recent raid his quartermaster, Captain Squeak, had sought him out to tell him it was time they returned to Port Jay. They had not brought sufficient supplies for a campaign as lengthy as this one was turning out to be and what remained was barely sufficient to get them back home.

"That will not happen," said Snivel. "Have you any idea the ridicule I'd be subjected to if we returned without having defeated these slaves?"

"At this point it wouldn't matter if we did defeat them," replied Squeak. "Once they surrendered we'd have no choice but to release them. We simply don't have the provisions to hold them captive."

"Release them?! What would that accomplish?"

Squeak didn't answer. The question held no interest for him. The whole campaign held no interest for him. His time was better spent in day dreams of his cottage in the old country. How he missed the pastoral bliss of his quaint back yard, with its amiable winding paths leading to the duck pond, freckled with lily pads . . . Oh well.

Famularis and Akoko, late in the day following a raid on one of the surrounding settlements, were sorting through the spoils. Famularis knew he was tipping his hand to Snivel every time he conducted one of these sorties, but it couldn't be helped. He'd been naive thinking the Forest would provide for their needs. The Forest had proven an unstinting source of malaria and that distemper they called 'the vomit,' of fevers and insects, but it did its best to withhold the food and protection his people required. He enjoyed the hours such as this one, spent with Akoko. She was the only one with whom he felt secure. Her talk had advanced beyond simple gestures of the hands and face first to a meager half-articulate speech, and now to the point where she could put her ideas into sentences and speak them aloud, though she didn't always use the right words.

"If I was them," said Famularis, "I would not mount another large attack. No, what I would do: I would send in a few men to shoot me dead first. Once I be down, who do they have to fear? But they seem not to do this."

"They are tools," said Akoko. "You are a fool. You have been shaped by density."

"You must try harder to get your words straight. You still have much to practice. They be the fools, and I the tool of destiny."

"But what are density's plans?"

"To learn this we must await events as they's unfolded to us."

"I dun't so stink. Often density must be taken in hand. It is an old man that does it."

"A bold man. Not an old man. Can you practice saying that?"

"A bold man."

"Good. You're learning." He held up a broad bandolier that carried many cartridges and looked at it admiringly. "Cast your eyes on this. I tell you bullets is more precious than rubies." A slave entered and bowed before him. "What is it."

"Two white men have entered the camp. Their weapons were taken from them and they are being guarded. They ask to speak with you."

"Did they give their names?"

"One did."

"What was it?"

"Fergus."

"I don't know this man."

"Shall we kill them?"

"Of course. But bring them to me first. I would learn what they know."

The slave bowed and departed.

"Perhaps these are the ones you spoke of. They've come to kill you."

"If so they wouldn't walk in and introduce themselves, would they?"

"I dun't know. Beyond your hard."

Day had been just on the point of turning to night when the traveling man, with Fergus at his side, had been met at the perimeter of the slaves' camp by a pair of burly, angry-looking Negroes. These were two hard working field slaves recently arrived in camp. Their master, thinking they cut notable figures, in a moment of levity had named them Archimedes and Euclid. These two now ordered the newcomers to dismount and turn over their weapons. The traveling man was struck right away by a number of differences between this camp and the one in which he'd first met Famularis. The most notable difference was, "That smell, what's it from?"

One of the Negroes answered, "The latrines have not been getting cleaned out on a regular basis."

The other added, "Also there's some dispute as to where the latrines are located."

"I'd think Colonel Snivel wouldn't have any trouble tracking you down. He could just follow his nose."

A runner had been sent to Famularis when the men first arrived, to find out what should be done with them. When the runner returned with word to bring them to Famularis's tent the two Negroes took charge of the white men and led them through the campsite. On the way, the traveling man had an opportunity to see how the newest arrivals were adapting to their lives as free men. They seemed to be still bunched into separate groups, just as they had been upon reaching the camp. No process of assimilation with the original band or other new arrivals was taking place. Some groups were composed entirely of young men, while others were just a couple, a man and a woman, with perhaps a child. Most of them looked quite forlorn and distrustful of their neighbors, whom they doubtless suspected were planning to rob them of the few possessions they had brought with them. And of course this was the case. Those who had been with Famularis a long time were particularly avaricious, feeling that having been supporters of freedom from the outset, they were justified in taking the clothes of the newcomers, their own garments having become so threadbare they could only be described as rags.

A shallow stream near the encampment was evidently the source of the water used for drinking and bathing, but at many points it was clogged with refuse. Some of the older and weaker slaves were lying listlessly on the ground, perhaps sick or trying to sleep. Also several young men with rifles, who were notably better fed and more alert than the others, could be seen walking the grounds or sitting on low-lying branches. The traveling man took all this in, unlike Fergus, whose attention was fully occupied by improvising on his harmonica, which he'd fallen back on ever since Fleet Cougar had destroyed his banjo, asking their guards from time to time, "Tell me, have you ever heard anything like this?"

"You I recognize," said Famularis when the two were in his presence. "But when I knew you before, you had both your ears. Now your right ear be missing. A man who loses an ear, someone was very displeased with him."

"I displease many. If you recall, I displeased you when I said if you didn't move you'd die. But you've learned that lesson well."

"Oh yes. And now the tide be in our favor. Our example draws others to us. You see how we's increased in numbers."

"This is how men were meant to love," said Akoko. "In my bold hand there were no jewelries of plaster and slave."

"Old, not bold. I's told you."

"Men were born free," said the traveling man, "but since the first moment of recorded time they've been trying to live in ordered ranks and files. However, this is about to change. The revolution is upon us.

Men will be retaking their old freedoms. We'll tear everything down, every last shard and shingle of the old regime."

"They be bold words," said Famularis. "But the time for words is passed. Now you must put them into effect."

"When last I left you I left a gift, a gift of blood. You know whereof I speak."

"Yes."

"There, you've felt it. That's freedom. Can words give you that? You can pass that gift on to your people."

"Yes . . ." Famularis drew the picture in his mind, and it pleased him very much. Slaves would run, but werewolves . . . "Are you proposing I create a fraternity of werewolves?"

"A society of werewolves. Not only brothers, sisters as well, all of you werewolves. What civilized force could stand against you?"

"You forget the one most disagreeable aspect of the werewolf. Before, when I was entirely a man I felt myself to be a man and I knew my strength and my power was mine every day of the month. But now, when I's more than a man, I feel myself to be something less, because I has my full power and my strength only one day of the month. On the other days I's trapped by weakness that wants me to waste away and die to no purpose, as if I's in a cage and the world and all I would do be locked away where I cannot get to it. So the gift you's given brings more disquiet than I would have otherwise."

"What then is your wish?"

"To be a man no longer. I wish to be a wolf always."

"That time is coming. Soon the moon will be full every night, and we will all be as we truly are. It is only necessary to throw off the last trappings of reason, and that work is well in hand. Tonight you must begin the creation of the army of which I spoke."

"Yes. It will be done."

"What will you do?" asked Akoko.

"You will be first." As he said this he took a knife and slashed a wound in the base of his hand. Blood oozed from the gash. He held his hand up to Akoko. "Drink."

Akoko looked at the bleeding hand with dread and trembling.

But what was that? Everyone was abruptly alert. Was that rifle fire?

"Was you followed?" Famularis demanded of the traveling man.

"I'm certain we weren't," he answered.

"I'm certain you was." Famularis burst from his tent. "Come! To me!" he called to those that were his followers. Now was when he should be a wolf, but he was only a man who felt the rage and passion of a wolf. "We will destroy these soldiers now!"

The first stars were twinkling in the sky, which was now quite dark, but not so dark that Colonel Snivel could not see to shoot. He aimed carefully through the sights of his rifle and pulled the trigger. One slave went down. He had them now. He put another in his sights. There was no question of finding an abandoned encampment this time. Blam! Another slave killed. These were not going to be rounded up and returned to their masters. Oh no. This was a hostile force. He was going to stamp out this slave rebellion and no question about it. There would be no survivors. He noticed Captain Squeak slowing down and turned to see why.

"I'm not so fast as I used to be," said Squeak with a put upon air. "And I'm a quartermaster. It's ridiculous I have to do any actual fighting." He watched as Snivel, with a contemptuous gesture, hastened towards some barricades that were still offering resistance, leaving him behind. He stopped and caught his breath. It's true the slaves were totally unprepared. It was just a matter of mowing them down, really. He could handle this. He saw Nero dressed in a soldier's red coat holding a rifle and running past him a few yards to his right. "Where'd you get that coat?" he shouted.

Nero couldn't be bothered to answer. He could hardly even be bothered to shoot the other slaves. He was looking for the tent of Famularis. He had a vivid memory of what it looked like. Since he was not stopping to aim and fire he quickly found himself coming to the center of the slaves' camp. A bullet twanged just past his ear. He sighted the slave who had aimed at him and fell to one knee. Quickly bringing his rifle to his shoulder he aimed and fired and was rewarded by the sight of his enemy falling to the ground. Now that he was kneeling he looked around and saw there were others like the one he'd just killed, slaves armed with rifles defending the camp. And there, he saw it, Famularis's tent. He looked behind for Snivel and the soldiers but all he saw was the trees and the backs of slaves. He was torn for a moment, wondering if he should rejoin the others and lead them to the tent, or if he should proceed on his own. He started crawling back, but just then he saw a short man in a broad-brimmed hat emerge from the tent followed by a red haired youth looking intently at the harmonica he carried in his hand. These two were not slaves, and he was intrigued as to what they were doing here. He crept closer to overhear what they were saying.

"It's time to get out of here," said the man with the hat.

"Well don't hold back on my account," said the youth. "Those bullets are a lot closer than I like."

"Look," the man with the hat was pointing to the sky, "the witches." Their dark profiles could just be made out fluttering between the clouds. "The coven is assembling. Hurry!"

They started off, just as Famularis, wearing a bandolier full of bullets across his chest, came out after them. "Wait," he said. The two paid no attention, hastening quickly away. "Seize those two!" he shouted. Two heavily muscled slaves burst from the tent and set off in pursuit. Famularis watched them for a moment before reentering the tent and then emerging a few moments later carrying his rifle. As soon as he did so he was confronted by Nero standing with a rifle aimed directly at his chest.

"Hold it right there, Romeo," said Nero, "and drop that gun."

Famularis, enraged, shouted, "Nero! What's you doing here?!"

"I said drop it!"

"Why's you pointing that gun at me? And what's you doing in that red coat? Has you sold yourself to the army now?" He laughed at the idea.

"I am not joking. I will shoot you if you don't put that gun down right now!"

"I never said you could have a rifle!" Famularis strode forward and ripped the gun from Nero's hands. "This is loaded! Who gave you a loaded gun?!"

Akoko now walked cautiously out of the tent. She was fearful on account of the darkness and the gunshots and the other sounds of fighting. "Who are you talking to?" she asked.

"This idiot has reappeared, just when we needed him least." He handed her the rifle he'd taken from Nero. "Here. Shoot him if he tries anything." Then he set off after the others.

Akoko held the gun uneasily on Nero. "Were you sin?"

"What?"

"You've been wrong penny plays. Were you sin all this dime?"

"You jabber like a monkey. Can't you talk like a person yet?"

"I talk like I talk."

"Tha's 'cause I didn' teach you. You got a lot to learn. Akoko, I'm a better man than he is. He's not even a man. I came back to rescue you."

"Putt I live him."

"Put down that gun and come with me. You deserve better than this."

"Pots! Dun't drum drear. I'll shoot."

"We're wasting time. I will make you a queen."

There was a burst of shooting nearby and many slaves ran past, firing guns and shouting loudly. Famularis stumbled back fatally wounded. "The stupid slaves just run away," he shouted, falling into Akoko's arms. Akoko wailed a lament, dropping the rifle. Muscles stood out like cords on her arms as she crushed him to her breast. "You run too," he urged her. "Don't let them take you."

"Come, my liver, come. We must escape."

"I can't. I'm dying."

"You will not die for a long time. You cannot die. I live you."

"Akoko, you's my greatest joy." Tears poured down Akoko's face as he went on, "They can kill me, but I made myself a man. They can't unmake me. My last sight be your beautiful face. Promise you'll never let them make you a slave."

"Never will I be a slave. I will die with you. Shoot me."

"I can't."

"Dun't leave me aloonly."

Famularis tried to raise his rifle to shoot, but Nero hit him and knocked him down. "Nero," he said, "go fight your foes . . . the men who's made you in their . . ." Then he breathed his last.

"Image," said Akoko. She renewed her sobbing.

The soldiers had the upper hand. The woods were dense with running figures, but Nero and Akoko stood motionless over Famularis's corpse. Slowly he walked to her and put his arm around her shoulder. She shook it off.

"Kill me too," said Akoko. "My love is not worse living."

Captain Squeak, meanwhile, had entered into a fighting frenzy and was busily finishing off any wounded slaves left behind when their companions fled. He almost fired at Nero before recognizing him in his red coat. "Nero, the day is ours," he said.

"The night is more like. Allow me to introduce you to Akoko. I have rescued her from the fate of her companions, and I have killed Famularis. His body lies here."

Snivel arrived with a platoon of soldiers. "Jasper, what are you doing?" he asked.

"I've captured these two and killed Famularis." He pointed to Famularis's body.

Snivel walked to where the body lay. "Yes, this is him. Good work."

"Actually, I was the one who killed him," said Nero.

"That's not possible. You're my prisoner. And take off that coat. Do you realize there are actual soldiers who don't have coats? And you're wearing this. It's a disgrace."

Just then a group of eight or nine slaves threw themselves at the soldiers' feet, crying, "We surrender. Please, don't shoot us." They threw their weapons, which amounted to an assortment of wooden clubs, hammers and other implements, to the ground and held out their open hands. Among the group were two women and a child.

Snivel looked them over. "We've won the battle," he said. This was a moment he'd looked forward to. "Gather them together," he told his troops. "Find all the slaves you can and bring them here. The battle's over. We've won . . . And get each one to bring some brush, or fallen branches – wood we can use for kindling."

The troops spread out, rounding up the demoralized slaves. Very few had any fight left in them. Most were happy to drop their weapons and give themselves up, as though they'd known all along this wasn't really going to work. Before long there was a considerable

crowd gathered together, mostly men, but also women and a few children, looking about disconsolately, some smiling and making small talk with the soldiers who surrounded them.

Squeak said, "We can't take prisoners. We have nothing to feed them. We don't have the men to take care of them and we don't have enough supplies."

One well-muscled black who took it upon himself to act as a spokesman for the rest said, "We'll find our own provisions. We'll find yours too."

"How? You think we'll let you loose to forage in the woods? You'll escape," said Snivel. He turned to Squeak, "There's nothing to do but kill them. It's actually merciful. We'll shoot them."

A number of soldiers seemed disturbed when they heard this. They looked at one another, exchanging confused glances in the ever-darkening glen.

"These aren't really people," said Snivel. "They're enemies."

"We've surrendered. You can't kill us," said the black, as it dawned on him why they'd been told to gather kindling. "We promise not to escape. If you let us, we'll all go back to our masters. We promise." There was general assent and shaking of heads at this from the other captives.

"Shoot them," Snivel gave the order.

A few of the soldiers brought their rifles to their shoulders and aimed, but most stood their ground, unwilling to shoot the captives milling uneasily in front of them. "Even the women and children?" one asked.

"Look, this can easily be worked out," said the black nervously.

"We can't feed them, they'd die anyway. You can ask the quartermaster." He turned to Squeak. "Isn't that right?"

"Oh, don't bother me. I don't care anymore. I wash my hands of this whole business."

"But that's murder," said the soldier.

"Not when you're wearing a uniform and following orders. Soldiers don't commit murder. This is war!" He gave a manic laugh and raised his gun. "Look, I'll show you." He shot the one who'd acted as spokesman. Immediately the slaves reacted by trying to rush the soldiers, or by running into the woods. The soldiers all started shooting. Some of the slaves tried to climb the trees, but this just made them clearer targets. One woman snatched up a child and bolted for cover. Snivel ran after her and shot her in the back. Then he smashed the child's skull with the butt of his rifle. He gave a silly giggle. His only wish was that this could all go on much longer, he was having such a good time. All around him slaves were falling to the ground amidst a clatter of bullets and a haze of gunsmoke.

Nero, horrified at the summary execution of unarmed men, women and children, grabbed Squeak's shoulder and shouted, "Why are you all so blood thirsty? There is good value in these slaves you are killing so unnecessarily."

"No," answered Squeak, "not after they're suspected of being werewolves. They've no value at all."

"Werewolves?! Only Famularis was a werewolf and he is dead."

In his exasperation Nero turned to Snivel where he was standing over the dead child, the light of insanity in his eyes. "You seem to be a man of sense. Why are you destroying these slaves when you could sell them and make yourself rich? Killing them is just a waste."

Snivel looked at him, his face freshly flecked with blood. "You're right. It is a waste. We should rape the women first." He cackled like a maniac.

Akoko stood up to him. "They said my husband was a peast. You are much worse. You are fluffy masqueraders! Have you no smart?"

"What are you saying? I'm worse than a priest? That's absurd." He marched off looking for others to kill.

"No! Kill me!" shouted Akoko. "I don't want to love!"

Nero grabbed her and hustled her away. "You're out of your mind. They're all out of their minds."

"No! No!" Akoko was hitting him.

"Lie low. I'm saving your life." He pushed her down and lay on top of her. Akoko continued to mutter and cry out, but she spoke in her native tongue, and the words she used would not endure translation.

In the end it was a bloodbath. With the brutality of a horde of butchers the soldiers waded through the mass of ill equipped, disorganized slaves, slaughtering them as they went. A few small groups escaped into the Forest, but the army of werewolves the traveling man had envisioned was never to be.

When the killing was over, and no more wounded were moaning their agony, the shooting stopped and an eerie silence descended. The soldiers looked in amazement at what they'd done. Snivel gave order to pile the corpses together and heap the dried kindling around them. He set a small piece of wood alight and was going to throw it onto the funeral pyre. The dancing flames were reflected in his eyes. At this point he hesitated. It occurred to him that the Forest was exceptionally dry and there was great risk of starting a wildfire. He stood for a moment and then, making the greatest effort imaginable, willed himself back to sanity. He looked around. He saw his troops transformed into maddened executioners; he saw his uniform soaked in innocent blood; and for one awful moment he was aware that he could have chosen otherwise. Then the flame, burning down the wood he held, reached his fingers and he involuntarily yelped and tossed the fiery brand into the kindling. The kindling caught alight and the flames spread rapidly, quickly consuming the funeral pyre. The burning flesh smelt sweetly as black clouds of smoke enveloped the clearing, shutting out all sight of the stars. The roaring flames cast sparks into the branches of nearby trees where they ignited dried leaves and twigs and soon the fire was spreading from the clearing into the surrounding forest. The blaze spread with an eager ferocity, erasing all traces of the massacre and threatening to surround the troops. Quickly Snivel called his force to order and began a hasty retreat, staying just ahead of the flames. They reached a river. It was not deep and they were able to ford it. On the other side they finally dared to rest, the river making a boundary between themselves and the fire. Elsewhere flames spread all that night and the next day and the next. To the north there'd been much rain, but here the Forest was dry to the point of being arid. The blaze spread, engulfing the neighboring plantations and many of the largest and the most grand were destroyed. Eventually the fire burned itself out, but not till much of the southern Panhandle had been reduced to ashes.

The area around Trento, however, was spared, so on their way back to Port Jay, Snivel's troops stopped at the Merriwether estate to deliver Nero and Akoko. Just as Nero had foreseen, Andrew Merriwether was delighted to have his slave returned to him. He resolved to make Nero an example that would deter any others who were thinking of escape. He made a public spectacle of breaking both his arms and both his legs before hanging him from a tall and many-branched elm tree. The body was allowed to dangle several days till it had been picked apart by crows and was starting to decompose. Akoko was taken in amongst the household slaves, where she found a place in the Master's bed. She was there on several occasions, until the next full moon, when Master Merriwether, after a tumultuous night, was discovered with his throat ripped open amidst the bloody bedclothes. A shattered window in the boudoir was the only clue to Akoko's whereabouts.

CHAPTER TWENTY-THREE
HEARTBREAK HILL

TAVISH AND KATIE moved on from the tavern and traveled the rest of that day. When night fell they still hadn't found a suitable spot so they pressed on. Katie was dozing as she sat Neddy's back and Tavish was plodding along beside her, putting one foot in front of another, on and on, as he'd been doing since they left Port Jay. As he walked beside her he fell under a spell cast by the freshness of the night air, the fragrance of the pine woods and the constant swish and tinkle of the saddle bags and bridle. He knew the man he was, and he thought of himself as one of those rare souls who can see himself without self-deception. He knew himself to be generous and compassionate, tender and sensual. He also knew these qualities were hidden from others, but they were his essential nature. He wanted to share them with Katie, but every way he'd tried, she'd blocked him. That was her essential nature. Yet he loved her so much. It wasn't because of her beauty that he loved her like he did. That had drawn him to her, of course, it drew everyone to her, but it was something else that made her so lovable and impossible to resist. And it was such a common thing there must be some word to describe what it was, but he was blank as to knowing what that word might be. And it struck him there were lots of things that existed and everybody saw them and knew what they were but what was the word for them? The thing about Katie that made it impossible for him not to love her was one. Whenever he tried to think what that thing was he'd get tongue-tied and end up falling back on something about how beautiful she was, but that wasn't it. That was just what you saw. There was something she had in addition. It was vain struggles like this to pin a word to what made Katie so desirable that his mind would contend with as he walked step by step beside the pony through the night . . . Moody . . .? Headstrong . . .? Whatever it was, that was what had gotten him so tangled up with her. Sulky – that didn't quite hit it on the head. But still, if he had to describe her in one word, that would be it. Or maybe sultry. Wasn't it queer that there were these things that must be clear to everyone but no one had thought to put a name to them? Like the pleasure Madam Lanchester always got from being displeased, what was the word for it? How she'd go about looking for things that didn't please her just so she could get all swelled up with it, whatever it was. He wondered if an educated man like Father Clumphy who'd read many books would know the word. But as he thought back to the words the Father used, words like sin, or morality, or pride, they all seemed to be about something else. He was sure that wasn't what he was thinking of. But these young women – that's what he kept coming back to – especially the ones that looked pretty – well, they all knew they looked pretty, why did that make them pretend they didn't want to look pretty – no, that wasn't it exactly – it made them screw their faces up so they didn't look pretty, but . . . Now he was losing track of his thoughts. He took a moment just to pace beside Neddy, and take in the night . . . The trees around here were different from the trees around Port Jay. He'd never paid much attention to trees before, but lately he'd been seeing so many he couldn't help but notice all the different kinds. And what would things be like in Kashahar, he wondered. He'd heard stories. The houses were built more with stone and less with wood. He wondered if they had the same kinds of stores and sold the same kinds of food as he was used to. And thinking of what they sold in the stores set him to thinking of things he'd bought for Katie and other girls before her and what it was, in his experience, was that anything you gave them wasn't good enough, like if you gave them something to wear it was either too big or too small, though as far as he could tell they looked pretty good in anything. Nothing was right for them and nothing annoyed them more than a friendly remark and they were cross with all the lads who admired them. And there he goes thinking of himself as a lad again. He was a grown man, damn it, why did he still have these thoughts? Though the girls seemed pleased by thoughts of being admired. They'd put their feet in shoes that didn't fit and walk all day with pains in their ankles just so they could be admired, but if you said anything friendly there went that face again. He couldn't make any sense of it. But that's what it was that had got him so tangled up with Katie. Tangled was the word he kept using. Was that the right word? He was sure it was. That word tangled seemed to have been thought up just to describe the way he was. So he had a word for that, but what had made him give up his old way of life entirely and become a thief and a wanderer just so he could be with Katie? There wasn't even a word for it he could use if he wanted to explain to someone why he'd done it. Not that there was anyone but himself who'd ask.

It was getting towards morning and they hadn't stopped yet when they saw an abandoned farmhouse. Chickens were running wild in the yard, and the place looked like it had just recently come to be neglected. Tavish took one of the hens and broke its neck and tied it to Neddy's saddle bags. But the inside of the house had such a sad and forlorn feel to it, they knew something bad had happened there, and they chose to move on.

Dawn's first light was filtering through the branches of the trees near that sorry farmhouse, falling on the travelers on the road, and also on a small campsite just inside the edge of the woods where a man lay asleep. This man had been here a few days, resting and recovering from a wound in his stomach. He hadn't had much to occupy himself with while he was recovering so, like Tavish, he'd been mulling over the events that had led him to the spot he now occupied. And as he mulled over those events he thought to himself, *What is a life? What's it for, and how should I use it?* He realized that the greatest moments of his life had in a way also been the simplest. They were the moments he'd spent at the top of a mast, taking in or letting out sail, with the ship rocking and the whole ocean below him and the wind tousling his hair, up among the seabirds with the whole wide world spread out for him to wonder at. There was nothing that compared to the way a man felt when he was up on a yard at the mercy of the gusty, blowing winds, the waves throwing him back and forth, hanging to the sheets for dear life. If he could have chosen any moments to relive, those would have been the ones, over and above even the sport of love. Why had he let those sorry buggers confuse him with their talk of a life on the land? That wasn't life. What he wanted was a ship, and an ocean to sail her on, and a breeze to blow her across the water, with nothing between himself and the horizon.

And now, his thoughts went on, now was the time he could have whatever he wanted. He had a lot of gold. He was very rich, especially now that Mr. Chips had bequeathed him his share. Now was the time to live the life he could imagine. And that life was far distant from the one he was living, here at a campsite in the woods. He had enough gold he could buy himself his own ship. The days spent lying on the ground, wearing dirty clothes and nursing a savage old wound were soon to come to an end. A man with as much gold as he had was a man who would make an appearance in the world. The first thing he needed was some new clothes. Then he'd need a pony too, to carry his gold into Kashahar. So when he'd recovered some strength he found a place not far from his camp where he buried most of his gold, and he made his plans to head into Kashahar, there to purchase his own sea-going vessel.

This morning he was feeling well enough he thought the time had come to put his plans into action. He'd watched as Crazy Dog tore the farmhouse apart and carved up the old lady and then moved further up the Coast Road. Now, while Crazy Dog was looking in another direction, was the time to move.

Till he could get new clothes he'd have to do the best he could with what he had. He tucked his shirt in so the tear wouldn't show. He hoped his hair and his beard didn't look too unkempt. He'd need to visit a barber. He set his knife in the scabbard at his waist. He filled his pockets with doubloons. And trusting his appearance wasn't too much that of a thief in the night, he headed into Kashahar.

Shortly after he'd gotten onto the Coast Road it went up a small hill, and on the hill he saw a man and a woman with just the pony he wanted. He hurried to catch up with them and when he was within shouting distance he yelled, "Ho there! I'll buy your pony."

The man looked around and came to a stop. Vincenzo caught up to him and held out his hand with two shiny doubloons. "Here," he said, "I'll pay two gold doubloons for the pony. I've not inspected him, but he looks a stout one. Sure two gold doubloons is more than he's worth but I'm in a hurry." He smiled.

Tavish and Katie looked at him. His clothes were dirty and bore some bloodstains. His hair was tousled and his beard was unkempt. He had a nasty scar on his face. A man like this with a lot of gold hadn't earned it in any respectable way. Of course they had long ago stopped expecting to meet anyone honest, but in this man they sensed a hitherto unsuspected measure of depravity. Tavish said, "Well, true enough. That would make a good profit on this pony, but I'm not sure we want to sell." He looked at Katie. Katie was looking very tired and she just shook her head no, so Tavish answered, "I'm sorry, but the lass says no. She'll not part with her pony."

"Whose pony is it?" asked Vincenzo. "Is it yours or hers?"

"We're in this together and sure we must both agree to sell."

"You mean she decides."

Now Katie spoke. "I'll not walk the rest of the way to Kashahar. I'm fatigued and my stomach is not settled. It may be a fair price for Neddy if we were standing in a market where ponies are sold, but I'll not part with him here for your two gold doubloons."

This vexed Vincenzo. He wished the man would take charge so a deal could be struck. "Very well then," said he, "I'll sweeten the pot. Here's a third doubloon." He was not smiling now.

"I think you're not understanding me," said Katie. "I'm not holding out for a higher price. The pony is not for sale. I've no need of your gold and I've a great need of Neddy."

"There's no reason you can't walk into Kashahar." Vincenzo was letting his impatience show. "And I need a pony."

"She cannot. Not in her state. *You* can walk into Kashahar," said Tavish, "and I'm sure you'll find another pony there will suit your purpose."

"Ah, the ponies they have in Kashahar, so I've heard. But why can she not walk?"

"She's with child. Surely she must have the mildness of the pony ride. To say naught of who would have to carry the saddle bags. And that's an end to it."

"I'm offering enough she could buy her own bed and a midwife in Kashahar and be set up like a real lady. Does she not see that?" He felt slighted. It wasn't just the pony. Only a few minutes ago it had been his plan to walk into Kashahar to purchase a pony, but now he'd seen this one it was like an omen. Sure some friendly spirit had put this pony in his way and he was bound to have it. Well if he couldn't buy it there were other ways he could get it.

"She sees that well enough, and sure she'll be cursing herself later for not taking your gold, but at this moment all she can think of is the gentle ride into Kashahar, and she cannot ride your doubloons."

"She's with child, is she?" He put his gold back in his pocket.

"Certain it is."

"Well something can be done about that." Pure spite it was. He hit Katie a brutal blow in her stomach and then pulled his knife on Tavish.

Katie screamed.

"Get her off that pony," said Vincenzo holding his knife to Tavish's throat.

Tavish was stunned by this sudden change and Katie was whimpering from the pain in her belly. Both were staggering from fatigue and had no strength to resist the attack. It took little time for Tavish to maneuver Katie off the pony and get her standing on the ground.

"Give me that musket also," said Vincenzo. He still held the knife pointed at Tavish.

Tavish looked at the knife. Then he took the musket from his shoulder and handed it to him.

"Oh God, I can't stand." Katie swayed and sank slowly to the ground.

Nimbly mounting the pony, Vincenzo said, "So you really didn't have to worry about who'd carry the saddle bags because I have them. And you don't have to worry about her walking into Kashahar with child. I've fixed that too. I've solved all your problems not that you'll thank me for it." He gave a mean laugh and took Neddy's reins in hand.

Tavish was leaning towards Katie, trying to comfort her, when just that moment they heard the sound of galloping hooves from behind.

Vincenzo, who was mounted and looking over their shoulders, was the first to see the new arrivals. Two men on horseback were pounding down the Road. One of them had a hook where his hand should have been. Vincenzo, recognizing who they were, gave Neddy a quick kick in the belly and hurried away fast as the pony could take him. But there was no chance he'd outrun the steeds of Barnacle Jack and his companion. Jack also had recognized Vincenzo and, elated at this sudden good fortune, was bent on running him down. The two horsemen passed Tavish and Katie in a blur and fell on Vincenzo, who was attempting to load the musket while still riding the pony. He was unable to fight them off and quickly succumbed.

"Hold your hands up," said Barnacle Jack dismounting and holding a pistol. "Elijah, go through his pockets." Elijah put his hand into Vincenzo's pockets, where he found many doubloons and pieces of eight. Vincenzo glared dead hatred at Jack the whole time. "Well, I think you're going to tell us where the rest of this gold can be found."

Vincenzo was silent.

"What's the matter? Cat got your tongue? There's things can be done about that."

Meanwhile Katie was squatting where she'd fallen. Tavish had ripped her dress off and she was passing copious quantities of blood and urine. Tavish took his own shirt off and laid it beneath her so she wasn't directly on the ground, but there was really little that could be done. She moaned and tried to lie down, then squatted again, her hands tearing at her own belly as if they could tear the pain away. It was an arduous ordeal, but in the end the baby's little body was flushed out also, with the blood and other tissues.

Tavish lay beside her and held her as she cried. She cried great sobs that shook her whole frame. He thought of the sulky girl he'd walked next to through the night now transformed into this grieving woman. He wanted to comfort her with his every last fiber, there was nothing he wouldn't have done to give her even the slightest consolation, but there wasn't anything to do except lie beside her and hold her as she wailed her grief at the naked sky. He whispered words of love in her ear though he was certain she'd never hear them. Her grief was beyond the depth that could be known, and she was racked by terrible sobs, and Tavish felt each sob as though it was a wound to his own body. Gradually, as time passed, the relentless outbursts of sobbing became more gentle. Slowly the moaning ceased. She wrapped her arms around her chest as though she was holding herself together. She moved her legs. She closed her eyes and from somewhere deep inside soothing waves of comfort came to her anguished soul. In time she slept.

Tavish still lay beside her, one arm trapped under her body that he didn't dare move. This tragedy had befallen them so unexpectedly, so needlessly, it was impossible to see any good in it. But of course there had to be good in everything. It was simply a matter of finding it. He was interrupted in his reflections by Neddy who, being ignored, had now wandered over to his old master and was nuzzling Tavish on the shoulder in expectation of being fed. Tavish carefully drew his arm out from beneath Katie and sat up. As he did so she stirred and whimpered something in her sleep. It took only a glance up the road to see that things weren't going well there. Vincenzo had made an effort to stab Jack with his knife and make an escape. But Elijah had grabbed him before he could get away and Jack had unloaded two bullets into his chest. With his last dying breath he'd told Jack he'd never find the gold where it was buried. Jack let out a roar because he realized he'd done for his source of information and apart from the gold Vincenzo had on his person the rest was still as tantalizingly out of reach as ever. He and Elijah searched through everything Vincenzo had been wearing, extracting a few more coins and a watch and other odds and ends and then, seeing that Tavish and Katie had remained where they were, they decided to find out what they could tell.

Barnacle Jack approached Tavish saying, "I'm sorry. It appears this gentleman has caused you some grief also. I would not disturb you at this time, but it is of some import to ask what you know of him. I doubt he was a friend of yours."

"Certainly not," answered Tavish. "I'd never cast eyes on him before today when he came to buy our pony, and finding we wouldn't sell, he stole him from us."

"Did he take anything else?"

"The pony and his bags, but those we've recovered, thanks to you. And that musket I see lying there, that was ours."

They were on a small hill, and the elevation gave them good views of the surrounding countryside. A small distance to the east they could still see the abandoned farmhouse they'd passed in the night. The Road stretched along by the shore, empty as far as they could see in both directions. To the south lay the Forest, and to the north the Sound, and on the horizon they could make out Lost Bastard Island. Jack looked all about and then asked, "Which direction did he come from?"

"He caught us up in the direction we were going, towards Kashahar." Katie opened her eyes.

"He had some of our gold on him," said Jack. "Pity I shot his lights out before he could tell us where the rest was hid but he was that nettlesome a caitiff I found I'd killed him before I'd thought on't . . .There were a few other knickknacks on his person; I don't know if any of these are yours?" And here he held out the items they'd taken from Vincenzo's pockets, among which was a watch which bore a design of knots and tangles. Katie's eyes went wide when she saw that. She took the watch and opened it, and inside was inscribed, "From your own darling Katie." At that she gave a cry, and tears burst from her, for she saw now that Tom must certainly be dead, he'd not have given that watch away. She saw it all now, that this man had killed him and taken it from him, this same man who'd given her the blow in the belly that also had killed Tom's child. And she wept. She saw that her travels had been only a terrible waste and that all her love and her care and her hopes were all come to nothing. And here on this small hill not far from Kashahar she knelt down and wailed her grief for all that had happened and for the emptiness that was all that was left in her life.

Jack turned to Elijah. He said they'd best go back the direction Vincenzo had come from, see if they could find his tracks that mayhap would lead to where he'd hid the gold. So they mounted their horses and rode back slowly, looking to see where he'd gotten onto the Road. The sound of their hooves soon faded into the distance.

321

Tavish found some blankets in the saddlebags he could use to cover Katie. She was in no condition to move. Also he found a couple carrots for Neddy. What with one thing and another he kept himself too busy to dwell on what would have to be done for Katie, or where it made sense to go now. He kept his head turned away from the corpse of Vincenzo lying on the road a little ahead. When he heard Katie's breaths coming steady he dug a hole to lay the little thing that was almost a baby in, then covered it up. He stood and cast his glance in all directions. Surely all the omens were bad except the ones that were worse. Was there a word for that he wondered.

Chapter Twenty-Four
Sorrow and the True Nature of God

Tom would have come to a bad end in a matter of days from starvation or some other cause had it not been that he was found by that one individual who values life in all its forms and who sees the good in even the worst and most downtrodden specimen. He was captured by a slave trader. It's a tale worth some telling.

From an early age Harry Blackstone had been certain that anyone as clever and good-looking as himself was destined to be more than just another street urchin in Kashahar. He had devised numerous schemes to rise above his lot and take a place among the elite. His first enterprise had been selling forged theater tickets. When that dried up he managed to walk away untouched and since then he'd served as a broker for stolen goods, a seller of rum without paying the tariff, a merchandiser of homes on land that didn't exist, and various other roles. At times the loot had come rolling in, but mostly it hadn't, and he'd never acquired the bankroll he needed to achieve his goal of rubbing shoulders with the city's upper crust.

When he reached his thirties, he began to have the feeling he should stop relying on his luck and instead find a job with a salary. He'd watched as the oafs and lackwits he'd grown up with had traveled that route and were now looking like getting established. Through a friend he'd made in the constabulary he was able to get a job as an assistant warden in the jail, where he'd found he could wear a uniform, act tough and be bone idle and get paid for it.

One day, as he was seated in his office, picking his teeth with a toothpick he'd whittled from the leg bone of a rat, he had an inspiration. A call had gone out from the great landowners. The slave trade had been disrupted and many slaves had escaped and now, at the height of the season, they needed slaves. Harry asked himself a most important question: what was a slave? Everyone seemed to think it was someone whose skin was black. But Harry realized that it wasn't the color of a man's skin that made him a slave, it was putting chains on him that did it. Why did the slave dealers go to the jungle to find their slaves? Because the men there were black? No. Because the men there could be put in chains. Well Harry looked around and he saw he had plenty of chains. And due to all the recent upheaval, many were the lost souls wandering across the land. If those plantation owners wanted slaves as badly as they said, they wouldn't quibble if a few weren't exactly black. Putting those facts together gave him a jolt that got him out of his seat and set him to pacing around. His cells were currently empty, with the exception of one occupied by a local drunk who made it a habit to sleep there almost one night in seven. Currently he was passed out on the floor. Harry walked to the bars of his cell, looked in at him and said, "Barney, you're a slave." He opened the cell door, roused Barney and clapped him in handcuffs. He then collected all the cuffs and chains he could find in the prison, loaded them into a sack on his back and led Barney out the door to begin the search for his next slave.

But first, the sack on his back was dragging him down so he decided to call on a pair of brothers who'd been accomplices in some of his previous undertakings. He liked these two because they were strong and didn't ask a lot of questions. They were stupid and sadistic too, but apart from that they were nice guys and always sweet to their mother. He explained how his new business operated and asked if they wanted to get in on the ground floor. They allowed as how they were open to the idea and they'd always wanted to learn how slave driving worked. The two brothers were named Dane and Bramij. Dane was the brains and Bramij was the muscle though truly none could tell the difference. Harry handed the sack to Bramij, but Dane said, "We've got a slave. What's he for?" So Barney ended up carrying the sack of chains.

Harry decided on a back and forth route in the woods around Kashahar that would allow them to pick up whatever stragglers could be found. Any who couldn't give a good accounting of themselves

– in other words, any who didn't fight back – were fair game. He planned to do this for a few days and then take them down to the slave market in Indradoon to be sold.

He was giving Dane and Bramij a little instruction on the fine points of his plan as they walked down a forest trail. The early morning mist was just rising from the ground. Harry enjoyed the sensation of being out of doors. Too many of his days lately had been spent surrounded by iron bars and walls of stone. Suddenly he saw a pair of young blacks skinning a deer in the woods. Harry stopped, put a finger to his lips and pointed out the quarry to Dane and Bramij.

"How do –" said Dane.

Harry shut him up and gestured to him to whisper.

"How do we catch those two?" whispered Dane.

Using hand gestures, Harry described how Dane and Bramij could sneak through the woods and approach the two from opposite sides. When they executed this maneuver the two blacks put up a good fight, getting in their share of blows, but after a brief scuffle they were cuffed and added to the chain behind Barney.

"Are you going to return me to my master?" asked one, whose name was Amos.

"You belong to me and I'm going to sell you to a new master."

"I'll never go back. You'll have to kill me first," said the other, whose name was Daniel.

Dane had taken a blackened eye in the fight and Bramij had wrenched his back. Now that the slaves were handcuffed, Dane took the opportunity to pay back the slave who'd hit him by punching him in the face.

"Hold it, hold it," said Harry. "You're mauling the merchandise."

"Look what he did to my eye."

"I don't care. But if *he* has a black eye that comes out of his price. I mean to sell quality goods, not someone all beat up." Dane looked crestfallen. "Look, you can't just clobber these slaves. That'll cost us money."

"Can I kick them?" asked Bramij.

"I guess that's alright. Just don't leave any marks."

So Bramij kicked them a few times till the pain in his back got worse. Then they resumed their back and forth trek, now with three slaves in tow.

That night they made a campsite by the side of the trail. Harry had saved the deer the two blacks had been skinning and had forced them to carry it for him. Now he made them build a campfire to roast it on. He enjoyed a succulent meal with Dane and Bramij while it was only water from a nearby freshet and whatever they could chew from the hooves and the marrow bones for the three slaves. Harry set Bramij to be guard for the first watch of the night and then he and Dane went to sleep. The slaves tried to do the same. The day's exertions had taken their toll on Barney. He had a bad tremor and his pants stank of urine. He'd noticed Bramij taking a few swigs from a hip flask and he pleaded with him to share what he had.

"Say one word more and you'll regret it," was all the answer he got.

Amos asked Barney how he'd gotten captured.

"I got drunk and passed out. When I woke up I was in chains. Didn't know they could do that – could make someone a slave. I'm not like you. You're a real slave."

"You mean I was born a slave."

"Blast your stinking ass I said keep quiet!"

"You were made a slave," Amos went on. Bramij walked over and hit Barney with his stick. When he went to do the same to Amos he just gave Bramij a look of contempt and said, "Don't try it on me."

"Then don't make me have to."

After this there was silence, only broken by the occasional rustling of the chains when Barney shook.

The next morning they overtook two Indians, one of them a squaw, accompanied by a white man in a cloak. These were cuffed and added to the chain gang. Harry quickly realized that the squaw, who happened to be young and of healthy appearance, created a worrisome complication. Dane and Bramij made no secret of their plans to rape her and it occurred to him the other slaves would likely do the same – he'd heard about the blacks. In principle he had no objection, but he foresaw a host of arguments that were certain to arise, so he announced that from now on there'd be two chain gangs, one for men and another for women. He was going to oversee the women's chain, while Dane and Bramij had custody of the men's. He added that everyone had to keep their filthy paws off the squaw, whose name was Breezy Woodchuck, and that she was his personal property. Bramij quickly objected, arguing that he had played the largest role in her capture, so by rights she should belong to him. Harry tried to make it clear to Bramij that in this business he had no rights; that rights were something only he, Harry, had, because this was his idea, and if Bramij was left on his own without Harry he'd soon see what a hopeless bugger he was. The conversation was a long one and very repetitive but, the exchange of ideas having been accomplished, everyone decided it was now the middle of the day and high time to get something to eat.

Barney and the blacks were almost fainting with hunger, but of course Harry had nothing for them. Barking Dog, the Indian, had a little fruit, which he shared. Harry took Breezy aside and told her she was not to mingle with the others or listen to what anyone else said. He told her she was his personal slave and no one else was going to touch her.

"You can put me in chains," she said, "but I am nobody's slave."

"We'll discuss this further tonight," he answered.

Meanwhile Dane and Bramij were amusing themselves with the cloaked man, who was attempting to recite a prayer. They'd let him get the first words out, then they'd hit him and tell him to shut up. That would make the man puke and lie down some, but he'd never shut up, so they'd just hit him some more and they were having lots of fun playing this game.

While they were doing this Barney asked Barking Dog if, in addition to his fruit, he happened to have anything to drink. "I could almost kill for a drop of the real thing, or even some wine." But Barking Dog had nothing.

The cloaked man, having recovered from his most recent beating, was back to his prayers. "Deliver me, o Lord, from the evil –"

"Blast your stinking ass!" said Bramij, bringing his stick down on his shoulders.

"—man; preserve me from the violent man; which –"

Dane hit him too.

"Keep quiet. You're just going to get yourself hurt," counselled Daniel. There was silence for a while, broken only by the sounds of Dane and Bramij eating. Then the cloaked man whispered, "—which imagine mischiefs in their heart –"

Dane put his face right up to his, almost eyeball to eyeball, and said, "You're a stubborn one, aren't you?"

"—continually are they gathered together for war." But after that he said no more.

They captured another that afternoon. He was wearing the uniform of a soldier, but he'd lost or thrown away all his weapons. He'd been a cobbler in Port Jay till his house burned and he joined the army. His name was Pete and he hadn't put up any resistance when they cuffed him and put him at the end of the chain gang. They stopped and took a break after this. Harry looked at his rag-tag band of creatures: one – two – three – four – five – six men and one woman. He still had a few chains in the bag Barney carried but he guessed this would represent a good haul, and soon it would be time to head towards Indradoon. He was pleased by how well his new business was working out.

Even though they'd been told not to talk, the slaves were introducing themselves to one another. "My name is Father Clumphy," said the cloaked man. "I used to be a simple parish priest till God exalted me and gave me a mission to spread the word of the Lord to the Indians. He made of my heart and tongue burning coals whereby He set alight the hope in their souls."

"You're really lucky I'm tired and don't feel like getting up," said Bramij, who'd taken a few swigs from his flask. "I have no doubt whatever you're saying doesn't matter worth a shit."

"What is wrong with talking? Surely our words are not a threat."

"I just don't like hearing that kind of talk."

"So that's what caused the Indians to rise up and attack and led to all the death and destruction in the Forest. And now I'm not sure if that was God's plan or not, and if it was, well . . ."

"How do you know God has a plan?" asked Amos.

"Maybe plan is the wrong word. But there must be some fundamental, guiding intelligence in the world. I myself have read the message God wrote and sent to mankind."

"What did it say?"

Clumphy grew very thoughtful. ". . . The actual words are not important. What is important is to know that the message exists."

"If I were God, and I wrote a message and showed it to someone I'd be disappointed if that person said the words of the message were not important."

"But you are not God. Of course the words are important, but the meaning of the words is not one that our minds can comprehend. Our minds were given to us to do things like find a mate and get a meal. But we try to use this feeble tool to unlock the mysteries of God's universe. Is it any wonder there is much we don't understand?"

"I'm standing up," said Bramij.

"Especially considering it's so unerring when it comes to finding a mate," said Breezy Woodchuck. She had mostly been keeping quiet, so when she spoke everyone looked at her.

"And getting a meal," Daniel put in. "I'm starved."

"And getting a drink," added Barney.

Then they all looked at Bramij and kept quiet.

Bramij hit Clumphy on the back with his stick. "I'm warning the rest of you," he said. Then he went to his place and sat down.

They traveled a little further that day and then found a place to camp for the night. Shortly after they'd finished their meal, Harry retired with Breezy Woodchuck to an area he'd set up apart from the others. Soon there were sounds coming from that direction. Clumphy decided he would distract them all from what they were hearing. "It's my opinion," he said, "that belief shapes the world. There are those who argue that seeing is believing. But without belief nothing can be seen. Believing is seeing."

Breezy Woodchuck's cries were becoming louder and more anguished.

"It's this attribute belief that we attach to some ideas and not to others that shapes the world. The world is really only this present moment we're sharing. Nothing else exists. Everything else is just things we believe, noise in our heads."

"Is no one going to do something?" pleaded Barking Dog.

"Does anyone disagree with that?" There was no response. The drama being enacted a few feet away was drawing everyone's attention. "There are many things we all believe, that's why we can live in the world together and talk to one another. Our beliefs create the universe. It's not the other way round."

No one seemed inclined to dispute this. Barking Dog just gazed into the shadows under the trees.

Shortly afterward Harry returned to the others. He was dragging Breezy Woodchuck behind him. Her clothing was torn and her hair was bedraggled. He said he wasn't sleepy. He'd take the first watch and let Dane and Bramij snooze. Everyone slept, or at least pretended to, and there were no more disturbances that night.

The next morning they captured Tom. They put him at the end of the line behind Pete where he lurched along, getting cursed at by the others every time he tripped over a rock or some unevenness in the path, which happened pretty frequently. He heard the voices of the other slaves in the chain gang and tried to sort them out. As they went along, Clumphy was constantly breaking out in prayers and getting pummeled. Harry had to intervene, noting that Clumphy was showing a lot of bruises. The walk that day felt endless to Tom, just one long nightmare of stumbling and cursing and beating. At one point Harry announced, "I think we've got enough now it makes sense to head towards the slave markets. There's a place near here where we can stock up on supplies, and then we'll get onto the Coast Road and take it as far as the branch for Indradoon." He had eight slaves altogether, and one of them a woman. It was a good haul. The Indian wouldn't bring top dollar on account of Indians being notoriously lazy, but he was worth something. The same went for the blind beggar. So long as he still had enough strength to walk he could be used as a pack animal, or he could pull a sledge or something. He wouldn't go to waste.

During the afternoon the slave drivers were pestering Harry about getting their turn with Breezy Woodchuck. He told them if they behaved themselves and stopped beating the merchandise black and blue, that would be their reward. They came to the spot Harry had mentioned and while he was bargaining for some bacon and onions, everyone in the chain gang took the opportunity to rest.

The minute Barney sat down his eyes closed. He was dead to the world.

Amos and Daniel had their heads together. They communicated mostly by darting movements of the eyes and fingers, accompanied by the occasional whispered word. None of the others knew what they mumbled about.

Barking Dog kept trying to justify himself for not taking action last night. He told himself Breezy had been Half Moon's woman, not his, so why was it his duty to defend her? But at heart he knew he was a coward. In truth, he didn't see what he could do to rescue her, but if he died in the attempt that would at least clear him of all shame. He just couldn't convince himself he really wanted to die in the attempt.

Father Clumphy was turning over what he'd said last night about seeing and believing. There were some things that could be seen without belief, and other things that couldn't. Maybe it was the difference between 'believing that' and 'believing in.' But God had vouchsafed him a clue. "I will not marry a wallaby." Somehow the more he contemplated that statement the more he felt his mind was no longer working. Some mysteries remained beyond the depths the human intellect could comprehend.

Pete was reviewing his experiences of the past few weeks and wondering how his life had gone so wrong so quickly. For many years he'd lived and worked in Port Jay. He'd supported a family, gone to church and been part of the neighborhood. If someone had told him a few weeks ago that he'd soon be dressed in the uniform of the colonial army, manacled in a chain gang to be sold as a slave he'd have laughed. He'd now come to see the world was a far more dangerous place than he'd ever imagined, and the people in it were far stranger than he could ever have conceived. His old life seemed like a dream from which he'd been awakened to a world of distress and terror, the everyday world we inhabit, all unknowing. And he was starting to take on the slave's hopeless hope. He couldn't let himself hope because it hurt to hope when everything in life was beyond his control. But how can one live without hope?

Tom removed his boot and massaged his injured foot. Whether it was on account of Elijah's salve, or due to some other reason, his wound was healing. He tried to sort out the voices he heard. The voice of the religious man sounded vaguely familiar, but he was sure he didn't recognize the others. He'd been afraid he'd be found by Crazy Dog; now he knew there were worse than him. The distrust, foul suspicion, hatred and vengefulness, which were all he saw in those around him, were giving him a very low opinion of humanity. It seemed impossible to imagine that people were worse than they actually were, and he feared whatever he saw in others was but a pale reflection of what was in himself. He saw that all men were driven by unjust anger and mad delusion, that they were at odds with all creation and their lives were just the long process of being devoured by evil rancor, till the very roots of life were eaten away and men were estranged even from themselves.

Breezy Woodchuck sat apart, where Harry had left her. She looked at Bramij, and he wasn't much to look at, but she said, "You."

"Yeah?"

"Where you taking us?"

"Indradoon."

"Indradoon?"

"You're going to be sold in the market there."

Breezy made a dismissive shrug. "That's not where you'll get the best price."

"What do you mean?"

"Have you been to Indradoon before?"

"Lots of times . . . Oh, you mean Indradoon? No, never been there."

"Didn't think so. If you had, you'd know at Indradoon they cheat like hell. They're all insiders there. They'll find a way to cut you out. "

"Really?"

"Really . . ."

"They won't cut me out. You'll see. I'm too smart for that."

"I know a better place. There's a place we Indians sell and get top dollar. It's a secret, but I can lead you there."

"Oh no. Don't do this. You're trying to trick me."

"Do I look like I could trick you? Someone like you, how could I trick you?"

"People always think they can trick me. I don't know why."

"Listen. Talk to Harry about it."

"Don't tell me what to do." His face grew thoughtful as he pondered his next steps. "I'm going to talk to Harry about it."

"You do that. If you're smart, you'll get –"

Here she was cut off. Harry had completed his bargaining. "Alright," he said, "I've got food for us all the way to Indradoon. And I'm keeping a tally by the way. What you eat comes out of the price we get at the end."

"Tell him," said Breezy.

Bramij just gave her a look and walked away. But she saw him thinking something over and whispering to Dane as they resumed their trek.

Late in the day they found a spot by the side of the trail and settled down for the night. Dane and Bramij were arguing about who was going to go first. Bramij said they should let the lady choose and Dane told him that was a barmy idea and why did it matter to her? They continued to argue as they prepared the meager dinner for the slaves and the blacks started a campfire. Harry was making a stew out of the supplies and getting a headache listening to Dane and Bramij. He finally got so annoyed he told them if they wanted any of the stew they could pay him by giving him another night with the lady. He wouldn't even take the food they ate tonight out of their tally. There'd be a few more nights before reaching Indradoon and they'd have their chance, but he'd changed his mind and decided he'd keep her for his own another night or two.

"You changed your mind?" said Dane.

"That I did."

"You changed your mind?"

"I went to a lot of trouble bargaining for these victuals. I should get something for that. Anyway she prefers me. She's scared of you two."

"If you're going to change your mind, maybe I'll change my own mind about helping you. You're not the only one with a mind he can change."

"Go ahead. Leave if you want. I'd like to see how far you get."

"Oh, I'll leave alright. And when I leave I'm taking her with me."

At this point, Harry pulled out his pistol. "You'll do nothing of the sort."

"Oh ho. You think that'll stop me? There's two of us and only one of you, right, Bramij?"

"Right," said Bramij.

"You showed us how to divide and attack from both sides." Bramij started creeping around to get in back of Harry. "Are you sure you don't want to put that pistol away?"

"I'll get one of you," said Harry. "One for sure."

"But the other one'll get you."

There was a tense silence. Then Harry put the pistol back in his belt. "There's no reason to act unfriendly."

"Then she's ours?" asked Dane.

You could see from his face this was going down hard with Harry, but he nodded his head yes. Breezy Woodchuck had watched all this with no expression, but at this point she looked at Barking Dog. Barking Dog lowered his eyelids and looked away.

"Dinner's served," said Bramij, putting a meager platter of water and some crusts of bread before the slaves.

"I'm not eating that. I want some of your food," said Breezy Woodchuck.

Now everyone was getting stirred up.

"You're a slave," said Harry. "You don't make demands."

"I told you, I'm no slave."

Clumphy stood up. "Peace, brothers," he said.

"Look, I'm not your bleeding brother," said Harry. "I own you. Now sit down." Then he turned to Breezy Woodchuck and told her, "Don't eat that if you don't want it. But that's all you're getting."

She spit in his face. He grabbed her and pulled her away. He started to slap her but then thought better of it. Instead, he turned to Dane and Bramij. "We've got a nice little proposition here. All we have to do is grab people and take them to the market and sell them. Once you've done that you'll get all the women you want. Don't get stupid and greedy now. You'll mess it up. Why do you have to rape the merchandise?"

"You do it."

"But I know how to do it so it won't lower the price. Christ, now the stew's burning. "

"I have an idea," said Bramij.

"That's dangerous for you, bro," said Dane. "I'll do the thinking."

"I was thinking Harry'd make a good slave."

"Christ almighty, do you want to wreck everything?" said Harry. Then he capitulated. "Oh hell, she's all yours."

"Peace, brothers," said Clumphy.

"Shut up!" Harry shouted at him.

Bramij said, "I want to eat first. I can't do it on an empty stomach. You take her."

Harry went back to the pot, which was now putting forth a very mouthwatering aroma. "Christ," he mumbled, "can't I even make a pot of stew without all of us trying to kill each other?"

"Peace, brothers," said Clumphy, "after the killing and destruc-tion we've endured, surely we've learned –"

"I told you to shut up!"

"—that fighting accomplishes nothing –"

He leapt at Clumphy and battered him. Clumphy went straight down, like a sack of potatoes. Harry stood over him till he was cer-tain he wouldn't be getting up again and then went back to the stew-pot, which was bubbling. "I think it's ready," he said.

Harry, Dane and Bramij sat down to eat, but it seemed they'd lost some appetite. The stew just sat in their bowls making a very juicy smell.

"I'm making a change," said Harry. "I'm not keeping her on a separate chain. Shouldn't have done that. I thought it'd prevent ar-guments, but it's just made them worse." He put a little food in his mouth. "I don't care who has her. Anyone can . . . We'll take turns."

"I can't eat," said Dane. He picked a place a few feet away and led Breezy Woodchuck there. For the slaves, it was honestly hard to know which was worse, the smell of the stew that was going to waste or the lamentations of Breezy Woodchuck. Harry just stared at his bowl, not eating. There were sounds of Dane hitting Breezy.

"Go further off," said Harry. Dane dragged her further away, but the Forest was quiet and the sounds they made were impossible to ignore.

When he was done, Dane returned with the squaw. "Your turn," he said to Bramij.

Bramij put his uneaten bowl of stew to one side.

"Christ, you bruised her face," said Harry.

"It's not bad," said Dane.

"It'll be worse in the morning."

"Maybe I'll bruise your face."

Harry just looked at him with malice in his eyes.

Bramij took Breezy Woodchuck with him into the woods.

"And move further off," Harry shouted after him.

Clumphy had now regained consciousness. Pete and Tom tried to comfort him. It was clear he wanted to talk. "Last night . . . there was a distinction I didn't draw . . ."

"Rest. You'll tire yourself," said Pete.

"There's one thing I can see and you can't . . . I see that God loves mankind . . . That's one of those things that can't be seen unless you believe . . ."

"There's no point in anything you're saying," said Tom. "Please rest."

Clumphy tried to sit up. "It's not like looking at that tree there . . . You see the pear tree . . . ?"

"That's a pear tree? Are you sure?" said Pete.

"Maybe you think it's something else. Maybe you think it's a juniper bush . . . We could dispute about it, but it's possible to see the pears and then we'd all agree . . . But looking at the universe, not everyone can see the love, not unless one believes . . ."

"I can't see any tree," said Tom.

"Pardon me for speaking of sight to a blind man . . . It's just the common word we use when what we mean is understand . . . Pete, bring us a fruit from the tree and then we'll know. That will prove it's a pear tree . . ."

"Sit down and shut up!" shouted Dane. Breezy Woodchuck's cries could now be heard again mingled with Bramij's grunts.

"Oh well . . . You'll have to take my word for it . . ."

"Alright, I'll believe it's a pear tree," said Tom. After a while Bramij had finished. The only sound then was the chirring of the crickets. Tom wondered what the crickets were saying. The world they lived in must be very different from the one he lived in, and yet it was the same world. *Do the crickets even know I exist?*

Bramij returned alone.

"Where's the squaw?" asked Harry.

"She got away," Bramij answered.

"She got away?!" Harry blurted out in complete disbelief. "She got away?!"

"She told me to close my eyes. When I opened them she was gone."

"What kind of an idiot are you?!"

"Um, let's see . . ."

"Well don't just stand there! Get her back!"

"You don't think I tried already?! She's gone, I'm telling you."

"Which way did she go?"

"I don't know. My eyes were closed."

"Well go get her! She can't have gone far."

Bramij showed no sign of moving, so Harry closed on him and hit him in the face. A fight broke out, with Dane coming in on his brother's side.

"Peace, brothers!" Clumphy stood. "Violence resolves noth –"

At this all of Harry's rage boiled over and he completely snapped. He turned to Clumphy and battered him in the face and the stomach. Then he grabbed a stick and beat him over the head till he'd collapsed, covered in his own blood. Once he was on the ground Harry kicked him viciously. It was possible to hear the ribs snapping. Eventually he wore himself out and fell to his knees beside his victim, who was gasping great shuddering sobs and moaning in pain.

The slave drivers and the other slaves just looked on. They were shocked by the sudden outburst and somewhat awed by the single-minded ferocity of Harry's fury.

Finally Harry stood and returned to his bowl of stew. He took one mouthful and then threw it out. "It's cold."

"Is that what you call not damaging the merchandise?" asked Dane softly.

"He'll be fine."

But clearly he was not going to be fine. He was rolling back and forth moaning, and blood was pouring from his nose and mouth. Pete and Tom tried to hold him and offer some comfort. "Do you have any bandages?" asked Pete.

"Do you think I'm a stinking doctor . . . ?! He'll be fine."

The argument with Dane and Bramij was now forgotten. No one spoke. The only sounds were the crickets, the low crackling of the fire and Clumphy's sobs. Clumphy looked as though he was trying to say something but Pete, who was cradling his head in his arms and whose clothing was soaked in his blood said, "Shh . . . Shh . . ."

Clumphy was breathing in shallow panting bursts. He closed his eyes and eventually the sound of his breathing quieted and the heaving of his chest subsided. He lay very still for a long time. Tom grew afraid that he'd died, but when he placed his head on Clumphy's chest he heard the slow steady thump of his heart still pounding away.

As Tom pulled his head away Clumphy whispered, "Imagine if you could do away with belief . . ." Clearly speaking required a great effort. Tom urged him to keep quiet, but he went on, "What if there were no such thing — ow, ow, ow, it hurts . . ." He moaned, then attempted a smile. "What if we all believed nothing . . . ? What would we share . . . ?"

"There'd be nothing to share," said Tom softly.

"We'd be sharing the dream . . . Our dreams are the same, it's our beliefs that differ . . ."

That was the last he said for a long time. Everyone lay down except Harry, who was keeping watch, and Barking Dog, who couldn't rest. He kept staring into the woods hoping to catch a glimpse of Breezy Woodchuck. How could she leave him alone?

It was late in the night before Clumphy spoke again. "When I used to prepare a sermon it always bothered me that I taught the

338

truth, but it was possible to come up with some little fact no one cared about that would contradict the point I was making . . ."

"Shh . . ." said Pete.

"It seemed like that would happen all the time . . . The truth is simple but facts are confusing . . . Now it's happened again . . . It doesn't spoil the point I made, but now I look a little closer I see it's actually an apple tree . . . Silly mistake . . ."

Tom, drowsy and barely coming awake, said, "Never mind. I still believe it's a pear tree."

In the morning Clumphy was dead. He'd passed sometime during the night without anyone noticing. The hands Pete and Barking Dog had held during the night were rigid and cold. Harry stood over his corpse and cursed. He said to Dane, "I ought to put you in his place on the chain. That'd be fair recompense."

"Me?!" said Dane. "I wasn't the one who killed him."

"All I ever wanted was a good, reputable business."

"What's this about?"

"And you guys mess it up."

Dane ejected a lot of water and mucus from his mouth. Then he unlocked the corpse from the chain and dragged it to the side of the road. Harry wanted the body buried, but Dane and Bramij didn't see any point. Harry insisted. He'd have blushed to admit it, but he was fearful of the uneasy spirit if the body was not properly laid to rest. Dane said he wasn't going to do any digging and anyway they didn't have any shovels.

"You could use your bleeding hands," said Harry.

"Too much work," said Bramij.

Then Harry remembered he was a slave owner. He ordered the slaves to dig a hole with their hands. This order was not received with much enthusiasm but after a few sharp blows from the slave drivers' sticks it was assented to and the hole was dug. They put Clumphy's body in and threw some dirt on top. Once that was done Harry thought he'd give the slaves a little breakfast that wouldn't cost him anything. "Bet you didn't know food grows on trees? It does. Here." He took some fruits from the tree and threw them to the slaves. "I don't know what it is, though. I never saw trees like this before. What is it? A peach? Anyway, it's probably not poison." The slaves ate the proffered fruit, which was bitter and tasted like lemons. Tom spat it out.

By the time they'd finished eating, half the morning was gone, so Harry said to make up for it there'd be no break in the middle of the day and they went on. Tom quickly found himself worn out as he staggered at the end of the line knocking his blistered feet against every root and protruding stone. Pete tried to help by warning him of obstacles, but Tom was so weary and his injured foot was in so much pain he could barely stand, let alone keep up the pace the others were setting. He thought he would just drop and he wouldn't mind whatever the slave drivers did. If they killed him that would just bring on the inevitable a little more quickly.

Around mid-day they emerged onto the Coast Road which was smoother and easier to traverse than the Forest paths. Shortly after entering onto the Road Dane said, "Look, there's someone sitting on that rock by the shore." The line stopped. Harry walked over to get a closer look. "Want me to grab him?"

"No, don't bother," answered Harry. "I'll show you how we get this guy." He shouted to the man they'd seen, "Hey, you! Get over here."

The man looked up in surprise. "Are you talking to me?" he shouted.

"Yes. I've got something for you."

The man stood up. It became clear that the rock they'd thought he was sitting on was actually his bottom, which was by far the largest part of his anatomy. "What is it?"

"Come and see."

The man seemed ambivalent, unable to make up his mind. "What if I don't like it? Can't you just bring it to me?"

"Listen, stupid, if you don't get here pretty soon I'm going to give it to someone else."

The man just waved his hand and sat down again.

Harry shook his head in disgust. "Well? What are you looking at? Go get him," he said to the slave drivers.

The two men ran down and grabbed Colophus – for of course it was he – and dragged him to the Road.

"It seems like you're going to an awful lot of trouble just to give me something," said Colophus. "What is it?"

"This." Harry struck him in the face and then clapped him in irons and attached him to the end of the line, behind Tom. "Alright, let's go." And the line started up again.

Tom found the going even more difficult now with someone behind him. He was constantly being pulled backward when he'd speed up, or being bumped from behind when he'd slow down. Also, he realized, the person behind him was talking to him.

"Tom," said Colophus, "is that really you?"

"I know that voice," said Tom. "Colophus?"

"Yes. Can't you see me?"

"I see nothing." Tom turned his head, revealing his eyeless sockets. His cheeks were covered with the gore and pus that oozed from his wounds and his beard was sticky with blood and vomit.

"Oh . . ." Colophus bumped into him. Then they didn't speak for a while, concentrating on keeping pace.

"So you're out of the leviathan too?" said Tom.

"Oh yes. When I gave up and set fire to my memoirs, everything went wrong. I found myself swept up with a lot of other refuse and deposited on the surface of the sea."

"So now you know what I said was true. We weren't in Purgatory. We were inside a fish."

"There's no contradiction. It was Purgatory. I just didn't realize Purgatory was inside a fish."

"But now you must realize you're not dead and you're still in the real world."

"Of course I'm dead. Now I'm in Hell . . . I didn't fulfill the tasks God gave me. I lost hope and God has seen fit to punish me. I've been sent here to suffer torment eternally. These are demons driving us on, craftily disguised as men."

"They're not. They're men. Demons would be more intelligent."

"And I see you've been sent to Hell too. Although your punishment is remitted to a degree. You've been relieved of the sense of sight." Just then Colophus tripped and fell, bringing Tom and Pete down with him. This led to a general stoppage of the line and when things had finally gotten sorted out Harry decided they'd take a short break after all. While they were resting, Colophus asked Pete if he knew what sins he'd committed that had caused him to be sent to Hell.

"Pretty much all of them, I guess," he answered. "I never took much notice. I was mostly busy fixing people's shoes."

"You fixed shoes and were sent to Hell. There's a pun on soles there somewhere," said Colophus.

"What sort of God sends people to Hell?" asked Tom.

"Maybe you should ask what sort of people believe in a God that sends them to Hell?" Colophus replied.

"What is God?" asked Tom.

"I whipped my son and said disheartening things to him. I felt bad about that for a long time, though I never said so . . ." Pete was sifting through his memories, not too proud of what he found. "Don't know where my wife and son are now. We ran different ways in the great fire. Maybe they're better off without me."

"Don't think that for a minute," said Tom. "They miss you very much. They need you. They're looking for you right now. Hold onto that. Without that you're just a slave."

Pete said, "I'm not a slave." He stood up. This movement jerked Tom and Barking Dog to their knees. "I have to —"

Dane hit him with a club. "Sit down."

"I'm not a slave!" he shouted.

"You're a slave!" There were more blows.

"I have to get to them . . ." he sank down and both slave drivers hit him. After he lost consciousness they hit a few of the others for good measure.

When the guards moved off they were all silent for a long while, hardly daring to breathe. Pete sat huddled next to Barking Dog, who had his arm over his shoulder. Everyone was thinking about Clumphy and hoping Pete wouldn't be next. Their drivers seemed to be becoming more harsh and irrational by the minute. After a while Tom repeated the question he'd asked earlier. "What is God . . . ?"

"You expect an answer?" asked Colophus.

"You may be the wisest man I ever met. When first I encountered you I thought you were a fool. Since then I've been through many troubles and I feel like I haven't learned anything from them. But I look at you, and you've been through troubles just like mine, and I feel like you've learned from them. So I ask you, what is God?"

"Everything I've been through, the beatings and the punishments and the trials I've endured, all this has been the process of acquiring wisdom?"

Tom ripped up a piece of grass next to him and threw it into the wind. "Certainly I think so. You've had to learn things you didn't want to understand."

"Then I would say after one has acquired a certain amount of wisdom one should have learned it is very foolish to acquire any more."

"That sounds like one of those wise old sayings people repeat. In fact, it may be a way of restating the proverb, 'Once burned, twice shy.'"

"But like all old proverbs it is also a contemptible falsehood. We are not twice shy. Constantly we burn our fingers, time and time again. And what is this great truth we constantly are learning, over and over? We learn that we don't like to get burned . . . And I don't think you are still the same. To me, you are different. So I'm sure you've learned much."

"What I've learned is that it's better to have eyes than to be blind."

"I'm sure you'd deduced that already, so this is not what we'd call an insight. Mostly the lessons experience teaches are lessons we already knew. In fact, now I think about it, that's the difference between being taught and learning. We can only be taught things we already know, but the things we learn are not the things we are taught. But I've digressed. What were we talking about?"

"I can't remember."

"You asked me, 'What is God?'"

"Oh, that's right."

"I don't know why you'd think my experiences would have taught me the answer. There are a few things I've learned. For instance, the fact that man's cogitative faculties reside in his buttocks. No one knew this till I discovered it. But the nature of God? Again, I think this is something we already know. God is the divine creator and ruler of the universe."

"But what sort of being is that?"

343

Colophus took a moment to ponder. "Maybe I know . . . What creates the universe and holds it in place . . . ? It's what that silly gospel was trying to tell us. God is language. And language is God. God puts meaning into the sounds that come out of our mouths. And that's what creates and rules the universe . . . It's all so simple when you think about it . . ."

"So our understanding creates the universe? It isn't the other way round?"

"We open our eyes and see what's there. What makes it the universe is God . . . Sorry to speak of opening our eyes."

"I have no eyes to open."

"Can you see anything at all?"

"Only when I sleep. In my dreams I see. When I wake I see nothing. It's like having my eyes closed."

"You see nothing when you close your eyes?"

"I have no eyes to close."

"When I close my eyes I see the congregation of the saints – I see God's angels, entwined in graceful community of complex form, celebrating in jubilant happiness all around me. And only I am alone and in Hell."

"Certain it is that I see nothing. Just black."

"If only I had your vision."

"Let's get moving," said Dane, hitting Colophus with his club.

"Blast your stinking ass," said Bramij. And so, with much quiet grumbling, the chain gang set off again.

That night they settled in a campsite by the side of the Road. The slaves had some watery gruel for dinner, but they could smell the sausages Harry and the slave drivers were roasting for themselves. It was a sweet smell, but one they couldn't sink their teeth into.

After the events of the preceding night, everyone seemed subdued. The slaves were left to their own devices, under the watchful eyes of their warders, and they curled themselves into a circle. No one seemed interested in enforcing the prohibition on talking that had been in effect on prior nights, so Colophus asked, "Can I tell a funny story?"

There was no objection.

"All the great truths that have been discovered and pronounced by the great philosophers have been in the form of statements."

"That comes as no surprise. What other form could they take?" asked Pete.

"They came wrapped in the eloquence of truth, and men acknowledged them to be great insights. But every statement calls into being its contrary, and inevitably its contrary is also found to be true. Indeed, it might almost be given as a rule that a statement is only true if its contrary is also true. However, this leads to a great deal of confusion and to a world where everything is allowed. But don't humans have a way of expressing truth that does not contain its own contradiction and that extracts from those that hear it the involuntary admission of truth? Yes, they do. It's called a joke. And the involuntary admission is laughter. Any truth that cannot be expressed as a joke and confirmed by laughter cannot be true. Statements are incompetent to state anything with finality or complete accuracy, but once you've laughed at a joke you've acknowledged its truth. This idea occurred to Cladibus, the Emperor of Demarest not long ago. It also occurred to him that mankind had struggled through several ages in its rise to civilization, when mastery of various different materials had been the road to the command of society. There had been the stone age, then the bronze age, the age of steel and so forth. He saw that mankind had entered into an industrial age, but he saw that this age would soon pass and was to be replaced by a new age which he believed would be the age of truth. After all, what could possibly be more valuable than truth? He who knew the truth would be master of the age. Furthermore, he knew how the truth was to be expressed. Not in the form of windy slogans that inevitably went out of date, but in the form of the jokes that could be told forever and which men were always involuntarily acknowledging to be true by laughing at them. So he decided to get rid of his treasury and replace it with a Department of Humor. He selected a Secretary of Humor whose job it was to tax the citizens, but unlike the taxes they had been accustomed to paying in the form of money, the taxes that would be collected would be jokes. So the Secretary of Humor set about going round to all the citizens and collecting their jokes and bringing them back to be stored in the old treasury building, which had been emptied of the gold coins and ingots of precious metals that had formerly resided there. The jokes were stored there instead to be used in case of drought or famine.

"Everything went along this way for several years and all the citizens were pleased to be able to pay their taxes in this new way. They all praised the genius of Cladibus who had foreseen this new age which surely must be the height of civilization, when all man's necessities could be provided for not by toil and labor and the sweat of the brow as formerly, but by telling jokes. However, eventually the drought and the famine arrived. When this happened all the citizens looked to Cladibus for relief. 'There is no grain in the granary, nor is there any treasure in the treasury, but I can tell you a lot of very funny jokes,' he said, slipping a custard pie from one of his sleeves. However, at this point the people did not find the jokes to be all that funny, and Cladibus was forced to acknowledge that when he had installed the new age of truth he had only been joking. But that joke was not found to be very funny either, so they chopped off his head, put it on a post and threw the custard pie at it. And they all had a good laugh at that.

"Did you find my story amusing?"

"No . . . not very," said Tom.

"Too bad. I was hoping it would cheer you up."

"What made you think I needed cheering up?"

They laughed.

That was the last Tom was ever to hear from Colophus. The next morning they came to a tavern on the site of a mill where the wheat that was grown locally was being ground. But this was an unusual mill. The wheel of this mill did not run in water. This mill had been constructed in such fashion that the wheel was turned by an ox that was driven round and round in a subterranean room, and this motive force was conveyed to the wheel which ground the grain. The miller was a feral looking fellow with a walleye that caused him constantly to squint. His ox had died the night before and although some oxen could have been found in the vicinity to take its place, Harry, who'd begun to worry that the blind beggar he'd acquired might not make it to Indradoon, saw an opportunity to get him off his hands. A price was agreed to and Tom was removed from the chain gang and handed over to the miller, who set him to work in the underground chamber where he was chained to a stout piece of timber that he had to push round in a circle. It was perfect work for a blind man so long as he could still walk. Round and round he pushed, hour after hour, goaded on with a sharp stick whenever he lagged, unseeing and unseen by any save the miller. There were brief intervals when he could rest and relieve himself and he was given the tavern's leftovers to eat and at night they unchained him and gave him a bed on some mildewed straw in back. His only prayer at night was not to wake in the morning. But death was busy elsewhere and chose not to come so quickly, and day after day Tom kept at his task, pushing the log in its eternal circular groove. There was no conversation with the miller. Not being accustomed to speaking with his ox it hadn't occurred to him to speak with its replacement. The only sounds were those made by their feet and the swishing of the log in its circular course and the grunts that were all the expressions needed.

Meanwhile Katie and Tavish resumed their journey. They arrived at Kashahar towards twilight, weary and saddened. Ever since leaving Port Jay Katie had been making plans for her arrival in Kashahar, picturing herself searching for Tom and seeking information at the docks, but now she had no use for her plans. Tavish had been trying to lead her gently, as he always did, toward making an accommodation to life. He saw the shape this accommodation would take, even if she didn't. At the moment they were looking for a place where they could find a bed for the night. A man in a tattered blue coat approached Katie and asked for money. Despite all her troubles still there was room for pity in her heart. The man had a little sea-captainish look to him, albeit dashed to devastation, so she fumbled through the few coppers she had and gave him one, but the man insisted he wanted all.

Tavish, who'd been watching this exchange, asked him, "You mean you're trying to rob us?"

"Yes. Your money or your life." He held up a blade to make his intentions clear.

This was more than Tavish could stand. "We've been robbed by better than you," he answered with a note of disdain. He dealt the man a blow which toppled him and put him on the ground. Then they moved on.

It might be noted in passing that this ineffective bandit was none other than our old friend Ramsey. Ever since he'd been battered and dismissed by Barnacle Jack he'd been trying to find some way to eke out a subsistence. He hadn't found any who were looking to hire a sea-going man of his demeanor, so he'd taken to robbery. But he was so decrepit, most of his victims took him for a beggar just as Katie had. Then, when his larcenous aims were made clear, they'd either cudgel him mercilessly or else just laugh and pass on. Eventually he found a living on the docks where, clad in a colorful loin cloth, he'd perform for young boys by diving for the small coins and other trinkets they'd throw in the water. One day, attempting to retrieve a coin that had been thrown an unusually great distance, he was swallowed in two bites by a hitherto unseen and unsuspected sea serpent. So that's how Ramsey came to his end, a man who never harbored malice for any, but was perhaps not so observant as he should have been.

Returning to Katie and Tavish, they found an inn with a room and a bed. There was a stable where Tavish unloaded the saddle bags and gave Neddy over to the ostler's care. Then he went up to his room where he found Katie seated on the bed, her eyes wearing the lost look they'd worn all day. He sat in a chair across from her and tried to get her to look at him, but the horizon she was surveying was a dim and a distant one. Her eyes seemed vacant, but her gaze was fixed. After some time he spoke to her softly. She tossed his words aside and asked, "When the little one came out, it must have been far enough along you could see it was a boy or a girl?"

"Certain it was."

"I never looked, but I wanted to know . . ."

"Shall I tell you?"

"If you'd be so kind."

"'Twas a girl . . ."

"Spared the little colleen a world of trouble . . . I would have called her Lacey. A brave name, is it not?"

"I don't know what made him hit you like that."

"It was just a random vexation, I'm sure. And that was the same man killed Tom."

"You don't know for certain he's dead."

"I do." They looked at one another. "I even think I know when it happened. It was the night Tommy Dog ran away. He died that same night . . . So what are we about then?" She rose and looked out the window at the street below. "Where am I to go in this world?"

He came and stood behind her. "We've about spent all we brought with us," he said. "We haven't sufficient to return to Port Jay, nor any idea what sort of shambles we'd find there. Tomorrow we must start looking for a situation here, in a rich man's house or a tavern, somewhere we could fit in."

"There's a place we fit in then?"

He put his hands on her shoulders. "Yes. We can fit in. We'll be alright," he said. "We're strong enough we can work, and I've no doubt there's work to be found here . . . Won't you turn and face me?"

She turned. He ran his hands down from her shoulders and let them rest on her hips. "Tavish," she said, "I can't . . ."

"Rest easy. I'll take care of everything. We're better off than many." He kissed her on the cheek. She didn't resist, so he slid his hands around her back and held her. He kissed her again on the lips. "I love you," he whispered. "Always, I've always loved you."

Katie, for her part, was frozen, but her body knew what to do. She felt the tiny hairs on her neck rise when he looked at her, and she felt her nipples harden as he caressed her back. Even so soon after all was lost, her flesh hungered for the sweetness of love, and she became moist at Tavish's touch. They spoke no words, their bodies communing with one another, conspiring together to give them what they were in need of. They undressed in silence. As she lay on the bed Tavish took a moment to admire her holy nakedness. She was skinny from lack of food; her face was drawn and haggard; there were shadows under her eyes and in her cheeks. Everywhere she showed signs of fatigue and care, of a burden borne past bearing. Her beauty, that he'd always thought so fragile, had never been so apparent, or so useless. He lay beside her on that old worn bed in that tavern in

Kashahar and as gently as possible, with every softness he knew, he took her as a man takes a woman.

When it was over Katie lay on her back and stared at the ceiling, oblivious to everything; her thoughts at that moment were a mystery to her. She asked, "What is love? Why does it have to be so big, and why does it ask for so much? Why is it the only thing there is, that makes everything else not matter? Why are we slaves to it . . .? And then when we're out of love, why is it all we want to do is fall in love again?"

Tavish, lying next to her, answered, "It's like falling into a pool of water that has no bottom. You keep thinking you'll hit the bottom and bounce back up. But you never do."

"Do you love me?"

Tavish thought a good while before he answered. His first thought was why does she have to ask. His second thought was he wouldn't dare ask her the same question. So then he knew why she'd asked. She knew the answer. Finally he said, "Love's too small a word for it. I adore you. I cherish you. Everything else inside me's been scraped bare to make room for you. You're the reason I get up in the morning. I wouldn't do anything for me if I could do for you instead. My every hope has been to be the man who'd light up your eye. Like if you walked into a crowded room and looked around and all of a sudden your eyes would shine when you saw I was there. That would be the height of everything I could wish for, just knowing I was special for you like you're special for me. I'd want to protect you and save you from every kind of trouble you could endure. And if life rubbed you too raw, I think I'd take my own skin off and put it on you . . . I don't know if there's anything else I'd ever want . . ." He looked at her to see how she was taking his words, but her eyes were closed and she was breathing steadily. So he let her sleep as he made plans for the morrow. And as his thoughts drifted this way then that he slipped into a dreamless slumber.

CHAPTER TWENTY-FIVE
IN THE DEVIL'S WORKSHOP

APART FROM A FEW scraggly pines, the white surface of the snow stretched unbroken from horizon to horizon. The only sounds were the wind and the shirring murmur it made in the branches. There was no sign of any animal life apart from Stuart Lovejoy and his horse. There were no birds, no tracks in the snow, no noises in the night. He was completely, absolutely alone, under a gibbous moon, in an alien landscape of pristine, unbroken white. Even time seemed to have come to a halt, as the moon stood stationary in the sky above. It was impossible to say how long he'd been traveling or how much distance he'd covered. He looked back and saw the tracks left by his horse, but as he watched they vanished under freshly fallen snow. It was cold, and when his horse stopped, the cold crept under his jacket and into his bones. So he kept moving.

Eventually he encountered something of the work of men. He came to a bridge across a deep ravine. It stood on three arches, the legs of which disappeared into darkness. Far below he heard what he thought was the chuckling of water over stones, though it could have been the gnashing of tireless teeth for all he could tell. He was unable to see anything on the other side and was uncertain whether to cross. Though of course in the end he did.

After crossing the bridge he saw a distant light that hadn't been visible before. Fitful at first, it soon took on a steady glow, warm and yellow like candle light, grateful in a palette of black and white. As he drew near he saw that it shone from a window at the top of a tower, as if it were a beacon, summoning him from the dark. When first he'd sighted the tower he'd thought it must be far in the distance, but as he approached he realized it was none of the biggest – scarce thirty feet high — and was actually very close. He came to its foot and dismounted, tying the reins of his weary horse to a post. He walked round the tower till he came to a door that stood open, so he entered and climbed a circular stair to the top where he found a large table and four personages seated around it. Actually, not all were seated. One of them, a young man with wings, who was facing the door at which Stuart stood, appeared to hover slightly above the table. He was looking in the Lieutenant's general direction but couldn't see him due to the fact that he was wearing a blindfold. He was holding a bow, and a quiver of arrows was strapped to his back. Seated to his right was the most beautiful woman in the world. Everything about her bore the marks of the most ravishing enchantment. All her grace and glory had been designed to reach the absolute peak of exquisite perfection at this exact moment and seen in this light and it was inconceivable that they would ever again be so overpoweringly magnificent, and yet every gesture, each slight turn she gave to her lips, or twist of her fingers, unfolded beauties unmatched by any that had come before, every heartbeat embodying a new loveliness. Reluctantly tearing his eyes away from her he looked at the one seated across the table from her, to the youth's left. This one's features bore every mark of the utmost idiocy. His oafish eyes peered in different directions and his witless mouth hung open, a line of spittle continually drooling from one side. He was dressed in motley like a fool and there were bells in his hat that jingled when he moved. The fourth figure sat across from the youth so that Stuart could see only his back. He appeared to be wearing a mask, at least Stuart could see the sides of the mask and the string that ran between them round the back of the man's head, but the head itself wasn't there, or rather what was there was a sort of nothingness that filled the space where the head would have been but which was constantly falling away. It's impossible to describe what it looked like because although it continuously filled the space where the head should have been it wasn't actually there any longer, as though it were a waterfall from which the water had been removed, leaving only the fall. The table they were sitting round bore a map of the Coast, rather like the large map in the war room in Port Jay, but this one was drawn so realistically that it actually looked like the Coast in miniature. Stuart could see water and forests and

352

what he took to be little creatures that were scattered about in some places and in other places were piled up in countless multitudes. It was curiously detailed and remarkably life-like, so much so that it gave the impression one was actually floating in space looking down at what was happening. Although the details were inconceivably miniature, when one looked at them closely, without becoming any larger, somehow they became more distinct and clearly visible, almost as though if one looked closely enough one could see each tree or individual exactly as it appeared, although the table must have been incredibly small in comparison to the landscape it contained. The four sitting around the table were all holding various cards and there were other cards scattered in piles around the edges of the table. They were also rolling a number of dice. As they rolled them they would engage in complex contortions, such as holding them over their head or shaking their hands from side to side, and then when they rolled they would utter exclamations like 'Heads over ends' or 'Quart tierce!' and then blow on their fingers, as though needing to cool them off. The number and size of the dice changed from roll to roll, but once a roll was completed one of the players – because they were clearly playing a game – would enact some business on the board and then hand the dice to the next person. The entire table was lit by a chandelier hung from the ceiling containing many candles, casting the table and the four players in a warm light, but leaving the corners and the walls in darkness.

Stuart watched for some time, letting the snow he'd carried in on his clothes melt in puddles at his feet. Eventually the one with his back to him turned around. He could now see the mask. It was a jovial face with dimpled cheeks and a wide smile expressive of gleeful hilarity. It was impossible to imagine the visage that was being masked because all Stuart could see through the eye holes and the mouth was the noth-ingness endlessly falling away. The man was dressed in black evening wear and wore a pair of white kid gloves, but between the gloves and the shirt cuffs, where his skin should have been visible, there was once again just the falling nothingness. He nodded to Stuart as though they were friends and then rose and came to greet him. Placing a monocle in one eye, he gave a small bow and said, "Stuart Lovejoy, I presume?"

"How did you know it was me?"

"I've been expecting you, ever since you opened the back gate. Come in."

Since there was no muscle in the mask's eye socket, the monocle fell out and dangled at the end of its string. When the man replaced it in the eye of the mask, it fell out again. This happened repeatedly throughout their conversation. He was constantly placing the monocle in one eye socket or the other and then allowing it to fall. Since, as far as Stuart could tell, the person behind the mask did not possess an eye, he wondered what the point was. However, the man seemed completely unperturbed, so Stuart decided to pay no notice.

"I don't recall opening a gate," he answered, entering the room.

"That's what we call it, though it doesn't look much like a gate. But allow me to introduce myself. I am Father Time." He held his hand out for Stuart to shake.

"This is an honor."

"This," pointing to the most beautiful woman in the world, "is Venus."

"Hello, darling." Venus turned to him and smiled.

Stuart fell trembling to his knees. "I adore you. I worship you. I would do anything for you."

"Yes, yes," said Time, patting him on the back. "We know you would. Here," gesturing to the blindfolded youth, "is her son Cupid."

Cupid, unable to see, smiled and waved awkwardly in the wrong direction. "Nice to meet you."

"The pleasure is all mine," said Stuart.

"And this charming fellow," said Time, pointing to the idiot in motley, "is Folly."

Folly gave a large fart.

"The four of us, as you can see, are playing a game, and this is a thrilling moment because you are one of the pieces in the game, and it's not very often that the pieces know where to find us."

"But . . . I didn't know where to find you," said Stuart.

"You knew the key to open the gate."

354

"I did?"

"Yes. Well I did help just a little, it was my turn you know." Time looked at Stuart, and despite the mask's fixed expression, he gave Stuart the feeling something was expected of him, something like the answer to a difficult riddle, perhaps. Stuart, however, had no idea what the riddle was. "It was those seven steps backwards, that's what opens the gate."

"Seven steps backwards?"

"You don't remember them, do you?"

"No."

"Well, you took them, and now you're here. You can't argue with that."

"I'm here."

"Yes."

"But where is this?"

"This place? This place is nowhere."

"I see. It's nowhere. But nowhere is not anywhere at all. Where actually is this place? And how did I get here?"

"I told you, you opened the gate and came in. And this is the precise spot where nowhere is located."

"Nowhere is here?"

"Yes."

"How can that be?"

"The universe is infinite in extent, so it follows that it must include all places, even places that don't exist."

Stuart was silent, trying to grasp this concept.

"Furthermore, it also follows that every place in the universe is the exact center of the universe. So the one place that can't exist is the one place that's not the center of the universe, which is nowhere, where we are now."

"We are?"

"Yes. And don't get me started on now."

Stuart thought this over. Then he asked, "Is there any possibility I will ever get back to where I was? You see, it's very important that I get to San Dorio."

"I think San Dorio is no longer, as they say, in the cards. Please understand, you've arrived at just the right moment to help fix a terrible problem."

"I have?"

"Yes. The Son of Light was killed. I know, it's not your fault. And it didn't seem like such a bad idea at the time, but ever since, all the love affairs have been going wrong. Why is that a problem, you ask. Personally, I don't care, but Venus and Cupid do and they work as a team. I know, don't say it, that's against the rules, but try telling that to the two of them. And all they care about is love affairs. That's why there are always so many damn love stories. Love stories are the cockroaches of the human narrative; there's just no getting rid of them. And those two are getting a bit miffed. We tried making another Child of Light, but that's gone wrong too and now they've said if they don't get the Son of Light back they are going to pick up their pieces and go home. And that would be it. The game would be over before it was finished. Well, we can't have that, can we . . .? Can we?" This second 'can we' was spoken a bit more insistently.

Stuart realized the question was not rhetorical. He'd been caught off guard looking at the mask with its expression of constant unchanging joviality. "Oh, of course not."

"No, of course not. Any simpleton could see that."

Here Folly farted again.

"Is that all he ever does?"

"Oh, you can't imagine. When it's his turn he never does anything sensible. Of course not. He's forever shoving dirt up his nose or setting fire to his socks. One turn he tried to set his shirt cuffs alight and the sparks got into the game board and caused no end of trouble."

At this Folly gave a big smile. The effect was slightly macabre.

"And his card play is actually worse than his manners if you can conceive of such a thing. Actually I think he eats the cards more than he plays them. You can see several that have been chewed on. The Pique Dame has recently gone missing and I suspect I know what's happened to her." Here Time placed the monocle firmly in his eye and screwed it in, so that it actually remained in place longer than a few seconds. He glared at Folly, who quickly wiped the smile from his face. "It's disgraceful. But to return to what we were talking about, it was just recently my turn and I used that turn to bring you here. You see I've devised a plan to help us with this problem. But first it's Venus's turn. Let me give her the dice while I explain."

He handed Venus the dice. She raised them over her head, giving them a vigorous shake and then, shouting "Snake eyes or bust!" rolled them on the table. There were a number of dice, none the same size or bearing the same number of sides. Some displayed various numbers of spots while others depicted what resembled alchemical symbols. All the players, excepting the blindfolded Cupid, leaned over and scrutinized them. Venus then drew a card from one of the piles at the edge of the board and laid it down. It bore a picture of a coven of witches gathered round a large bubbling cauldron at a crossroads in the middle of a blinding thunderstorm at night. Underneath were the words, 'The Witches' Sabbat.' Venus now turned her attention to an area of the Forgotten Forest and as she looked at it, without its becoming any larger, it grew more detailed till it seemed to fill the entire room, and in it they could see a clearing in the woods and Deirdre standing on a raised dais. Around her were gathered many witches. She upheld her arms and spoke.

"Sisters, the hour of our triumph is upon us." This was met with many screeches and much wailing. "God is to fall from his pedestal, the Devil will triumph, and all will be free!" A number of small, menacing horned demons were popping into and out of existence around her where she stood.

"This is the sort of thing Deirdre gets away with now the Son of Light is no more, and there's nothing Venus can do to control her," Time whispered in Stuart's ear. "Sometimes these game pieces suffer from delusions of grandeur, which at the moment are not appearing particularly delusive. So we've got to bring him back. And you're the right one for the job. You were practically on the spot when he was done away with."

"I was?"

"Do you recall purchasing a nosegay to present to Stephie Eliot the night you'd arranged a tryst?"

The sudden change of subject caught Stuart by surprise. It took a moment. "Yes. I acquired it from Madam Fortunata. Something of a hedge witch, but I'd heard good things about her."

"Just as you were making that acquisition the Son of Light was being done away with round the back of her cottage. So we've got to go backwards in time and see that that doesn't happen. But now it's Cupid's turn. Let's see what he does."

Cupid felt around the surface of the game board till he'd gathered a fair number of dice. He shook them and tossed them in the air. They landed all over, some on the table and some on the floor. Everyone except Cupid kneeled down to find the scattered dice and then carefully preserving the side that had landed on top, placed them on the game board. When they reemerged from under the table they saw that the card Venus had placed earlier had changed. There was now a man they hadn't seen before dressed in a scarlet coat with silver buttons. And the words at the bottom of the card had also changed. Now they read, 'The Devil's Workshop.'

"Oh, I just hate it when the cards change on their own, don't you?" It wasn't clear whom Venus was addressing. Stuart just stared into her eyes and was overcome by a wave of awe and adoration and the certainty that the whole purpose of his life was simply to do anything for this woman.

Time brought him back to earth by muttering, "Look at the board now."

He saw that next to Deirdre there was a short man in a broadbrimmed hat and a youth with red hair. The man was addressing the witches. "It's been a great deal of work and the time it has taken has been far more than I'd have thought. The seeds of compassion and human empathy had grown roots deeper than one would have believed possible, but they're pretty much torn up by now. This is the time when we—" He suddenly looked up as a shadow passed overhead. Venus had waved her hands over where the traveling man was standing and a huge bird of prey was descending, its talons thrust out to grab him.

"She's cheating!" shouted Time. "It's not her turn! She always does that. And she's not even doing it to help herself. She does it to help her son."

"Well he needs the help," said Venus. "He's blindfolded."

"You see," declared Time, "she always does that. The two of them gang up. It's not fair."

Meanwhile, on the game board, the large bird of prey was now accompanied by other smaller birds on the lookout for quarry of their own. The short man ran off grabbing for his hat as it blew away. A great gusty wind from the flapping of the wings rippled through the trees and the witches' robes. Fergus dashed off and mounted his black stallion, tearing away into the trees to escape the birds pursuing him, but the traveling man, under the shadow of dark wings, had no such luck. The great bird of prey clasped him in its talons, then flew away across the sea, out of view of the players. In the place where he'd stood there was now a man in a scarlet coat with silver buttons. It was almost impossible to look at him because he was coming apart and falling together all at the same time. He strutted majestically in front of the witches, making artful gestures with his hands.

Cupid flapped his wings, rising above the game board. He reached for an arrow in his quiver, but became entangled with the chandelier. He attempted to lower himself while placing an arrow in his bow. His wings flapped more slowly as he revolved in the air, the arrow pointing at one person after another as he rotated counter clockwise. When he'd reached a point where the arrow pointed at the coven he released it. It struck one of the witches in the breast. She immediately turned to the witch next to her and embraced her. Cupid took more arrows and shot them also at the witches. When the witches were struck they would gibber deliriously and fling themselves wantonly into their sisters' arms, or run to fall breathless at the Devil's feet in a bacchanal of Satanic lust.

Meanwhile, Time picked up the thread of what he'd been telling Stuart earlier. "You'd be surprised all that goes on round Madam Fortunata's cottage. That's our major pivot point for controlling what happens down below."

"You mean Fortunata is actually a powerful witch?"

"Oh, no, she's just an old fraud. It's Henry we rely on. He's a good chap and he's been around for years and years. Very dependable."

"Henry . . .? I don't recall any Henry. There wasn't a man around."

"No? An old man with a large nose and spectacles, bent over, wearing a gray coat with long tails and –"

"Oh, Henry! That's her parrot. He's just an old, dirty parrot. He doesn't do anything."

"How can you be so sure?"

"All he does is sit on her shoulder and repeat the gibberish she speaks. Honestly, I don't know why she keeps him."

"Oh . . . Well I suppose that explains a few things. But now it's Folly's turn. Let's watch."

Folly picked up the dice. He tried putting one or two in his mouth. Time slapped his hand away. "None of that. Now roll." He turned to Stuart and said, "You see what I have to put up with. What with Venus's cheating and Folly's imbecilities it's amazing the game hasn't fallen into an absolute mare's nest long ago. It's a good job everyone can rely on me to keep things moving steadily along. However I'm afraid we're going to have to throw a little crimp into that too."

"But I don't see any sign of you actually doing anything," Venus stated angrily. "We're not going to stand for it forever. We said we'd leave and we mean it." She took Cupid by the hand. "Come, honey, we're going. This has been the worst game we've ever played. Amor vincit omnia my ass." She snatched her cards together and then went about picking up some of the pieces. Just then everyone was startled by what sounded like a drum roll of ominous thunder, but was only Folly letting loose a mighty fart as he picked up three of the dice and tried to juggle them. He was unsuccessful and the dice fell to the table. Once again everyone except Cupid leaned over to scrutinize the throw.

Folly said, "Horse piss," and then laughed uncontrollably. Stuart started to say something but realized what he'd been about to say was meaningless. He sounded the words he was going to speak in his mind, marveling at how the intonation went up and down, sometimes accompanied by a breath of air or a clicking of teeth, straining to catch at what the significance of it all had been. Folly gave a big grin and snapping his fingers produced a spark setting one of the cards alight. On the game board, the people were deflating, as if the air had been let out of them, sounds running down their sides like candle drippings, their eyes and mouths sinking into their faces. Folly lifted the burning card to his head, as if trying to set his cap on fire. Some untidy locks escaping from the cap's edge began to sizzle. Trees near the Devil started to burn. Shadows just beyond the edge of the board grew deeper and shifted, taking on shapes, eldritch, cruel, deformed beyond imagining. He felt giddy and he gripped, as figures toppled, tumbling lengthwise along the ground, spinning inside veils of congealed lightning, vanishing in dust – they were on top of him, hitting with hammers, hitting him crashing against the ground – the veils rode up – howling with beautiful rage stepping on and crushing – running to a high spot, turning around, the silence broken by the voice, "And just in the nick of time, if I do say so myself, it's my turn." Dice rattling like the choreography of ritual combat, he reared high above the trees and knocked them to one side – the faces of all the dice were completely blank. Dragged by shoulders like a toy soldier, away from the vanishing board, roaring in clouds, ahead the walls of the world buried in sudden darkness, a dimly lit tunnel, stamping of colossal feet. All the vacancies inside him reared up becoming monstrous buildings – impression of traversing vast distances – diamond-tufted gardens flicker past, minarets of foam. Swept up masses of discarded time huddled against the wall of the tunnel, dead things, skeletons shrouded in cobwebs, but he couldn't see any of them distinctly enough to be certain. Also, as they moved further from the game board the sounds started to become intelligible. Stuart realized there was some meaning associated with the changes in modulation given to the various hoots and whistles Time was making. He realized Time was talking about something, something that mattered. He was talking about how to go back in time, and he was giving directions. Stuart tried to listen closely since he was sure this was all very, very important.

". . . and I hate to do it since one of the rules of the game is that you can't go back in time, but I've found, the longer I play, that you don't actually know what the rules are until you've obeyed them, up till then the rules aren't real rules, they're only rule-like."

"What does that mean?" asked Stuart.

"Well that means, it's kind of hard to explain, but I'll try. You see, when we started this game there were five players, not four. The fifth was my daughter. Would you like me to tell you a story about her?"

"Yes, please."

There was a rather long pause. Stuart saw that the walls of the tunnel were changing. Now there were windows through which he could see rows of poplars and elms laid out with grand paths between, and marble fountains spraying jets of crystal water into bright, sunlit air. Then Time asked, "So, do you understand?"

"Understand what?"

"How we go back in time."

"I thought that's what you were going to explain."

"Well, that's the best explanation I can give. You see I can get to any instant in the past or the future. The only instant that's really tricky, that I seem to keep just missing, is now." Time gave him a wink. You're probably wondering how he did that. So was Stuart. "Here we are in Madam Fortunata's cottage."

Stuart turned around and there was Madam Fortunata presenting him with the nosegay for Stephie.

"Be certain to give this to her the moment you meet, and have her wear it on her collar."

"I will do so. Here's your payment." He handed her a silver guinea.

"Oh, and a very handsome payment it is. For this you can be sure the effect will be everything you could wish for."

"Thank you." He saw Henry on his perch in the background.

"And now," said Time, "instead of exiting through the front door as you did on that occasion, I am going to lead you to the back door. Just one slight change, and it effects so much."

"I didn't know there was a back door."

"Oh, but there is. This is one of the most important things in life. There must always be a back door. Even front doors aren't required in all cases, but a back door always." Time was now leading him down a stairway into a cellar. He could see chains and hooks hanging from the ceiling.

"Isn't this going to create a big muddle? I'd imagine changing things in the past would be very dicey. If you're going back to change something that's already happened, that would mean that part of the past is now in the future, or it will be in the future, or – oh, I think I'm getting a headache."

"Don't worry. Everything's been taken care of."

"And now I'm going to be here in the past, which is now the present, instead of in the future where I belong. Won't that cause problems?"

"I told you not to worry. I can assure you everything will be alright."

"But isn't that the paradox with time travel?"

"You're getting worked up."

"Someone could go into the past and shoot someone else, who perhaps is his own father, but then how could he ever have come into existence?"

"But what if the one going into the past wasn't the one doing the shooting?"

"What do you mean?"

"Oh, all I can say is that I've thought the whole thing through and it's very clever what I've done. I don't want to explain it all. It would spoil the surprise." They had now reached the back wall of the cellar. "Oh, one other thing. You're going to have to wear this jacket." Time helped Stuart out of his military coat and into a black jacket. "Let's see how you look. Here, you can put that nosegay down. That's splendid." He turned Stuart around so that he faced the wall, as if it were a mirror. But there wasn't a mirror. What he saw was a wooden statue of a hooded man in bas-relief. "You see this statue? This is the back door. This part of the wall is on a swivel. There is another identical statue on the other side. When the wall is swiveled, by giving a little push here, the statues change places, and the statue here, in the interior, will then be on the exterior. By holding onto this statue, when I swivel the wall you will be conveyed to the opposite side. It will seem as if you walked through the wall. Anyone who doesn't know the trick will have no idea how you got there."

"I understand I am supposed to prevent the murder of the Son of Light. But what exactly do you expect me to do? Can you tell me?"

"There's no need. You'll understand the situation. I'm sure you'll know just what to do. Now, we're a few seconds early. I'm sure you've seen this invention. It was the cleverest thing you humans ever did. It's called a watch. It comes in handy sometimes. Stand here, and on my count . . ."

"Should I draw my sword?"

"Entirely unnecessary." Time continued to stare at his watch.

"Surely there'd be no harm done if I arrived just a few seconds early?"

Time held up one finger while looking at his watch. ". . . Now. Good luck." He swiveled the portion of the wall where Stuart stood, instantly conveying him to the street outside. A man had just run past the spot where he stood. Stuart turned to see what the man was running from just in time to be shot in the chest by a short man with a broad-brimmed hat, as the Son of Light disappeared round the corner. Stuart fell lifeless to the ground. The short man came up and surveyed his body in the dim evening light.

Queer how a man looks different when he's dead. He looked Stuart over for several moments. Then he dragged the body to the cart he had nearby and placed it in a long wooden box he'd provided for this purpose. He closed the top of the box and then picked up a hammer. Looking about, he muttered, "Nails . . . Damn it . . . What a thing to forget . . ."He put the hammer down. *Oh well, it's not as if he's going to try going anywhere.* He took a box of snuff from his waistcoat pocket, allowing himself the pleasure of a long snort. He was sneezing as he crossed the street to a tavern on the other side. He entered to a scene of shiny brass spigots and a flurry of faces, some pink, some veined, some wattle red.

"I need a man who'll help me with a job I have tonight. It's a good bit of work but we'll be finished ere dawn. Fifteen silver dollars in your pocket now and another fifteen when the job is done. A man can't be fairer than that. Who'll work with me?"

Tom put down his drink and came forward. "Lord knows I like the sound of thirty silver dollars for a single night's work." The two shook hands and left together.

As to Stephie Eliot, she waited over half an hour outside the Bar Sinister before she was certain she'd been jilted. Determined not to waste the evening on her own she'd contrived for herself she entered the saloon and sat on a stool next to a sailor who was drinking alone, as she concluded that after all, Stuart Lovejoy really wasn't her type.

CHAPTER TWENTY-SIX
LOVE CONQUERS ALL

AFTER FATHER TIME, Venus had her turn.

Katie woke betimes to the sound of footsteps in the cobbled street outside and the smell of fresh baked bread. She reached for her stick but it wasn't at her side. Tavish was asleep beside her, his softly indrawn breaths wrapping the morning in a tender hush. She rose and looked out the window. Already bustling traffic was moving up and down, people with errands and things to do, unhesitant to acquit themselves this day as they did every day and all day, simply and solely giving themselves to the hard strife and gain of living. *I'm ready to start my new life*, she thought to herself.

Tavish rolled over and got to his feet. The two of them looked at one another and smiled. It felt like a good morning. After all the expectations they'd had were gone, there was almost a sense of relief. They got their things together, washed and dressed, rubbing up against one another in a natural way they'd been inhibited from before. It made for a minor miracle of mildness. Katie didn't exactly recognize what she felt but perhaps it was what goes by the name of hope, while Tavish was assuaged by a jocund remembrance of the past night. *Yes*, he thought, *there's a brightness in her eye, and that's because of me.* Of such slight and thin stuff is happiness made.

"Shall we look in the town?" she asked. "Or might there be better chances round about?"

"What were you thinking of?"

"I saw many a nice looking house, and taverns too, as we approached the city."

Tavish felt since they were both city folk they might be more comfortable in the town. On the other hand the long walk they'd done had left him changed. He felt more comfortable out of doors;

perhaps he could even see himself with some chickens or maybe a goat. "I think I might like to see what's outside the town myself."

So they made their way to the outskirts of Kashahar and looked around. There were mansions scattered on the outlying hills, some looking a bit seedy but mansions nonetheless. They knocked on a few doors through the morning, inquiring what services might be wanted, if it was for cleaning or painting the walls, moving furniture about or whatever. Tavish had had a knack for carpentry, and Katie could do a wash, they were open to almost anything, but it seemed the service most in demand was just to leave. One of the houses they knocked at was that of a baker. The fellow thought there might be a need for a baker's boy.

"A baker's boy?" asked Tavish.

"To pound the dough and sift the flour, ye ken. But I'd not have a position for your wife in any case."

"We're not married," Katie spoke up before Tavish could put in a word.

"Oh, are you brother and sister, then?"

"No, we're . . ."

"We're companions," Tavish finished for her.

"Your companion then, but if you're going for a position round here the people are mostly very high on their morals. I can't see you finding a place if you're not man and wife."

Tavish didn't dare give Katie a look when he heard this. But he did please himself with some thought of the two of them growing old together.

Come the afternoon they turned to the taverns. They knocked at a couple, seeing if there was need for a barmaid or a cooper or anything of the sort. Though they hadn't yet found a situation, they were of good cheer that one would soon turn up, and Katie was feeling much her old self, certain the comforts of knowing her place and a place where she was known were soon to be hers.

Near the end of the day they came on a place that held itself slightly apart. It felt as if a little shadow hung over it, which had caused them to approach it last. It was a tavern but also a mill, though it hadn't the customary mill wheel. When they entered, the miller's daughter gave them a smile and led them to the miller, a fellow with a very foul squint. He looked the two over and then asked Tavish if perhaps he was a man who could drive his ox.

Tavish allowed as how he'd not done it in the past, but he'd seen it done in the fields and he had no doubt he could drive an ox as well as another.

"This ox of mine is not in the fields," said the miller, attempting a sly grin, though it came out more like a scowl. "Want to see him?"

"That I do."

The miller led Tavish and Katie along a hall and down some stairs to a dimly lit room in the cellar. They didn't know what they were seeing at first. They saw a great log moving in a circle, turning the massive axle at its center that stood on the floor and projected through a hole in the ceiling. The only light was that which filtered through the hole, so it was next to impossible to make anything out when first they entered from the well-lit room upstairs.

"Where's the ox?" asked Tavish.

The miller chuckled. "That is he."

They saw a man clad in nothing more than a loin cloth pushing the log round and round. His hair and beard had been let grow, and his cheeks were covered in something reddish dark and murky that after a moment they saw was dried blood. He was thin to the point of scrawniness, but his rope-like muscles stood out as he strained at his task. He slowly drew near where the others were standing.

"That's no ox," said Tavish.

"He's my property. I paid for him and he'll be what I like." The miller punctuated this remark by spitting on the dirt floor.

"No, I've no stomach for that. Find another to drive your ox." They turned to leave. Tavish and the miller had started up the stairs and Katie was following behind. She had her foot on the first step but something tugged at her, something in the stance of the man pushing the log that awoke a faint recollection of a man standing under a tree, wincing when the rain drops fell from the branches. She went back to get another look. He was on the opposite side of the room now, but as he drew near in his circular track she made out his face. "Tom . . . ?" she breathed the name, barely more than

368

a whisper. It was a hopeless hope and it wounded her to wake it, knowing it would be crushed. But she heard herself saying the name again, more loudly this time, "Tom . . . ?"

The man slowed, and came to a stop. He'd gone past where she stood, so his back was to her. "That voice . . ." The words emerged slowly, as if he spoke in a daze. "That sounds like one I know. But never could she be here." He swayed and fell to his knees. "Sure I'm dreaming."

Tavish looked on in consternation. "Come, Katie," he said, reaching for her. But she didn't reach back; she stood where she was, staring at the nearly naked man on his knees as he turned in her direction.

The miller came bustling down the stairs. "Now look what you've done. He's stopped." He went to Tom and poked him with his stick while he said to Katie, "You shouldn't be interfering."

Katie's knees gave way. Then she struggled to her feet, her arms outstretched for Tom. The miller made to interfere but Tavish stepped over to where he stood and wrenched the stick from his hands. When the miller complained, he threatened to strike him. Katie took Tom in her arms.

Tom, feeling her arms about him and the warmth of her breath on his face, said in a strangled voice, ". . . No, it can't be . . . But it is you. Oh Lord, oh Lord, let this be no dream."

Seeing he didn't lift his face, Katie said, "Tom, Tom. Look at me."

He raised his ruined eyes. "I can't. But sure I know your voice. It's that of an angel, sweeter far than any in Heaven."

Katie cried aloud, the tears running from her eyes. "Tom, my own Tom, I've found you."

The miller, held back by Tavish, looked on, uncomprehending.

"Oh, Katie, ever since I left you I've been searching for you. I thought my search was ended here, and here I've found you."

"Tom, Tom, I'd lost all hope I'd ever get you back."

"If only I could look on your face once more it would be all I'd ever ask. But I have no eyes."

Endless and enormous, soundless and shameless the tears ran down Katie's face. They traced rivulets next her nose and mouth, trembled from her chin, then fell in their abundance on her breast, and from there onto Tom's eyeless sockets. And there a miracle was accomplished. As the sweetness of music can ravish the ear, so his eyes were ravished by the sweetness of her tears, and there where his eyes had been, when Katie's tears fell on them, the lustrous jelly slowly returned, and where all had been dark there was now a little light. As more tears fell, the light invaded his astonished soul. In the darkened chamber he saw again, first a shape only, outlined by the light, then more clearly, and the first he saw was Katie's face. It was her face as he'd pictured it through all the days of his pitch black night, but now he saw it lit by unexpected joy. The two of them clasped one another.

"That's my ox you're holding," protested the miller.

"Unchain him," said Tavish.

"Do you want my ox? If so, you'll have to find me another, or pay me for this one."

"I won't give him up," said Katie. "I'll never give him up."

"We haven't aught we can pay," added Tavish. "We're near skint, but I'll work for it. Any odd job you can name. I'll work to earn the price of an ox."

"I've no work for you other than driving this ox. So I'll ask you to give me back my stick and give me back my ox and I'll show you to the door." He grabbed Katie's shoulder and made to pull her away. At this Tom rose up. The slow burning of his anger at last was ignited, as it had been that time on the Road. He hit the miller in the face, knocking him to his knees and then stood glaring at him.

"You're no longer blind," the miller gasped in unhappy surprise. "You can see!"

Tom hit the miller again and he moved away. Tom tried to follow, but was held back by the chain. "Come here and let me beat you!" he shouted.

The miller looked at Tavish, expecting his support, for he knew his cause to be rightful. "You want a job?" he asked. "Then knock him down. He's my property."

"This man is no one's property," Tavish answered. "He was a free man in Port Jay. He was never born a slave and I don't know how he became one."

Now the miller's daughter, hearing the shouting and the noise, rushed in to see what was the matter. "Oh, Da," she said, "what are you getting up to?"

"They won't let me beat my slave," her father answered.

"Is it the blind man you chained to the wheel?"

"Yes, but he's blind no more. They've worked some magic on him and now he wants to be free."

She looked to Tom in some amazement, and saw that what her father said was true. "Well you shouldn't have done it," she said. "Sure I was ashamed of you when you did and I'm ashamed of myself also for I never said a word."

"But he's my ox!"

"He's a man; he's never an ox. Sometimes, Da, you're a stubborn old fool. If these people told you to unchain him they were right to do so and it's a pity it took them coming here to make us see what we should have seen all along."

"Give me my stick," the miller said to Tavish. "I have to beat my daughter."

"Go ahead, Da, all you'll be doing is showing the world what a stupid chowderhead you are. Go on with you and your ox. You're a stupid man. I doubt you even know how to spell ox."

The miller just stood where he was and looked at his daughter. He'd have stood up to the world for what was rightly his, but he knew he couldn't stand up to this young woman when her choler was roused. And indeed, all of them looked at what had been done, and it was almost as if a black cloud was lifted from their minds. What had they been thinking of, that a man was a beast of burden? Truly it wasn't right. They knew a man was a nobler thing than that. How had they forgotten?

"Unchain him," said the young woman, and the miller obeyed. Then he blushed when his daughter gave him a kiss for doing it. All were made happy and they left the dim chamber underground and climbed back to the room above. Here the miller dispatched his daughter to purchase an ox from a nearby cattle farm.

Katie and Tom sat with one another and told of all the events that had passed since last they'd been together. There were many

371

marvels to speak of and much that had to be explained. When Katie came to tell of the death of the baby she cried all over again, feeling the sorrow of it.

"I so wanted to bring you your child, but I failed in my quest."

"Take comfort. There will be time for more babies yet to come."

"But all else that was lost is now found. Look." She told of the death of Vincenzo and drew forth the watch he'd carried with him. It was the same she'd presented to Tom that morning long ago, but now when they looked at it they saw the knots were all untied, and the tangles all made straight. It was a wonder to open it and see the second hand still ticking round and the inscription that had been engraved there, "From your own darling Katie," brought the tears to their eyes once again.

Tavish sat in the corner and watched. He'd been forgotten altogether by the two of them as they relived their days of anguish, and he wondered what change this all foretold.

Just as the dark shadow of the night had retreated here, so it seemed elsewhere, all along the Coast, that daylight had come. Everywhere people were waking up, as if from a bad dream, and seeing now clearly what was to be done. It must have been Cupid's arrows that did it, fired in profusion wherever hearts were wistful. In encampments beside the River of Tears husbands and wives held hands and blessed the day that had brought them to this spot where a little industry could supply their needs and a family could be raised. In the depths of the sea, the long calamitous war between the mermen and the mermaids was quickly patched up and harmony restored. In a bower deep in the Forest, where many tireless young women pranced skyclad before a figure in a scarlet coat with silver buttons, a pause came to the dance. The motions they were making ceased, and all was suddenly still. A few trees in the background ignited in sparks but then the sparking ended and the fire died. The Devil looked about in dismay. He was not a creature to be seen by daylight. Then, in a sudden access of love the witches left the clearing, running to find the habitations of men. Wherever they encountered them, in Indian camp or settlers' village, they embraced the young men they found, joyfully propagating a love unbound. It was everywhere a holiday of happiness and requited desire and it was a day the memory of which many lucky young men were to treasure for the rest of their lives.

Even in a darkened cottage, in the midst of a burned out city, where scavengers roamed, some light was cast. Madam Fortunata recalled the honeyed days of her youth and, as if invoked by the recollection, a young man in a flowing gray coat with long tails came downstairs and took her in his arms. The two of them embraced and reenacted the deeds of a happy past. And when it was done, and the young man had retreated to his post, Fortunata lay long in her rumpled bed, ravished past the edge of desire, hovering on the verge of a dream as a hoarse voice from the shadows called, "Come again."

CHAPTER TWENTY-SEVEN
BUTTOCKRACY

AND THEN it must have been Folly's turn.

When General Hobsbawm finally came fully awake it seemed as though his prayers had been answered. He was lying in a hospital bed in Port Jay. After the battle had turned against the colonial army his doctors had conveyed him hither in some haste. He'd been recovering from his wounds, for the most part tranquilized by the laudanum his doctors had prescribed, and receiving briefings on the progress of the war. He'd learned that the Indians had been cut to ribands by Colonel Milquetoast's force, which had arrived on their rear just as the troops under Hobsbawm's command had been retreating in disarray. Milquetoast had caught the Indians unprepared and unequipped and they had been soundly vanquished. The pincer action which had so pleased Hobsbawm had worked like a charm. He'd written an account of the battle and included it in a report to the King. In order to get it to the King the report had had to be carried by messenger to one of the ships of the line under Colonel Milquetoast's command, as the docks at Port Jay had not been rebuilt since the great fire.

Colonel Snivel's force had also recently returned to Port Jay with the gratifying news that the slave mutiny had been put down. It had been a glorious victory. The slaves had been massacred and the resulting fire had only destroyed less than half of the leading plantations. It was starting to appear very much as though things were on their way to getting back to normal.

This morning Snivel was seated next to General Hobsbawm's bed. The windows were open. Sunlight poured through and a gentle breeze was playing with the coverlets. Snivel was eagerly describing a new project he'd undertaken. He'd decided that the victorious campaign against the slaves should be memorialized in a book, and of course he would be the author. "It would be a real book, you know, with dedications to notable individuals, prefaces, forewords, the works. And of course an index. I love a good index. I might make the index a separate volume."

"Yes, I've seen books such as the one you're describing."

"And a frontispiece of course, a picture of me, emblazoned with the Snivel family arms."

"All you need now is something to put between the forewords and the index and you'll be all done."

"Oh, that's one of the abstruser parts of the book. Gentlemen of wit and discernment generally don't peruse those passages."

". . . How have you ascertained the habits of gentlemen of wit and discernment?"

"By ascertaining my own, of course."

"It was my understanding that that portion of the work was the one in which the author took the greatest pains, where he sought to display in the best light his learning, judgment, eloquence and wisdom."

"Which is precisely why those passages are ignored. My word, you show an astounding ignorance of the publishing profession. I've even selected an appropriate citation for the title page." He produced a paper and read, "'*Basima eacabasa eanaa irraurista, diarba da caeotaba sobor camelanthi.*' It's from book one of Irenaeus, chapter eighteen."

"What does it mean?"

"I have no idea. I don't know Latin."

They were interrupted at this point by the unexpected arrival of Colonel Milquetoast and his staff.

"Ah, how convenient," said Milquetoast. "You are both here." The members of his staff took up positions blocking the exits.

"Colonel Milquetoast, allow me to congratulate you on a well-executed campaign. I would have come in person to deliver these felicitations, were it not for the grievous wounds I sustained in defense of the realm."

"Yes, of course."

"So it is very gracious of you to come here and allow me to praise you face to face."

"I have come because I opened the report you wrote for our royal monarch."

"Of course you did. My missives to the King are of a highly secret nature. No doubt they've been read by every messenger and sub-adjutant between here and Kashahar."

"I read it and destroyed it."

"Then I will have to be at some pains to write another. I wish you hadn't destroyed the first one."

"What was in it?" asked Snivel.

"A description of the battle fought against the Indians," said Hobsbawm.

"Yes," said Milquetoast, "one which said the Indians received their greatest harm from the Hercules cannons. But this was not the case. It was I who defeated the Indians. So I replaced it with this letter that tells the true story." He produced the document from the briefcase he held at his side.

"You can't tell the King the truth. He will never believe it."

"Very well. I have included some fictions also. I included an account of General Hobsbawm's death and the battlefield promotion of Colonel – now acting General – Milquetoast."

"I see."

"Snivel," said Milquetoast, producing a pistol from that same briefcase, "you can go along with this and retain your current rank, or else I can retire you as well."

"You're not going to murder General Hobsbawm in cold blood are you?" asked Snivel.

"I don't think of it as murder. I think of it as earning a promotion." Hobsbawm snorted. "Also seeing that justice is done."

"Justice? And what is it I'm guilty of?"

"You're guilty of withholding assistance from an entire city that was burning. You're guilty of sending Colonel Dunder and the Eighteenth Regiment to their doom. You're guilty of allowing the Hercules cannons to be destroyed. I'd say that's enough."

"This is ridiculous. It was Dunder who led the Eighteenth Regiment to its doom and it was you who allowed the Hercules cannons to be destroyed. I really thought better of you than this. Don't you see the precedent you're setting by allowing your staff to witness the execution of your commanding officer? Put that pistol away. You're not going to use it."

Milquetoast remained where he was, suddenly indecisive.

"Come on, Milquetoast, we're soldiers," said Snivel. "We follow orders. That's the way to get promoted. Not by shooting your senior officer every time he does something stupid."

"Yes, having come all this way, now I'm finding I can't pull the trigger. I actually feel sorry for you somehow."

"Shooting me was a good idea," said Hobsbawm. "It's probably the first idea everyone comes up with around here, and then you all stop trying to think of anything better. It doesn't take much thought to come up with an underhanded and devious plot. On the other hand, it takes a great deal of thought to come up with something blindingly obvious. So let me spare you the effort of thinking and present you with the perfect solution. I will rewrite the report you so hastily destroyed and bring it in person to the King. I will be feted as a living, breathing hero. Have you any idea how starved the world is for heroes? I've managed to put down a slave uprising and an Indian attack while the city was being burned to the ground. I've been wounded in the service of my country. I shall be promoted and made the head of all the King's generals. This will of course leave an opening for you here, Milquetoast. You can take charge of this colonial misery with my blessing."

"I see," said Milquetoast putting his gun away. "Your plan does seem to work for all of us."

So it was done. Colonel Milquetoast returned to his headquarters, accompanied by General Hobsbawm who then departed for the old country on a man of war, while Milquetoast got down to the work of restoring order to the Coast. There were still many bands of criminals and vagrants making the roads unsafe, and the task of rebuilding Port Jay had to be taken in hand.

Also there were the pirates of San Luno Bay to be dealt with. Barnacle Jack, once he arrived back at the Seahawk in Kashahar spent some time with Ruby, the second mate, below decks. The two of them emerged, as the Seahawk was sailing to its rendezvous with

Crazy Dog, having put together a plan to take the old pirate down a peg or two. It had to be done. This whole venture was turning out to be near a disaster. They'd lost the emerald, as well as most of the booty from the Queen of Bel Harbor. They'd suffered severe losses in their battle with the priests of Slothikay, not to mention the lads that had been murdered by Vincenzo and his accomplices. And now Crazy Dog wanted to sit on some despot's throne and rule the world? Maybe it was time to head back to San Luno Bay.

Crazy Dog meanwhile was passing the time amusing himself with Blanche, the tavern keeper's daughter. He told her all the many ways he was going to do her in in between bouts of frenzied lovemaking. He took a great thrill from her terrified eyes as he told her he would hack her to pieces even as he lunged between her legs. The exhilaration he felt during the days spent awaiting Jack's return was winding him up to undertake something desperate.

When the Seahawk pulled in to the slip near the tavern, Crazy Dog, with Blanche on his arm and a fresh coat of blue on his beard, walked proudly aboard. He was greeted with cheers from his crew and both Barnacle Jack and Ruby snapped salutes and called him Captain. The first thing he did was take Jack and Ruby with him down to his cabin, which he found they already had made use of.

"So, Jack," said Crazy Dog, "how quickly will you be removing your possessions and these other knickknacks?"

"There's no hurry," said Ruby.

"This is the Captain's cabin. And did I not hear you call me Captain?"

"Well sure, if you're the Captain, I'd —" Jack began but Crazy Dog cut him off pretty quick.

"If? Did I hear if? If I'm the Captain? This did not used to need an if."

"I'll put it plain before you, there's been naught but hard times and ill use ever since we first saw Cutthroat Bay. This venture has not been a prosperous one, nor has it been properly managed."

"And are there some think they could have managed it better?"

"Aye, there be some." There spoke Ruby.

Crazy Dog reached for the knife at his belt. He held it up before the others in the room. "You see this blade. This was the blade did in old Chitty Face when first I took command of this vessel. I slit his throat and then slept in his bed that night, this bed here." He threw the knife so it stood trembling in the wall, notching a tiny gash in Jack's cheek on its way thither. "I always said when the time was come I was no longer feared or heeded there'd be one who'd take that knife and do the like to me. Well, there it is. And here," he stretched his collar down to give them a good look, "is my throat. If the time's come you think you'll be better off without me then do it." He stood there, but no one moved. "There's no trick. Do it. Blanche, that holds for you as well."

All three looked at one another, but none went for the knife.

"Alright, you made your point," said Jack. "We called you Captain and we want you for our Captain. But not like it's been this bloody summer. Can we not get back to the ways of pillaging and plundering as we did before?"

"You'd not set your sights higher than that?"

"Your grand plans and your higher destinies are all very well for them with the stomach for them, but for me I'm content to skim the cream and murder the merchants. Let's away from this place and no more trying to steal the reins from history's hands."

Crazy Dog laughed. He took his knife from the wall and returned it to his belt. "I knew you wouldn't do it. None of you have the stomach. You need me. Your lives would be piddling little things were I not in them and well you know it. I promise you a day will come when I'll murder the three of you, but that day is not this day. So let's away." He strode out of the cabin and up the hatch. "I feel the tide has turned. Affairs here are no longer fit for a man of my stature. San Luno's shifting currents call to me, so let's set sail for a friendlier shore."

Sail was let out and the Seahawk went on its way west. And whether they came to San Luno Bay, or whether they sailed across the Ocean and defeated the cannibals and conquered the Isles of Pearls, or whatever other idiocies they got up to, this tale has naught to tell.

CHAPTER TWENTY-EIGHT
OBSESSION

THAT NIGHT THEY STAYED at the tavern, and Tom did not sleep on the straw in back. He and Katie went to bed together upstairs. Tavish spent the night in a spare room on the ground floor, but sleep did not come near him. He remembered the night before and the kisses they'd shared. He rose from his bed and opened his door, but then went to bed again. Now he knew how sweet she was, and how much sweetness hurt.

There were two windows and he looked out of each, but the views they held left no impression on his mind. It was a lesson he'd learned: one can never have what one wants too much. He saw he'd left the door open, so he rose and closed it.

May, the miller's daughter, in a room of her own on the ground floor, was in a bit of a turmoil over a lad she'd fancied. When she heard the noises from Tavish's room she plucked up her courage, and after he'd shut the door there came the littlest knock, he thought he mayn't have heard it, but was sudden certain Katie had tired of Tom and come to him, so he listened to see if the knock would come again and sure enough he heard it once more.

He opened the door and there stood May in her nightgown with a taper to light her way. He knew at once why she'd come.

"Can you not sleep?" she asked.

He saw her hair was the color of straw. Her cheeks, which had looked white and pasty by day, were gentled over by the taper's light. He saw her great breasts under her gown. He looked at her face again and her eyes were brown in the candle light and he thought she wanted to smile but wasn't sure. He wanted to tell her he knew what ailed her and he didn't want her near because he couldn't mend it, but what he said was, "I can't . . . Well don't just stand there. Sure you've made your mind up to disturb me, so come in."

"I wouldn't if I was disturbing you." She came in, and the smile now came with her. "Are you unhappy?" She kicked herself. Why had she said that?

"Sure I've made my mind up to be unhappy. I'm as unhappy as I want to be." He also had no notion why he'd said that. Was it true, he wondered.

"Well, since neither of us is sleeping, there's no point doing it on our own. We'd do it better if we did it together."

They stood where they were, looking at one another, trying to discover what would happen next.

"Have you any brothers or sisters? Or is it just you and your father lives here?"

"It's the two of us. My Ma died, so I look after Da." Then she added, "There's a few lads we hire sometimes. One left today . . . Mostly it's my Da and me."

He could have held her face and kissed her. Instead he said, "It's a lot of work for two people."

"Not if you keep your mind on what's to be done." Seeing something in his face, "Shall we sit?" she asked. "I'm getting tired standing." So they looked about but there wasn't a chair.

"There's room on the bed."

"Are you sure?"

Was he sure of anything? "It's a comfortable bed," he said, sitting on it.

"But not one you can sleep in." She sat next to him. Their hips touched. A feeling of warmth rose and burst like a bubble, but didn't vanish.

"Not the bed's fault." He could smell her scent.

Silence like a secret stretched, till, "Where did you come from?" she asked.

"Port Jay."

"What made you come so far?"

"I don't know . . ."

"You must know. Otherwise . . ."

"There was a lady. I thought she needed protection from the troubles on the Road." He pulled away. Had someone put her up to this? Was this some kind of joke? Oh, wasn't he that tired of women and their ways.

"Did she need protection?"

"She probably needed protection from me."

"Why, are you that wicked a man?" She inched closer. He gave her a long look. ". . . I'm sorry if you thought I was calling you wicked. That's not what I meant."

"I know what you meant." He wanted to put his hands on her. Shame covered him like a wound. He said, "I am that."

"Oh . . ." There was a pause. "Would you like some wine? I could get some."

He thought about it. "That would be nice."

"Ever since my Ma died, my Da has been lonely. It's done something to him . . . There's many men are lonely and undesired." She paused and looked at him.

Tavish wondered if she'd finished. Just then the taper guttered and went out, leaving them stranded in the starlight. They laughed like they'd been caught at something.

"Well, I'll get that wine." She rose, but instead of going to the door she looked out a window. "This is one of my favorite rooms. I love this view."

He got up from the bed and stood next to her. There was a pond and a little hazle-brake. She stood there like she was waiting for something. Unexpectedly he ran his hand quickly down her back. Tentatively. She didn't move. Then she looked at him. It's unclear what she saw, but finally she said, "I'll be right back." She left, closing the door after herself.

He sat and waited. His fancies ran to thoughts of this young woman and what would pleasure her. *I'm cursed*, he thought. *Must I want every woman that comes near me? And what will Katie think?* No, he couldn't do it. He was deluding himself. He tossed it to and fro and realized he knew nothing was going to happen. He waited for her to come back.

It took a long while, but finally he realized she wasn't coming back.

Early in the morning, when Tom and Katie came downstairs, Tavish was up, waiting for them. He asked Katie if there was aught he could do for her. She had to think, for truly there wasn't. The two of them walked to the stable, Tom allowing time for their good byes.

"Is Neddy trim and able to go? We'll need him, for we'll be finding a place to live. I think it'll be just the two of us. We won't have more need of you. If there are supplies in the saddle bags you want, or there's something else feel free to take it. I think we'd want you to have it." It was a little smile she gave him.

He said to himself, *Now I know the word for her. For sure the word is impatient.* "I guess I'll take the musket.

"Good luck to you, Tavish. You were the best companion I could've asked for on the Road." She put her head close to his and leaned her forehead against his brow. "Don't think of me. Lord knows I'll remember you often, but don't think of me. I'm afraid your heart will be sore if you do." She sought for more to say, but there was nothing, so she kissed him on the cheek and led Neddy away, but he walked beside her unwilling to let her go.

"Shall you be going back to Port Jay?" she asked.

"I've not thought of it," he answered.

They were come now back to the tavern and Tom was there. He put a hand on Tavish's shoulder and led him a step away. "Katie told me all you did for her," he said. "I'm more grateful than it's possible to say. I know I'd be a dead man had you not brought her here."

"I couldn't let her go on her own."

"Of course not."

"There's many times she'd have been dead or worse."

"I know, she's told me all you did . . . After the troubles I've come through I feel myself to be a changed man. And so I forgive you. The weight of any resentment is too much to carry. I forgive you with a full heart. I really do."

"And what is it I'm being forgiven for?"

"You know." And here they looked hard into each other's eyes. "Let's not be aught but honest. I no more hold you at fault than I'd hold a dog for stealing a bone. No, that's not a good way to put it.

Never mind. We're both men." He gave him a pat on the back and returned to Katie.

But Tavish was not to be gotten rid of. The thought came to him he should hit Tom and ask if he'd forgive that, a dog would know no better, but instead he walked with him back to where Katie stood, as though he meant to go with them where they went.

"This will not do," said Katie. "It would not be right for you to be serving us, it would only keep the wound still bleeding for you. Can you not see that? It's best you go away. If you do not see the two of us it will not prey on your mind. And if you loved me like you said, you'd be happy for me."

"But where am I to go?"

"You can go wherever you want."

"Where I want to go is where you go."

Tom put his hand on Tavish's chest. "Not this time," he said.

Tavish knew he was lost but couldn't do other than he did. When Katie and Tom walked away he still walked with them. Then Katie took her stick and she poked him with it. "Go away," she said. "Did you really think I'd want to be with an old troll like you? Go away." She hit him.

This time when she walked away Tavish stood where he was. He watched them leave together. Neither turned back to look, and after some while they'd gone, vanished down the road. He stood for a long time after they'd gone, the spot where Katie had kissed him burning his cheek, before he finally went and gathered up his musket and his other possessions. When he did the thought came that Neddy needed tending, but then it hit him they'd taken Neddy too. For some reason that made him cry, when nothing else had.

Tom and Katie headed back down the Road, retracing the steps they'd recently trod. They came to the little hill where Katie'd lost her poor baby. This was where she'd given up all hope. In her heart she'd abandoned herself to Tavish then, and that was why she'd had to hurt him, which was the one pure drop of poison in her loving cup of bliss. Tom saw her upper lip quiver and he put his arms around her and they hurried on. When they did, Tom found himself walking past Agata's old farmhouse. It looked much sadder than he remembered. Had he been alone he would have tried the door, but as it was he kept his arm round Katie and hastened past.

The next day they came to the tavern where Tom had been blinded by Crazy Dog. Tom was fearful of the spot till he reflected that all he'd lost had been recovered. But as they went past he also saw where he'd run into the wood and been caught by Connor. A little shiver came over him because that was where he'd lost his hope, and the last of his luck had left him. What a sorry fool he'd been.

When they came to San Dorio they asked if there was any habitation they could make their own. They were told there was nothing in the town itself, but in the woods not far was the hut that had been home to the hermit Trogle. The holy man had recently departed, none could say where, and the hut now stood empty. Following the directions they were given they trudged through the woods till suddenly the trees fell apart to reveal a broad sunlit greensward. At the center of this clearing stood the hut. The building itself was small, with but one door and one window, but the grounds and the walls held still an aura of beneficence cast by the hermit's sanctifying hand. Inside it had been roughly partitioned into two rooms, one for sleeping, the other for preparing and eating food. The walls and the frame of the door were solid and well-built. The roof was thatched with straw. It wasn't much, but they didn't need much, apart from one another. It was just the place they wanted and they felt almost as if it had spoken to them words of invitation.

They settled in and found it a soothing spot, where nature offered itself in guileless abundance. A stream of clear water ran nearby, and often its lively chattering was heard amidst the constant sounds of birdsong. Sometimes deer would walk fearless right up to the door, and the squirrels would bring nuts to their hands.

The morning they moved in Tommy Dog came to the door to greet them, as though he and Trogle had been acquainted. It was a joyful reunion. The times were happy after all their troubles and they treasured the days spent in this retreat tucked away from the turmoils and travails they'd so long endured. Also they were in love and this above all set them apart from the rest of the world. But Tom had never yet encountered a coin with only one side, and he knew trouble unlooked for was sure to come, so he acquired a rifle, which he kept in the hut where it remained unused and unregarded for many a day.

Tavish they'd left behind. After he'd gathered his possessions he stood a long time gazing at nothing. But there were actions he had to take and the first he took was to mark the spot where they'd parted. When she was ready to come back this would be the place she'd look for him. He wouldn't follow her; he'd let her come back on her own. He'd be ready for her when she was ready. But he couldn't waste his days standing in this spot, and what if she came back when he was somewhere else? She'd need some sort of trail to follow so she could find him, but he was uncertain how to give her one. He thought he could leave something there and then come every day to see if she'd taken it. It had to be a special token, something she'd know was his. He had a little wallet he'd made for himself; she'd often seen him with it. He could leave that. It bore a 'T' on the front for Tavish. He took out the wallet, emptied its contents into his pockets, put something in telling her where to look for him, then laid it on the ground. It looked peculiar, though he figured that was the point. But surely anyone could come along and take it. There were many problems. He walked a few steps away and looked back. The wallet lay just where he'd put it, looking sad and abandoned, as if it was him. So he went back and picked it up. In the end he decided to return every day to this same place. When she wanted to come back, if he didn't happen to be there at the time, he was sure she'd find a way of letting him know.

That day he returned two times. He looked, but he didn't see her or any sign she'd been there. The second time he thought he saw her just leaving, but when he caught up to the woman he thought was her, it was someone else. He lived several days like this, unwilling to go far, because he knew she'd come back. During this time he ate as little as possible, only taking small bites at day's end to stretch what he had. He hadn't the will to provide for himself. The thought of finding work was disagreeable to him. All he thought about was Katie, and the quotidian tasks of struggle and survival seemed like relics from some unrecognizable past. He didn't want anything coming between him and his need to return every day to the spot where he waited for her. He slept under the stars and came to know the streets and sidewalks in that vicinity. There were others he saw regularly, living the life of an outcast like himself, but he would have nothing to do with them. Most of them spent their days begging. Tavish was too proud to beg, but he knew he couldn't live as he was very long. He thought of working as a baker's boy, but the thought didn't please, till finally one day he put his dignity to the side and returned to the baker. But the baker spurned him, seeing he'd grown dissolute and dirty, and wouldn't allow him in the house.

There'd been occasions when, seeing young women of about her size, he'd imagined they were her. He'd grown familiar with the constant craving he felt and how it could lead him to see things. So it came as a shock, one that nearly took his breath away, when, one evening in a tavern on the outskirts he actually did see Katie again. He knew her like he knew the teeth in his mouth. She was seated beside another man, not Tom, and she was wearing a hat. He hadn't known her to favor hats, but it was her face, her smiling eyes, her lips, her hair escaping from the back of the hat. He watched as the two of them talked together in a familiar manner, and the unbreachable dikes he'd built to keep his feelings out just crumbled, the wounds of his desire opened and he drowned in torrents of jealousy and anguished memory. Above all else he wondered who was this new man? She'd left Tom already – he'd known that would happen – but she hadn't returned to him? He watched as they shared the food on one another's plates, for all the world as though they'd had a long acquaintance. He saw their fingers touch. The pain of seeing her with another, so uncaring of himself, so casually intimate, was heart shattering. He continued to watch every move she made to see if she'd look in his direction, but she seemed unaware of his presence. As he gazed at her he felt again all they'd shared and how they'd cared for one another on the Road. He saw her mannerisms he knew so well without realizing how well he knew them, the way she'd pinch her face to make a point, or squeeze her fingers together for emphasis. All these things she did, gesturing with her hands, as she talked to the man next to her. He couldn't sit still and he stood to go to her side, but then held himself where he was, still watching. He didn't want to talk to her in front of that man.

Then she rose and went into another room. She moved gracefully between the tables, not once casting a glance in his direction. Her companion remained where he was, comfortable in whatever his reflections were. This was his chance. Anticipating her return, he moved nearer to the path she'd taken. She might come next to him and he'd look up, 'Oh what a surprise –' But no, it was no surprise. Surely it was destiny. He'd known it was fated the two of them would meet again. He tried to prepare something to say. And then she was returning. He looked down and just as she went past he looked up to speak and it wasn't her. It was a different woman by several pounds and many years. He watched as she returned to her seat, resuming her conversation with the man she was with, the two of them casual in their attachment. Looking at her now he saw she was a different person, not Katie at all. He stood and left.

On the pavement outside he looked at himself and realized he had almost reached the point of madness. Examining what he felt he found naught but hunger and anger. He realized that was all that had been inside him for many days now, and only now he'd seen it. He'd been too taken with looking for Katie to see what was happening to himself. But now he saw the rage that was growing. He couldn't leave the vicinity because he had to be here when she came back, but what could he do? He'd spent the last of his money. He had to do something and in his current mood he could take no responsibility for what it would be. He was beyond any bounds he could control. In a flash of hatred he wanted to find Tom and kill him. This was pure hatred, anger refined and directed to a point, as consuming as love and as unquenchable. He was going to stalk him down and do away with him.

A man was sauntering down the other side of the road. He was well dressed in an orange tawny jacket like a merchant, and was absorbed in the contemplation of some papers he held in his hand. He had that contented look Tavish wanted to defile, the look of someone who had it in his heart to forgive. The man paused for a moment and produced a faded rose from the papers he was holding, then resumed his progress in the direction he'd been going. He wore a dagger in his belt. In one violent moment of thought Tavish saw himself taking the man's knife and using it to rob him. He'd do it just as Vincenzo had done to him and Katie. Surely this was the way the world worked.

He followed the man, who paid no attention to him, wrapped up in his own thoughts; and then Tavish saw there was another, a Negro, in a shadow at the corner, with eyes on the same prey. Yes, now he was certain this was how things were done. He met the Negro's gaze and it was as if they both agreed. Together they jumped the man. The Negro put his hand over his mouth to keep him from calling out while Tavish whipped the dirk from his belt. The papers and the flower he'd been holding fell scattered to the ground. He tried to protest but could only get out a muffled yelp. For one hallucinatory instant he wore Tom's face, his lips mouthing, 'I forgive you.' Tavish slit his throat, while the Negro grabbed his purse. They left him dying and ran away.

The minute they felt safe they crouched together to see how much they'd taken. It was less than they'd hoped for, but it would see them through the next few days. They shook hands, concurring in the deed and sharing the proceeds. The Negro was an escaped slave named Archimedes. From that day forth he and Tavish worked as a team. Archimedes was accustomed to being ordered about so Tavish took command. They lived together and prowled the streets by night, looking for victims. In those unsettled times there were many uprooted, with nowhere to call home. These were their prey.

After a robbery they would retire to a hidden clearing in the woods and assess the take. On one occasion when they did this Archimedes' temper was grim and forbidding. He didn't like being a robber but saw no alternative. "I am marked by my skin. Any who see me can capture or kill me as they please. But why have you chosen this way of life? It is not one in which a man will last very long. I am grateful I am not alone, but you could find a position in one of the mansions, or a tavern. How comes it you have not done so?"

"I could be a baker's boy and pound the dough. But I would liefer do summat for which I cannot be forgiven. I fear it's the only way to wash the stench of forgiveness from my soul."

"I would ask who put that stench on you. And I suspect this has something to do with that spot you return to every day."

So Tavish told all the story of him and Katie and how they'd left Port Jay and arrived at Kashahar. It was a tale he'd kept to himself, but he felt a relief now he'd told another.

Archimedes pondered on this tale and gave his head many grave shakes. "I know the woman you describe," he said. "I see her with the eye of my imagination. You cannot see her. You are blinded by love. But I will be your eyes and teach you to see. She is a shrewd and a selfish wench. She knows you will do anything for her so she uses you. Her trick is to ignore you till you can think of nothing but her. And all the time she ignores you also she watches you and she knows all she has to do is give you a smile or a little twinkly look with her eyes and you will do what she wants. And what she is thinking is, 'What a fool. I can get him to do anything.' I know these pretty women."

"You have no idea what she's like."

Archimedes wrinkled his brow and smiled, as though he'd remembered something funny. But what he said was, "The world is full of many like her. But I put them in their place. I let them know I understand the game they play. But when someone is in love he will do crazy things, things for which there is no explaining . . . So I thought there might be something like this. Is there nothing that would make you stop loving her?"

"No, that's impossible."

"There is one way for sure; it always works."

"What's that?"

"If you marry her."

Archimedes laughed, but Tavish remained sullen. "It's no use. I'll always want her, though I fear I've lost her. I've not the first hint of an idea where she's gone. Far enough from me, I'm certain."

Archimedes put his hand on Tavish's knee. "If you want her that bad, we should get her for you. There are two of us now; I will help."

"What would you do?"

"What *we* would do is we would find her and kill the man she is with, and then bring her here and keep her here. She will have to be nice to you."

Tavish knew she would never come, nor would he ever force her to be a mere robber's jilt, but he kept these thoughts to himself. "I don't know . . . She lives in me, but truly I fear she's lost."

At that moment an arrow flew to stand quivering in the tree trunk next to Tavish and a rough voice said, "We have you in our sights. If you do not do what we say, the next shaft will kill."

"Where are you?" asked Archimedes.

"You are surrounded. Stand slowly and leave your weapons on the ground. Then move away from the clearing and you will be allowed to live."

"Come out and let us see who you are," said Tavish.

The answer to this was another arrow standing in the ground between Tavish's feet. "The next will not miss. Now move! We grow impatient."

Archimedes and Tavish stood, letting it be seen that their hands were empty, and then they walked slowly and with great reluctance out of the clearing, leaving their booty behind.

"Now run, if you value your lives."

They ran, making as much noise as possible so their attackers would know they had gone. After those sounds died away there was a long silence. Nothing moved in the clearing or the surrounding trees. After close to twenty minutes had passed an Indian crept out of the woods and gathered up the loot the robbers had left behind. This took a little time, but clearly he was very pleased. Suddenly Archimedes and Tavish erupted from the trees and fell on him. After running a short distance they had stealthily crawled back to see who had ambushed them. Seeing only a single man they had resolved to take back what was theirs. Archimedes wrapped his powerful arms around the Indian while Tavish asked, "Where are your companions?"

"They are coming," said the Indian. "You can still run away and be spared." But Archimedes and Tavish were laughing now at the Indian's audacity and the low trick he'd tried playing on them. The Indian, knowing he'd been seen through, said, "I should have shot both of you when I had the chance. Now I am punished for being soft-hearted."

"Yes, why didn't you kill us?"

"I was hoping you would keep stealing more and I would take that from you as well."

In the end the three of them formed a friendship. The Indian, whose name was Cunning Fox, had fought under Half Moon, but after the Indians were defeated, soldiers came with fire and guns and destroyed the village where he'd lived, killing the rest of his family. He alone had escaped, and had been prowling the Forest, living off the game he could shoot with his bow. He hadn't been brave enough to risk going near the towns of the settlers, but when he saw these two alone in the wood he'd devised his plan to take advantage of them.

So Tavish and Archimedes welcomed Cunning Fox into their little society. They would hunt as a pack. Three of them together were enough to ambush any of the small convoys that carried cargoes up and down the Coast Road. They became notorious and were known as the Three Bandits. Tavish forgot the man he'd been, translated by melancholy, longing and bleak despair into an outcast and a desperado. He thought each day might be his last, and in every episode of banditry a savage portion of his heart was hoping he'd be killed. This made him a peerless brigand, brutal and unafraid. Often he thought of Katie. Since he no longer returned to the spot where he'd seen her last, he worried that when she wanted to come back she wouldn't know where to find him. So he made sure to leave his name at the scenes of their crimes, often writing "Tavish was here," on the skin or clothing of his victims, trusting his ill fame would come to her ear. Archimedes and Cunning Fox spent their days hiding out in the woods, but Tavish would come into the towns and mingle with the crowd on days of feast or at the market, learning of the goods that were to be shipped and looking at all the women, but never seeing the one he sought.

One day in the woods Tavish came to a very large, lichen-covered rock, and seated on the top of the rock was a woman. She was attired in dark cloth of subtle tissue and her hair also was dark. She wore a silver belt round her waist and on it thirteen silver bells. Tavish did not see her at first on account of the rock being so large and her being on top of it, so when he did see her it crossed his mind she must have been watching him and waiting for a while. He'd heard tales of meetings such as this and knew it for a sign that he was soon to die. This didn't disturb him overmuch. He found his way up and came to her. He saw her eyes were bruised with sadness and a little despair.

Deirdre – for it was she – smiled and opened her arms, inviting, but he held back, knowing her for a deceitful baggage. "I've a gift I can give," she said. "I'll take the memory of her away and the hurt goes with it. You'll know nothing of her. Were you to meet again it would be for the first time. Come, lie with me and your past will be forgot."

Still he held back. "Sure it is I can't. If it went, my soul would go with it. I'd not be myself, just some unhappy bugger who couldn't remember anything."

"And you would never know what was gone, nor would you miss it."

"The only gift I'd ask is to tell me where I might find her."

"She will not come back to you."

"She may not come back to the Tavish who loved her. I fear that man is dead. But certain I am she will come back to me."

She looked at him after he'd said this, holding his eye with hers. He'd grown bold staring down the men he killed, and was accustomed to what he'd read in their eyes when they knew their time had come. But he was not prepared for what he saw in Deirdre's eyes. Truly it frightened him, and he found himself looking away. "You'll find her in the hut of Trogle the hermit. She's a garden planted there. She's been there just so long the seeds she's sown are coming in to bloom." He turned his eyes to look at her again, but he saw where she had been was only a fold in the granite, and that had been her eyes were two bits of mica sparkling in the sun, and the tinkling of the silver bells was the lonely calling of the birds. He was by himself, his only companion a chill breeze wafting from the nearby trees.

CHAPTER TWENTY-NINE
STORY'S END

HOPE IS A FOOLISH and futile possession for any man, especially one as experienced as Tavish. Nevertheless, on the day following his meeting with Deirdre, he told his two companions he was going on an expedition to Trogle's hut. He told them what he expected to find, adding that when he returned, they would make a plan to get Katie. However, it was not his intention to return. He planned to kill Tom and then embark on a new life with Katie, but this he kept to himself.

When he got to the hut, he saw it was as Deirdre had said. He watched from the shelter of the surrounding trees, following Tom as he went about his errands, but keeping his eye always on Katie. He was a practiced observer of her, and seeing how she acted around Tom he became convinced she had tired of him already. Tom would have to be killed, Archimedes was right about that. But Tavish wouldn't carry her off against her will, though he wasn't certain how to convince her to come to him. He loved her so devoutly with every fiber of his body, he was sure she had to love him back. But how to make her see that? Slowly a plan formed in his mind, but it was one that would involve his two companions, so on the morning of the third day after he'd arrived at the hut, he returned to Archimedes and Cunning Fox.

He told them how things stood. It seemed simple. The hut was isolated, far from any town. It had but the one door and only one window. There was no back door; anyone inside would be trapped. The trees had been cleared all around, so there was no way to sneak up, but that would pose no problem. Archimedes favored coming by night and cloud. The three of them would creep stealthily up to the hut. They'd kill the man and abduct the woman. Nothing could be easier. It would take no more than a few minutes.

"What about the dog?" said Cunning Fox. "The dog will bark."

"Kill the dog quick," said Archimedes. "He won't bark long."

But Tavish insisted that wouldn't be right. A deed such as this should not be made simple. It would be done by day. Tom was to know who killed him and Katie was to watch him die.

"So you're wanting to make it into a grand drama," said Archimedes. "That's a foolish plan."

But Tavish was not to be brought round. He had it his way in the end. Also, there would be no carrying off of Katie. He would convince her to come on her own. But the way he imagined doing so was something he didn't share with the others.

Tom and Katie, having no suspicion of the malice planned against them, were as blithe a pair of lovers as any in fairyland. The time passed quietly, one perfect day following another. They were just the two of them, sufficient to themselves. Every morning they woke aching for the other's kiss and all day they rode the currents of desire. Love was the theme and melody of every singing hour and nothing in the loving world held them back from giving everything they had. Only to love forever was all they asked, and forever was only now. And when the sun dropped below the horizon, they'd lie together, limbs entangled, as the mysterious night engulfed them, the low horned moon edging the clouds, a few pale stars strewn across the sky, and a low wind running to and fro, like the children they'd once been, not knowing where to go.

"Wherefore are there more than you and I . . .?

"Tell me again about everything . . ."

"And all the world inside . . ."

"The living world . . ."

It happened on a warm sun-dappled morn that Tom rose from an empty dream to see Katie standing mother naked, feeding a doe and a hart that had come to the window. He rose to stand beside her, taking in the pleasance of the sunrise and the friskiness of the breeze. Thrushes were cooing in the thatch. Tommy Dog was pretending to chase a brace of conies who'd scamper when he came near, more in play than earnest. Katie looked up and he took her in his arms. They made themselves happy in kissing and comforting one another, and when they were done, they dressed and turned their thoughts to the cares of the day, little and few as they were. Tom paid a visit to San Dorio to barter the beans and onions he'd grown in return for bread and cider. His mind was on the passing of the summer and the preparations for autumn. The leaves on the maples were turning a deep bloody red, and soon he'd have to look out for warmer clothes. But the chill was not yet. His foot still ached. The wound had never entirely healed with all the walking he'd done, so he had to endure the occasional throb of pain, but all in all it was better than it had been.

Katie sat in her chair, looking at her garden out the window. So many times she'd sat this way. She thought about the dreams she'd had on the road and it came to her maybe this was all another dream. Maybe she'd wake back in Lanchester Mansion and she'd have to go downstairs and put on her apron and set out breakfast. Had that person really been her? Life was so much simpler now, and there wasn't much in it that displeased her. She'd await Tom's return, till then she savored the peace.

Tom concluded his bartering and set off on the long walk home. He felt tiredness in the muscles between his shoulders: it was the jug of cider that weighed him down. On this day there was one who followed him, waiting for the choicest moment to make him a victim, but of this he was unaware. He'd been shadowed through the woodland paths, till he neared the hut and then, the moment having arrived, a musket was fired and he fell on the broad greensward.

The man who'd fired the musket shouted, "Do you forgive me for that?"

Tom's mind was muddled, not having taken in what had occurred. "I'm afraid something stupid's happened and I've spilled the cider," he called to Katie.

Katie rushed to his aid, but as she ran to the door an arrow suddenly stood in the doorpost and another voice shouted, "You cannot come out. If you do you'll be killed."

So she knew they'd been ambushed and were being robbed. Tommy Dog barked at the trees and ran a little way on his crippled legs towards Tom where he lay, then ran back. She took the rifle and pointed it out the window, looking for the faces of those who sought to harm them. All she saw was trees.

Tom was struggling to stand. She saw him about thirty yards from where she sat at the window. He'd been shot in the shoulder and as he got back up, first he kneeled on one leg and then rose on the other, but as he did the musket fired again, hitting him in the knee and he fell once more. Katie screamed, but she couldn't come to him; her role was to do no more than watch as he bled to death.

"Alright, whoever you are," she shouted to the woods. "What is it you're wanting?"

"We want you to watch him die," came an answer. "And when he's dead you can come out to us."

She now thought very deeply what she should do. The voice that had answered her was one she thought she knew. "Tavish, is that you?"

"Certain it is."

"Please, let me just have Tom. We've hardly begun. Don't kill him."

"I've got to kill him. Else I'll die for your love."

Well she couldn't think of anything to say to that.

"Tavish, come out of the trees for one minute, so I can see you," she shouted.

"Why do you want to see me?"

"Maybe it's a sight I've been missing. Let me see your face."

Slowly he stepped out. He stood visible to her on the edge of the grass. His aspect was changed since she'd seen him last. His eyes glittered from a dark brown face that bore a beard the color of rain-spoilt hay. He smiled. As he remained there she took a shot at him which missed, but sent him scrambling to hide in the brush.

"You've had your chance," he shouted. "You'll not get another."

She fired a few more times into the woods near where he'd disappeared, but then stopped, mindful of wasting bullets.

Tom strove to crawl to Katie's door. As he was doing that, Tavish shouted to him, "Do you still forgive me?"

"Yes, whatever you've done, always . . . always I will forgive . . . Can you not see that nothing good will ever happen if we cannot forgive one another?"

Katie had had a thought. "Tommy," she said to the dog, "go find Tavish for me. Show me where he is."

Tommy barked and ran out of the hut. He ran directly to the spot where Tavish stood and bared his teeth and growled. Tavish kicked him, but Katie fired a shot that nearly hit Tavish in the face, missing only by inches. So he aimed his musket at Tommy Dog and shot him. Then he moved away, finding a different tree to hide behind. Tommy was mortally wounded and had no place to go to die but to where Tom was lying. Tom held the dog's face in his hands and Tommy Dog spoke for the second time, saying, "All love leads to death," and then died in Tom's arms.

Katie decided she had to risk the arrows, so clutching her rifle, she came running to where Tom lay. As she did, an arrow from Cunning Fox tore through her cotton blouse, grazing her breast.

"No!" shouted Tavish. "Don't hurt her!" He raced to where the other two were hidden and chastised Cunning Fox angrily.

Katie came to Tom.

"Katie, my love, I had so much to say, but now my life is ending."

"Your life will not end today. It's only Tavish, and his aim is lousy." The jest was on her lips, but foreboding gazed from her eyes. Tom was losing a fearsome amount of blood. She got him up and moving, leaning on her. The pair of them managed a strenuous stumble towards the hut and the protection it promised while Tavish and Cunning Fox were carrying on their dispute.

At this point Archimedes put his hand on Tavish's arm and said, "Stay calm, my brother. I will take care of everything." Seeing Tom was wounded and Katie was too busy with him to do anything else, he strode boldly out of the trees and walked to where Katie and Tom had now gotten, which was just outside the door of the hut. Taking his great knife he stabbed Tom in the chest. A plume of blood erupted and Katie screamed. Archimedes then knocked the rifle out of her hands and grabbed her by the hair, so he could carry her to Tavish. Tavish broke off his argument with Cunning Fox when he saw Archimedes dragging Katie towards him. Archimedes shouted glad tidings to Tavish, confident the job was done. Tom was dying, choking in his own blood, and they would carry Katie away. But

Tavish had been cherishing a secret plan of his own, and saw now its time was come.

"Katie, I would never let any hurt come to you," he said.

He aimed his musket and fired. Katie screamed. Then Archimedes fell dead.

Turning quickly to Cunning Fox, Tavish loaded and aimed his musket again. Cunning Fox could make no sense of what was happening. Tavish said, "Drop your bow and arrow."

"What are you doing? You shot Archimedes."

"I said drop them!"

Cunning Fox did as he was told.

"Now step out into the open."

"Have you gone mad?"

"I said step out or I'll shoot you!" Looking at Cunning Fox's face, Tavish was no longer certain he could go through with it. He had to get this over quickly.

Cunning Fox left the shelter of the trees and stood on the greensward, visible to Katie.

Tavish stepped out also. He could see Archimedes' body sprawled brokenly on the grass. Pointing to Cunning Fox he said, "This is the man who almost killed you with his arrow. But I would never let him hurt you."

Cunning Fox blurted, "You told me –"

He said, "Cunning Fox, forgive me," and fired again.

"Shr – fr –" whatever he tried never got said. Cunning Fox fell to the ground.

Tavish turned to her. He groped in his mind for a formed idea but it was empty. He literally couldn't think what he was doing. "My own true friends they're dead now and I killed them, all so you'll know there's nothing to fear." He opened his arms. "Come to me, Katie."

Katie looked in horror. "You're a vile, evil man. I'll have naught to do with you." She ran to the hut, where Tom now lay gasping his last. "Stay with me, Tom," she pleaded with him. He looked at her, but couldn't speak. He'd loved her always with all that was in him. There wasn't much in him now, but his love had no bounds and his eyes told all he felt. His heart pumped the blood from his chest in great, pulsing bursts. Katie knew he was almost gone. "You've always been my one, my only. You're all the only thing that's true. You're–" she sobbed. "Stay with me. My Tom. Oh my Tom!" She tried to keep it up so he'd have her voice to hold onto, but in the end her words failed and she could only watch through her tears as the last light of life left his fading eyes and she knew he'd passed away forever.

Then she picked up her rifle and aimed it at Tavish. She fired, but her trembling hands betrayed her and she missed. Tavish stepped back and concealed himself. "Don't shoot me," he shouted. "Come and be with me." He added, "I've no one else I can kill for you."

But she'd never come out. "Show me your face," she shouted back. "Show me so I can send your sorry soul screaming straight to Hell!"

But he wouldn't. Instead he shouted, "Talk to me, Katie."

There was no answer.

"Katie. I love you, can't you see I'm protecting you still. Always I've protected you. Can't you see?"

Now she answered that with a bullet.

He despaired. His plan had come to nothing. Nothing, nothing, nothing. He might as well step out in the open and let her kill him. Sure it was what he deserved. Poor Archimedes. And poor bewildered Cunning Fox. He saw Cunning Fox's bow at his feet, where he was almost treading on it. He picked it up, and as he did a notion came to him. He found the quiver of arrows too. He knew how he could force her out. He ripped off the bottoms of his trousers and tore them to make rags. He wrapped the rags round one of the arrows. That done he used his flint and steel to make a spark that set the rags alight. He let them burn long enough to be certain the flame had taken. Then, aiming his bow up to the sky to compensate for the weight of the rags, he shot an arrow into the air. It flew up then down and landed on the grass the other side of the hut. But now he had the range. He tried again, and this time his arrow landed on the hut's thatched roof. The flame was hesitant at first, but then a wind fanned it and the thatch caught and the fire was burning merrily. He thought one more for good luck so he lobbed another burning arrow into the sky. Soon the roof was burning in two places.

Katie caught sight of a little flame coming from the roof. Oh no. She caught up a bucket with water and tried to dowse the burning, but seeing the flames in many spots and smelling the smoke, she knew she couldn't put it out. The whole hut was going to burn. If she left, he'd have her. She saw no way around it but to remain in the hut and let it burn. She fell onto Tom's bloody corpse but his heart was still and she tasted the bitter heartbreak of good-bye forever. She gave a wail of grief for all her love had come to, but she wasn't one to feel the burning, and all she wished was that all was done, so as the flames closed around her she turned the rifle to her head and pressed the trigger.

Tavish heard the shot from the burning hut. "Come out, come out," he called. It was no use. The whole hut was burning now and down it all came in a savage blaze, casting logs and many sparks onto the grass. He came out from the woods and approached the remains of the hut, which now was a torch incinerating everything he'd ever valued or treasured. He came as near the flaming heat as he could and called, "Please come out. Come. Be with me . . ." But nothing burned but his dreams, and all his hopes were ashes.

THE LAST CHAPTER
A MEDITATION ON LADYBIRDS

OBADIAH RUMPLE had fled from Port Jay on the night of the great fire, and found his way to the sleepy fishing village of San Dorio. He'd retained his Bible, as well as a large supply of smuggled rum, so he felt confident he'd be made welcome in his new surroundings. He erected a small house on the edge of town, put a cross over the door and called it his chapel. As Chaplain Rumple he set about ministering to the spiritual needs of the people of San Dorio. They were a stolid lot, living on the cycles of sun and storm as men must have done on these shores for centuries. Embarking on the offshore winds in the morning, returning with the onshore breeze at eve, it was a simple life, bounded by the tides and the horizon. Each day, like the clouds above, was a little different but still the same. Rumple wasn't made particularly welcome at first, although the rum did help open a few doors.

He made the acquaintance of the Sheriff, who gave him a tour of the jail. He was pleased to see the cells were being kept clean and reasonably free of vermin, and was a bit surprised, at the tour's conclusion, that he hadn't seen a single prisoner.

"We don't get a lot of criminals around here," said the Sheriff. "It used to be the main point of my job was to keep the Indians out, but even they haven't been raising much hell lately."

"When you do have criminals, what happens to them?"

"There used to be a circuit judge who'd do the rounds. He'd come and hold a trial. We have a man in the village who's studied some law books, so he'd help. But with all the disturbances lately, the judge hasn't been coming round."

"Then it's just as well you have no criminals. Seems like a waste, though, having so many cells and nobody to put in them."

"Well we're sure to round up a few. When we do you can come and pesterize them."

"Yes, 'tis a well known fact every jail needs a chaplain. And I think the word is proselytize."

Rumple spent some of his time tracking game in the woods when he was hungry for something other than fish. One day he was almost knocked over when three men came hastening out of the Forest. They had a panic-stricken air about them and their clothes were torn and dirty, as if they'd been many days in the trackless woods. Rumple, seeing they were in need of some succor, brought them to the town square where they could sit and have a cup of tea, and then summoned the Sheriff, who listened to the tale they had to tell.

It was a strange one. They'd been caught up in some sort of squalid slavery and murder spree. Two men named Dane and Bramij, together with a third named Harry, who'd thought he was the boss, had caught them and put them in a chain gang, along with some others, with the intention of selling them as slaves.

"It sounds like these were some enterprising lads," said the Sheriff.

"Too enterprising, I'd say," said one of the men, who was sipping his tea with an air of distaste. "They grabbed us and brought us down to Indradoon. When they got there they wanted to sell us, but the man who ran the market saw some of us had no black skins, nor any stamp of the jungle, so he asked where they'd gotten us."

"What did they say?"

Here another one of the men, a portly one with a huge posterior, interrupted and said, "They answered like true philosophers. They held it as a maxim, which at the same time could be a universal law, that if they could beat a man up that made him their slave, so they'd beaten us up and brought us there and now they wanted to sell us. The auctioneer thanked them deeply. He said he couldn't recall ever having had the moral basis of human society explained quite so succinctly. Then he went on to tell them that due to a tremendous fire — of which he was startled to learn they'd taken no notice, considering the sky had been black with smoke for days — many of the largest plantations had recently burned to the ground and as a consequence there was no longer any need for slaves. 'In fact,' he went on, 'many landowners have asked us to sell their slaves at ridiculous bargains so as to avoid the cost of feeding and housing them.' Well, you can imagine that left our lads feeling a trifle foolish."

"So did they set you free?"

"No," said the third man, who wore the tattered remnants of an army uniform. "They should have, but they didn't. They were afraid of what we'd do once we were free. All we'd have done would have been to get away, but they debated what to do, whether they should just massacre us, or maybe chain us to some trees deep in the Forest and let us starve. While they were arguing, it came out that one of the Indians had told them there was another place where slaves were sold, and she'd offered to lead them there. The only problem was the Indian who'd told them this had escaped. However, they had another Indian, and since obviously all Indians would share this sort of arcane information, they were sure this other one could tell them where to find the place."

"I'd doubt such place exists."

"Which was exactly what the Indian told them," said the one who'd spoken first. "He said the whole story was a lie. He said there was nothing to it, and that anyone with a brain the size of a pea could have seen right through it. But when they threatened to shoot off his toes he suddenly remembered how to get there. So they took us barging around in the woods, letting this Indian lead them in circles, till finally they ran out of supplies and then there was a big fight. Dane got hold of the only pistol and used it to shoot Harry and the Indian, while the rest of us escaped. There were a couple others, I don't know where they went, but the three of us stuck together till finally we found our way here. By the by," he asked Rumple, "is that a bottle of rum in your pocket?"

They gave the three some supplies, then let them go their way. The next day Dane and Bramij came into town and the Sheriff, knowing his duty, arrested them and threw them into his jail. Once they were there, he wasn't certain what to do with them, but he thought the circuit judge was bound to come round sooner or later and till then they'd just have to wait.

Chaplain Rumple found these two to be a sad warning of what men could come to when their imaginations were smitten with sin. "These men are like those trees that stand out yonder. You know the tall ones I'm speaking of?" he asked the Sheriff.

"Certain I do."

"Well men are like those trees. Their branches reach up to the sunlight, but their roots are planted in deep gloom far below." He considered this commonplace an awfully shrewd insight, showing the conformation of all parts of a man, from the dust beneath his toes to his angelical aspirations. He took great relish in repeating it.

A day came when a pillar of smoke rising over the woods led the Sheriff to the scene of an horrific crime. When he arrived at the source of the smoke, he found Tavish crouched on the ground that surrounded a charred pile of rubble that had been Trogle's hut. He knew him at once to be one of the notorious Three Bandits, and he found the bodies of the other two nearby, as well as that of a dog. Once the embers had cooled, an investigation of the ashes revealed the remains of two others who must have been burnt in the hut. The prisoner made not the slightest resistance when he was put in cuffs, only muttering that he'd murdered them all, without saying any more.

The Sheriff put Tavish in a cell well away from the other two so they'd not be able to talk to one another. The Sheriff found his prisoner to be a man of few words, who complied with every order he was given. He willingly told them where all the plundered loot was stashed, heedless of the value this could have held as a bargaining chip. He had little motive force of his own, and was content to sit idly in his cell and let the hours pass.

Chaplain Rumple's rounds took longer than before, now there was a third prisoner. He didn't quite know what to make of this quiet, sad-eyed ambassador from a desolate heartland who looked at him out of a ruinous face. He sat on the stool in Tavish's cell and asked him if there were any steps he felt the need to take, to reconcile him with his maker.

"And why would I be doing anything of the sort?" Tavish asked.

"God placed you on this earth for a reason; you're a part of His plan for all of creation. If you have not acted worthily in His eyes, it's never too late to ask forgiveness."

"Do you honestly believe that?"

"It's a belief that brings me great comfort, knowing I'm doing my best to walk in the path He laid down for me."

"And what is the purpose of this path?"

"To help my brethren, my fellow pilgrims through this shadowed vale of life. If I can ease the burden for just one, I'd rejoice in a life well spent."

"That's why we're here? To help others?"

"When you come to the end of your life and look back, only those things you've done to help others will be of value in your eyes."

Tavish thought this over. Then he said, "If we were logical, and of course we aren't, far from it, but if we were logical and we wanted to do the one thing that would be of the greatest benefit to others, I think we'd kill ourselves. Remove ourselves entirely from the competition for the good things in life. That would be a real help. Anything else is just selfishness."

"You think all that's in your life is only yourself? You'd be best off if your fellow creatures were dead and there was just you, the only one in all the world?"

"Of course . . . Apart from myself, what is there?"

"That's an evil logic if you ask me."

"Logic is just logic; it's not evil unless you think it is."

"I'd not have your thoughts for any money in this world. 'Tis said an idle mind's the Devil's workshop. Before I leave, might I provide aught to exercise yours? Maybe a deck of cards?"

"No thanks. My mind is sufficient for itself . . . Except for my dreams."

So Rumple left Tavish alone with his thoughts. He knew he wasn't really a good chaplain, he knew everything he said was just silly nonsense, and anyone who was determined to feel bad would find a way around all he could say. But he also knew his silliness brought hope to people. He saw it in the village fishermen he spent time with. Where did they get their hope? Surely not from the drudgery of their daily existence which left them disemboweled with care, fearful to grasp any joy, knowing before it can be theirs it will have been snatched away. They got their hope from him. And there was always the rum.

And Tavish, in his own thinking, knew there was no way out of the senseless logic that was all he could make of life. As he sat in his cell sometimes thoughts of Katie and Tom came to trouble him. He remembered how he'd loved her, and he'd call up again his hatred for that bastard Tom, but he no longer felt those things directly. Love and hate were only words. It felt like his life was over, as if he'd been buried alive, unable to see past the coffin lid inches above his eyes, awaiting the final suffocation. There was no longing in him anymore. He was truly empty, hollowed out.

Then one day there was the sound of hammering and sawing coming from the town square. Rumple arrived with news that a gibbet was being erected in anticipation of the long-awaited arrival of the circuit judge, which was expected tomorrow. He'd arrived yesterday in Kir-a-Vanta, a few miles down the Road. There he'd taken matters in hand. He was a hanging judge and had not acquitted any. In fact he'd hung the witnesses as well, and the bailiff, even the old lady who unlocked the courtroom door. None were innocent in his eyes, and all deserved the hangman's noose.

Tavish spent that night considering what was likely to be done the following day. He tried to picture the judge and the courtroom. He thought again about the conversations he'd had with the chaplain concerning guilt and innocence, and the reasons for punishment, but it all seemed like some obscure joke that would have to be explained to him. And then of course it wouldn't be funny. He lay on his bed idly watching the moonlight from his window creep across the wall, wondering how many other men had slept on this same bed, and what their dreams had been, and if any were still alive.

The Judge arrived in the morning. He was a solitary traveler; no others were required since his person embodied also the roles of jury and prosecuting attorney. It had been found that this precluded any number of tiresome legal shenanigans.

He dealt with the two brothers first. It didn't take long. When Tavish was brought in he saw the Judge seated behind a raised desk. He was a short man and his face was shadowed by the broad-brimmed hat he wore, but when he looked at Tavish he set the hat aside and put on a pair of spectacles, hooking the temple ends over his ears.

He spent some minutes regarding Tavish sternly. A young man in a dark suit came in and sat next to Tavish. Also the Sheriff found a seat in the back.

"Looks like we're all here," said the Judge, as he banged his gavel.

The young man in the suit stood and said, "May it please your Honor, the defendant is entitled to a lawyer to aid in his defense."

"Where's the sense in that?" asked the Judge.

"The defendant, not being an expert in the law, requires the advice and guidance of one who is, in order to assure that none of his legal safeguards are overlooked or given short shrift."

"That argument would carry some weight if the law played any role in these proceedings, but in this court the law matters no more than a hen's fart, so I see no need for a lawyer."

The young man looked at Tavish and smiled as if to say, "Well I tried."

"Call the first witness," said the Judge.

"The witness must first be sworn in."

"There'll be no swearing in. It matters not a fig to me if the witness be truthful or no so I'll spare him the pangs of conscience."

The first witness, who was none other than the Sheriff, took the stand.

The Judge said, "I have but one question for you. Is the defendant guilty?"

"Guilty as sin, your Honor," said the Sheriff.

"Objection," said the young man. "What is he guilty of?"

"I hold it to be a widely acknowledged fact that all men are guilty," intoned the Judge. "The doctrine asserting that guilt is a consequence of a specific malfeasance is a tawdry legalism of recent invention. Guilt existed before there were laws. In fact, there was guilt long before even the possibility of innocence had been hinted at. Guilt is a habit, one we imbibe with our mother's milk." He then turned to Tavish and asked, "Have you anything to say in your defense?"

"I won't waste my breath. The world will doubtless be a better place once I'm no longer in it."

"Then I pronounce you guilty. Were I a cruel man I'd sentence you to life imprisonment, but I'll be merciful and condemn you to hang by the neck until you are dead. As the gibbet has not yet been perfected in its construction the sentence cannot be carried out just at present, but will be deferred to sunrise tomorrow, which," here he consulted a calendar, "is the last day of October." He banged his gavel again and that was that.

As he was led away Tavish said, "Hardly seems worth the trouble of having a judge come out. He could just send us his verdicts on a post card."

"There has to be a judge," said the Sheriff. "Otherwise it'd just be a lynching."

Chaplain Rumple came to him that night. He said, "Do not think about death. Death itself is nothing. It's thinking about it that brings grief. Be nothing but life, right to the end."

"I've naught but contempt for a man who imagines that those who are to be hanged in the morning can occupy their minds with thoughts of something other than their demise. Get out. Do not sit on my stool. I have no use for you or your consolation."

So the chaplain departed, but then Tavish felt a slight remorse when it struck him that now he'd be all alone till they took him out to die.

The night passed slowly. There were the constant sounds of hammering and muffled conversation coming from the town square as they worked on the gibbet. But the night passed very slowly. It's true that clocks lie. Not every increment of time is of the same duration. There are moments that rush past in a blur, and others so sluggish they will not give way to the next, but have almost to be shoved aside. It was those latter moments that made up Tavish's night. He thought it odd that the last few hours of life seemed to drag on forever. He'd imagined that if one had only a few hours to live, those hours would seem hopelessly short, flying away into the past before he'd had the opportunity to treasure them. But he had no use for life. The hours of the night loomed before him like endless obstacles he would have to endure in suffering and perseverance. Eventually he drifted off to sleep, realizing he'd done so when he came groggily awake as the first light of dawn crept through his window.

So this was it. Soon they'd be coming for him. But they didn't. His aching senses were dimly aware that the sounds of hammering and sawing that had been going on through the night were still going on. So the gibbet wasn't ready yet. *Delays, as usual. What did I expect?*

He closed his eyes and willed his mind to go blank. It did no good. His thoughts still needed something to occupy them. He reopened his eyes and took an inventory of his cell. Let's see: there was a stool, a bed, a couple of weeds, a window through which he glimpsed the top of a tree. He looked at the weeds again. It struck him that these were his fellow prisoners, locked in the same cell, but their lives would continue after his was cut short. He decided he would pull them up, but didn't do it just yet.

They were so ordinary he hadn't paid them any attention. In their ordinariness and their insignificance, did they remind him of himself? No, not really. He imagined an artist painting the scene of his last hours. He'd show the jail cell and he'd display Tavish's anguished self, wearing a brave expression. He'd show the window and the tree outside. He wouldn't show the weeds. They'd be blotted out, otherwise it wouldn't be art. The only time anyone pays any attention to a weed is when he's going to pull it up and throw it away, as Tavish was going to do to these. Now that he looked at them he saw the two weeds were the same type of plant. Where had they come from? Apparently two seeds had found their way, blown into the cell from who knows where, and finding a little dirt and moisture in the cracks between the flagstones they'd sprouted. It was really a tale of adventure and endurance. And now he was going to pull them up.

He stood and took a closer look. Each had a light green stem with two flat orbiculate leaves at the base and a leafless head at the top. He was forced to concede they were remarkably unattractive, but doubtless this was a sturdy and invasive weed, impossible to stamp out. He had the feeling he'd been looking at weeds exactly like these all his life without ever actually seeing them. He was pleased to think at least he'd been spared long enough finally to take notice. And as he took notice he saw the plants were being approached along the floor by one of those speckled beetles that for some reason are called ladybirds. He decided to sit back down and watch.

The ladybird moved slowly across the flagstones in the direction of one of the plants. It marched in a straight line, negotiating with some difficulty the cracks between the flagstones, but ultimately staying on course. Tavish felt almost godlike, observing a singularly humble event, but one doubtless of great import in the microscopical world of the beetle. At any moment he expected to be hauled off to his death, but he hoped he'd be allowed time to learn what the ladybird beetle was doing.

The ladybird was moving in a straight line, approaching the plant it was nearest to. It reached one of the leaves and continued its march across it keeping as closely as possible to the same direction. It was not aiming at the stem of the plant; its ultimate objective seemed elsewhere. Watching the beetle he saw that the surface of the leaf was rough and uneven, causing the ladybird's path sometimes to deviate from a straight line, but after each deviation it caught itself and returned to its original direction. Having crossed the first leaf the beetle returned briefly to the flagstones before it encountered the plant's second leaf, which it then traversed just as it had the first. He wondered what its goal was or, for that matter, if it had a goal.

The hangman, his black hood over his face, was at the bars of Tavish's cell. It was just the Sheriff dressed to kill. "Are you Mr. Tavish?"

Tavish was dismayed that he was not going to learn what the beetle was doing. He looked up. "You know damn well who I am."

"You're to be hanged today." The hangman stood there looking at him. Tavish wondered if he expected a reply. Then the hangman moved off, saying, "I'll get the other two first."

Given a brief reprieve, Tavish returned his attention to the ladybird, seeing that it had finished crossing the second leaf and was heading across the flagstones again. He thought now he could see what its objective had been all along. It was heading straight for the stem of the other weed. When it reached the base of this weed it proceeded to crawl vertically up the stem. Having climbed a distance of perhaps an inch or an inch and a half it paused. This was the first moment since Tavish had sighted the beetle that it was motionless. Up till this point it had moved steadily along, surmounting obstacles, seemingly determined to arrive somewhere, wherever it was headed. Had it reached its goal? Was it going to do something? Tavish watched in suspense. The ladybird started moving again, resuming

411

its ascent of the plant's stem. The stem was perhaps eight inches tall, and the beetle was now undeterred, climbing steadily upwards. Just as it neared the top, the ladybird transformed. It opened its spotted shell to reveal a pair of wings, and flew away. It cycled lazily a couple times round the cell and then soared out the window.

As Tavish sat back, a host of questions came to his mind. Why had the beetle bypassed the nearer plant in favor of the one further away? Both seemed identical. Then, what was its goal in climbing up the stem? Presumably it intended to reach the top, but then why had it flown away? What were its motivations? And what had the beetle accomplished? You'd think such a tiny creature would be altogether devoid of reasoning power and would be guided entirely by instinct. But if that were the case, wouldn't its goals be unambiguous and its actions clearly designed to achieve them? Wouldn't it have gone to the nearest plant instead of the one further away? Surely that's what a sensible beetle would have done. But that was not the case. In fact, its actions had been entirely unpredictable. The events Tavish had just witnessed must have encompassed an enormous episode in the very short life span that would be the beetle's, perhaps comparable to his trek from Port Jay to Kashahar with Katie. And as he thought of that, all he'd felt came back from the oblivion where it had hidden, and his heart broke again, aching for the stupid, pitiless loss of it all. All the pain he'd tried to escape, all the anguish that was his, now fell onto him and he wondered, if God had been looking down on him, had all his actions conveyed the same air of perplexing pointlessness? And what had he accomplished?

It was clear the ladybird could not have been guided by instinct. It had been guided by considerations of content and discontent. It had rejected one plant and selected another, and then had changed its mind once more and flown away. It had made choices that revealed a senselessness and lack of purpose that could only be the results of rational thought. In fact, it was impossible to deny that the beetle was a reasoning being moved by its own free will. But if that were the case, then every tiny insect, every mote and glume of life must be just the same. They were all freely making an infinitude of choices. And the resulting universe was shaped by the unpredictable whims of every organism acting chaotically on its own. There could be no grand, eternal plan. Everything was senseless. Life wasn't a predetermined path of cause and consequence, yet he'd felt shackled to the past, a fly dangling in the iron web woven of regret. Why? He felt he was glimpsing an important truth, one that changed everything he'd ever believed. If a coin was tossed a thousand times, and every time came up heads —

He was interrupted again by the hangman, this time with Dane and Bramij in tow. "Mr. Tavish, you must come and be hanged."

He led Tavish out of his cell towards the gibbet to which the final touches had at last been applied. As they approached the town square they came to a spot with a view of the surrounding countryside and the nearby Sound. He saw a man with a pony. The pony's nose was deep in its feed bag and the animal was munching happily away. *What ever happened to Neddy?* he wondered. Over the Sound it was raining. He could see the falling rain, and through it a distant patch of blue sky. The effect was of a shade of azure he couldn't remember ever having seen before. He paused and stared. It gave him the feeling all of nature was speaking to him, it had always spoken to him, all his life, and there was a meaning behind all the things it had ever said, and all the things it had ever said meant the same thing, and what it meant was –

"Blast your stinking ass," said Bramij.

The hangman gave him a poke from behind. "Sorry to disturb your meditations, but we're behind schedule."

"Ah, no matter, I was only thinking about ladybirds."

FINIS

Acknowledgments

I would like to acknowledge people who read some early chapters and offered criticism: Andrew Alford, Tom Cantillon, Todd Honeycutt, Bill Mingin, Jason Radak and Johanna Rodda. And of course, I owe a big debt of gratitude to Dario Ciriello, without whose advice and guidance this book would never have seen the light of day.

Author's Note

If you enjoyed this story, please take a moment to post a review, however short. Tell your friends about this book, or mention it on social media. Since indie authors like me depend on our readers to spread the word, every mention helps.

I also invite you to drop by my website at donnallymiller.com, where you'll find information about me, free stories, and my blog.

97577422R00235

Made in the USA
Columbia, SC
16 June 2018